Also by Paige Toon

Paige Toon

the LAST piece of my HEART

**SIMON &
SCHUSTER**

London · New York · Sydney · Toronto · New Delhi

A CBS COMPANY

First published in Great Britain by Simon & Schuster UK Ltd, 2017
A CBS COMPANY

1 3 5 7 9 10 8 6 4 2

Simon & Schuster UK Ltd
1st Floor
222 Gray's Inn Road
London WC1X 8HB

www.simonandschuster.co.uk
www.simonandschuster.com.au
www.simonandschuster.co.in

Simon & Schuster Australia, Sydney
Simon & Schuster India, New Delhi

A CIP catalogue record for this book
is available from the British Library

Paperback ISBN: 978-1-4711-6255-8
eBook ISBN: 978-1-4711-6257-2
Export Paperback: 978-1-4711-6302-9

Typeset by M Rules
Printed and bound by CPI Group (UK) Ltd, Croydon, CR0 4YY

Simon & Schuster UK Ltd are committed to sourcing paper
that is made from wood grown in sustainable forests and support the Forest
Stewardship Council, the leading international forest certification organisation.
Our books displaying the FSC logo are printed on FSC certified paper.

For I and I.
This one had to be yours.

A Letter To My Readers

Dear Reader,

Thank you very much for buying this book. I hope you enjoy reading it as much as I enjoyed writing it.

The Last Piece of My Heart is Bridget's story. This is a brand new, standalone book, but Bridget herself is not a new character. You may already be familiar with the Prologue because I wrote it as a short story for my club, *The Hidden Paige*. And I didn't want to stop there, as you can see…

I can honestly say that I've never enjoyed being inside a character's head quite as much as I did Bridget's. In fact, I still don't want to let her go, so stay tuned to *The Hidden Paige* for a spin-off story later in the year. You can sign up at paigetoon.com if you haven't already – it's completely free.

I love hearing from my readers, so if you'd like to drop me a line, please get in touch via the social media details below.

I hope Bridget captures a little piece of your heart, too.

Lots of love,

Paige Toon x

www.paigetoon.com
#TheHiddenPaige
Twitter @PaigeToonAuthor
Facebook.com/PaigeToonAuthor
Instagram.com/PaigeToonAuthor

Prologue

The problem with giving your heart away to someone is that you never fully get it back. Long after you've fallen out of love with them, they still own a little piece of you. That's why first love is always the strongest: it's the only time you ever love wholeheartedly. And I do mean that literally.

I came up with this theory a few years ago when I was belatedly reflecting on why on earth I had ever broken up with David, my boyfriend at university. He was great, but *something* was missing, so I called it off and started a new search for the complete package. Over a decade later, I'm still looking.

It's not that I haven't been around the houses. I have. And the caravans, apartment blocks and skyscrapers, to boot. At the end of the day, it all comes down to Elliot Green. He's entirely to blame. He was my first love and he took a piece of my heart – and my virginity, while he was at it – and then emigrated to Australia with his parents at the age of sixteen, never to be seen or heard from again, once his initial frenzy

1

of letter writing had died out. I figured he'd found a fit Aussie bird and had forgotten all about me, so I tried to forget about him, too. Many moons later, I'm still trying.

It doesn't help that I'm currently in Sydney, where he moved all those years ago. I've been daydreaming about bumping into him here and melodramatically declaring, 'You've got something that belongs to me,' before demanding that he give me the piece of my heart back.

Never in my wildest dreams did I think I actually *would* see him again, yet there he is, completely oblivious to me gawping as he has a beer with some mates at a harbourside bar.

Despite his changed appearance, I recognised him instantly. His long, lean body has broadened out and his arms are tanned and muscular. His brown hair is the same unruly length, but he now has sexy stubble that's bordering on beardy. From where I'm standing, Elliot Green is hotter than ever. And now he's looking at me.

He's looking at me!

And now he's *not* looking at me.

Before I can register disappointment, he does a comedy double take and his blue eyes widen. His face breaks into a grin and then he's on his feet and my heart is threatening to beat out through my eardrums.

'Bridget?' he asks with disbelief, opening up his arms.

'Hello, Elliot,' I reply warmly, as he crushes me to his hard chest. *Oh, my God, he smells amazing.* What was it that I was supposed to say to him again?

'You've hardly changed at all!' he exclaims, withdrawing and holding me at arm's length as he takes me in.

My figure hasn't altered a lot since he last saw me. I'm tall and fairly slim and my eyes are, obviously, still blue – more of a navy, compared to his lighter swimming-pool shade.

He fingers a lock of my dark hair. 'Even your hair's the same,' he comments.

It comes to the midway point between my chin and shoulders, which is more or less how I wore it as a teenager.

'I've been growing it out, actually,' I say with a shrug. Turns out blunt-cut bobs are high-maintenance. 'Was that an Aussie accent I heard?'

'Maybe,' he replies with a grin.

'It *is*! That's so weird.'

He laughs and shakes his head at me. 'What are you doing here?'

'I'm on my way home.' I nod towards the ferries chugging in and out of Circular Quay.

'You live in Sydney?' he asks with amazement.

'Sort of. I'm here for a year.'

'Seriously?' His eyes dart searchingly between mine. 'Do you have to rush off? Can I buy you a drink?'

'No, I don't have to rush off, and, yes, I'd love a drink.'

He smiles at me and the words pop into my mind from out of nowhere: *You've got something that belongs to me.*

Of course, it's immediately apparent that I'll sound like a right idiot if I say them out loud, so I follow him mutely to his table instead.

Over the next couple of hours, I sit with Elliot and his mates, drinking and laughing and establishing that he is excellently single. When his friends call it a night, Elliot and I stay, and, as the white sails of the nearby Sydney Opera House glint gold in the setting sun, and bats swarm out of the nearby Botanic Gardens, I'm ready.

'So,' I say, swirling the ice around in my glass of vodka tonic, 'I have a theory.'

Elliot cocks one eyebrow and listens with amusement as I enlighten him.

'And that's why I haven't found The One,' I conclude.

He looks confused. 'But you've been in love since we went out, right?'

'Yeah,' I scoff. 'Loads of times.'

'Well, if that's true, you'd better hunt down all of *those* guys and demand that they give you their pieces back, too.' He takes a gulp of his beer and plonks the glass down on the table, looking a little too pleased with himself.

Is he right? Have I whittled my heart down to such a small chunk that I'm never going to be able to fall hook, line and sinker for *anyone*? Damn.

'Your theory is flawed,' he adds annoyingly.

'No, no, no.' I shake my head with renewed determination. 'You were my first love. You've got the biggest piece. The most important piece. And I want it back.'

'What if I don't want to give it back?' he asks.

I force my brow into a frown, while secretly thinking it's adorable that he's indulging this silliness. 'Why would you want to keep it?'

'I don't know.' He shrugs. 'Maybe I like having it around. And anyway, if you want your piece back, then it's only fair that you give me mine back, too.'

'I have a piece of your heart?' I ask with surprise, hoping no one is eavesdropping on our bonkers conversation.

'Of course you do,' he replies, barely refraining from adding, '*Duh!*'

I think about this, the alcohol muddling my brain. 'I suppose we could do a straight swap,' I mutter eventually.

His lips tilt up at the corners as he stares across the table at me with those very blue eyes of his. Momentarily I'm back in the past with him and butterflies are going berserk inside me.

'Shall we continue this discussion over dinner?' He slides his hand towards mine and touches the tips of my fingers with his. A shiver runs down my spine and I can almost feel fresh perforation marks being punched into my body's most vital organ.

'All right, then, if you insist,' I reply with a smile.

If he wants to tear off another piece, I don't think I'll stop him.

Chapter 1

'Hello again!' my literary agent, Sara, exclaims as we air kiss each other's cheeks. Her smile is a hundred watts brighter than the last time I saw her back in February. 'Thank you for coming in.' She directs me to a seat. 'How's it all going? I see you've topped ten thousand followers on Twitter!'

'Yes, last week,' I reply. 'And the comments on the last post were off the scale.'

'That was the Gabriel reunion?'

'That's right.'

'Oh, I loved that one!'

'Good!' I grin. 'It cost me enough to get to Brazil.'

She laughs. 'You sounded like you had a lucky escape with him. What a chauvinistic pig! *How* many children did he have again?'

'Nine.' I grimace. 'I felt so sorry for his poor wife.'

'Whoa, did *she* have her work cut out for her! Were those kids really as badly behaved as they sounded?'

'I'm sure they have their good days,' I say benignly, wondering why I'm here.

It's been three months since our last meeting when I pitched Sara an idea for a book, but it wasn't as well received as I had hoped it would be.

'Forgive me, Bridget,' I remember her saying, as she eyed me shrewdly. 'But, when you asked for a meeting about a book, I assumed you'd be pitching an idea about your experiences of navigating the globe, not your experiences of navigating men.'

It was a fair assumption. I was – *am* – a well-established travel writer.

'I *do* plan to take the reader on a journey,' I said with what I'd hoped was a winning smile, 'and we *will* travel all around the world together, but our voyage will take us, yes, via all of the men I've ever been in love with. Travel writing will feature prominently, but, ultimately, this book will be about love.'

She smirked. 'Are we *really* talking about love, here? You're thirty-four, and you say you've been head over heels in love with twelve different men? Some weren't simply holiday romances or one-night stands?'

I waved her away dismissively. 'Oh, there were *loads* of those, too. But I could probably spin a couple out if I'm stuck for material,' I added with a grin, as she blanched at me.

It was Elliot who gave me the idea, when I bumped into him in Sydney, a year ago last December. That night was the start of something new and beautiful between us, and I'm delighted to announce that we're still together.

At least, we're together as a couple. We're not together literally, because I'm now back in the UK *sans* visa and he's on the other side of the world in Australia. I could move over there if I married him. But that would mean one of us asking.

I'm slightly scared of him asking.

I love Elliot so much, but, when we were sixteen, my feelings for him were all-encompassing. He meant *everything* to me.

The love I feel for him now is not as powerful, and I'm worried that it's because I've become jaded over the years. Have I had too many relationships to believe in happy ever after?

Maybe I've just grown up. Maybe love as an adult can never compare to that of a teenager.

Or maybe something *is* missing. And maybe there's a chance that I can get this *something* back...

That night we met up again, Elliot put forward the tongue-in-cheek notion that perhaps I needed to hunt down all of the men I've ever loved to ask for their pieces of my heart back. Before I left Australia, he brought up the idea again, but this time he was serious. He knows that I'm struggling to commit to him wholeheartedly, but he believes that, if I use this time apart from him to revisit the past, I might be able to make more sense of the here and now. He suggested that I write about all of my encounters, and then he came up with another genius idea: if I could get a book deal, my time and travels would be funded in the form of an advance.

I should point out here that my boyfriend is not the jealous type. This was one of the first questions Sara asked when I put the idea to her back in February.

She also said that I needed to blog about my reunions and raise my profile before she'd consider approaching publishers, so that's what I've been doing for the last three months.

My readers have joined me on voyages to South Africa

(David), Iceland (Olli), Spain (Jorge) and Brazil (Gabriel), and, of course, I've also written about how Elliot and I rekindled our relationship in Australia. I'm yet to meet up with Dillon in Ireland, Freddie in Norway, Seth in Canada and Beau, Felix, Liam and Vince here in the UK.

My contacts in journalism have helped to spread the word about my blog, and, if you just ignore the trolls, I'd say it's all going swimmingly.

Elliot, meanwhile, has been hanging onto his piece of my heart. It's still the biggest piece – the first *and* last piece – and, once I get the other bits back, my path will lead me back to him. A walk down the aisle really would be the happiest of happy endings.

Late yesterday afternoon, Sara's assistant called and asked me to come in for a meeting as soon as possible. Apparently, my agent had some news and she'd explain in person.

I got a little bit excited.

I know that Sara has started talking up my blog to publishers, but while the feedback so far has been good – they like my style, they like my wit – no one has wanted to commit to a relationship-blog-turned-book in the current market. Sara claims that publishers won't be able to argue with the numbers if I keep growing my readership, so I intend to crack on. But has something changed in the last twenty-four hours?

'You must be wondering why you're here,' Sara says to me now, reading my mind.

'I'm pretty curious,' I admit.

'Yesterday, I had lunch with Fay Sanderson.'

The name isn't familiar to me, but Sara explains that she's an editorial director at a top publishing house.

'She's been avidly reading your blog and was raving to me about how well you strike the balance between warm and likable, and feisty, funny and fresh. She *loves* your voice. She *absolutely loves* it,' Sara stresses, and there's something about her tone that has me sitting up straighter in my seat. *Am I about to be offered a book deal?*

'She has a proposal,' she continues. *Yes!* 'Have you heard of Nicole Dupré?'

'Er, that name sounds familiar,' I reply.

Sara swivels on her chair and takes a book down from the shelves behind her. 'Nicole had a runaway bestseller with *The Secret Life of Us*, which was published last autumn. It took us all a little by surprise, to be honest.'

'I remember hearing about it.' I pick up the novel she's placed in front of me. The cover has a photograph of a lone girl standing on a beach in Thailand. I turn over the book and scan the blurb. It's about a travel writer who falls in love with two different men on two different continents.

Where is Sara going with this?

'Nicole passed away shortly after that was published,' Sara explains, her tone growing sombre.

I breathe in sharply and glance up at her. 'Oh, God, that's right, it was in the news. Was she one of your authors?' I ask with surprise.

She nods.

'I'm so sorry. I had no idea you represented her.'

'It's okay. It was very sudden,' she tells me. 'She had a brain aneurysm. She was only thirty-one.'

I shake my head, horrified. That's three years younger than I am now. 'That's so tragic,' I murmur sympathetically.

11

'Nicole was writing a sequel,' Sara continues, drawing my attention back to her. '*Secret* ended on a cliffhanger. The readers are crying out for more. And, Bridget…?'

I haven't been sure up until this point what any of this has to do with me, but, from her more upbeat tone, I sense I'm about to find out.

'Fay thinks your voice is perfect!' she concludes, triumphantly.

There's a long moment where neither of us says anything.

'To write the sequel.'

She thinks she's clarifying it, but I'm even more confused.

'I don't understand,' I say, shaking my head. 'Fay loves my blog?'

'Loves it!' Sara repeats. 'She thinks your voice is spot on!'

'I thought you were about to tell me that she wants to sign me up.'

Sara clears her throat. 'She does. For the sequel to *The Secret Life of Us*.' She points at the book I'm holding.

What?

'Nicole was about a quarter of the way in,' she explains. 'She left behind a stack of notes. Fay's been trying to find the right person to complete it.'

'She wants me to be a *ghostwriter*?' I splutter. 'But what about *my* book?'

'You'll still write it,' Sara says evenly. 'Think of this as a stopgap, your way in. This is your chance to get your foot through the door of a major publisher. You can write your own book alongside this one while you continue to build your profile, and the advance you'll get will pay for your travels. It's the *perfect* solution.'

12

'But…' I'm still reeling. 'What makes anyone think I'm up to the job? Surely there are a million other more qualified authors who could do this?'

'Oh, I'm sure there are, too,' she says smoothly. 'But Fay wants you. She's even read the novel you wrote a few years ago. The plot wasn't quite there,' she says hurriedly, quashing any hope of resurrecting my old romantic-fiction dream, 'but the point is, Fay knows you have it in you to pull off fiction. She thinks your style is fabulous.'

'She does?' I allow myself to feel a little flattered, as well as incredibly daunted.

'Have you read *The Secret Life of Us*?' Sara asks.

'No,' I admit, studying the book in my hands.

'Take that copy,' she says. 'You won't be able to put it down. The protagonist is a travel writer just like you, so you should be able to identify with her brilliantly. It is the biggest compliment that Fay believes you can carry Nicole's baton to the finishing line.'

'I just… I'm not sure…' I'm struggling to get my head around all of this. A young woman, dying so abruptly… A bestselling author leaving behind an unfinished sequel… Me – *me!* – being the one to complete her work…

'Read the book,' Sara urges, and I sense she wants to wrap up our meeting. 'And keep in mind, Bridget, this is a *great* opportunity. Give me a call as soon as you've reached the end so we can discuss the finer details. I'm around all day tomorrow.'

She seems very confident that I'm going to go along with this hare-brained scheme.

Her conviction is founded, because I call her back first thing.

Chapter 2

It's a beautiful sunny day in early June when I step off the bus in Padstow, Cornwall. The tide is out and the view stretches right over the Camel Estuary as I climb the hill, revealing a series of long, smooth sandbanks punctuating the clear, bluey-green water. The smell of fish and chips wafts through the air, making my tummy rumble. My appetite will have to wait. It's already three thirty in the afternoon and Nicole's husband, Charlie Laurence, is expecting me.

When Sara explained that Charlie wanted to oversee the writing of his wife's book, I was apprehensive. The job was already going to be challenging enough – would he make it even more difficult?

I come to a stop outside a modest, terraced, redbrick house. A narrow, slate-topped veranda stretches across the front, sheltering a charcoal-grey door and a bay window. Apart from a lavender hedge bordering the wall adjacent to the street, the tiny paved area is devoid of plants.

Movement catches my eye at the window, so I quickly walk up the path and knock on the door. There's not even time to check my reflection in the glass before it opens to reveal who I'm assuming is Charlie.

He looks to be in his early thirties, and is around six foot tall and slim, with green eyes and shaggy dark-blond hair held back from his forehead with a mustard-yellow bandana. He's wearing a faded orange T-shirt and grey shorts, and his face and limbs are sun-kissed the colour of honey, all the way down to his bare feet.

Wow.

'Charlie?' I check hopefully.

'Hello,' he replies with a small, reserved smile, holding back the door. 'Come in.'

I don't know what I was expecting, but it wasn't this.

'Tea?' he offers.

'Thank you, that'd be great.' I jolt as the door closes with a clunk. I'm nervous.

Charlie gestures down the hall, indicating that I should lead the way. The television is on in what I presume is the living room, but I don't look in as I pass, and a moment later we spill out into a galley-style kitchen. It continues onto an extension containing a two-seater sofa backed up against the left wall and a round table at the end.

He fills the kettle and gets out two mugs. 'How was your journey? Did you drive?'

'No. Tube from Wembley to Paddington, train to Bodmin, and bus to here.'

'Sounds harrowing.'

He's polite and well spoken, but he hasn't made eye contact with me once since I stepped over his threshold.

A noise sounds out from the direction of the living room. 'Excuse me,' he says, exiting the kitchen.

I take a deep breath and force myself to exhale slowly while taking in my surroundings.

The internal walls are exposed and the bricks have been painted with thick, white masonry paint. The worktops are fashioned out of old railway sleepers, sanded and varnished to a dull shine. French doors at the end open up onto the back garden. It's neat and tidy in here, but it looks like a right tip out there. My attention drifts to the table and the wooden chairs encircling it.

Two chairs.

And one highchair.

That was another thing Sara neglected to mention at our meeting last week.

When Nicole died, she left behind not only an unfinished manuscript *and* a grief-stricken husband, but a five-week-old baby daughter, as well.

Life can seriously suck.

Charlie is talking in low tones in the living room. Another wave of nerves washes through me.

Babies freak me out. They don't seem to like me, and I don't particularly like them. What if I make them cry? What if I make *this* one cry? If she takes offence at me, Charlie probably will, too, and he may well pull the plug on this idea.

Earlier this week, I met up with Nicole's editor, Fay. She's a lovely, warm woman in her late forties and she revealed that the decision to go ahead with the sequel came down to Charlie. He wasn't at all sure, from what I gather, but he felt a responsibility towards Nicole's readers and in the end, gave the go-ahead, as long as the job was done well by the right person. I'm still not convinced that I'm the right person, but, after reading Nicole's book, I'm as keen as anyone to find out what happened next. Even if I have to write it myself.

The prospect is admittedly terrifying, but I'll cross that bridge when I come to it. If this meeting with Charlie doesn't go well, there won't be a bridge to cross.

The kettle boils, so I distract myself by pouring hot water into the mugs. A moment later, Charlie returns.

'CBeebies only distracts her for so long at her age,' he says, knowing he doesn't need to explain his circumstances because I've already been made well aware of them. 'Milk?'

'Yes, please.' I move away from the worktop to give him some space. 'How old is your daughter?' I ask.

'Eight and a half months. Sugar?' He flicks his eyes up to meet mine.

'No, thanks.'

'My mum was supposed to be here, but she had an emergency at work,' he reveals, stirring two teaspoons into his own cup.

'What does she do?' I ask.

'She and my dad run a campsite. They had a burst water main or something.'

'The campsite on the hill?'

'No, they're about an hour away. A couple of mates of mine run the one on the hill. Do you know it?' Charlie picks up his cup and finally looks at me properly. I thought his eyes were green, but they're getting on for hazel.

'Only because my dad mentioned it. He's stayed there a few times in his campervan,' I explain.

His daughter cries out again.

'We'll go through,' Charlie says quietly, nodding at the door. I wait until he leads the way.

I see her legs first, bare and chubby and kicking back and forth like nobody's business. Then the rest of her comes into view – her pastel-coloured babygrow adorned with bunnies, and fine, slightly curly, light-blond hair. She's strapped into a bouncy chair in front of the television, and Charlie drags the contraption across the wooden floor towards him as he takes a seat on the sofa nearest to the bay window. He pushes on the back of her bouncer to make it move and she giggles.

'This is April,' he says, sticking his tongue out at his daughter before nodding at me. 'That's Bridget,' he says more civilly.

'Hello, April!' I reply, cringing because my voice sounds too loud and overeager.

April looks over her shoulder at me, her expression vacant. Then her mouth breaks into a toothy grin and she says something unintelligible. Charlie pushes on the back of her bouncer again and she happily returns her attention to him.

I'm tense as I sit down on the second sofa, hoping she'll ignore me from here on in.

'Where are you staying?' Charlie asks, back to making courteous small talk. He picks up the remote control and turns the volume down on the TV, not quite muting the ludicrously enthusiastic and eccentrically dressed man doing something bizarre with an egg carton.

'A B&B in Padstow. It's cheap and cheerful. My bus leaves early in the morning.'

'You're only here for one day?' He seems surprised.

'Yes, but… Obviously I can come back if…' He looks at me expectantly, waiting for me to complete my sentence. 'If I get the job,' I finish awkwardly.

'Oh.' He averts his gaze and takes a small sip of his tea. 'Fay said you're a travel writer.'

'That's right.' I smile with relief. This territory I can talk about for hours. 'My mum works on a cruise liner so I grew up seeing the world in my school holidays.'

'Bet that was an interesting childhood.'

'It was. I lived with my dad during the term, but we visited Mum pretty regularly.' He nods, listening. He doesn't ask any more questions, so I carry on pitching myself to him. 'I used to write about the places that I saw, then I built my own website and eventually started to pester magazine and newspaper editors for work. I can pretty much get work writing about anywhere, these days.'

'That would've been Nicki's dream job,' Charlie says with a fond smile. *Nicki, not Nicole*, I note. 'Before she got a book deal,' he adds.

And before her life was cruelly stolen from her.

He breaks the long, awkward silence. 'So you liked her novel?'

'I *loved* it!'

He smiles properly now, a smile full of pride, but its light reaches his eyes only briefly.

How bad do I feel? He shouldn't have had to prompt me – I should've been raving about his lovely wife's book from the moment I got here.

'I *really* loved it.' I'm trying to make up for my gaffe, and for the next few minutes it's all I can talk about.

In Nicole's novel, the heroine, Kit, is a travel writer who falls in love with two men at the same time: Morris, a laidback surfer-turned-entrepreneur from right here in Cornwall, and Timo, a sexy Finnish rock climber who is based in Thailand. At the end of the first book, Kit goes to Thailand to break up with Timo because Morris – her first love – has proposed to her. But, before she can come clean, Timo asks her to marry him, too. And she says yes.

I know! WTF, right?

'I detest cheating with a passion, so I shouldn't have liked this book on principle,' I tell Charlie, arguably too honestly. 'But somehow Nicole made it… I don't know. It's so believable. She wrote in such a heart-wrenching way that I couldn't help but be swept up in the story. I felt like I was inside Kit's mind, feeling every emotion she was feeling and somehow understanding the crazy decisions she was making. It was…' I shake my head, finally, yes, *finally* lost for words.

I think I've said all the right things from the look on his face.

'Do you know what was going to happen in the sequel?' I ask. 'Do you know who Kit was going to end up with?'

He shakes his head. 'I'm not sure even Nicki knew.'

I feel a surge of disappointment. Charlie leans back to put his empty mug down on the windowsill behind him. 'But, if she did, the answer will be in her notes. She made lots of them. Let me show you her office.'

April seems to be content sitting in her bouncer for the moment, so Charlie turns the sound back up on the television and leads me upstairs. He walks straight ahead, pushing open the door to a small room that looks out over the messy back garden. Any view of the estuary would be from the other side of the house. A large desk fills the area under the window, and there are bookshelves and filing cabinets lining the walls. A slick Apple computer takes pride of place in the centre of the desk. The room is tidy, but I can see from here that the computer screen is dusty from underuse.

Charlie pulls open the top left desk drawer to reveal a series of notebook crammed inside.

'Nicki was always writing in these,' he says.

He closes that drawer and opens the next to expose more notebooks.

'I haven't gone through them.' From the tightening of his voice, I take it he hasn't wanted to. 'But all of her research is in here.' He opens another drawer. 'She also used to keep diaries when she was younger. Her dad moved to Thailand for work and she'd visit when she could. A lot of what she wrote about back then made it into *Secret*. I think you'll find clues as to where she planned to go with the sequel.'

I look up at the crowded bookshelves and notice several Post-it notes sticking out of the tops of some of the books. What pages did she mark? Were they significant?

Nicole did a couple of interviews around the time *Secret* was published last October, so I already knew that her father is a French chef called Alain Dupré, and that she wrote under her maiden name. But, as she died just two weeks after her book was released, before the sales had taken off, her readers and I don't know much more about her – it's very surreal to be standing here in her office.

'Did she leave notes on her computer, too?' My mind boggles. *Where would I start?*

Charlie hesitates almost imperceptibly before reaching

21

behind the screen and feeling for the ON button. The computer fires up with a loud *dong*.

'I would've thought so,' he says.

His back is to me, his posture tense. I stare at his frame and out of the blue think of Elliot. It's been almost six months since we've seen each other and, on the whole, I'm coping. But suddenly I miss him intensely.

April lets out a cry downstairs, making Charlie start. 'Take a seat and have a look,' he mumbles, leaving me to it.

Is he sure he doesn't mind? Uncertainly, I pull out the chair and sit down. The screen in front of me lights up and then I'm looking at a small photograph of Nicole, under which is a request for her password.

She's laughing and her slim, oval face is basked in warmth from the sunshine. She has dark hair that brushes her shoulders and her eyes are sky-blue. Across her head is a familiar yellow bandana headband that doesn't quite obscure her fringe, and a sprinkling of freckles dusts her nose. She looks happy. I find myself wishing that I had known her. The posed black-and-white publicity shot on the inside cover of her book doesn't do her justice.

'It's *Thailand*.'

I almost jump out of my skin at the sound of Charlie's voice from behind me.

'The password is *Thailand*. Uppercase *T*.'

'Oh!' I type it in. I press ENTER and Nicole's desktop swings into view.

I hear Charlie inhale sharply and know better than to turn around.

An image of him holding a newborn baby has filled the

screen. His hair is shorter and he's gazing with love at the tiny bundle in his arms.

'I've barely been in here since we lost her,' he says softly.

'We don't have to do this now,' I murmur. His wife died just over seven months ago. I'm not at all sure that he's ready for this. I'm not sure that I am.

'It's fine,' he says, leaning in and taking the mouse. I scoot my chair over to the left, watching as the arrow hovers over a blue folder on the dock at the bottom. The name comes up: 'SECRET'. Charlie moves the mouse to the right and clicks on a folder called 'CONFESSIONS'.

'Is that the title of the sequel?' I ask, alight with interest.

'*Confessions of Us*,' Charlie tells me. 'Sara wasn't sure about it.'

Sara was Nicole's agent, too, of course.

'I like it,' I tell him, peering more closely at the contents of the folder: *Characters… Confessions… Research… Synopsis… Timeline…*

'You'll have to check out her *Secrets* folder, as well. I'm not sure she moved everything across.'

'Okay.' I nod.

'If you want the job, that is.' He lets go of the mouse and straightens up.

'Isn't that up to you?' I ask him carefully.

He stares down at me. 'I've read a couple of your blog entries,' he replies instead of giving me an answer. 'Fay was right. Your tone of voice is very similar to Nicki's.' Charlie leans against one of the filing cabinets and folds his arms across his chest. 'But are you sure you have the time to take this on?'

'Absolutely,' I state. 'This will take precedence over all of my other work,' I assure him. 'I can blog in my spare time – I don't have a deadline and there are no other pressures on me.' I take a deep breath before announcing, 'I think I'd do a good job.'

He eyes me thoughtfully as the seconds tick past, and then he finally nods in what I hope is agreement. 'I'll speak to Fay.'

Chapter 3

'I don't *do* camping, Dad!'

'Campervanning is not camping, Bridget. There's a fold-down bed, for Christ's sake! You'd love it. Don't you remember how much you once adored messing around in your little playhouse? It's not so different to that.'

'That was back when I used to make mud cakes.'

'I'm not advocating you make mud cakes in *Hermie*. In fact, I'd rather you didn't.' He pauses before being sure to add, 'I'd *definitely* rather you didn't.'

Hermie is the name he gave to his seventeen-year-old Mercedes Vito campervan. Originally *Herman the German* – chosen by his now ex-girlfriend when he brought it over from Germany a few years ago – the name swiftly morphed into the far cuter variation. And *Hermie is* kind of cute. I just don't want to live in the bastard for two months.

'Charlie *really* liked you,' Sara effused after my recent trip to Cornwall. I suspect this was a bit of an overstatement. 'He definitely wants you on board,' she added.

'Really?'

'Yep! There's just one little thing…' she said.

Apparently, Charlie panicked when Sara asked him if he could box up Nicki's things for a courier to collect. She assumed it could all be delivered to me in London, but Charlie wasn't ready for Nicki's diaries and notebooks to leave the house. The solution? I go to Padstow and work from her office.

It's just as well I don't have much of a life at the moment. I don't even have an apartment. I'm staying with Dad in Wembley because my place in Chalk Farm is still being rented out to the people who took it over when I went to Australia. I say *my* apartment, but it's technically Dad's – he bought it as an investment, although he accepts only enough rent to cover the mortgage. The current tenants pay way more, so, when they asked if they could extend their lease until October, Dad suggested I move in with him to save money. He knows I struggled financially in Australia, but really he just likes my company. We're very close. He raised me practically single-handedly from the age of six.

I love hanging out with him, but there's something a little bit creepy about living at home at my age. So I came around to the idea of Cornwall pretty quickly. After all, who wouldn't want to spend their summer at the seaside? I only really started to stress this morning after calling around and discovering that all the B&Bs and hotels in Padstow are booked out, if not completely, at least for a good part of the summer.

I gave up and came straight to the pub. Not to drown my sorrows, mind. Dad owns the place. It's a medium-sized, definitely-not-a-gastro-pub that's a fifteen-minute walk to Wembley Stadium in one direction and about the same distance to his house in the other. On game and gig days, it gets pretty hectic, but right now it's quiet, save for a couple of regulars.

'Honestly, darling, that campsite on the hill is really lovely,' Dad says, coming back over to me after taking an order for two scampi and chips and a lasagne.

As I say, not a gastro pub.

'I can just see you climbing the hill and having a drink while watching the sunset.' He pauses, cocking his head to one side. He still has a head of thick, bushy hair, but it's dark in colour now, thanks to his regular Just For Men habit. 'You'd be able to hook up some solar-powered fairy lights,' he continues, 'and fill up the fridge with mini-bottles of Prosecco.'

Now he's talking!

'You could even take the attachable tent and portaloo,' he adds.

'Portaloo?'

'So you wouldn't have to walk to the toilet block in the night.'

'You've got to be kidding. I can hardly get my head around sleeping in a car for two months, let alone emptying my own shit.'

He laughs and shakes his head at me.

I'm not the sort of travel writer who relishes slumming it. I didn't mind so much in my early twenties, but these days I write more about top-notch honeymoon destinations and five-star hotels.

It's a hard job, but someone's got to, and all that.

'To be honest, Bridget, I'm jealous,' he says, propping himself up at the bar. 'I'd give anything to be able to jack in this job for the summer and join you at the seaside.'

'Hold your horses, Dad. You know I love you, but your *house* is only just big enough for the two of us. Don't go getting any ideas about squeezing into *Hermie* with me.'

He reaches over and musses up my hair good-naturedly. I bat him away and rest my elbows on the bar top, rapidly taking them off again because it's sticky. I should know better at my age.

'It'll be an adventure,' he says. 'And, if anyone loves an adventure, it's you.'

I'm counting on it.

Chapter 4

It's early August by the time my contract is sorted and I'm able to get back down to Cornwall. In the next eight weeks I plan to do all of my local research for the scenes that are set in this part of the country, and I also need to go through every book on Nicki's bookshelves, every notebook and diary in her drawers and every single document on her computer. The intention is that I'll gather enough material to be getting on with so, by the time October rolls around, I should be able to move straight back into my flat and write the majority of the book from home.

I set off from London at the ungodly time of four a.m. on a Sunday to avoid traffic, but it still takes me six hours with breaks. *Hermie* is a bugger to drive – the clutch is stiff, the steering is heavy and it's also a left-hand drive – so, by the time I reach the campsite in Padstow, I'm exhausted.

Charlie's friends, two warm and boundlessly enthusiastic hippies called Julia and Justin, welcome me with open arms.

29

I try to take in what they're telling me about the amenities, but resolve to put most of my brainpower into working out where my pitch is.

The campsite comprises three different levels: two flat, grassed paddocks separated by a tall hedge and a small, steep hill, and one huge open field on even higher ground. I'm in the first paddock, which doesn't have a view, but is closest to the toilets. Despite Dad's warning that I'd regret it, I did not bring his portable toilet. I could barely fit in my bags as it was.

I pull up on Pitch 9, cut the ignition and reach for my phone, typing out a brief message to Dad. He worries about me.

'*Here at last and in one piece – both Hermie and me. Love you, call you later xxx*'

I press SEND before realising there's no phone reception.

And, *oh no*! That means there's no data reception, either!

It's a veritable disaster.

I get out of the van and look up at the field on the third, highest level, pinning all of my hopes on its big, steep hill. There's a flight of steps just across the internal campsite road, so I lock up and set off in desperate search of a link to the outside world.

Several tents have been erected around the perimeter of the field, and, as I trudge uphill through the long summer grass, I pity the poor sods who have to sleep on the sloping ground. I'm out of breath by the time I reach the halfway point and then I stop. Time for the big reveal – so far I've resisted looking over my shoulder.

I spin around.

Now *that* is a view.

I can see right out to the open sea. In the nearby distance is the estuary, flanked by Padstow on one side and lush green coast and the town of Rock on the other. The tide is in at the moment and the water glints in the morning sunshine. Boats that, when I was last here in June, were marooned on the sand are now floating in the green-blue water, and flocks of white birds soar through the clear summer sky. I look at my phone screen and sigh with relief.

4G. Thank Christ for that.

I press SEND again on my text to Dad and then plonk my bum down on the grass. The time difference in Australia makes speaking to Elliot tricky, but now is good. I FaceTime his number.

'Check out my view,' I say upon his answering, turning the phone screen around to face the estuary.

'Nice,' he says.

I turn him back to me. 'Not bad, eh?'

'This one's even better.'

'Soppy git,' I tease.

He's sprawled out on his brown-leather sofa at home, with one arm folded behind his head.

'Are you watching telly?' I ask.

'Nah, there's crap all on,' he replies, glancing to his right, where the TV is, before returning his attention to me.

I know the layout of his living room like the back of my hand. I practically lived with him for the last half of my stay in Sydney; I was there for a year in total.

'Are you wearing the jumper I bought you?' Charcoal-grey wool is just coming into view below his neck.

He holds the phone higher so I can see his outfit properly. 'Yeah, it's really cold here now.'

We speak so often that we rarely have big news to share, but the boring, everyday stuff makes being away from each other strangely more bearable.

'Wish I was there to warm you up.' It's winter in the southern hemisphere now.

'I wish you were here, too,' he says in a sleepy, deep voice. 'I've been missing you today.'

'Have you?'

'Yeah. I went over to Bron and Lachie's for lunch. He roasted a joint on the barbecue, flashy bastard. Wasn't the same without you.'

I feel a pang of longing as he talks about our friends. I miss them, too.

'What have you got on?' he asks me.

I hold the phone over my head to show him.

'Man, those shorts…' His voice trails off longingly.

He likes my legs – he says they're sexy – so my cut-off denim shorts became my staple wardrobe item in Sydney. This is the first time I've worn them this year, though. It was cold and dark when I set off this morning, but I'm an optimist – the weather forecast in Padstow was predicted to be twenty-two degrees and sunny. I probably should've changed once I got here, judging by the dribbling looks I kept getting from truck drivers in petrol stations on my way here.

'You're as tanned as you were when you left,' he notes.

'Aw, and you're all pale and pasty.'

'I'm not, am I?' He peers down the inside of his jumper.

'Show me your abs,' I prompt.

'Bugger off,' he replies.

We grin at each other, but his smile fades away. 'How much longer before you come back to me?' he asks pensively.

I sigh. I wish his eyes would look at me properly. It's the thing that really bugs me – we can't make actual eye contact because we're staring at each other's face on the screen, not at the tiny camera lens that catches our images.

'I don't know, El. Now that I'm writing this novel, it could be March or April by the time my edits are done.' My dead-line to deliver the manuscript is the end of January, but there will no doubt be a lot of work to follow. 'Weren't you going to try to come and see me this summer?' I ask.

Now *he's* the one to sigh. 'I've got so many projects on at the moment.' If only I could reach through the screen and stroke his dark, stubbly jaw. 'I just don't think I'm going to be able to get the time off, however much I'd like to. You know what a ball breaker Darren is,' he says.

Darren is his boss and he's a bit of an arse. Elliot is a senior civil engineer at a big firm and they work him incredibly hard, but it's too good a job to quit.

'Anyway, it sounds like you'll be too busy to entertain me any time soon,' he says. 'Now you've got *two* books to write.'

'True,' I say. 'But I'm never too busy to entertain you,' I add with a wicked grin. His own smile widens.

'You want to do something about that now?' he asks meaningfully.

I look over my shoulder. 'Er… I'm in a field in full view of people in tents, so I don't think that's a very good idea at the moment.'

'Go back to your campervan,' he urges.

My face falls. 'I can't. There's no reception down there.'

'Are you telling me we can't do sexy stuff while you're in Cornwall?' he asks with disappointment.

'Where there's a will, there's a way,' I assure him cheekily, but I'm as gutted as he is.

When Elliot and I have said our goodbyes, I head back down to the paddock to get set up. The wide side door of the van opens to reveal a grey and yellow Westfalia interior – which, according to Dad, means something impressive. In front of me is a small open space of about one metre squared. Let's call it the living room. To my left is a grey bench seat that folds down to form part of the bed – a.k.a. the bedroom. And ahead is what I'd loosely refer to as the kitchen: two cupboards crammed with goodies, a small top-loading fridge under one yellow worktop, and double gas rings and a teeny tiny sink under the other. The layout takes the meaning of 'open plan' to a whole new level.

The driver and passenger seats turn around 180 degrees to face the bench seat, so I decide to tackle them first. With quite a bit of jiggery-pokery, I manage the task, before straightening up and bashing my head on the ceiling. Ouch. The roof pops up – *pop* is a debatable word – but, with a bit more manhandling, I've enabled some standing space. Just need to put up the table and I'll be sorted. It stows away in the side door and it's a while before I can figure out how it clicks into place – Dad did talk me through all of this, honest.

By the time I'm done, I'm even more knackered than I was before. Is ten thirty in the morning too early for a glass of Prosecco?

I decide, regrettably, that it is and elect to make a cup of tea instead, filling up the kettle from bottled water stored under the bench seat, firing up the gas with matches I manage to find in one of the cupboards, and then repeating a similar search in my hunt for teabags and a mug.

I'm sure I'll get used to all of this eventually.

As I don't want to waste one minute of precious sunshine, I decide to sit outside on the grass, but have to unpack half of the boot to get to one of the two camping chairs that are buried under my bags. By then the kettle is whistling like a demented blackbird and I almost burn my hand trying to turn the gas off.

Christ, how do people do this?

Let me rephrase the question. *Why* do people do this?

Finally – *finally* – I'm able to sit down and stretch my legs out in front of me, clasping a hard-won hot mug of tea in my hands.

Behind the tall hedge in the next paddock, I can hear children playing badminton. A middle-aged couple in the campervan a few pitches away are making genial conversation to the young couple opposite them. A family of four cycle up the campsite road beside me, huffing and puffing and bickering among themselves. High on the field, a man and a small boy are trying to launch a kite into the air. Birds twitter and chirp in the hedge adjacent to *Hermie* and I just sit there and take it all in.

The sunshine beats down on the top of my head as I sip at my tea and, I have to say, it's the best cuppa I've ever had.

Chapter 5

Do you know what? This isn't half bad. It was actually kinda cosy in *Hermie* last night with the curtains drawn. I lit the candles in the lantern and read in bed, and, when I went out for one last loo stop, I came back to find the solar-powered fairy lights I'd hooked up around the outside of the van had twinkled into life. I slept well – considering – and this morning I got ready at the refreshingly clean shower block and ate a bowl of fruit-and-nut granola at my little yellow table. Making up the bed was a bit of a faff, as was putting it away again, but, on the whole, I think I might be more cut out for this camping business than I thought.

Of course, there's always tomorrow.

And the next day.

And the next sixty after that.

Hmm.

I'm sure Charlie will have Internet connection, so I don't bother going up the hill to check my emails. Padstow is just a short walk away from here on the Camel Trail – the one-time railway route that runs right alongside the Camel Estuary – and I smile as I make my way along the picturesque path, moving aside for the occasional cyclist, my rucksack slung over my shoulder. The sun is out and it's another beautiful day. I can't wait to get started.

Unfortunately, it all goes pear-shaped from then on in.

Behind Charlie's front door, April is screaming her head off. I consider walking away again, but Charlie clocks me from the living-room window, where he's pacing the floor with a phone to his ear.

A moment later, the door whooshes open and the volume inside the house goes up a notch.

'Hi. Sorry, I'll just be a minute,' he says to me, covering the mouthpiece. 'Come in.'

He steps back to let me pass. I do so, reluctantly.

'I don't *know*, Mum.' He speaks again into the receiver, raising his voice over the din. He jerks his head towards the kitchen, so I lead the way, horribly aware that we're heading *towards* the noise. 'Yeah. Calpol *and* Nurofen,' I hear him say.

April is sitting in a square playpen that wasn't there the last time I came, screaming at the top of her lungs. Her face is red and puffy and she has a river of snot trailing down from her nose. She looks up and sees me.

I step away from the playpen.

'I don't have any. I don't *have* any!' Charlie shouts to make himself heard. He looks incredibly harassed as he grabs the kettle and fills it up, cradling the phone to his ear. 'Tea?' he mouths at me.

'I'll do it,' I mouth in return. He lets me take over.

I try not to look as alarmed as I feel. The kitchen is a tip, with plates piled in and by the sink, and food and drink spills over the worktops and on the floors. The sofa opposite the playpen is crammed with toys, clothes, babywipes and other baby paraphernalia. It is a far, far cry from the last time I was here.

'She won't *go* down!' Charlie says loudly into the receiver, freezing in motion to listen to whatever it is his mum is saying in reply. 'All right, I'll try.' Pause. 'I said *all right*, I'll *try*!' He huffs and listens again. '*Thank* you,' he says acerbically. He ends the call and mutters something under his breath, barely looking my way.

I get a couple of mugs out from the cupboard. 'Do you want one?'

'I think I need a shot of tequila,' he replies.

'It's a slippery slope,' I tease, but he doesn't find it funny.

He goes to the playpen and I glance over to see April holding her arms up to him while she screams. He lifts her out of the pen and walks out of the room, taking some of the noise with him.

I probably let the tea brew for a few minutes longer than necessary, but, by the time I tentatively appear at the living-room door, the screaming has quietened to hiccuppy breathing. Charlie has April over his shoulder and is jigging her around. She notices me and turns her face away to bury it in her dad's neck. I place the tea on the coffee table.

'Is she okay?' I ask in a whisper.

Charlie closes his eyes briefly in resignation and nods.

'Shall I go and get started?'

He nods again.

Nicki's computer screen has been dusted since the last time I came here and her desk has been wiped down, too. But, if Charlie has a cleaner, she hasn't been this morning.

I switch on the computer, and, while I'm waiting for it to fire up, I get my notepad and pen out of my rucksack. The first thing I want to do is read the beginning of the sequel. I'm hoping to find some clues as to where Nicki was going with it.

Ten minutes later there's a knock on the door.

'Come in,' I call, swivelling in my chair to see Charlie enter.

'Have you got everything you need?' he asks. His face is racked with exhaustion.

'Yes, I'm fine. I'm reading *Confessions*. The first few pages are great,' I think to add.

He nods, but I can tell he's not in the mood to hear about Nicki's book.

'How's April?' I ask.

He sighs and leans against the doorframe. 'I managed to get her to sleep in her pram. She's been up half the night.'

'You must be knackered.' His eyes are tinged red.

'Mmm. Turns out she was, too. She wouldn't normally nap until ten.'

He rubs the heels of his hands against his eyes. He hasn't shaved this morning.

'She usually goes down like clockwork. Mum reckons she must be teething again.'

'A clockwork baby? I didn't think they existed,' I jest, hoping he can take it.

'Neither did I,' he replies wryly. 'Nicki's sister, Kate, got

39

her into a routine a few months ago. Wrote out a timetable for me, told me to stick to it. Mum thought it was rubbish, but it worked.' He tuts and looks away. 'Well, it does work, usually.'

'Where does Nicki's sister live?'

'Essex, where Nicki's mum lives, too.'

'That's a long way away,' I say unnecessarily.

'Funnily enough, when Nicki moved back here, she didn't think it was far enough.' Pain darkens his features, killing off his momentary amusement. 'Have you got everything you need?' he asks brusquely, and I adapt my expression accordingly. He doesn't want my sympathy.

'Yes, I'm fine.'

'Well, I'm going to get on with some work while she sleeps. I'll be outside if you need me.'

'Okay, thanks.'

A short while later, a scratching sound comes from outside the window. I curiously peer over the computer screen to see Charlie, in a white vest and frayed khaki green shorts, sanding a large tree branch in the back garden. I wonder what he's doing with it. I watch him for a moment, noticing the taut muscles on his tanned arms.

And there I was, lamenting the absence of a sea view from this side of the house.

I told Elliot all about Charlie the same day that I met him. He called me when I was at the B&B in Padstow, about to go to bed. He wanted to know what Charlie was like and I knew he meant both in manner and in appearance, so I told him honestly, a goofy grin plastered all over my face. He chuckled and told me to go and take a cold shower.

I love that he doesn't get jealous. He trusts me and I trust him, and neither of us has issues over the other admiring some eye candy if it crosses our paths.

I think of Vince and shudder. He's one of my ex-boyfriends whom I'm really not looking forward to meeting up with again. He used to get insanely jealous. I try to put him out of my mind.

I'm completely caught up in Kit's world again as I read the early pages. I know the words will come to an abrupt end, but it's still a shock when it happens.

The Secret Life of Us concluded on a cliff hanger, but *Confessions* stops right in the middle of the story, right in the middle of a *conversation*...

It's staggering to think that Nicki died at this point in the book. Where was she when it happened? Was she working, sitting here at the desk where I'm sitting now? A chill trickles down my spine at the thought.

How did Charlie and April cope, losing her so suddenly? April was only five weeks old, a tiny baby, needing her mother. I can't even begin to imagine how Charlie managed to pick himself up and be a father to her. His grief must've been utterly debilitating. It doesn't bear thinking about.

I take a deep breath and exhale loudly. I think it might be time for a coffee break— No way! Is that the time? It's twenty past one! The morning's flown by. Maybe I'll take a wander into Padstow for lunch.

I stand up and stretch, looking out of the window. I've been so lost in the story that I didn't even notice Charlie had stopped sanding.

The house is quiet as I wander downstairs. I poke my head around the door to the living room, but it's deserted. There's no one in the kitchen, either.

'Charlie?' I call out in case he's lurking somewhere. No answer.

I frown. I didn't hear him come upstairs, not that I was paying attention. I look around, but there's no note to say where he's gone. He hasn't given me a key, so I won't be able to get back in if he's out for the day.

I'd better check upstairs.

'Charlie?' I call out quietly as I walk back up. I don't want to wake April if she's still asleep. How long do babies nap for? Surely she'd be awake by now.

Aside from Nicki's office, there are three other doors on the first floor and they're all open. The first is the bathroom – empty.

I go to the second and knock on the door. 'Charlie?' No answer. I peek in and find April's bedroom. Her cot and furniture are wooden and painted white, and her curtains and blanket are pale pink. There's a large seahorse on the wall, made out of sticks, and the small table beside the cot is crammed with higgledy-piggledy, white, wooden photo frames. I can see from here that some of the photos are of Nicki, and, although I'd like to study them, I already feel that I'm snooping. I call out Charlie's name once more before knocking on the last open door along the corridor. When there's no answer, I cautiously peer inside. The large double bed dominating the space is unmade, and there are more photo frames on the side table, but that's all I take in of Charlie's bedroom before backing out.

The house is empty. I am alone. And I am ravenous.

When will Charlie be back? When can I go for lunch? I really don't want to risk getting locked out.

I decide to make another cup of tea to tide me over, and then I get back to work. I plan to read over the rest of the contents of Nicki's computer and take notes.

I start with the *Confessions* synopsis, but it's disappointingly brief. Kit continues to plan two weddings, but the pages end with the question, 'Will she go through with them?' so I have no idea if Nicki intended her character to choose between the two men, get dumped by either or both of them, or marry them both. When I'm done with the synopsis, I move on to the next file in the folder.

Whereas the morning flew by, the next hour and a half passes in slow motion. Eventually, I can stand it no longer and go back downstairs in search of food. There's a loaf of bread in the breadbox, so I guiltily slice off a couple of pieces and pop them into the toaster before raiding the fridge and cupboards for condiments.

While I'm waiting for my toast to pop up, I tidy up a bit. There's a dishwasher, but, upon investigation, I discover it needs unpacking, so for now I just take the dirty plates from the table and relocate them to the pile already in and by the sink. After I've eaten, I wipe over the worktops and wash up the dirty dishes by hand. Hopefully that will do as payment for my stolen lunch.

It's almost five o'clock before Charlie comes home with April – I left the office door open so I could hear them returning. I'm a bit confused that Charlie went out without leaving me a key – or even so much as telling me – but maybe he doesn't want me to have open access to his house yet. I guess it must be weird having a stranger here at all, but he was the one who asked it to be this way. I'll bring lunch with me tomorrow.

I gather my things together and shut down Nicki's computer. At least I've had a productive day.

On my way downstairs I can hear Charlie talking to April in the living room. I poke my head around the door to see him changing her nappy. She's lying on a mat on the bay-window sofa, gazing up at him.

'Hi.'

He jolts and looks at me over his shoulder. Nicki's yellow bandana is back in place around his forehead.

'I'm going to head off.'

'Okay.'

'I nicked some of your bread for lunch, sorry. I'll replace it.'

'There's no need,' he says with a frown, smoothing down April's red dress and sitting her up.

'I'll see you in the morning?' I say. 'Nine o'clock?'

'Sure.' He stands up and lifts his daughter into his arms. She smiles at him.

'She seems happier.' I linger at the door.

'I think the teething gel helped.'

'Your mum's idea?'

'Yeah.' He comes over to me, so I step out of the room and head towards the front door. 'Everything all right today?' He sounds tense.

'Yes, good. I'm just reading everything in the *Confessions* folder.'

He nods curtly and opens the door. 'See you tomorrow, then.'

'Yep, see you then.'

The door closes with a loud clunk before I've even made it onto the footpath.

Chapter 6

The same thing happens the next day, but this time I came prepared. I go downstairs to the empty kitchen and clear away the breakfast things before eating my sandwich at the table overlooking the back garden. At least I'm not missing out on sunshine. The sky is completely overcast.

What I previously thought of as a bit of a dumping ground, I now realise is some sort of outdoor workshop. The trampled grass is carpeted with sawdust and wood chippings and there are workbenches peppered with tools and wooden planks lined up on the ground. Charlie was sanding a branch again this morning and there are several smooth, finished branches lying under the veranda. I wonder what he's making.

When he comes back at the slightly earlier time of three forty-five that afternoon, I go downstairs to make a coffee and to ask him.

'Some recreation equipment for a local primary school,' he tells me, popping April into her pen. She immediately squawks and hauls herself up to a standing position, her chubby fingers clutching onto the side of the pen as support. 'Play with your toys for a bit,' he says to her.

She cries out with annoyance, but he ignores her, opening the dishwasher.

'You set it going,' he says to me, seeming almost perplexed by the sight of clean dishes.

'Yes.'

'You don't have to tidy up after us.'

'I don't mind. I needed a break from staring at a computer screen.'

He's oblivious to my pointed statement.

He starts to unload the dishwasher while I make myself a coffee, trying to take a leaf out of his book and ignore April's insistent cries. Eventually, Charlie gives up and lifts her out of her playpen, sitting her on her nappy-clad bottom on the floor with a saucepan and a wooden spoon to play with. She bashes the utensil against the pan. *Ow, my ears!*

I walk over to the French doors and look out while waiting for the kettle to boil.

'Is that what you do?' I call over my shoulder. 'Make stuff out of wood?'

'Yep.'

'Like what?'

'Play kitchens, houses, tree houses, that sort of thing.' He has to raise his voice over the racket April is making.

I'm always impressed by people who can make things with their hands. I turn away from the doors. 'Do you always work when April is asleep?'

'Yep. But how much time I get varies.' He casts a wry look

47

at his daughter. She gazes up at him and he narrows his eyes at her.

Whack, whack, whack.

'Water's boiled,' he notes absently, glancing my way.

I get on with my task and leave them to it.

'Tell him to give you a key!' my friend Marty exclaims the following evening when I call her from up on the field. I've come here to catch up on my emails and check the comments on my blog, but I got bored after a while and decided to call my best mate instead.

Marty and I were introduced in our early twenties by a colleague who worked at the same travel magazine as me – Marty, herself, is a travel agent.

I'd just broken up with my boyfriend, Vince, and we clicked straightaway. We flat-shared for three years, although I lived with her only on and off, as, once I went freelance, I travelled around quite a bit. We've been great friends ever since.

'I can't ask for a key,' I reply. 'Not yet. He barely knows me. I don't want to go to him with a list of requirements.'

'A key is hardly unreasonable, especially as he asked you to work from his house.'

'I *will* ask him for one, just not yet. Maybe next week.' I smile at a woman as she trundles down the steep hill towards the toilet block with her onesie-clad daughter, before returning my gaze to the estuary. The tide is on its way back in. 'I sat out on his front wall for a bit today. It was really hot.'

'What's wrong with his back garden?' she asks, so I explain.

Charlie was hammering earlier, as well as sanding. He

seems to be making basic structures out of wooden planks – at the moment he's working on a play kitchen. I don't know where the branches will come in.

'Is he shaggable?' she asks suddenly.

'Highly,' I reply with a smirk, then immediately feel guilty for being so flippant considering the circumstances that brought me here.

'Does he look anything like Ross Poldark?' Marty asks eagerly, blissfully unaware of my altered mood.

'No,' I reply firmly. 'You're *obsessed* with that series!'

Poldark is set in Cornwall, so she does have a reason for bringing it into our conversation.

'Yeah, I am. Aidan Turner is insanely lickable.'

'Lickable?' I ask with a laugh, as our conversation goes off on a bizarre tangent. Nothing new, when it comes to Marty.

'Don't you just want to climb through the TV screen and lick his face?'

'Can't say I've ever wanted to do that,' I reply, presuming she's talking about the guy who plays the lead character. 'How did we get onto this?'

'You were saying Charlie is as fit as fuck and I asked—'

'Stop!' I cut her off. 'I did *not* say that! You're making me feel bad. The poor guy only lost his wife last October.'

'That really is properly shitty, isn't it?'

'I'd say that's putting it mildly.' I sigh heavily.

'Are you all right?' she asks. 'You don't sound like your usual chirpy self. Is it depressing, being there?'

'Not as depressing as it could be, but I do feel a bit like I'm intruding,' I admit. 'Yes, even though he wanted me here,' I say before she can chip in. 'He only really talks to me if it's about his daughter. I've tried to make conversation about his work, but he's not what you'd call chatty. I guess it's only early days. It'll be fine. I'll perk up. Hang on a sec.' I place the phone down on the grass and crack open a mini-bottle of Prosecco before putting the phone back to my ear. 'Cheers,' I say, taking a swig. The bubbles fizz right up my nostrils and make me cough.

'Are you drinking on your own?' Marty asks with alarm.

'No, I'm talking to you. I consider that company.'

'When you said you were going to perk up, I didn't realise you meant you were going to get shitfaced on the phone to me.'

I burst out laughing. 'Oh, Marty, do you really have to go on holiday to Greece for two weeks with that boyfriend of yours? Can't you come and see me instead?'

'I promise I'll come and see you when the lovely Ted and I get back,' she assures me.

'You really do love him, don't you?' I say wistfully.

'I really, really do,' she replies even more wistfully.

'All right, now you're making me want to throw up.'

We're still giggling when we ring off.

I take a deep breath of the damp, salty air, inhaling the scent of seawater and long, summer grass. The sun is setting and the sky is a canvas of mauve, orange, rose and blue brush-strokes. I stay up on the hill until the first star comes out and then I return to *Hermie*, climbing into bed without bothering to take off my make-up.

Chapter 7

I'm a bit over it now.

And, yes, I know this does not bode well for the coming weeks.

I had to make a midnight loo stop thanks to my old pal Prosecco, and my stomach muscles were at it all night long because I kept rolling off to one side – obviously the ground is not as level as I thought. I slept terribly, so I'm knackered and I woke up this morning with crusty eyes and clumpy lashes.

I look like hell. And I don't even care. I'm not even sure I can be bothered to go to the shower block.

I lie there in bed until eight forty before pulling myself together.

Sort it out, Bridget. Charlie is expecting you.

Grabbing my washbag, I climb out of the van. I really *do* need to wash my hair today. Grease is the word.

The showers work with tokens – it costs 50p for a good

five minutes. I got a stack of them when I arrived, but can I find any of the little gold fuckers in my washbag when the shower cuts out halfway through rinsing my hair? No, I cannot.

I wrap my towel around my body and unlock the shower cubicle, hoping to find a sympathetic passer-by. Luckily I see Justin heading away from the toilets, so I call after him.

He comes over, grinning like a loon, his dreadlocks happily piled up under his cheerfully coloured hat.

'Run out of tokens?' he asks.

'Yes. Can I owe you one?' I beg.

'Course you can,' he replies with a wink. 'Back in a tick.'

The skies are back to being overcast and, on the return to my pitch, it starts to spit with rain.

'Oi, Bridget?' a little voice calls out, stopping me in my tracks.

'Morning, Roy,' I reply, trying to inject some enthusiasm into my voice as my next-door-pitch neighbour emerges from his campervan. He and his wife Shirley introduced themselves to me on my first day here. They seem like a sweet enough couple, if a little chatty and overeager.

'Er, Bridget,' he says, shuffling to the edge of his awning in his slip-ons. 'I hate to be a killjoy, but…'

Oh dear, what have I done?

'Your music kept Shirley awake last night, and she's recovering from an op, you see.'

'Oh, I'm so sorry!' I say, genuinely mortified. 'Is she okay?' I only put it on to cheer myself up.

'She's fine. She has dicky knees, but she's on the mend now.'

'That's good to hear.'

He shifts from foot to foot. 'You do know that the rules of the campsite say no music?'

'I'm sorry, I won't play it that loud again, I promise.'

He laughs uneasily. 'You really shouldn't play it at all.' He taps his finger on the side of his nose. 'But I won't tell anyone as long as you keep it right down.'

'Okay, thanks, Roy.'

He nods at me graciously and a little bit patronisingly. 'No problem at all, Bridget.' He peers up at the sky. 'Looks like rain today.'

'It's already started.' I hold my palms up. 'I'd better get back under cover.'

'Right you are. Have a good day.'

'You too,' I call over my shoulder as I head back to *Hermie*.

Now, where did I put my raincoat?

It's just as well I find it, because the heavens throw everything at me on my way to Charlie's.

By the time I get there, my jeans are soaked and I am *late*.

Charlie doesn't look too impressed when he answers the door.

'Sorry I'm late,' I mumble, feeling like a naughty schoolgirl as I remove my dripping raincoat.

'There are towels in the bathroom,' he says as I take off my Vans.

'Can I put these on the radiator?' I ask, indicating the one under the coat rack.

'Yeah, I'm just on the phone.' He heads back down the corridor.

Phone? I didn't see him with a phone.

The voice of a young woman on speakerphone rings out as I follow him into the kitchen. She's talking in a cutesy voice to April, who is standing in her playpen, bouncing up and down on her feet as she stares fixatedly at the phone lying flat on the sofa opposite.

'I'm back,' Charlie says loudly.

'Hi,' the voice in the phone says. 'Was that the ghostwriter arriving?'

'Bridget, yeah,' he replies. 'She's here.' He glances at me and jerks his head towards the phone. 'I'm talking to Kate, Nicki's sister,' he explains quietly.

'Oh,' I whisper. I did notice the Essex accent.

'You want to make yourself a cuppa?' he asks.

I nod and get on with it.

'Charlie?' Kate says as he wipes down the table.

'I'm here. What were you saying?'

'Do not put her to sleep in the pram today, all right?'

'I don't have time to do it any other way,' he replies, sounding agitated. 'I'm so behind on this job.'

'When do they want it?'

'Next week.'

'Next week?' she scoffs. 'School's not back until September.'

'The caretaker's going away. He wants to get it installed before he leaves.'

'Oh. Fair enough. But listen, she'll sleep better in her cot, and, if you slip out of your routine, it will come back to bite you. Believe me, I know.'

'Yeah, I know,' he mutters, rinsing out the sponge at the sink. 'How are the kids?'

'Driving me insane,' she replies. 'School holidays.' She pauses. 'Do you want me to come and help out next week?' Her tone is tentative. 'Mum could have the kids.'

'No, it's fine,' Charlie brushes her off. 'I'll get it done. My mum reckons she'll be able to spare some time in any case.'

'Do *not* let her use the pram for naps,' Kate states firmly.

'Have you tried stopping her?' he asks drily, picking up the phone and slumping onto the sofa. He presses the button to turn off speakerphone and puts the phone to his ear, rolling his eyes at something Kate says.

'Exactly,' he states.

I pick up my mug and go upstairs, grabbing a towel from the bathroom to sit on until my jeans dry out.

I've been working in silence so far this week, but today I need a pick-me-up, and nothing does that for me like music. I switch on my prized Bang & Olufsen Bluetooth speaker – I brought it with me from the campsite – and then search through my iPod Touch for the perfect song, pressing PLAY and turning the sound up. If I have to wear headphones in *Hermie*, I may as well use my speaker here – I think it's my favourite possession.

I don't hear Charlie knock because the next thing I know he and April are in my office. Nicki's office. *Our* office.

I turn the sound down and swivel to face him. 'Is it too loud?'

'No. I'm putting April down for a sleep now. You might hear some crying.' He glances at my speaker. 'Or maybe not.'

'Do you want me to turn it down? I can turn it down.'

'Honestly, it's fine with the door closed.'

'Okay, cool.' I smile at him. I am *much* happier. That's what

'Tainted Love' by Marilyn Manson, 'U Can't Touch This' by MC Hammer and 'The Sun Always Shines on TV' by A-ha does to me.

'Are you going out today?' I ask as he starts to leave the room.

'Sorry?' He pauses with his hand on the doorknob. He's wearing a light-blue bandana today – another one of Nicki's, I'm guessing.

'Are you going out today?' I repeat my question.

'Er, probably.'

'Do you know roughly when?'

He furrows his brow. 'When April wakes up. Eleven, eleven thirty. I usually take her into town for lunch.'

Must be nice to get out of the house…

'Why?'

I shrug. 'I was thinking about going into town for some lunch myself,' I say casually. His eyes widen. 'I didn't mean with you,' I say quickly, sensing his alarm at the thought of me inviting myself to join them. 'I meant for a wander. But it's raining today so I probably won't bother.'

'Okay.' He looks awkward. April starts to whinge and he jigs her up and down. 'I'd better put her down,' he says, kissing her forehead. She lays her head back against his chest, her blue eyes staring at me sleepily.

'Sure. See you later,' I whisper after him.

That went well. I didn't even ask him what time he'd be back.

At lunchtime, I take my speaker with me downstairs to the deserted kitchen and dance along to Billy Joel's 'It's Still Rock and Roll to Me' while I'm tidying up, clicking my fingers, having a bit of a jive and bashing out the big drum roll on an invisible kit. Vanilla Ice comes on after that and I'm well away. There's no point attempting to eat my sandwich while 'Ice Ice Baby' is on. It's impossible to rap with your mouth full.

Every evening since I've got here, I've picked up fish and chips, scampi and chips or something else fried and fishy on my way back to the campsite. Then I've sat on a bench overlooking the estuary and watched the tide roll back in while tucking into the very best Padstow has to offer.

But this evening I make a decision: I can't live on Rick Stein's forever.

I mean, I *really* can't live on Rick Stein's forever. The cholesterol will kill me.

I *will* cook at some point, just not tonight. Because Thursday is Pizza Night at the campsite.

Get in.

At six o'clock, two guys rock up with a converted horse trailer that's been painted green and contains a wood-fired oven. I place my order for a cured-meats pizza and wander back in the rain to the bombsite that is my home for the next seven and a half weeks. I'm counting down.

I turned *Hermie* upside down in my search for my raincoat this morning and now there are clothes strewn everywhere. I really have no idea what I'm going to do with them all. I gather everything together and cram it into the footwells belonging to the driver and passenger seats. I'll deal with that mess later. Right now, I just need to make sure I've got a table to eat at.

I didn't have time to make up the bench seat earlier and there doesn't seem to be much point now as I'll be going to sleep in a couple of hours. I wonder if the table will still click into place with the bed down. I decide to give it a whirl and discover that it does. And that's how I roll with it: my legs dangling over the edge of my bed, stuffing my face with pizza at *Hermie*'s bright-yellow table while the rain pelts down over my head.

Could be worse.

Chapter 8

Honestly, the weather is up and down like a frigging yo-yo. On Friday it's sunny again. Not that I'm complaining.

This time I manage to nab Charlie at eleven forty-five as he attempts to back out of the house with April in her pram.

'What time will you be back?' I ask him, distractedly smiling at April as she gazes up at me. She's too intent on finishing whatever indeterminate white and gooey round thing she's eating to smile back.

'I'm not sure.' He frowns. 'Why?'

'I might nip into Padstow for some groceries. I don't want to get locked out.'

'Oh.' He looks surprised. Has the thought not even occurred to him that I can't leave his house and get back in if he's out? 'I was going to try to put April down in her cot at two today,' he says.

'Okay, great. I'll tie my walk in with you, then.'

'Okay,' he says.

'Okay,' I say.

He goes out of the door and pulls it shut behind him.

I decide to take a break and eat my Pot Noodle early, turning my music right up and singing along to 'Unbelievable' by EMF while I'm waiting for the kettle to boil. It's not even noon, but I won't leave the house before one if I'm taking an hour's lunch break. I'm over by the French doors punching the air when Charlie calls my name.

'*Holyfuckingshit*!' I gasp, clutching my hand to my chest as I spin around to face him.

'Sorry,' he replies with a smirk. He's standing in the kitchen doorway. 'Forgot nappies.'

He looks – dare I say it? – amused as he roots around in the cupboard, pulling out what he's after. 'See you later,' he calls over his shoulder, a blindingly gorgeous grin on his face.

I reel backwards. That's the first time I've seen him smile properly when it wasn't at his daughter.

Or at the memory of his wife.

'Freedom' by the lovely, late George Michael is playing at top volume on the stereo inside my head when I finally make it out of the house. The sun is shining, the sky is blue, and Padstow is *absolutely rammed*. I can barely make my way along the footpaths because they're so packed with locals and tourists, so I walk on the road instead, hoping I'll be able to avoid death by motor vehicle. The water in the small harbour is dotted with sailing boats, and a flock of seagulls are going berserk over something a small, gleeful boy has thrown to them. I can see two ice cream vans from where I'm standing, and I passed a crêperie van on the way here, too. Grey-stone, light-blue and cream-painted shops, restaurants and cafés follow the curved line of the road to my left, and, across the other side of the harbour, a hill stretches away from the town, creating a pretty green backdrop to the buildings.

The sweet smell of fudge wafts out of a confectionary shop as I pass, mingling with the aroma coming from the Padstow Pasty down the road. I think there's a Co-op around the corner. If this is anything like the other posh seaside towns I've visited, there'll be a White Stuff, Joules, Fat Face or Seasalt here, as well.

I find all four. If Marty were around, we could've made that a drinking game.

I miss her. In truth, I've been missing her for a long time. I'm glad that she's happy, but, when I dicked off to Australia for a year, I didn't expect to come back and find her living with a guy I hadn't even met. I like Ted – he's a good 'un – but seeing my friends so loved up and popping out babies makes me pine all the more for Elliot.

Not that I want a baby.

After I've picked up a few bits and pieces from the super-market, I nip into Joules and try on a couple of things. I get a bit of a shock when I discover the size 12 is a little on the tight side – damn my Rick Stein's addiction! – so, on my way back to Charlie's, I take a detour via one of the bicycle-hire places. The Camel Trail is excellent for cycling, apparently, so I reckon I'll go on a few bike rides this weekend and try to burn off some excess calories.

I arrive at the house to find that Charlie hasn't yet returned, so I sit on the wall in the front garden and wait for him, twiddling stalks of lavender and absent-mindedly sniffing my fingers.

A girl with a red T-shirt and matching headscarf pushes a pram along the footpath towards me.

Bandana Central.

'Are you the author?' she asks, smiling brightly as she comes to a stop in front of me. She has warm, brown eyes set within a round face, and her legs are surprisingly stick-thin. With her red T-shirt, she reminds me a little of a kindly robin.

'Yes, Bridget,' I introduce myself, liking the ring of *author* way more than *ghostwriter*.

'I'm Jocelyn,' she replies. 'And this is Thomas.' She nods at her son. 'We live across the road.'

'Hello,' I say, smiling at her baby. He looks to be about April's age.

'Is Charlie out?' she asks.

'Yeah, he went into town. I'm just waiting for him to get back.'

'Don't you have a key?' she asks with surprise.

'No.'

'Oh.'

Awkward.

'How's he getting on with the school job?' she asks, as though I'd know.

I'm a bit embarrassed that I don't, so I pretend otherwise. 'Okay, I think, although it's a bit tough without childcare.'

She looks dismayed. 'I can have April! I keep offering, but he never takes me up on it! Will you remind him? Thomas and I are free this afternoon for a couple of hours.'

'I think he wants to put her down in her cot at two o'clock for a nap, but he might give you a shout later.' Again,

I bizarrely feign knowledge of the situation. I don't know what's got into me.

'Urge him to,' she says. 'I'm a teacher at the school he's making it for,' she explains, whispering conspiratorially, 'I put the job his way.'

Eek, I hope I haven't just landed him in it.

'Well, it's all looking fantastic so far,' I enthuse, overegging it a bit. 'The kids will *love* it.'

She smiles. 'I know they will. Charlie's pieces are works of art.'

She and Thomas have gone into their house by the time Charlie appears.

I hop down from the wall. 'I just saw Jacqueline, no, Evelyn, no—'

'Jocelyn,' he helps me out as he pushes the pram up to the door.

'That's the one. Nice lady. She offered to babysit April for you if you need some help.'

'That was nice of her,' he murmurs, leaning over April to put his key in the lock.

'She meant it. I could tell,' I state, wheeling my bicycle up the path behind him, my shopping hung over the handle. 'She's around this afternoon,' I add, looking around for something to lock the bike to.

'Okay, thanks,' he says as he pushes the pram over the threshold.

I can tell by the tone of his voice that he's not going to accept her offer of help, but I don't know why.

'What is *that*?' he asks, stopping so abruptly that I almost ram into him. He turns around to face me.

63

'A bike.'

His face breaks into a sudden, surprising grin. 'Where did you get it?'

'Bicycle-hire place.'

He laughs, and I realise I should probably be annoyed that he finds the idea of me on a bike so funny, but the sight and sound of him laughing is so lovely that I find myself giggling in return.

'What?' I ask, mock-affronted. 'Is it so strange that I want to get some exercise?'

'Not at all.' He shakes his head, trying to keep a straight face as his green – or hazel, still can't decide – eyes sparkle. 'But you'll look like a right div on that thing. Bring it indoors,' he urges. 'There's nowhere to lock it up out there.'

He moves the pram out of the way and holds the door back for me, so I wheel the bike into the hall.

'You know what? Return it,' he says suddenly. 'You can borrow Nicki's bike while you're here.'

I freeze, my smile locked in place as my eyes grow rounder. He immediately sobers up.

'No, I couldn't.' I shake my head.

'Yes, you can,' he mutters quietly, shutting the door behind me. 'It's in the shed. I'll get it ready for you this weekend.'

'Honestly, I—'

'It's a good bike,' he interrupts. 'Practically new. She bought it with the money from her book.'

I continue to protest.

'I want it to get some use,' he says, cutting me off again, and I know he's had enough of my arguing.

'Okay, thanks,' I say edgily.

He shoves his hand deep into the pocket of his shorts and pulls out a set of keys.

'I should've given these to you earlier.' He drops them into my palm. 'You can come and go as you please. Let me talk you through the alarm. I don't usually bother setting it, but I should.'

As he goes through the instructions for the keypad on the wall, my eyes drift over the wood dust coating the light-blond hairs on his lean forearms. He notices me noticing.

'No time for a shower.' He brushes his hands over his arms and I stiffen with embarrassment, trying to focus on the rest of his instructions.

Chapter 9

Right, that's it. I'm going out for the day. It was all very nice tootling along the cycle path yesterday on my, yes, admittedly chunky hired bike, but today I fancy a drive. And it has nothing to do with the fact that my leg muscles are sore now as well as those of my stomach.

Nicki's 'Research' document mentioned a Morris-and-Kit scene set in the Lost Gardens of Heligan, so that's where I'm headed.

I stand on the grass outside the van's wide side door and stare in at the mess. I'd better make up the bed and store the table at the very least. I should probably also wash up so I can put away the plates and cups. Plus, I need to turn the driver's seat back around, so that will mean clearing the clothes from the footwell. Christ, I need to take off all the fairy lights as well.

Urgh. What a faff.

I start with the table and bed, then decide to tackle the

footwell. But, when I go around to the driver's side of the van, I see to my dismay that the back left wheel is completely flat.

Ah. So *that's* why I've been rolling off to one side for the last few nights.

My shoulders slump. I've never changed a tyre in my life.

I set off to the office in search of help and find Julia sitting behind the desk.

'Hey,' I say.

'Hey, Bridget!' she replies, far more chirpily.

'I don't suppose you or Justin knows how to change a tyre, do you?'

Her face falls. 'Have you got a flattie?'

'Yeah.' I roll my eyes.

'I'm afraid not. We don't have a car. We cycle everywhere. Neither of us can even drive, to be honest.'

Bloody hippies.

'Give Charlie a call,' she suggests, perking up. 'He's very handy.'

'Oh, no, I don't want to bother him.'

'Don't be silly.' She picks up the phone and dials a number.

'No, I *really* don't want to bother him,' I reiterate, waving my hands at her in a panic.

'Hi, Charlie?' Julia says into the receiver, blatantly ignoring me, even as I continue to wave my hands wildly at her. 'It's Julia.' Pause. 'Hello! Listen, I've got Bridget here and she's got a flat tyre on her campervan.' Pause. 'You're a star. Thanks, darling.'

She hangs up. I stare at her, mortified.

'He's coming right over.'

'You didn't have to do that.' It's a struggle to contain my frustration.

'It's no problem,' she replies with a sunny smile.

I get as far as showering and washing up my dirty dishes when Charlie pulls up at my pitch in a silver Mitsubishi pickup truck.

'Sorry about this,' I say as he climbs out of the vehicle.

'It's no bother,' he replies, getting a tool bag and a jack out of the back before seeing to April. She's sitting in her car seat, eating another one of those gooey round things. I think they're rice cakes.

He frees her from her harness and puts her down on the grass, brushing sticky white globules of puffed rice off her yellow cotton dress. He's wearing washed-out grey cargo shorts and a white T-shirt. April holds her arms up to him, so he stands her on her feet and she gamely snatches his hand.

'No, Daddy's got to stay here,' he says firmly as she tries to lead him away. He scoops her up and carries her over to my camping chair, propping her beside it so she has something to lean against. She clutches the armrest and bends forward, clamping her mouth over the green material. She's like a little puppy. She releases her mouth and grins up at me. I giggle at her, despite the fact that she's just slobbered all over my chair.

'Can you keep an eye on her?' Charlie asks over his shoulder as he heads to the other side of the van.

April holds her hand up to me and lets out a cry, her brow knitting together. I take her hand and she sets off, toddling unsteadily across the grass.

'Where are you going?' I ask.

'Urghn,' she replies, leading me to a flowerbed. She reaches down and cheerfully beheads a red geranium.

'Ooh, no, I don't think we should do that,' I say light-heartedly. 'Shall we go and see what Daddy's doing?'

She looks up at me and nods – a big purposeful nod. There's something quite cute about her, I guess.

As babies go.

'Where's Daddy?' I ask as she leads the way. 'Can you hear him?'

We emerge around the side of *Hermie* to find Charlie jacking up the back right-hand side of the van. He's not wearing a bandana today and his dark-blond hair is falling into his eyes as he winds the handle on the jack. Not even a nun would be blind to the way his muscles are rippling in that T-shirt. He straightens up and shoves his hair off his forehead.

'She'll give you a backache if you let her do that for too long,' he warns, nodding at his daughter, who's still holding my hand.

'I don't mind,' I reply.

'Is the spare tyre in the boot?'

'Yeah.'

He follows slowly while I walk at April's pace round to the back of the van. When I open the rear door, half of my wardrobe falls out.

'Whoops, there go my clothes.'

Charlie swings April out of the way, breaking our hand contact. 'Give me a sec,' I say, wiping my now-sticky hands on my jeans and gathering up a big armful. I walk around to *Hermie*'s side door to find it closed.

'Er, Charlie?' I call out apologetically. 'Can you open the

door for me?' I look back to see that I've dropped three pairs of knickers. At least they're clean.

He appears around the back of the van, his eyes darting to my underwear and his lips twitching as he opens the side door.

I step forward and dump everything in the living space – on top of everything else.

'Whoa!' he exclaims, surveying the mess. 'How do you live like this?'

'*You* can talk,' I joke impertinently. 'What about the state of your kitchen every morning?'

He looks surprised, and I'm not sure that he realises I'm teasing. 'I'm doing the best that I can,' he says.

'I can't believe you're pulling the widower card on me.'

He freezes.

'Did I just say that out loud?' I ask with alarm.

He lets out an incredulous laugh, his eyebrows jumping practically into his hairline. 'Yes, you really did.'

'Oh, shit! Sorry. Please don't fire me,' I blurt.

He shakes his head and then laughs again, but this time it's a full-bodied belly laugh. My insides warm, despite the internal freak-out that's also going on.

'I don't know how I've lived this long, saying the first thing that comes into my head,' I mumble. 'I'll just get the rest of my clothes.'

I continue to walk April around while Charlie changes the tyre. My back does begin to hurt from stooping, but luckily April gets bored and wants to explore my so-called living room. I gather all my clothes together for what feels like the fiftieth time and relocate them to the grass; and, while she coasts along the edge of the bench seat playing with the freshly washed plastic dishes, I stand just outside and begin separating clean clothes from dirty. I fold up the former and place them in a neat pile on the camping chair. I really should do some washing today. I fear the Lost Gardens of Heligan will have to wait until next weekend, at the rate I'm going.

'Do you want a cup of tea?' I think to ask Charlie after a while.

'That'd be great. I'm pretty much done.'

I enter the now relatively clear space and fire up the gas, unwittingly creating a health and safety risk. *This is exhausting*, I think as I return April to the great outdoors.

'You've still got a bit of a lean going on,' Charlie comments a little while later, peering into the van as he sips his tea.

'Have I?'

'Yeah, can't you see? The back end is sloping down.'

'That's nothing compared to the poor bastards in those tents on the hill.'

He smiles past me, looking at the field. 'Nicki and I camped up there a couple of years ago when we were doing building works to the house. It was a wreck when we bought it.'

'It looks great now,' I say.

'Thanks. We thought camping would be more fun than living in a shithole,' he says with a smirk, adding with a glance my way, 'It wasn't.' He nods at *Hermie*. 'Is this your dad's?'

'How did you know?' I ask with surprise.

'The first time we met you mentioned he'd stayed at this campsite.'

'Oh, that's right. Yeah,' I say. 'He loves it. Hasn't used it much since he broke up with his last girlfriend. They toured all around Europe together.'

'When did your parents split up?'

'They divorced when I was ten. It was amicable.'

But not amicable enough for Dad to continue to want to spend his every holiday on a boat with his ex-wife. My aunt Wendy – Mum's sister – took me after that. That arrangement lasted for a good few years until Mum screwed it all up by having an affair with a married cruise-ship captain. Wendy was so incensed that she refused to take me the following summer out of principle.

Every cloud has its silver lining: that was the year I met Elliot.

'So your mum worked on a cruise ship.'

'She still does. That was how my parents met,' I tell him. 'Mum was a dancer and Dad was a bartender.'

They fell in love after a whirlwind romance, but when Mum got pregnant with me, her contract was promptly terminated. Dad quit too. They cheerfully tied the knot and moved to north London, where Dad worked in a pub and Mum retrained as a beauty therapist in her sister's salon.

But, as time passed, Mum's feet got itchy and no amount of Scholl foot spray was going to cure her.

Dad supported her decision to return to work on a cruise liner, this time as a beauty therapist in the on-board spa.

I was less pleased about it.

I was only six years old when my mum became mostly absent from my life. The only time I'd see her would be when Dad and I visited her on a boat or she was between jobs, when she'd come home for long stints at a time. During these weeks – sometimes months – she'd become so bored that she was never very easy to be around.

But, when she was working, she seemed happy.

Every summer holiday, and most Easters and Christmases, Dad and I would visit whichever cruise liner she was currently contracted to.

I grew used to her not being around much, and, eventually, so did Dad. He was the one who asked for a divorce.

'She's a cruise director now,' I tell Charlie. 'Worked her way up the ranks.' From dancer to beauty therapist to hostess to assistant director to where she is today.

'Sounds like a fun job,' he says.

'She likes it.'

'Do you get to see her much?'

'Not that much.'

I survey my clothes. 'Guess I'd better put this lot away.'

He downs the rest of his tea and puts his empty cup on *Hermie*'s table, pausing and squinting at the inside of the van. 'Don't you have any levelling blocks?'

'Oh, do you know what? I *do*,' I say, remembering. 'Dad told me about them. They're in the boot.'

'Let me give you a hand.'

'Really?' I follow him to the back of the van. 'I've already taken up enough of your time.'

'It's okay. We didn't have much else on. Are you going to take that back, by the way?' He gently kicks the hired bike I've locked up to the pitch sign.

'I feel a little uncomfortable about using Nicki's bike,' I admit cagily.

73

'Don't be stupid about it,' he chides. 'I'll leave it for you in the hall tomorrow morning.'

'Where will you be?' I ask.

'I'm taking April to my parents' place. My mum's going to look after her for a few hours so I can crack on with my job.'

I open the boot and rummage around for a bit, before pulling out a dark-blue bag. 'I think this is them.'

'Looks like it,' he says, taking the bag from me. 'You driving?'

'I just have to turn the seat around. Er, and clear the footwell…'

Charlie gapes in disbelief when I open the driver's door. 'Are you seriously a travel writer? I would've thought you'd have packing lightly down to a T.'

'This *is* me packing lightly,' I tell him. 'You should see me when I go abroad.'

'How do you cope?'

'I'm not usually in any rush. I'd rather wait at a conveyor belt for a bit than make do without my essentials.' I scoop up my clothes. 'Yeah, I know, I've got a lot of essentials.' I head back around the van to my clothing pile.

'You could do with a tent to put everything in,' he calls after me.

I sigh on my return. 'Dad wanted me to bring one. I didn't think I'd need it.'

'I've got a tent you could borrow.' He pauses for thought, adding, '*Somewhere…*'

I grab my second and final armful. 'I'll be fine. I'll just shove everything back in the boot.'

'Doesn't it get in the way when you have to put the bed down?'

'Yeah, I have to move it all again. It's a pain in the arse, to be honest,' I call over my shoulder. 'The ridiculous thing is I went shopping on Friday and almost bought *more* clothes.'

'You're a nutter,' he says with a grin as I reappear.

I shrug. 'Best you know that early.' I climb in the car and start up the ignition, closing the door and putting down the window. 'What do I do?'

He goes to the back of the car and lays down one of the levelling blocks. 'Reverse backwards about twenty centimetres.'

Well, *that's* easier said that done. It takes several minutes of going backwards and forwards, moving a little to the left and a little to the right, before Charlie is satisfied that the van is on level ground.

'Do I really have to do that every time I go out in this bloody thing?' I ask.

'If you want to sleep well at night,' he replies.

I'm starting to understand why Julia and Justin stick with cycling.

Chapter 10

I do sleep better that night – so much so that I'm going to be late if I don't get a wriggle on. I wash my hair and leave it to dry naturally.

I feel as if Charlie and I bonded a bit yesterday, and I'm actually quite looking forward to seeing him this morning. It's only when I get to his place and there's no answer that I remember he's dropping April to his parents. Luckily, I have the keys, so I let myself in.

There's a purple bike in the hall. A pretty purple bicycle.

He meant it, then.

I dropped off the hired bike yesterday after Charlie left, figuring it wouldn't be too much of a pain to rent another if he changed his mind.

I run my hand over the bike's frame and find that it's shiny and dust-free. There's even a helmet clipped to one of the handlebars.

I sit on the bottom stair, staring at the bike. I don't know why I suddenly feel so sad.

Has Charlie still got everything that belonged to Nicki? Is her wardrobe still full of her clothes? Is the television cabinet still full of her DVDs? Are there chutneys in the fridge that he can't bear to throw out because they're hers, even though he hates the taste of them? Her office seems untouched since she died. How long does a person wait before they let go of the one they love?

And Charlie clearly loved her very much, as she did him. No one can write about love so beautifully – so believably – without experiencing it themselves.

Panic rises up within me as, not for the first time, I worry that Nicki's publisher made a mistake in hiring me.

How am I going to pull off this novel? How am I going to write about love the way Nicki did?

The protagonist is a travel writer just like you, so you should be able to identify with her brilliantly, Sara said.

But I need to connect to Nicki's heroine, Kit, at a far deeper level, and I don't know how I'm going to do it.

I get up and sigh loudly, picking up my rucksack and heading into the kitchen. I pull out my speaker and iPod and look for a suitable song. It's not long before I'm head-banging to Def Leppard's 'Pour Some Sugar On Me'.

My hair will be dry in no time.

I don't hear Charlie come back because I'm in the office with my music turned up, so the first I know of his return is when I see him out in the back garden.

I'm a little surprised – piqued, even – that he didn't come to say hello after yesterday, but fair enough if he's keen to crack on. I watch as he carries one of the sanded branches out from under the veranda and sets it across two workbenches before glancing up at the office window. I shrink back instinctively and then want to kick myself. Why didn't I just wave? Obviously, I don't want him to think that I'm spying, but it's hardly a crime for me to notice he's back.

I stand up and open the window to try to cover up.

'It's a bit warm in here today,' I say, pausing my music.

The way he shades his eyes to look up at me makes me think he probably didn't even see me before.

'Hey, thanks very much for the bike,' I say.

'No worries,' he replies.

'How was the rest of your weekend?' I ask.

'Pretty quiet. Yours?'

'Same.'

He nods.

'I'll let you get on,' I say eventually.

'Thank you.'

I sit back down again, feeling on edge. Maybe we didn't bond as much as I thought we did. I sigh, then switch my music back on and try to focus.

Where was I? Oh, yeah. Diaries.

I haven't been able to find that much plot direction from Nicki in her *Confessions* or *Secrets* folders, but it's occurred to me that maybe the key to connecting with her characters really lies with connecting to Nicki herself.

Sorting through all of her diaries and notebooks, I've worked out that she wrote her first diary when she was fifteen.

As the years went on, the diaries became less confessional and rather all-purpose notebooks, with random thoughts and general musings. She was only thirty-one when she died.

I lean back in my seat, put my feet up on the desk, and begin to read. Time to get to know the person behind the stories…

At the first mention of Charlie's name, I sit bolt upright and put my feet flat on the ground, my pulse racing. I had no idea that Nicki and Charlie went to secondary school together.

Morris and Kit went to secondary school together, too, and the similarities don't stop there. Both Charlie and Morris are from Cornwall, they're both blond and good-looking and they both run their own businesses.

Morris is a laidback surfer with ambition. I don't know if Charlie surfs. I don't even know if he's laidback – it's kind of hard to tell. I wonder if he has ambition.

I look out of the window and watch for a moment as Charlie drives a long nail through the wooden structure, two more nails at the ready between his lips.

It's only when he finishes hammering in the third nail that I realise I've been staring, but, before I come to my senses, he lifts up the bottom of his T-shirt and wipes his brow, revealing a maddeningly sexy stomach, all tanned and taut, with a dark triangle of hair disappearing into his waistband. My skin feels hot.

It is so not funny that my boyfriend lives ten thousand miles away. All this eye candy and no chance of action is doing my head in.

I stand up and turn down my music, needing a break from Nicki's messy handwriting. At that very moment, Charlie looks up and locks eyes with me. My scalp is prickling as I head down the stairs, walking into the kitchen at the same time as he steps through the French doors.

'You have got *seriously* eclectic music taste,' he comments drily.

That's why he looked up: he could hear my music. 'It has been said,' I reply with a grin.

'What was the song before last?' he asks.

'The Avalanches?'

'Is that who it was?' He sounds surprised.

'Yeah. "Frankie Sinatra" is the name of the song.'

'Bonkers,' he says.

'You mean catchy.'

He shakes his head. 'Maybe I need to hear it again.'

'I can play it for you if you want,' I offer, quite genuinely.

He shrugs and then meets my questioning gaze for a long moment. 'Go on, then.'

I return with my speaker and iPod.

He leans against the worktop with his arms crossed and stares at me directly as a 1940s Calypso singer goes on about Frank Sinatra not having '*the voice to sing calypso…*'

There's something unusual about Charlie's eyes. I've thought that before, but now it comes to me: there's no darker line around the outside of his irises. The greeny-hazel colour is clear, like bottle glass, and goes right up to the whites.

His mouth tilts up at the corners and I jolt, my concentration returning to the song. I suppress a strong urge to giggle at his expression, and then the rap kicks in and I can't help singing along. He throws his head back and laughs at me.

I really, *really* like making him laugh.

'Catchy, huh?' I nod at him significantly as the chorus returns.

'Catchy,' he confirms. 'But bonkers.'

'Oh, yeah, it's totally bonkers,' I reply in agreement.

He picks up my iPod Touch. 'Don't you keep your music on your phone?'

'Some, but I can't fit fifty thousand songs on there.'

He looks at me. 'You have fifty thousand songs?'

I shrug. 'Yep.'

'Bloody hell!' He studies my iPod again. 'I didn't even know The Avalanches had a new album out.'

'Last year,' I reply. 'Sixteen years since their first one.'

'They took their time.'

'You never listen to music while you work?'

He shakes his head. 'It used to distract Nicki.'

'She never listened to it either?' I ask as he places my iPod back on the wooden worktop.

'No, she couldn't concentrate,' he says softly, and I'm pained to hear the joy seeping out of his voice.

The happy song seems out of place now, so I reach for my speaker and turn the sound down until it's muted. I can never bring myself to end a track midway.

Charlie goes and fills up a glass of water from the sink.

'Do you want a tea?' I ask, remembering what I came down here for.

'Nah, I'm good, thanks. Better get on.' He heads back outside.

Chapter 11

If Charlie is Morris, then who the hell is Timo?

I find out in the next diary.

Nicki was sixteen when her parents divorced and her father – a French chef – took a job at a five-star Thai resort. She and her sister were devastated, but, while Kate's sorrow metamorphosed into anger, Nicki pined for her dad terribly. When he invited his daughters to join him for Christmas, Kate – Nicki's older sister by three years – refused, opting to stay home with their mother instead, so Nicki went alone.

Nicki and Charlie were just friends at this point, although Nicki did have a crush on him. She'd recently broken up with her boyfriend – a little shit called Samuel who'd stolen her virginity and then messed her around so much that I'd been screaming at her to break up with him weeks ago.

Well, pages. Honestly, her diaries are *riveting* – I'm properly invested.

So, when Nicki goes to Thailand, she's single. Charlie, meanwhile, is going out with 'Too Perfect Tisha' – Nicki's nickname, but I agree: it suits the girl.

I remember parts of Thailand from when I was fifteen, which was the last occasion Wendy took me to see Mum on a cruise ship. But Mum cruised around Asia for only two years, and, by the time I was old enough to visit her unaccompanied, the married captain had dumped her and she'd got as far away from him as possible.

The way Nicki writes about Thailand makes me want to book my ticket straightaway. And I really might have to. I'm here in Cornwall, soaking up the atmosphere, which is perfect for the Morris section of the story, but I know I won't be able to write well about a country I'm not familiar with.

But back to Nicki's diary... Her dad is working a lot of the time, so he books his daughter onto a rock-climbing course to keep her occupied. This is where Timo – a.k.a. Isak – comes in.

Isak, the course leader, is from Sweden – not Finland, as in *The Secret Life of Us* – but it hardly takes Sherlock to put two and two together.

He's twenty-one and absolutely gorgeous, with grey eyes and short, dark hair, and seventeen-year-old Nicki is smitten from the get-go. Even I'm captivated as I, along with her, read between the lines and try to work out if he likes her too.

She goes into excruciating detail about their every touch, their every exchanged look, their every conversation. When the course is finished, she states that she's going to continue to go rock climbing, and then I turn the page to see an entry written at two o'clock in the morning, and I know that something big has happened.

Her excitement spills right out of her pen onto the page as she recounts the events of the night before. After her rock-climbing session she got chatting to Isak and he casually invited her for dinner with him. He took her to the rundown village where he lives – on the same island, a fifteen-minute walk away. Nicki was scared about leaving the resort without so much as telling her dad, but her irritation over his lack of time for her made her rebel.

Isak showed her a side of Thailand that was very different from the five-star luxury of the resort – and, despite her initial fear, she found the excursion thrilling. Later, when he walked her barefoot along the sandy beach under the stars, he pulled her to a stop and gave her the most swoonworthy kiss she'd ever had.

We're seeing him again tonight. I can't wait.

Between one of my songs finishing and another beginning, I hear the door slamming downstairs. I lift my head up and look out of the window. No Charlie. What's the time? Three o'clock! I've read straight through lunch! I wonder if he's gone to get April.

I go downstairs and make myself a piece of toast before returning to the office to continue reading.

I have to tear myself away from the pages at five o'clock and, by then, Nicki has filled up another diary and is onto her third. She's still in Thailand – as I said, she goes into detail – and she and Isak are having a secret affair. She's in agony over the thought of leaving him in two days' time.

There's no one in the kitchen, but there's a saucepan on the hob, its contents merrily bubbling away beneath the lid. I put my empty mug in the dishwasher and then jump with fright when I realise April is standing in her playpen, staring dolefully up at me. She bounces on her feet a bit, steadying herself with her chubby little hands on the side of the pen.

'Hello,' I say, wondering where Charlie is.

She holds her arms open to me. A split second later, she falls backwards onto her bum and starts to cry.

'Hold on, hold on.' I look around for Charlie, then, against my better judgement, reach into the pen and lift his daughter out.

Her cries stop instantly, her face breaking into a full-beam smile.

'All right?' I ask, grinning back at her.

She reaches up and pulls my hair.

'Ow!'

She giggles, so I let her do it again.

My squawk this time prompts her to laugh like crazy. Huh. I don't want to get ahead of myself here, but I think she likes me.

'Okay, that's enough now, you cheeky monkey,' I say, trying to untangle her fingers from my locks before she bruises my scalp. She grins at me, her chubby cheeks widening to chipmunk-like proportions. Maybe it's her blue dress, but her eyes seem bluer today.

The lid on the pan begins to vibrate violently and both April and I turn our heads at the same time to stare at it. With one arm holding her to my hip, I go over to the stove and carefully take off the lid, grabbing a wooden spoon and stirring the red sauce within. The toilet flushes inside the hallway cloakroom and Charlie emerges.

'Thanks,' he says, coming into the kitchen. I jut my hip towards him, expecting him to take April, but he goes to a cupboard and begins rooting around.

'What are you making?' I ask.

'Spaghetti Bolognese.'

'For you or April?'

'Both,' he replies, unscrewing a jar of dried herbs and shaking some into the pan, flecking the red sauce with green. 'Just have to blitz hers in the food processor first.'

'Ew.' I pull a face.

He smirks at me as he screws the herb lid back on.

'How's your work coming along?' I walk over to the French doors and look out.

'Getting there,' he replies.

'Is that driftwood?' I ask, studying the twisted structure that's beginning to form around the outside of the play kitchen's frame.

'Some of it is. It can be pretty brittle, so I tend to use pine for the base and fix branches and driftwood on top to give it character.'

'Do you get it from the beaches yourself?'

'Yeah.' He materialises at my side. 'And my friends and family sometimes pick it up when they see it.'

'It reminds me of the seaside,' I say. 'I like the colour.'

'Yeah, it's been bleached by the sun. I like the shape,' he says. 'It's been knocked about in the water for so long that the waves have smoothed away most of the rough edges. And I like not knowing where it comes from or how long it's been adrift at sea.'

I smile at his reverential tone, and he in turn, smiles at his daughter, reaching across to tweak her nose. She giggles.

'Well, I guess I'd better get home,' I say, offering April over with more purpose this time. I still seem to have her attached to my hip.

'Do you want to stay for dinner?' Charlie asks casually, finally getting the hint and taking her from me. 'I've got plenty.'

'Oh, no, thank you,' I reply automatically, and then frown at myself as I walk away from him. It's not like I've got anything better to do – and I like a bit of spag bol – but he doesn't repeat his offer.

Nicki's bike is still resting in the hall and the sight of it makes me nervous.

I'm reluctant to pick up her helmet, and even more so to pull it over my head, but I do. The fit is good, but the straps don't quite meet under my chin and I'm struggling to loosen them.

I honestly would be so much happier on hired equipment.

'Let me help,' Charlie says, putting April down and coming to my aid. I didn't know he'd followed me out here.

I'm not sure where to look as he fiddles with the straps, so I focus on his jaw, trying not to flinch as his rough fingertips brush against my throat. His jaw clenches and my eyes dart up to his, my breath freezing in my lungs – his pain is palpable.

'Charlie, I—'

'Done!' He interrupts me, taking a step backwards and forcing a bright smile.

'Seriously, I don't want to—'

He covers his hands with his ears. 'Blah, blah, blah,' he says, going over to open the door.

I roll my eyes at him to lighten the mood as I wheel the bike past.

'Height okay?' he asks when I reach the road and swing my leg over the frame.

'Fine,' I reply, wondering if he's already adjusted it. I'm pretty tall at five foot eight.

He nods. 'Ride carefully.' He pats the doorframe with an air of finality and goes back inside, shutting the door behind him. I'm glad he didn't wait to see me set off. I'm feeling on edge enough as it is.

Chapter 12

A few days later, on Friday, I meet April's grandmother, and, if I didn't know that she was going to be there, I'd probably still guess who she was from her identical chipmunk cheeks. Like April's, they bulge brilliantly when she smiles.

'You must be Bridget!' she exclaims, opening the door to me. If she weren't so warm and welcoming, I wouldn't feel at all comfortable wheeling her late daughter-in-law's bike into the house. 'I'm Pat.' She offers her hand as soon as mine is available.

She's of medium height and build and dressed colourfully in a print blouse and trousers the colour of sunshine. Her champagne-blonde hair is long and curly, falling to well below her shoulders.

'It's lovely to meet you,' I reply, shaking it.

'Charlie's taken the play equipment to the school,' she says, the wooden beads around her neck clattering together noisily as she shuts the door.

He told me he would be setting everything up today. The finished articles were quite beautiful – like something out of a fairytale with their twisted, wooden structures and asymmetrical lines.

As well as a long, low play kitchen, complete with sink and pegs to hang utensils on, he made a table for sand play, several wooden stools, a series of stepping stones and a small play house – all gorgeously characterful pieces.

'He should be back around lunchtime. Cup of tea?'

'Thank you,' I say, liking her even more than I already did.

I follow her into the kitchen. I think I might've just met Charlie's cleaner: the place is immaculate. As mothers go, this one clearly rocks.

'How are you getting on?' Pat asks, and it's more than just a conversational question: it's concern.

'Really well,' I reply, although I'm not sure that's entirely true. I'm still reading Nicki's diaries. I can't tell yet whether that's getting me anywhere.

'Is there anything I can help you with? Anything at all?'

I furrow my brow. 'I don't think so,' I reply. 'To be honest, I'm still going through everything, hoping to find some clues as to what Nicki had planned. It's a bit of a one-man job.'

'I was hoping to come and say hi to you before now,' she confides as she moves swiftly around the kitchen, from the sink to the kettle and over to the cupboards. 'Charlie's not much of a talker. And he finds it very hard to talk about Nicki. So, if there's anything you need to know about her, them, whatever, then you can always ask me.'

'Er, thank you,' I say, surprised. 'I'm all right so far, but I'll keep that in mind.'

'Good.' Pat smiles at me. 'I'll give you my number so you have it if you need it.'

Was that a bit weird? I ask myself as I head upstairs to the office. I think she's just trying to help, but I'm pretty sure that, if I don't feel comfortable asking Charlie something, I won't feel right asking his mother. Although I guess that remains to be seen.

I've been on quite a journey with Nicki this week. When she left Thailand, she was heartbroken. She had assumed she and Isak would stay in touch, but, on their last night together, he confessed that he didn't want to try to make a long-distance relationship work. She told him she loved him and they were both emotional, but he didn't back down. He would likely still be in Thailand the next time she came, he said, but she mustn't wait for him.

Back in the UK, Nicki grew resentful, knowing Isak also meant that *he* wouldn't wait for *her*. She tortured herself by imagining how many other girls he was having holiday flings with.

Meanwhile, her sister, Kate, gave her the cold shoulder about Nicki going to Thailand to stay with their dad. She thought Nicki was being disloyal to their mum, and their mum didn't do a whole lot to reassure her younger daughter. Nicki felt very alone.

Charlie broke up with Too Perfect Tisha and flirted with Nicki at a party, but she was sworn off men, which, of course, only made him want her more. Over the following weeks he got several mentions in Nicki's diary, but she continued to claim she was over her crush.

Kate put increasing pressure on Nicki not to return to Thailand, but she held fast, and went back for the Easter holidays. Part of her reason for wanting to go again so soon was Isak – despite her bitterness, her thoughts were still consumed by him. She didn't know if he would be there so when, on her very first day, she spotted him up one of the limestone cliffs, tackling an overhang, her heart skipped a beat.

She sat on the beach and watched him for an hour. He clocked her as soon as his feet hit solid ground, his face falling right off the cliff he'd just been climbing.

At first she was cold and distant, and he seemed nervous around her, but she didn't refuse when he asked her to go for a drink with him.

That night he confessed that he hadn't been able to stop thinking about her and vowed he hadn't been with anyone else since. Regardless of the hurt she'd felt when he hadn't wanted to keep in touch, they pretty much picked up where they left off. But at the end of the holiday, the same thing happened, with Isak vehemently stating that long-distance relationships don't work.

When Nicki returned to school in the UK, she was so incensed with Isak that she ended up snogging Charlie in retaliation. They were both drunk, so she was surprised and apprehensive when he called her the very next day and asked her to go to the movies with him that evening.

Isak had insisted they were not tied to each other, so she went, but, when Charlie kissed her again that night, she still felt as if she was cheating on Isak. The days turned into weeks and Nicki's feelings for Charlie grew, as did her guilt over the two men. She felt as if she was deceiving them both.

The summer holidays and another trip to Thailand were fast approaching, and one night she wrote an emotional entry about having come clean to Charlie. He was very upset with her for not telling him about Isak and he wanted to know if she still had feelings for him. She was honest and confessed that she did. Charlie walked out on her and refused to speak to her – she didn't know if they'd broken up or not.

They hadn't – it later transpired that he was extremely hurt and understandably worried about Nicki going back to Thailand for the whole six weeks of the summer holidays. She promised she'd be faithful to him and they agreed to speak on the phone regularly.

Kate still had issues with Nicki wanting a relationship with their father, so Nicki was pleased to be escaping her older sister's wrath that summer when she came home from university.

In Thailand, her Isak infatuation returned in force. Isak was crushed when she told him she had a boyfriend, but, even though she tried to avoid him, they kept bumping into each other. He was still running the rock-climbing course for the resort, so he'd be on site regularly, picking up his next group and dropping them back after their climbs. One night he caught her arm as she was passing and begged her to have dinner with him – as friends. Against her better judgement, she accepted.

I wanted to hurl the diary at the wall at this point.

Isak told her he loved her, that he was in agony seeing her every day and not being able to touch her. He sincerely regretted letting her go, and would do anything to be given another chance – he swore he would try to make a long-distance relationship work at the end of Nicki's time in Thailand.

Nicki broke up with Charlie over the phone. Her tears smudged the ink on the pages of her diary as she wrote that entry.

Charlie wanted nothing to do with her when she returned to the UK. He soon got another girlfriend, but could barely bring himself to speak to Nicki for the rest of their time in sixth form. She was still pining the loss of their friendship when she set off to university in Coventry a year later.

Isak and Nicki went through plenty of ups and downs over the course of their time together. Eventually the long-distance strain got to them both and they broke up in Nicki's second term of university.

April is wailing in her bedroom when I emerge from the office. I listen out, but can't hear Pat, only the TV in the living room.

'Pat?' I call down the stairs. There's no answer. I can see from here that the living room door is closed.

I walk over to April's room and push open the door. She's standing in her cot, tears streaming down her face. She calls out in a panic as soon as she sees me, stretching her arms up and begging to be lifted out. She looks like she's been awake for a while – I had my music on, so it's hard to tell how long.

I go and pick her up and her cries soften. She buries her face against my neck and hugs me tightly.

'Aw,' I say, patting her back as she snuffles wetly against me. 'There there.' Isn't that what people say to babies? 'Shall we go and find Grandma?'

Pat is sitting on the larger of the two sofas in the living room with her feet up on a pouffe, watching daytime TV.

'Oh!' She leaps up when she sees me. 'She's awake!'

'I heard her in her cot,' I reply, handing April over.

Pat looks stricken as her granddaughter begins to cry again. 'I forgot to bring her blasted monitor downstairs with me!' She clutches April and jigs her around a bit. 'I'm sorry, darling,' she murmurs. 'Did Nanna not hear you?'

Nanna, not Grandma. I make a mental note.

Pat follows me out of the room to the kitchen, talking away to April as she fixes her some warm milk. As Pat is here, I reckon I'll get out of the house today and wander into Padstow. It's drizzling, but I could do with some fresh air.

'Good morning?' Pat asks, cuddling a now-quiet baby as the milk warms in the pan on the hob.

'Yes, great.'

She nods at me expectantly and I find myself saying more.

'I'm reading through Nicki's diaries. Trying to get to know the person behind the characters,' I explain, leaning against the kitchen worktop.

'That sounds rather voyeuristic.' She purses her lips.

Funnily enough, Sara said the same thing when she called to touch base with me yesterday. I wasn't mad keen on that description then, either, so I make a noncommittal 'mmm' sound.

'Could you just hold her a sec while I get her milk ready?'

I do as she asks. I'm starting to feel more comfortable with April now – or, at least, less scared. She hasn't thrown a paddy on me so far.

There's still time.

I sit on the sofa, placing her on my lap, facing me. I gently bounce her up and down on my knees and she looks so elated, I bounce her a little more vigorously. She cracks up laughing as if it's the most hilarious thing that's ever happened to her, and her reaction makes me laugh, too.

'You'd better get the bouncing out of the way before she's had her milk,' Pat says shrewdly, 'not after.'

She gives me a smile as she passes me a bottle.

Oh, am I doing this?

I take the bottle from her, slightly surprised to find that I am. April makes a sudden, eager grab for her milk, so I cradle her back in my arms and pop the teat in her mouth. She begins sucking in earnest as Pat pulls damp clothes out of the washing machine and places them in a basket.

I'm supposed to be going into Padstow. Should I not be a little put out? I search my inner feelings and discover that I'm not.

April is gazing up at me with her pretty blue eyes. I stare down at her, my chest expanding in an unfamiliar fashion. She clearly got her eyes from her mother.

And her chipmunk cheeks from her grandmother…

Yet, there's something about her face that reminds me of Charlie.

'I'm just going to hang up the washing,' Pat says, walking out of the room with the washing basket.

Feelings check: still not annoyed.

Bizarre.

Charlie comes back at three o'clock and I turn off my music, interested to hear how he interacts with his mother.

'The head came in and the caretaker was there, too.' It sounds like he's telling her about the job.

'And were they happy with everything?' she demands to know.

'I think so.'

'Of course they were,' she replies, haughtily. 'How could they not be? Your work is *stunning.*'

'Thanks, Mum,' he says in a low, amused voice. 'Is Bridget okay?' His question carries right up the stairs.

'Yes, she is. She seems nice.'

Her voice grows quieter as they head into the kitchen – I don't hear Charlie's reply.

About an hour later, there's a knock on my door.

'Hello,' I call.

I'm not expecting Pat.

'You might be gone by the time I get back,' she says. 'So I just wanted to give you this.' She hands over a Post-it note with her phone number on it. 'And to wish you a good weekend,' she adds.

'Thanks, you too.'

'Any plans?' she asks keenly, hovering by the door.

I shrug. 'I might go and check out the Lost Gardens of Heligan, do some exploring.'

'Oh, wonderful,' she says.

'How about you?'

'My other son, Adam, is arriving back from India this evening, so I'm cooking the boys an early dinner. I'm just nipping off to the supermarket to do some shopping.'

'How long has he been away?'

'Four months. He's been teaching English to local children. I can't *wait* to see him!'

It wouldn't surprise me if she started clapping and jumping up and down on the spot.

'Aw, have a great time,' I say. 'I'm sure I'll see you soon.'

'Oh, you will,' she agrees. 'But, until then, you have my number.'

She nods at the Post-it note I'm holding.

'Thank you,' I reply. I still think I'm unlikely to ever use it.

When she's gone, I go downstairs to get a drink.

'Do you *want* a tent?' Charlie asks as soon as he sees me. He's lazing on the sofa with his arm around April, his ankle resting on his knee.

'Sorry?' We haven't even exchanged hellos.

'Do you want a tent to put your things in? I remembered where mine is,' he explains as April shakes the colourful cloth book she's holding. It makes a rattling noise.

'Oh! Um, maybe, I don't know.' His question caught me off guard, but now that I think about it… 'Actually, yes, that would be great. Really?'

'Sure. I just need to get it back from my brother.'

'Aah, you lent it to him to go to India, did you?' I lean against the worktop and fold my arms, looking down at him.

'No, he didn't take it with him.' He doesn't seem surprised that I know about Adam. Guess he's aware that his mother's a chatbag. 'He's had it for ages,' he tells me. 'When I drop him home tomorrow, I'll grab it and bring it over.'

'Cool! I'll actually have room to move. That's a luxury. Is your brother older or younger than you?' I ask.

I now know from Nicki's diary that she and Charlie were in the same year at school, which also made him around the age of thirty-one when she died.

'Younger by three years,' he replies, taking the book from

April and squeezing one of its cloth pages. It makes a squeaking sound that impresses her.

'Is he your only sibling?'

'Yeah.' He smiles affectionately, then glances up at me. 'Do you have any?'

'No, I'm an only child.'

I can tell from his expression that he feels sorry for me, which also tells me that he loves his little brother a lot. I'd like to meet him.

Chapter 13

Unfortunately, I have to set off back to the campsite before Charlie returns from Bodmin station with his brother. Adam is coming in on a London train at five thirty that evening, but I've left at five pretty much every day since I got here and I don't want to be hanging around like a bad smell.

After dinner, I climb the hill to catch up on my social media. There's a group of friends camping in tents behind me, and I feel like a right Norman No Mates sitting there, working, while their barbecue smells waft down the slope towards me. Eventually, I return to *Hermie* and continue writing a blog I started earlier about Beau, the guy who stole the eleventh piece of my heart and who used to live right here in Cornwall, but I give up and call it a night early.

I have every intention of getting my arse into gear and heading to Heligan the next day, but when I wake up I feel a bit low.

I'm a sociable person. And I've been here for two weeks now without proper company. I really hope Marty is up for a visit soon. She gets back from Greece on Friday, so that rules out next weekend. I'll try to persuade her to lock in the one after.

I traipse up the hill to call Elliot, but when he doesn't answer, I make the decision to go into town for a pick-me-up breakfast. The gardens are only about an hour away, so I'll still have most of the day to explore.

It's a cool, partly cloudy morning as I walk along the Camel Trail into Padstow. The town is buzzing, but the streets are far from crowded, and I'm glad I don't have to fight the tourists for footpath space as I wander past the small harbour. I make a beeline for the café on the other side – I've been there for lunch, but thought the breakfast menu looked good, too.

It's a small, cosy venue with windows facing onto the water and a counter just inside the door crammed with cakes, pastries and ice creams. It's only when a waitress is about to show me to a table that I see Charlie. He's sitting right at the back with April – and Adam, at a guess – but, before I can walk out again, he clocks me and lifts his hand up in a wave.

'This way, please,' the waitress says, setting off with her single, sad little menu.

I can't really do anything but follow her.

As Charlie beckons me over, Adam swivels in his seat to look at me. Despite his heavy stubble and bleached-blond hair, the family resemblance is striking.

'Would you like to join us?' Charlie asks politely, placing his hand on the chair belonging to the empty table beside him. Adam grins up at me in a cheeky fashion as the waitress waits for my response.

'I don't want to intrude,' I say, awkwardly.

'You're not,' Charlie replies, swinging the chair into place between him and his brother.

April is in a highchair opposite. She tries to communicate with me in baby talk as I sit down and smile at her, self-consciously.

'Can I get you a drink?' the waitress asks.

'A latte, please.' The coffees on the table are steaming. I don't think they've been here long.

'I'm Adam.' He offers a big, rough hand to me and gives me a wide grin. His eyes are brown, not green, I notice, and he's more tanned than Charlie, with freckles sprinkled over his nose and cheeks.

'Bridget,' I say in return. 'It's really good to meet you. Have you guys ordered?'

'Only just,' Charlie replies.

'I'll go for the pancakes,' I say out loud, not bothering to look at the menu.

'How do you like Cornwall?' Adam asks me as Charlie flags down the waitress. I'm quite touched to hear him ordering on my behalf.

'It's great. But I haven't seen much of it yet,' I admit. 'I had a flat tyre on my campervan last week.'

'Oh, I heard all about your campervan,' Adam replies knowingly.

'What have you heard?' I ask innocently.

'About how you need my tent.'

'It's not *your* tent,' Charlie interjects.

'Whatever.' Adam brushes him off. 'It's just as well you don't have a boyfriend. Be a bit of a squeeze, from the sounds of it.'

My eyes widen.

'I didn't say she didn't have a boyfriend,' Charlie says. 'He lives in Australia.'

'How do you know that?' I turn to him, taken aback.

He shrugs. 'Your blog.'

That's right… He told me he'd read a couple of entries when I first came here. But why were they talking about whether or not I have a boyfriend?

Charlie must notice the unspoken question on my lips, because he explains.

'Adam was giving me grief about making you come to Cornwall for the summer.'

'I just wondered if there's a bloke you had to leave behind,' Adam clarifies.

'No.' I shake my head. 'Three hundred miles don't really make a difference when you're already talking ten thousand.'

'Still, you must have friends in London, right?' Adam persists.

'I should hope so,' I reply indignantly.

'Aren't you lonely?' he asks.

'You're a nosy little bugger, aren't you?' I tease.

Charlie laughs. 'You tell him, Bridget.'

Adam grins, but pink spots form on his cheeks. I didn't peg him as the type to embarrass easily.

'I do miss my friends,' I admit, trying to appease him. 'Eight weeks is a long time to be away.'

Charlie picks up his teaspoon and stirs his coffee, staring down at the spinning liquid.

'Told you,' Adam goads his brother.

Charlie glances up at him and I'm surprised to see that his lips have formed a straight line.

'I didn't mean to make you feel bad!' I exclaim at him. 'I'm fine! It's fun! Thank you!' I gush at the waitress as she places my latte in front of me. 'Christ, I'm just going to go and sit over there, all right?'

Charlie grins at me and the tension dissipates.

'How are you today, April?' I smile at her from across the table. Her brow knits together and she holds her arms out to me, making a sound of annoyance. Oops, what have I done?

'No, you have to stay in your highchair,' Charlie says to her. 'Your pancakes will be here soon.'

'Snap,' I chirp. 'Are you having pancakes too?' I ask her cheerily.

'Urrrn!' She really wants to get out.

'Here they come!' Charlie says with relief as the waitress appears, laden down with plates. 'Just wait a minute while I cut them up,' he chides his daughter.

As Charlie attends to April, Adam chats to me.

'Got any plans for today?'

'I was thinking about going to Heligan.'

'Oh, yeah?' He tucks into his fry-up. 'Just felt like a day out?'

'Yes, but it's also for the book.'

'Nicki's book?'

I nod at him, unable to answer with my mouth full. I

wonder if Charlie has told him I'm writing my own book as well. 'I need to visit a few places for research,' I add.

'Like where?'

I look up at the ceiling, thinking. 'Tintagel—'

'That's not far from me,' Adam interrupts.

'Where do you live?' I ask, distracted from replying.

'Bude.'

'I had a boyfriend who came from Bude,' I say as Charlie returns his attention to us. Beau, the guy I coincidentally started writing a blog about last night.

'Surfer?' Adam asks.

'He was, actually.' Bude has some great surfing beaches. 'Do you surf?' I ask him. He looks like a surfer.

'Course.'

I glance at Charlie. 'How about you?'

'Not so much any more.'

Aah, but he *used* to! Another Morris similarity confirmed.

'Now he's a boring dad,' Adam comments drily.

Charlie stares at him. 'I can't believe I actually missed you when you were in India.'

Adam chuckles and carries on eating.

I wonder if April is his only reason for stopping surfing. I imagine Nicki's death stole all of the fun out of his life, too. For a good long while, at least. It's a sobering thought.

'Are you set on Heligan today?' Charlie asks casually as we make our way out of the café after breakfast. He has a big black rucksack slung over his shoulder and Adam is carrying April up ahead. He's slightly taller than Charlie, slightly longer and lankier. 'I have to take my brother home and collect the tent, but I could take you to Tintagel on our way back through. I wouldn't mind visiting that beach.'

'Driftwood?' I ask as we spill out onto the busy pavement.

'Yeah, and April could do with some fresh air. She was cooped up inside all day yesterday.'

I think about the offer as he takes April from Adam and moves out of the way of passing people. He lowers her into the backpack and clips her into a harness, then glances up at me, his hair falling into his eyes as he awaits my answer. 'What do you think?' he asks, straightening up and swinging the baby carrier – and April – onto his back. He slides his arms into the armholes, his biceps flexing as he adjusts the weight on his broad shoulders. 'Would save you having to get your campervan out.'

'What's this?' Adam asks, interrupting.

'Just wondering if Bridget wants to do Tintagel today instead of Heligan. I could take her there on my way back from yours.'

'Guilt trip,' Adam says under his breath.

'Seriously can't believe I missed you,' Charlie replies, deadpan.

I decide to go along with the plan because, well, why not? So we walk back to Charlie's place together. While he heads indoors to change April's nappy, Adam carries his bags out of the house and puts them into Charlie's silver pickup.

'You sit in the front. I'll go in the back with my niece,' Adam urges, opening the front passenger door for me. 'I don't get to see her enough.'

We sit and chat about India until Charlie emerges.

'You'd better not keep her awake,' Charlie warns his brother as he buckles April into her car seat.

'I won't,' Adam replies chirpily, tickling April's ribs and making her giggle.

Charlie sighs and climbs into the driver's seat while I smile to myself, enjoying their banter.

'Do you mind if we swing by the campsite so I can grab my camera?' I ask. I always try to photograph anything that I might need to reference later.

'Sure,' Charlie replies.

'So tell me about this boyfriend from Bude,' Adam says cheekily, dangling over my seat when we're well into our journey, zooming along the A39. April is fast asleep.

'Can you put your seatbelt back on?' Charlie asks impertinently.

'All right, Dad,' Adam mutters, buckling himself back up.

'What do you want to know?' I swivel to face him.

'What's his name, how old is he, when did you meet him?'

'Jesus, am I on *Blind Date*?'

'Dear old Cilla,' he says affectionately.

'His name is Beau, he was twenty-five when we went out and that was six years ago. I was twenty-eight,' I add.

He grins widely. 'You like younger men?'

'She has a boyfriend,' Charlie interjects wearily.

Adam leans forwards and gently cuffs his brother over the head. Charlie bats him away, smirking. Adam looks out the side window, tapping his fingers on the doorframe. I suspect he's one of those people who have so much energy they can't keep still.

'I had a girlfriend once who dumped me for a guy called Beau,' Adam says thoughtfully.

'Who?' Charlie asks him, looking at him in the rear-view mirror.

'Michelle,' he replies.

'Aah,' Charlie says.

'Seriously?' I chip in.

He nods. 'Yeah.'

'It's just that I need to hunt Beau down and he's not on social media. I haven't tried very hard, admittedly, but it would be great if I had a lead.' There can't be that many Beaus in Bude.

'Why do you need to find him?' Adam asks.

'It's for my blog.'

From his vacant expression I gather he doesn't know anything about it, but, as he listens to my explanation, his features change from bemused to confused.

'Does your boyfriend know about this?'

'Of course!' I spin out my usual line about how it was his idea and how he's not the jealous type. I have a feeling I'm going to get bored of people asking me this question.

'How long have you been together?' he asks.

'Just over a year and a half,' I reply. 'But I've been back in the UK since the end of last year.'

'Are you going to move over there or will he come here?'

'Not sure yet,' I reply.

'How's the long-distance thing working out for you?'

'He really is a nosy little shit, isn't he?' I say to Charlie, who laughs and nods.

We fall into a light-hearted silence that lasts all of fifteen seconds.

'Hey, let's go out next weekend,' Adam says, leaning forward. 'We'll get Mum to babysit.'

'Mmm,' Charlie replies.

'Come on!' He clamps his hands on his brother's shoulders and gives him a small shake.

'Can you stop messing with me while I'm driving?'

'I mean it,' Adam states, letting him go. 'You need a night out.'

'Do I?' Charlie asks. He doesn't seem convinced.

'Yes, you do,' Adam says seriously. 'It's been too long. You can come, too, Bridget,' he adds, his tone turning flippant. 'Don't want you to perish from loneliness.'

I laugh. 'Gee, thanks.'

'Are we on?' he demands to know of us both.

'Depends on my workload,' I reply when Charlie doesn't answer. I'm flattered that Adam asked me, but I'm not sure how reliable he is when it comes to seeing things through.

'Bloody hell, no wonder you two get on,' Adam mumbles.

Do we?

'Here at last,' Charlie says loudly as he pulls into a small car park outside a large, cream-brick apartment block.

'You guys coming in?' Adam asks.

'Only to get my tent,' Charlie replies, turning to me. 'Do you mind waiting here with April? She could do with a bit longer.'

'Sure.'

She's still out cold.

Adam comes around to my door, so I wind down the window.

'If I see Michelle around, I'll ask her about Beau,' he tells me.

'That would be great.'

'What's his surname?'

'Riley,' I reply. I don't print surnames on my blog, and in most cases I change first names too. Usually my exes insist on it.

'See you next weekend.' He gives me a meaningful look as he walks backwards up the footpath.

Chapter 14

'Right.' Charlie restarts the ignition once the tent is safely stored in the back of the pickup. 'Tintagel.'

'Thanks for doing this,' I say as we set off back in the opposite direction. '*Hermie* isn't the easiest thing to drive.'

'*Hermie*?'

'*Herman the German*. My dad's campervan.'

'Ohhh,' he says slowly.

'Do you mind if I turn the radio on?' I ask after a few moments pass.

'Go for it.'

'It won't wake April?'

'I doubt it. She needs to wake up in a bit, anyway.'

I feel a twinge of guilt at the memory of her tear-stricken face yesterday. I still want to kick myself for having my music on so loud that I couldn't hear her wailing. I know it was Pat's responsibility, but that doesn't make me feel okay about it. How long had she been awake for her to be crying like that?

I feel like I should confess, but I don't want to land Charlie's mum in it. *Or me, for that matter...*

Tintagel is a cheerful village with colourful bunting stretching across many of the roads, and pubs and cafés lively with punters spilling out onto the pavements. After an overcast morning, the sun has broken through and the town is bustling. We park in the village car park and Charlie clips April into her baby carrier before we set off on the footpath towards the castle.

The Atlantic Ocean, cold and blue, stretches out in the distance as we walk along the dusty, stony path, surrounded by grassy plains on every side. The castle itself is a ruin – built in the thirteenth century by Richard, First Earl of Cornwall, after Cornwall had been subsumed into the kingdom of England. It later fell into disrepair.

What remain are walls – crumbling and ragged, with many lying low beneath shaggy carpets of grass. Parts of the ruins allow the imagination to run wild, conjuring up what might've been there before. A jagged wall peppered with tiny lookout holes steps down from the steep cliff face, and, across the path below, an arched stone walkway is formed. As I lift up my camera to take a photo, I can easily imagine Kit and Morris kissing beneath it.

Charlie bids me farewell and sets off down the stone steps to the beach, leaving me to focus on my reason for coming: work. I get out my notepad and pen and decide to walk up to the highest point to take some photos of the view.

The colours all around sing out with vibrancy. The deep

blue of the sea fades into aquamarine as it reaches the cove. A streak of rusty-red seaweed bleeds into the water that laps the shoreline, and acid-yellow lichen clings to some of the rocks.

Green grassy hills slide into rocky grey cliffs that jut outwards into points, like spears warding off ancient enemies. Everywhere I turn there are ruined walls, the remnants of a castle that stood long ago.

Down in the cove I can see Charlie with April in the baby carrier. He stoops to pick up the occasional small piece of driftwood and puts it into a white plastic bag he's carrying. The beach is tiny and I don't fancy his chances of finding many decent lengths, if any.

I think of Adam muttering 'guilt trip' and wonder if he's right. Did Charlie offer to bring me here solely because he felt sorry for me?

He really did seem uncomfortable about me having to come to Cornwall for the summer. I wonder how his initial conversation with Sara actually went – maybe she made the suggestion to appease him, without his actually requesting it. Who knows? There's no point dwelling on it. I'm here now, anyway.

'Find anything good?' I ask Charlie on our way back to Padstow.

'A few bits and pieces,' he replies.

'Can I have a look?'

He seems nonplussed. 'If you like.'

I stretch backwards and grab the plastic bag resting on the seat beside April. She's playing with some toys suspended on a cord stretched over her car seat and doesn't so much as look at me as I settle back into position.

'What will you use these for?' I ask Charlie, peering into the bag to see a whole bunch of small twigs and sticks.

'Something for April,' he replies.

I think of the seahorse on the wall in her bedroom, formed out of tiny, smooth pieces of wood. 'Did you make her the seahorse?' I ask.

'Er, yeah.'

'Aah, it's really pretty.' It suddenly occurs to me that he may wonder why I've been into her bedroom.

'I heard her wake up from her nap yesterday,' I explain, trying to keep my voice sounding casual as I dig myself out of a hole.

'Oh, right,' he replies.

His eyes are focused on the road, so I'm looking at his side profile. He has a very straight nose.

'What will you make for her this time?' I ask.

'A heart. I was mak—'

'Sorry?' I ask when his words cut abruptly short.

His Adam's apple bobs up and down. 'I was making it for Nicki,' he says, his expression stark.

'Oh.'

We fall silent. I wish I were better at this sort of thing. I'm not expecting him to carry on talking.

'Figured I should finish it,' he adds quietly. 'That's if I can find it. I only remembered it the other day. It's probably in her wardrobe somewhere.'

So he has kept all of her things…

'How's the writing going?' he asks after a while.

'I'm still researching,' I tell him. 'It's going to take me ages to get through everything. I've read through the contents of Nicki's computer and now I'm onto her notebooks.'

I don't say 'diaries' because the word feels too intimate.

'Find anything helpful?' he asks.

I wriggle in my seat. 'I guess I'm just trying to get to know her. I want to make sure I'm able to write the story that she would have wanted. It helps if I can, I don't know, get inside her head.'

'That makes sense,' he says.

'Does it? Good.'

'So you're reading her diaries, too?'

'Er, yeah,' I admit.

He nods, his jaw twitching as he stares out of the front window. 'Well, if there's anything else you need to know, you can always ask me.'

'Really?'

'Why do you sound surprised?'

'Er, your...'

'My...?' he prompts, casting me a quick sideways look.

'Your mum offered the same thing.'

'Did she?' He appears alarmed, then shakes his head. 'Seriously, you can ask me. I'm not as fragile as she thinks I am.'

'I wasn't going to ask her anyway,' I say, then giggle. 'I'm sorry, that sounded really petulant.'

He smirks. 'She brings out the teenager in me, too.'

'I like your mum,' I say with a smile.

'Yeah, she's all right,' he replies fondly. 'I'm lucky to have her.' A beat. 'Even if she does annoy the fuck out of me sometimes.'

I burst out laughing and he grins.

'My mum always annoys the fuck out of me,' I say, then jolt and turn around to look at April. 'Should we be swearing in front of her?' I whisper at Charlie.

'It'll be a while before we need to worry about that sort of thing. She can't even speak yet.'

'Phew.'

When we arrive at the campsite, Charlie parks up by the office and gets April out.

'I'll bring the tent over in a bit. Just going to say hi to Julia and Justin.'

'I'll take it,' I offer.

'You sure?'

'Yep.'

As he passes me the bright-blue tent bag, I wonder if this is goodbye.

'Be over in a bit,' he says.

I'm pleased. I've enjoyed the company today.

I get back to *Hermie* and unzip the bag, lifting the tent out. Hmm… Now what?

'You look like you're having fun,' Charlie says a few minutes later, wandering over with April.

'Do I seem like the sort of person who knows how to put up a tent?'

'You seem like the sort of person who can do anything she puts her mind to,' he replies matter-of-factly, putting April down on the grass.

Whoa, was that a compliment?

'Where are you putting it?' he asks, getting straight down to business.

'I'm still undecided,' I reply. 'Do I want to step into it from *Hermie*'s door or have it off to the side?'

'Well, if you step into it from the door, you'll be locked within a campervan/tent hole forever. It only has one entry and exit point.'

'Oh God, what an idiot. Just as well you're here to help me.'

'I'd put it here,' he says, dragging the flattened-out tent – that's as far as I'd got – to the back left of the campervan. 'That way, it's clear of the door, but still close enough for you to not get too wet if it's raining.'

'Do you reckon I'm allowed to have a tent as well as a campervan on this pitch?' I ask.

'Yeah, Justin said it's fine. It's no bigger than some of the awnings other people have.'

'Did you check with him?'

'Yeah.'

Aw.

'What do you think?' he asks, nodding at the tent's position.

'Great,' I reply. 'What shall I do?'

He passes me a bag. 'You can fit the rods together.'

The tent is up in no time – it's not very big, but it'll make a huge difference when it comes to my living space. I'm actually excited about the prospect of tidying up a bit. Maybe I could get some more fairy lights to wind around the outside of the tent. Or I could just relocate *Hermie*'s ones. I'm going to need to take them off anyway if I'm ever going to drive the bloody thing anywhere.

'Do you want a beer?' I ask Charlie hopefully. I'm not ready to go back to being Norman No Mates just yet.

'Erm…' He checks the time on his watch and glances at the tent. The door opening has been tied back and April is crawling around inside. She seems happy enough. 'Yeah, okay,' he decides. 'One won't hurt. I'd better not stay too long, though. April will be getting hungry.'

'I can make her something if you like. I've got pasta,' I offer.

I'm clearly *desperate* for company.

Charlie thinks about it for a minute and I'm sure he's going to say no, so I'm pleased when he nods.

'That would be cool, if you don't mind.'

'Not at all.' I go into *Hermie* and lift up the bench seat. 'Twirls?' I proffer up a packet of fusilli.

'Great.'

'Pesto?' I pull out a jar.

'No, better not. Too much salt.'

'What shall I put on it, then? I've got some broccoli.'

'Perfect. I can mix in one of her veggie pouches.'

My tummy rumbles as I set about boiling water. I realise I haven't eaten since breakfast.

'Did April eat lunch?' I ask with concern.

'Yeah, I fed her when we were on the beach.'

'Oh, good. I'm starving,' I admit. 'Think I'm going to do some pasta with pesto for myself. Do you want some?'

'Sure, why not?'

Smiling, I grab a couple of beers from the fridge and hunt out the bottle opener, cracking them open and passing one to Charlie.

'Have a seat.' I nod at the single camping chair and sit down myself in the side door opening, my feet on the grass. 'I've got another camping chair in the boot, but it's a bit buried.' I cross my legs as Charlie swings his chair around to face me.

'Yeah, probably better you don't go opening the back of this thing again.' He smirks and puts the bottle to his lips, taking a swig before looking at me levelly with his clear, unusual eyes. 'So why does your mum annoy the fuck out of you?'

I raise my eyebrows. 'I might need a few more beers if you really want the answer to that question.'

'That bad?'

'She isn't the most maternal of people.' I take a sip of my beer and shrug. 'Obviously, I love her, and we get on well enough. But she was only young when she had me and she hasn't grown up much since. Dad's the only real parental figure in my life. He's awesome.'

I look over my shoulder to see that the water in the saucepan has come to a boil. By the time I've added pasta and returned to my perch on the edge of *Hermie*, April has emerged from the tent.

Charlie bounces her on his knee, making her laugh hysterically.

As dads go, this one's all right, too, I think with a smile.

Chapter 15

On Sunday it pours down and the winds are so strong that I'm worried that my new tent is going to blow away. In the end, I hunker down and work on my blog, giving up on any plans for another daytrip. Heligan's gardens may well be lost again by the time I reach them.

I keep finding myself wondering what Charlie and April are up to. He probably feels he's done his bit for me now – I doubt we'll be going out again any time soon. The realisation is a bit of a downer, so to cheer myself up, I decide to plan a trip to Ireland the following weekend. Time to pay Dillon a visit.

The rain doesn't let up on Monday. It's still very windy and making my way along the cycle path is treacherous. At one point I'm almost blown into the estuary.

'You all right?' Charlie asks with alarm when I push Nicki's bike through the front door, looking like a sodden rat.

'I think I should've walked today,' I state.

'I would've thought so,' he replies pointedly.

'What do you do on days like this?' I ask, taking off my raincoat. The helmet didn't exactly keep my hair dry, but I console myself in thinking that the hood of my raincoat would've blown off my head in the wind, anyway. 'How do you work outside?'

'I have a pop-up gazebo I sometimes use, but, yeah, I tend to give the outdoor stuff a miss when it's like this. I need to sort out my accounts, anyway.'

I check my appearance in the hall mirror. My dark-brown hair is an interesting mix of wet and dry stripes. 'This is a good look,' I murmur.

'How was the rest of your weekend?' he asks with a smile as he goes into the kitchen.

'Fine. A bit boring, actually,' I say. 'Hello, April!' She's sitting underneath the table, munching on a squeaky toy. I turn back to Charlie. 'Just did some writing,' I add.

'Of your own?'

Squeak, squeak.

'Yeah. I'm going to Ireland this weekend for my blog.'

'Who's this for?'

'His name's Dillon. He's an Irish musician.'

Charlie narrows his eyes at me before shaking his head and getting the milk out of the fridge.

'What?' I sense he was going to say something.

'Nothing,' he replies.

'What?' I repeat.

'Do you really— No, forget it.' He shakes his head again. 'I'm telling you, Elliot doesn't get jealous. He trusts me,

121

and he's right to. I would *never* cheat – never have, never will.'

His lips tilt up at the corners as he listens to me.

'Are you done?' he says when I've finished.

Squeak, squeak, squeak.

'Yeah.'

'I wasn't going to ask about Elliot.'

I frown. 'What were you going to ask, then? Spit it out, Mr Laurence.'

He studies me for a long moment. 'Do you really buy into all that crap?'

'All what crap?'

'Your blog. The pieces-of-your-heart crap.'

I let out a laugh. '*Crap*?'

'It's just… You don't really take it seriously, do you?'

'I think I liked you better when you barely spoke to me.'

Squeak, squeak.

His eyes widen and his lips form a startled 'O'.

I wave my hands at him. 'I'm only joking.'

'When did I barely speak to you?' He glances at me with his bottle-glass eyes.

'When I first came here.'

He looks thoughtful.

'Anyway, to answer your question,' I say, moving on, 'no, I don't take it *that* seriously. I just thought it would be a fun idea for a book – hunting down all of my exes around the world.'

He nods and I think he's satisfied, but then his brow furrows again and he cocks his head to one side.

'What?'

'It's just… the pieces-of-your-heart stuff. That thing you wrote about wanting to love someone wholeheartedly.'

'Yes?'

'You really think you're going to be able to do that, just because you've met up with all of your old boyfriends and demanded that they give you a chunk of your heart back?'

'Okay, well, for a start,' I say matter-of-factly, 'obviously I'm not deluded. I know you can't ask for something like that back and simply get it.'

'Exactly, so, by a piece of your heart, you mean they still own a part of you. You still have feelings for them. Not romantic feelings,' he says quickly when he sees my face, 'but you haven't completely – I don't know – let go of the relationship.'

'Right. Yes, that's right.' *By Jove! I think he's got it!* 'And seeing them again gives me – I hate this word – but in some cases it gives me closure. It allows me to put the past to rest. It sounds wanky when you say it out loud, but I guess my heart does feel a little lighter after each reunion – as if it was weighed down before.'

He nods, accepting my explanation. But then he looks confused. *Here we go again…* 'But the wanting-to-love-wholeheartedly bit. You don't really believe that you can love someone any less just because you've loved other people before.' His eyebrows pull together. 'Do you? I mean, if it's right, it's right.'

I'm glad Elliot's not around to hear this…

'Now I know why no one wants to give me a book deal. The idea sucks,' I say sardonically.

'It doesn't suck. Lots of people will like it.'

'But you don't.'

'Well, erm…' He gives me a sheepish look. 'I'm not exactly your target audience, though, am I?'

I flick on the kettle. It boiled ages ago, but we've both been talking so much that we haven't got far with tea making.

Charlie stays where he is, leaning up against the counter with his arms folded. He's got jeans and socks on today, which shows how much cooler it is.

Squeak, squeak.

'Did Nicki talk to you about her book ideas?' I ask cautiously, focusing on the mugs as I fill them up with water.

'Sometimes.' He sighs. 'She used to hate it when I gave her my two cents' worth,' he adds in a heavy voice.

'Really?' I glance at him to see that he's staring at the floor. 'I bet she appreciated your honesty, too, though,' I say gently, fishing the teabags out.

He blinks rapidly. 'I hope so.' He makes a slightly frustrated sound at the back of his throat and unfolds his arms, resting his palms on the worktop behind him. He pushes off from the worktop and falls back against it before looking at me.

'Sorry if I wasn't nice enough when you first came here.'

His comment takes me aback.

'It's fine. You were fine. It was just a bit awkward, that was all.'

He nods. 'It was awkward for me, too.'

'I know. I mean, I can imagine,' I say – awkwardly.

'It's not awkward now.' And then he grins, and I *really* like the way his face lights up. 'You're all right. I actually quite enjoy having you around.'

'Don't get used to it, I'll be gone in six weeks.' I pick up my mug with both hands, the warmth in my palms paling in comparison to the warmth I'm feeling inside.

I walk out of the kitchen, casting him a smile over my shoulder. He's still blinding me with the force of his grin.

When Charlie puts April down for her morning nap, I switch off my music, not wanting a repeat of Friday.

'No music today?' he asks when I come down for lunch. He's feeding April at the table. I heard him go and get her, but I didn't hear her crying.

'No.' I give him an inquisitive look. I know he can hear my music from the window, but he hasn't been working outside.

'I didn't hear it playing when I came up to get April,' he explains.

'Are you sure it doesn't bother you?' I check once again.

'No, I like it,' he replies. 'Want to put some on now?'

'Yeah?'

He nods. 'Yeah.'

I return a short while later, scrolling through my songs as I walk into the kitchen. 'What do you feel like?'

'You choose,' he says.

I press PLAY and frown at the weather outside the window. It's tipping it down.

'I might make a cheese toastie,' I say. 'Do you want one?'

'I'd love one,' he replies, seeming pleased as he puts another spoonful of something green and disgusting-looking into his daughter's mouth. He nods at my speaker. 'What's this?'

'"Hold Tight!" by Dave Dee, Dozy, Beaky, Mick & Tich.'

'*Who*?'

'Dave Dee, Dozy, Beaky, Mick & Tich,' I repeat. 'Try saying that when you're drunk.'

April starts to bounce in her highchair, wiggling her bum from side to side.

'Look at her, she likes it,' Charlie says with a smile.

'You should get a radio in here.'

'I should,' he agrees. 'I haven't really listened to music since Nicki died,' he adds in a quieter voice.

April is still wiggling in her highchair. She looks so cute, I can't help but smile, even though she has green gunk all around her mouth.

'Can you chuck me the baby wipes?' Charlie asks me.

All too gladly… I go and get them from the sofa and pass them to him. A moment later, he lifts his daughter out of her highchair and puts her on the floor. She pushes herself up next to him, her hands on his knees, and bounces along to the music while grinning like a proper nutjob.

'Downtown' by Macklemore & Ryan Lewis comes on next. I can't help but dance along while I'm making our toasties, rapping along to the occasional line.

After a moment, I realise that both Charlie and April are watching me with identical grins on their faces. I laugh at the sight of them – they look so alike – and then the chorus kicks in and I just *have* to sing.

April holds her hands out to me and lets out a cry, so, on impulse, I go and get her, swinging her into my arms and jigging around the kitchen with her.

Charlie leans back in his chair and chuckles at us.

'She likes me,' I say, gleefully, handing his daughter back to him after a bit.

'She likes everyone,' he replies fondly, sitting her on his lap.
Now *that's* annoying.

'You don't have to be a dick about it,' I joke crossly.

He grins up at me.

'Can't you just let me wallow in her obvious adulation for me?' I continue. 'Babies don't usually like me. This is a big thing.'

'What do you mean, babies don't usually like you?' he scoffs.

'They don't. I usually make them cry.'

'What do you do, pinch them?'

I laugh. 'Nah, I think they can just tell I'm not a baby person.'

He frowns. 'How are you not a baby person?'

'Stop distracting me. I need to get on with lunch.'

Duran Duran's 'A View to a Kill' comes on.

'I haven't watched a Bond film in ages,' Charlie says, getting up to join me at the oven while I grill our sandwiches. He's wearing battered, worn jeans with a rip across one knee, and his T-shirt is dark grey, but I have a feeling it used to be black. It's frayed around the hem.

'Dad and I watched *Skyfall* for the third time the night before I came here,' I reveal, remembering to check that our food isn't burning. I peer into the oven. 'We love a bit of 007. I grew up on Bond. God, I miss television,' I say out of the blue, straightening up. 'Especially on days like this.' I look out of the window.

'You can watch TV here, any night you like,' he offers.

I glance at him. 'I wasn't trying to invite myself over.'

'I mean it. I actually miss watching telly with company.

127

The amount of times I used to argue with Nicki about what to watch… I used to encourage her to go out sometimes, just so I'd have the remote control to myself. Now I'd give anything to have her back, giving me shit because I refuse to watch *The X Factor.*'

My heart contracts at his sudden look of devastation, but, before I can say anything, he rearranges his face. 'You won't want to watch *The X Factor*, will you?'

'No,' I say, swallowing. 'It's not on at the moment, anyway.'

Later that afternoon, he knocks on the office door. 'When was the last time you saw *Octopussy*?' he asks.

'Ooh.' I lean back in my seat, thinking. 'At least seven years, I reckon. Why?'

'It's on tonight. I'm making a curry. How about it?'

I smile at him. 'Yeah?'

'Go on,' he says.

I don't take any more persuading.

Chapter 16

'We're not getting out of it,' Charlie says later that week. It's Thursday afternoon and he's just got off the phone to Adam. 'He wants a night out.'

'I can't. I'm in Ireland this weekend, remember?'

'You're leaving Saturday morning, though, right?'

I nod.

'He's talking about tomorrow night. Mum can't babysit on Saturdays – it's the busiest day at the campsite. She's coming here at six. Up for it?'

'God, yes. Wow,' I muse. 'An actual night out with proper drinking and everything. Are you sure you guys don't mind me gatecrashing?'

'Of course not. Just watch out for my brother. He'll probably make a move on you before the evening's out.'

'He'll get a slap around the face if he does,' I say indignantly.

'I would give *anything* to see that. *Anything.*'

*

Pat arrives half an hour earlier than promised on Friday night.

'Well now, that's a jolly sight,' she says warmly, coming into the kitchen.

I'm sitting at the table with April, feeding her chicken and veg. She can use a spoon, but it takes her forever to eat and Charlie wanted her sorted quickly. I took his place when he went to let his mother in.

Pat comes over to give her granddaughter a kiss on the top of her head and then puts her hand on my shoulder in greeting. April has been bopping along to the music blaring out of Charlie's new radio. I've plugged in my iPod because we couldn't find anything we wanted to listen to.

'Is this Johnny Cash?' Pat asks, raising her eyebrows when 'One Piece at a Time' comes on.

'Yep,' I reply, spooning finely chopped chicken into April's willing mouth. I've obviously developed an immunity to the mush, because it no longer makes me want to throw up. Small steps.

'Oh, I do like this one.' Pat sits in the empty chair beside me.

'I don't think I've heard it before,' Charlie comments.

'Listen,' I prompt him. 'He's building a Cadillac, nicking all the parts from the garage where he works. Check out the description of the car he ends up with.'

Charlie leans against the wall and smiles down at me as he focuses on the lyrics.

'That's brilliant,' he says eventually.

'Isn't it?' I return his smile.

April makes a swipe for the spoon.

'Oops, sorry, I'm getting distracted.' I feed her another

mouthful and glance at Pat to see she's wearing a slightly perplexed expression on her face as she looks between her son and me.

Charlie nods at my seat. 'Swap?'

'Sure. I'll go and get ready.' I walked here this morning and brought my going-out stuff with me.

'You go, too, love,' Pat cuts in before he can sit down. 'I'll feed April.'

'Okay, cool, I'll just jump in the shower.'

'Yes, you've got sawdust in your hair,' she notes shrewdly.

He's been working on a tree house this week, but it's unlike any other tree house I've ever seen. It looks absolutely incredible – the ladder steps and supporting posts are made out of gnarled-looking wooden branches, and he's even thatching a roof for the top. I thought it was almost finished, but Charlie says he probably still has another week working on it to go. I can't imagine how productive he'd be if he had more help with April.

The sun is still high in the sky and it's warm and clear when we walk into town that evening. The wind and rain from earlier on in the week are a distant memory.

'Why don't you take anyone up on their offers to help with April?' I ask Charlie. I've seen Jocelyn around a couple of times since that first day out on the street, and yesterday I overheard her telling him that she'd be happy to look after April any time. He replied with a grateful thank you, but said he was managing fine.

He said the same thing to his sister-in-law, Kate, when she called earlier this week, and, when Charlie was out of the room and Pat and I were talking about his tree house in the garden, Pat confided that she'd offered to have April at the campsite on Mondays and Tuesdays, but Charlie had said no.

'I just… I don't need to. If I'm up against it, maybe, but I'd rather take on less work and be around for April. At least for this first year. I know Nicki would have wanted that.'

'But April adores your mum. Does she get on with your dad, too?'

'Oh, she *loves* him,' he replies. 'It's a shame you haven't met him, yet, but one of them has to stay behind at the campsite in case anything goes wrong.'

'So April might quite like to spend Mondays and Tuesdays with her grandparents?'

'*I* wouldn't like it,' he mumbles.

'You'd miss her,' I realise, smiling.

He shrugs. 'Yeah. She's my world.' A beat. 'That sounded really corny.'

I flash him a sidelong smile, but he's staring down at the footpath. His hair is still damp from the shower and partially falling into his eyes. It looks darker when it's wet.

'To be honest, if it weren't for Nicki's book, I wouldn't have a choice,' he confides. 'I'd have to take on more work to make ends meet. It's probably just as well the sequel is going ahead.'

'Did you take some persuading?' I got that impression from Fay.

'Mmm. To be honest, I was shocked when Fay asked me about them drafting in a ghostwriter. I think Nicki would've hated the idea of someone else finishing the story she'd poured her heart and soul into.'

I feel a bit sick listening to this.

He casts me a sideways look. 'Sorry, perhaps I shouldn't have told you that.' He can sense my discomfort.

'It's fine, go on,' I reassure him, even though it's not fine and I'm not sure I want him to go on.

'It was Kate who swayed me,' he continues without further encouragement. 'She showed me some of the reader reviews. I couldn't believe how many people desperately wanted a sequel. Kate thought that I had a responsibility to them. She felt that Nicki would've agreed with her.'

'Maybe she's right,' I say, feeling grateful to Nicki's sister for convincing him. Nicki's teenage diaries haven't given me the best impression of her, but they were both only young when Nicki wrote about her, and she's obviously very supportive of Charlie now.

'Yeah.' He sighs. 'Anyway, the additional money coming in from *Confessions* means that I can work less and look after April. I *know* Nicki would have prioritised her daughter over her book, so I guess someone else finishing it might be what she would have wanted, after all. I've been consoling myself thinking that, in any case.'

'That makes sense,' I say as he takes a deep breath. I think he wanted to get that off his chest.

I hope he feels better for having done so, even if his confession has made me feel queasy. If this were a film, Nicki would probably haunt me into getting the sequel exactly how she wants it. Christ, what a thought! It's just as well I don't believe in ghosts.

'Thanks,' Charlie says. 'Now we should probably talk about something else or I'll end up crying into my pint.'

No argument from me, there. I'm more than happy to change the subject.

'This is my first night out since she… since we lost her,' he adds.

My eyes widen at his revelation. No pressure to make tonight a good one, then.

Chapter 17

'You're here!' Adam jumps to his feet and engulfs his brother in a bear hug, before giving me one, too. He's found a table outside the pub in the early-evening sunshine. 'So glad you guys made it. What are you drinking?' He digs into his pocket for his wallet.

'I'll go,' Charlie says.

'Sit down,' Adam replies firmly. He takes our orders and heads inside.

Charlie climbs over the bench seat facing the pub's courtyard and I slide in opposite him, looking up at the quaint buildings lining the other side of the road. Adam returns a couple of minutes later, spitting out two packets of crisps from between his teeth, and settling himself beside his brother.

'Cheers, you bastards, here's to a good night!' he says.

We chink pint glasses and then he rips the crisp packets open and sets them in the middle of the table.

'What have you been up to this week?' he asks, and the first pint slides down to the sound of amiable general chitchat.

Pint two is a bit different. 'That girl over there looks really familiar.' Adam frowns as he stares past me.

'Which one?' I ask nosily.

'Light-blonde hair, black top, two o'clock my time. Don't make it obvious.'

'I won't, I'm good at this game.' I oh-so-casually tuck my hair behind my ears, turn my head, and give the two o'clock tables a quick once over before returning my gaze to Adam.

'Pretty,' I say, nodding.

He's still frowning with the effort of trying to place her. 'I think I might've shagged her once,' he says.

Charlie puts his pint down. 'How can you forget someone you've *shagged*?' he asks.

'Because I'm a great big slag,' Adam replies with a grin. 'It's all right for you, you've only had sex with two people, they're easy to remember.'

'Fuck off,' Charlie replies with annoyance.

'I haven't had a shag in *way* too long.' Adam gives the girl across the courtyard a lustful look. After a moment, he purses his lips and gazes into his pint.

'I give it an hour,' Charlie says, raising his eyebrows at me.

'Before he hits on her?' I don't need a reply because Adam's cheeky face says it all. 'Best of luck,' I say sarcastically. 'I'm sure she won't be in the least bit offended that you don't remember having sex with her. But of course, there's also the very real possibility that you were completely forgettable, yourself.'

Charlie laughs and Adam sneers at me. 'I'm unforgettable.'

The Last Piece of My Heart

'Sure you are,' I reply, putting my legs up on the bench seat in front of me and crossing them at the ankles. I'm leaning against the wall. It's quite comfortable here. I could stay here all night. Maybe I will.

'How long has it been since *you* had sex?' Adam asks me.

I know I don't have to indulge his line of questioning, but I don't actually mind. 'Well, I haven't seen Elliot since December, so that's…' I count on my fingers. 'Eight months.'

'Ouch.'

'It's all right. I've gone longer. You know the thing I miss most?' I look at them both and they stare back at me quizzically. 'Hugs,' I state.

Adam laughs. 'Hugs?'

'Yeah, actual human bodily contact. I really miss hugs.'

'I'm going to the bar,' Adam says with mock disgust, standing up and walking away from the table.

Charlie and I grin at each other. After a moment he nods and looks down at the table. 'I get that,' he says, drawing a circle around the line of condensation left by his pint glass. 'I miss them, too, that feeling of having another person in your arms.'

'A nice, warm, actual other person,' I say nostalgically.

'Did you know, you're supposed to hug for at least seven seconds to get the full benefit of it?'

'Really?' I ask.

'Yeah, I read that recently. Apparently, seven-second hugs stimulate the release of serotonin, the feel-good hormone.' He smiles and looks down at the table. 'Nicki was an awesome hugger.'

'I wish I'd known her,' I say quietly.

137

'I wish you had, too.' When he looks up at me, his eyes are shining.

'Are you okay?' I whisper, my heart breaking for him as he tries to swallow the lump in his throat.

'Yeah, I'm fine.' He looks down again and draws another condensation ring, even though the water has almost dried up. 'Don't worry, I'm not about to start crying into my pint. I'll be all right for at least another couple, I reckon,' he jokes.

'Okay, I'll try to get you home before your fourth.'

'Don't do that,' he says with alarm. 'I'm having fun.'

'Are you?' I ask.

'Yeah.' He gives me small smile, though his eyes are serious. 'And anyway, I'll be the one getting *you* home.' He shrugs and downs the rest of his pint.

'Don't be silly, I can walk back on my own.'

'There's no way you're doing that,' he states in a not-up-for-debate tone of voice, and then Adam returns, juggling three glasses.

'That was my round,' I suddenly remember. My stomach has gone slightly squirmy. Am I hungry? I think I might be hungry.

'You can get the next one,' Adam says with a shrug.

'I think we should order some food first,' I reply.

Chapter 18

Three pints and a pie-and-mash later, Adam starts to pester me for information about the guys from my blog.

'Charlie doesn't want to hear this.' I frown in his general direction.

'Sure I do,' Charlie replies. 'I'll start you off. Elliot.'

'Okay, well, he was my first proper boyfriend,' I find myself saying, before adding in a slightly dreamy voice, 'Utterly gorgeous, totally devastated me when he moved to Australia.'

'How old were you?' Adam asks.

'Sixteen.'

'Same as me,' Charlie reveals, and I presume he means he was sixteen when he had his first proper girlfriend.

'Too Perfect Tisha?' I ask, giggling when he looks perturbed. 'Nicki's diaries,' I remind him.

He blanches. 'I forgot you've been reading those.' He doesn't look too happy about it.

'What's this? You've been reading Nicki's diaries?' Adam looks back and forth at us in disbelief.

'Yeah.' I shrug. 'You did give me access to them,' I point out to Charlie, defensively.

'Yeah, I know, I know.' He brushes me off.

'Ooh, that's freaky,' Adam interjects, still shaking his head.

'Shut up,' Charlie and I both say at the same time, but Charlie's the one to continue. 'She needs to understand Nicki if she's going to do her characters justice. Nicki would've wanted that. And there's stuff in there that relates to the new book.'

'Have you really never read them?' I ask.

He shakes his head. 'No, but she was pretty open about what they contained.'

I wonder *how* open.

'Anyway.' I move on.

'Who's Number Two?' Adam asks.

'Jorge. I used to go and stay with my mum when she was working on various cruise liners around the world. When I was seventeen, she was doing Europe and it was the first summer I'd been aboard on my own – before that my dad and aunt used to take me. Jorge worked in the casino. He was from Barcelona – a twenty-one-year-old, hot-blooded son of a matador,' I add with a grin.

I loved that cruise. I'd been gutted about Elliot's letters drying up, so, when Mum asked me to come and join her, I agreed. As the daughter of a staff member *and* a paying customer, I had exactly the same perks as the rich kids, while also being allowed to hang out in the staff areas. I was caught between two worlds – above and below deck – but this wasn't purgatory: it was heaven.

Most of the staff were crazy, young and fun and seemed to come from every country under the sun. Mum was busy hostessing, so I had to occupy myself, and, as she'd told her boss that I was over eighteen, I went wherever I wanted, from the casino to the pool, with nobody batting an eyelid. It was all very civilised.

Below deck was a different matter.

The staff were at it like rabbits. It was a place of rampant sex and late-night drinking games – Aunt Wendy had been right to keep me well away from it.

But Aunt Wendy wasn't there. Aunt Wendy was in Wembley.

At first I was scandalized by what went on behind the scenes – I was only seventeen, after all – but I was a pretty fearless seventeen, and was capable of fending for myself.

I fancied Jorge the moment I saw him, but it was forbidden for staff to hook up with passengers, and I was a hybrid of the two, so he was wary of me.

My breakthrough came one night during a pool tournament when we both found ourselves playing each other in the semi-final. Dad had pool tables at the pub where he worked, so I'd already wiped the floor with several of the kitchen boys.

I shared the rest of my beer with Jorge, and, when he later won the tournament, he took me to the staff bar, claiming to owe me a drink. We ended up kissing on the deck under the stars as he walked me to my room. We were in each other's pockets for the rest of the summer.

'Three?' Charlie prompts.

141

'Gabriel. Another cruise-ship romance. I was nineteen,' I explain. 'His dad was a wealthy property developer in Brazil who'd recently remarried. Gabe was pissed off at having to spend the summer on a boat when he could have been home with his mum and his friends. I was actually at university studying journalism, but Mum had swung a job for me, working with the cruise coordinating team that summer. I helped to organise the various tours for passengers to take at the different ports. Anyway, staff members weren't meant to have flings with passengers, so Gabe and I did a lot of sneaking around. I think he felt like he was getting back at his dad by slumming it with me.'

Charlie pulls a face.

'I met up with him a couple of months ago. He was even more of a spoiled brat than he was when he was twenty-one.'

'Four?' Adam prompts.

'David, my university boyfriend. He was lovely,' I say with a smile. 'He had a girlfriend in his first year, but they split up after the summer and we were already friends. We were together for about a year and a half. But... I don't know. I just stopped fancying him. I've never really been able to work out why because he had so much going for him. He's now living in South Africa with his wife and three kids. I caught up with him recently and he seemed very settled and happy.'

'Five?' Adam asks.

'I'd better speed this up or we'll be here all night,' I say. 'Am I boring you yet?'

They both deny it, so I carry on.

'Five was Freddie. I'd decided to go travelling around

America for a bit, and I met him on the road. He was a Norwegian wildlife photographer.' As wild and free as the animals and landscape he photographed. He snapped off a piece of my heart as easily as breaking off a KitKat finger. 'He encouraged me to buy a camera and taught me how to take photographs so I could submit pictures along with my articles.'

He had loads of contacts, too, which he generously shared. I'd been writing for years about the places I'd been visiting, working from the ship's internet café during my downtime, but I hadn't had much published. Freddie changed all that.

'He really helped kick-start my career. He was a bit older than me.'

'How much older?' Charlie asks with interest.

'I was twenty-one and he was twenty-eight. I loved him desperately. I was heartbroken when things fell apart and he went back to Norway.' I smile sadly and shrug.

'Six!' Adam chirps.

I groan. 'Vince. When I came back from America I decided to try to get a job at a travel magazine, but knew that would probably involve doing unpaid work experience, so I helped behind the bar at my dad's pub to get by. Vince was a regular.'

Or, at least, he became a regular while I was working there. He was a landscape gardener doing a big job on a house nearby. He'd come in every day after work for a pint of beer, and I liked that he always looked a bit grubby from a day's hard labour.

'He had a certain arrogance about him that initially wound me up. Freddie and I had only recently separated, so I wasn't looking for anyone else, but I soon warmed to Vince. He was

143

funny and confident, and, even though I'd sometimes call him a twat to his face, he never gave up.'

Charlie and Adam grin. You can tell a mile away that they're brothers when they're side by side and smiling like this.

Eventually, my dislike of Vince was only pretence. I used to inwardly smile when he walked through the door, while outwardly rolling my eyes. When he asked me out on a date on the eve of his job finishing, I agreed. It had been a month since he'd first sat down at the bar.

He was twenty-seven, stable, settled and not about to fly off to a far-flung country and desert me.

Looking back, I see I've bounced between settled, stable boyfriends and wild, free, untamed men all my life.

'Dad had started seeing someone while I'd been away, and, even though she was always nice enough to me, she wasn't thrilled that her partner's grown-up daughter had invaded their love nest. I stayed more and more at Vince's, and, before I knew it, I was living with him. He turned out to be a proper arse, though. Very controlling.'

Charlie looks concerned. Adam looks bored.

'Right, that's it,' I say, taking the hint. 'My round, and then we'll talk about something else.'

'No!' Charlie protests.

'Yep. Six is halfway. That's a good end point.' I get up and go to the bar.

When I come back, Charlie is sitting alone.

'Where's Adam?'

'Over there.' He nods at the two o'clock table. Adam is surrounded by four girls, including the pretty blonde. He looks like he's in his element.

'Good work,' I say, impressed, climbing onto the bench seat properly and facing Charlie.

'Come on, then, tell me about the others.'

'No, no.' I shake my head. 'I've talked enough.'

'I'm curious. Seven.'

'Are you sure? Okay, then. I met Olli on a press trip to an Icelandic Ice Hotel. He worked in hospitality.' And he looked after me *very* well. 'My boss, who'd gone off on maternity leave, had come back around this time and it felt like I'd been given a whopping great demotion, so, after meeting Olli, I resigned and went freelance. Mum was now an assistant cruise director and touring the British Isles, and, as Iceland was one of their stops, I decided to go back to cruise coordinating so I could drop in on Olli every few weeks. I blogged in the staff Internet café in my spare time and sold off my articles to magazines and newspapers.'

'I think I read your Olli account,' Charlie says.

I remember him saying that he agreed with Fay about Nicki and me having a similar tone of voice. 'Olli was the one who couldn't remember me,' I remind him.

'That's right. He sounded like a total dick.'

I laugh. 'Yeah, he was. I think he's got a whole jar of hearts somewhere, like the Christina Perri song.'

He gives me a blank look.

'"Jar of Hearts"? By Christina Perri? Never mind. Anyway, after Olli dumped me, Mum and I went and joined the Caribbean cruise set. I played the field a bit during those twelve months. It was hard not to, working on that ship. I didn't fall in love again for another year.'

'How old were you?' he asks.

'Twenty-five. That was Dillon.' I'm hit by a wave of anxiety. 'I can't believe I'm going to Ireland tomorrow to meet up with him. Ooh!' I put my hand on my belly.

'You all right?'

'Yeah, fine. I'm just nervous.'

He looks surprised. 'I thought you took it all in your stride.'

'God, no! It stresses me out massively.'

'Why do you do it, then?'

'You've got to step out of your comfort zone sometimes.' I take a gulp of my beer. 'Anyway, I started feeling homesick after so long away so I went back to do the British Isles to be a bit closer to Dad. Dillon was part of the ship's entertainment crew – a musician. I fell so hard for him that I ended up handing in my notice and going on tour with him and his band of merry Irishmen.'

On board he'd played jolly folk music for our passengers. Off board, the band's music had more of a rock edge. Dillon played the guitar and the banjo and was one of three singers.

'He was very sexy, a bit of a bad boy. The girls used to go mad for him. I walked away after a few months before he cheated on me – I was certain he would. He was *not* happy,' I state, remembering how he refused to accept that we were over. He said that I'd live to regret it.

I thought twice about contacting him prior to my visit, just in case he told me to go jump, but in the end I risked it and got a surprisingly warm email in return. We're meeting at a pub tomorrow night – he's got a gig a few doors down.

'What am I on now? You still want to hear this?'

Charlie nods. 'I think you're up to nine…'

'Okay, super quickly. After I left Ireland, I went to work for another travel magazine in London. That's where I met Liam. He was a picture editor. Very sweet, very sexy. We tried to keep our relationship under wraps for a while, which was fun, but we were together for a good eighteen months.'

'You like the whole forbidden-love thing, don't you?' Charlie comments drily.

I grin. 'Yeah, I do, actually. At least, I did. I've grown up a bit now.'

He smirks at me.

'After Liam came Seth. I was twenty-seven and I wanted to get away from London for a bit, so I joined Mum on the Japan route. It all went a bit pear-shaped. I won't bore you with the details. Eleven was—'

'Wait,' Charlie interrupts. 'How did it go pear-shaped?'

'Urgh, seriously, I'll tell you another time if you really want to know.'

'Okay.' He seems intrigued.

'Eleven was… Beau!' I say brightly. I cast a quick look at Adam over my shoulder. 'I wonder if he's seen Michelle to ask about him.' I turn back to Charlie. 'Beau was fun-loving and gorgeous. The perfect antidote to Seth the Wanker. I'd be so happy if I could track him down while I'm here,' I say. 'And, finally, there was Felix. I was twenty-nine and had agreed to do a freelance lifestyle piece on unusual forms of exercise. Felix was a free runner. He was also a dental hygienist.' I laugh. 'He was always looking at my teeth, which could be really annoying. We broke up about three times, but kept getting back together. I think I just wanted to settle down at that point, but it was a couple more years before I found Elliot.'

Charlie raises his eyebrows. 'So that's your twelve?'

'That's my twelve,' I confirm. There were others, but no one I loved enough to give a piece of my heart to.

'How many have you met up with?' he asks.

'Five: David, Olli, Jorge, Gabe and, of course, Elliot. Seven more to go, and another ticked off after tomorrow. Ooh.' I clutch my belly again and then reach for my beer, downing another nice, big mouthful.

'Could've brought mine over,' Adam says suddenly, placing his hands on my shoulders and making me jump so violently that I spill my drink. He slides onto the bench seat next to me and reaches for his pint glass.

'No luck?' Charlie enquires derisively.

'Nup. Night's still young.' He slides a little closer to me on the bench seat. I place my hands on his biceps and waist and push firmly until he starts to slither back in the opposite direction. The look on his face is priceless.

'Did you ever ask Michelle about Beau?' Charlie asks Adam when he's stopped chuckling.

'No, I haven't see her. I know where she works, though, so I'll pop in this week. What number guy are you on?' He glances at me.

'I'm finished,' I say. 'That's my talking done for the rest of the evening.'

'It better not be,' Adam replies. 'We're going to another pub to do some karaoke after these drinks.'

'Are we really?' I ask with glee, ignoring Charlie's objections. 'Singing is *not* talking...'

Chapter 19

I'd forgotten how breathtaking the Ring of Kerry is. It's almost taking my mind off my hangover.

It's Saturday afternoon and I've been driving for two hours. I flew from Bristol, arriving in Cork at just after two o'clock. Because I'm not meeting Dillon until this evening at a pub in Killarney, I decided to take the scenic route via Kenmare, Moll's Gap and the Killarney National Park. It doubles my driving time – from one and a half to almost three hours – but it's worth it. It's actually a pleasure to be behind the wheel of a normal hire car after wrestling with *Hermie*.

The first time I did this route was with Dillon when he was touring with his band. I remember being so blown away by the scenery that I couldn't believe I hadn't heard about it before. It felt like a big secret that the Irish had cunningly kept from the rest of us.

It's a gorgeous sunny afternoon, and as I make my way along the gently winding roads with the window down, I breathe in the cool summer air and sigh with happiness. All around me are the most stunning rocky hills, cast with both light and shade from the sun and the cotton-wool clouds in the sky above. The grey of the rock blends with the green of the patchy grass, so that the colours come across as muted, like the palette of a painting by a centuries-old landscape artist. I look through the white trunks of birch trees to a lake that's as still as glass and just as reflective. The ground is covered with a carpet of moss and fern and, on impulse, I pull over.

I get out of the car and climb carefully down the hill to the stony shore. Great slabs of smooth grey rock slope into the water's edge and all around are big boulders of various shades of grey. I sit down on one and stare out at the water, taking a minute to appreciate the beauty around me.

Despite my pounding head, I smile every time I think about last night. I can't believe we managed to get Charlie to do DJ Kool's 'Let Me Clear My Throat'. It was hilarious.

I giggle to myself, even as I sit there on my own. Ouch. I wish my head didn't hurt so much.

Both Charlie and Adam ended up walking me home. We almost fell into the estuary with all the zigzagging that was going on. Adam kept teasing me about the three different men who'd tried to pick me up. I don't know why I always pull guys on dance floors – I'm not even trying, and most of the time I'm not interested.

When we arrived at the hill at the bottom of the campsite, Adam let out the biggest groan and collapsed on the side of the road.

'I can't walk up there,' he stated.

'I'll take it from here,' I replied gallantly.

But, by God, that incline is steep. I swear I almost cart-wheeled back down the hill. Charlie saw me struggling and came to my aid, pushing me up from behind. I've never laughed so much in my life.

Well, I probably have. But it was a very funny night.

I still can't believe he rapped.

It's five thirty by the time I make it into Killarney and check into my hotel. I have two and a half hours to kill, so I decide to go for a wander.

As soon as I'm outside on the street, I'm approached by a wily-looking chap offering a horse-and-cart ride down to the lake. He has a mouth full of crooked yellow teeth, gigantic ears and a brilliantly bushy moustache, and he's wearing a sweater with 'IRELAND' embroidered on it underneath a green shamrock.

There are several other younger and less on-the-verge-of-death-looking horse-and-cart drivers standing in a group across the road, but none of them are touting for business. Quite frankly, I admire Paddy's enthusiasm – and the fact that he's fantastically called Paddy – so I find myself agreeing. I figure it'll give me something else to write about.

As I follow him and climb onto his green-and-yellow-painted cart, I notice the smirking faces of the other drivers.

'All right, Paddy?' one of them calls.

'Yeah, you're all right, lads,' he calls back, waving them away.

I soon realise what the joke is.

Paddy's horse is so old and slow that I could walk twice as fast. Paddy keeps waving vehicles past, sometimes right into the path of oncoming traffic, and I wince as a bus almost collides with a car. All the while, Paddy chats amiably, geeing his horse along every so often, prompting her to trot for about four seconds before she reverts to snail speed. Despite appearances, though, Paddy is as sharp as a stake.

When we finally make it into the park, he asks me if I'd like to take a boat ride out to the derelict abbey on Innisfallen Island. It sounds appealing and Paddy even says he can call ahead and have his friend waiting, but, having longingly counted seven other horses and carts happily trotting past us – all with smugly smirking drivers – I decide I'd better decline.

Back at the hotel, I don't even have time for a shower, but the smell of horse manure is up my nose, and, just in case that scent has spread to the rest of me, I decide to have a quick one.

By the time I get to the pub, I'm fifteen minutes late and bricking it. I take a deep breath and walk into the crowded venue, scouring the room for anyone remotely resembling Dillon.

I can't see him anywhere. Has he stood me up? Has he already walked out again?

My pulse is racing as I squeeze into a narrow space left by two bulky blokes in black-leather jackets at the bar. I still feel rough, so, much as I could do with some Dutch courage, I order a soft drink and then find a quiet corner of the pub. With one eye on the entrance, I wait, and, as I do so, a memory comes back to me…

We'd dropped in on Dillon's parents, who lived in Dalkey, southeast of Dublin, on the coast. That weekend it was raining across the whole of Europe, but Ireland was in the midst of a rare heatwave. Dillon wanted to take me to the beach, so we parked in Killiney Hill Park and walked hand in hand down the cliff pathway. The blue of the sky melded into the blue of the ocean and the coast was bursting with wild-flowers. The view made me think of the French Riviera – it was outstandingly beautiful.

Down on the beach, the sand was grey and murky and the water so cold that it almost froze my toes off, but, somehow, Dillon managed to go swimming. I sat there and laughed at him, while behind us a train chugged back and forth – offering its passengers the most incredible views of the ocean. I remember thinking that I would be happy settling there, and, if I had to commute to work in Dublin, the coast train would be the way I'd want to travel.

I fell hard for Dillon that weekend, seeing him interacting with his parents, witnessing him at home in a happy, stable environment. I almost believed that one day we could have that, too.

But then we went back on the road again, back to the bars, back around drink, drugs and rock and roll – not to mention the girls – and I convinced myself it was a pipedream.

'You are not leaving me,' he said, and the look in his dark eyes still haunts me.

'It's already done. I've taken a job in London.'

'Then I'll come with you.'

'No. You'd miss your band. You're not ready to settle down. I'm not sure *I* am. Let's quit while we're ahead. Let me go before we end up hating each other.'

'If you leave me now, I'll hate you for the rest of my life!'

My thoughts return to the present. Half an hour passes. I don't know if Dillon is coming, if he's already been or if he's simply getting back at me for dumping him.

But, luckily, his band are playing a gig a few doors down. Time to revert to Plan B.

I see him as soon as I walk into the bar. He's right at the back at a table crowded with pretty girls and drunken band members.

Not much has changed, it seems.

They're all laughing raucously and shouting and I watch as Tezza the fiddler pours whiskey into shot glasses and they all knock them back.

Dillon relaxes into his seat and casually drapes his arm around the shoulders of the girl next to him. His hair is chocolate-brown and messy and falls haphazardly off to one side, just like it used to.

The next thing I know, his dark eyes have locked with mine and his easy smile dies on his lips.

The girl in his arms turns to look at him with confusion – presumably because he's gone rigid – then she follows the line of his sight until she's staring at me, too.

I smile and shrug. *Ta-da! Here I am!*

I am completely faking my nonchalance. My heart is pounding ten to the dozen.

I casually jerk my head towards the bar. *I'm getting a drink. You want to join me?*

As I turn away, I see him slide out past the girl.

He's coming.

I feel, rather than see, him standing behind me.

'Can I get a vodka, lemonade and lime please?' I ask. So much for not wanting alcohol today. 'Drink?' I look over my shoulder at Dillon.

He shakes his head abruptly. He is still incredibly good-looking. He has lines around his eyes that weren't there the last time we stood face to face, and salt-and-pepper strands of hair around his temples.

'What are you doing here?' he asks me in a low, heated voice.

'You told me I was welcome to come,' I point out with a calmness I don't feel. I used to love hearing him talk in his lilting Irish accent. Even angry, he sounds sexy.

'I was drunk when I wrote that email.' He stares sullenly at the bottles lined up behind the bar.

'Well, I'm here now. Are you sure I can't buy you a drink?' I raise one eyebrow.

Charlie's question from last night is ringing around my head. *'Why do you do it, then?'*

'Fine.' I inwardly breathe a sigh of relief as he changes his mind. 'Make it two,' he tells the bartender.

Dillon meets my eyes again for a long, painful moment. It's a struggle to not look away.

'Is that your girlfriend?' I ask gently, when the hardness in his expression finally begins to soften.

'Just a girl,' he replies quietly, nodding at the bartender as two vodkas appear in front of us. I hand over a tenner and pick up my glass.

'Bottoms up,' I say cheerfully.

He downs half of his drink in one.

'Urgh.' I pull a face, and I've had only one sip. 'Got such a shitty hangover today,' I reveal. 'I don't know why I ordered this.'

He places his glass back on the bar and leans against it, facing me.

'Why are you here?' he asks directly, folding his arms.

'Don't you know?' I reply. Has he read my blog?

'You think I will have looked you up?' He sounds defensive.

I shrug and avert my gaze. 'I thought you might've after getting my email.'

'Maybe I did, maybe I didn't.'

I grin at him.

'What's so funny?'

'You sound like a little boy.'

'Piss off, Bridget, I don't need this.'

'Dillon, chill the fuck out. You're still so feisty.' I keep my tone light and eventually his fury morphs into mild humour.

'You're still so...' He screws up his face, thinking. 'Annoying.'

'Ha! Yes, I *am* still annoying. So come on, have you read my blog or not? Or do you just want to make this difficult for me?'

'I *definitely* want to make this difficult for you,' he says, but I can tell he's not completely serious.

'Okay.' I take a deep breath. Honestly, five men down – I should be used to this spiel by now. 'I've come to ask you for your piece of my heart back.'

I know instantly that he *has* read my blog. He knows exactly what I mean and precisely why I'm here. There's not even a hint of surprise on his face.

'I'm afraid that's impossible,' he says, downing the second half of his drink. 'I don't have it any more.'

'What did you do with it?' I demand to know, going along with him. He's obviously thought about this.

'I threw it away.'

'For God's sake, Dillon! How could you?' I pretend to be angry with him.

'You left me, I was hurt, I thought, Fuck you! So I threw it away,' he says facetiously, a trace of a smile on his lips.

'Where did you put it?'

'I don't know.' He shrugs. 'Some lake somewhere. It sank straight to the bottom. Hard and heavy as a stone, it was.'

I'm trying very hard to keep a straight face.

'A heavy heartless heart,' he adds and I can't help it, I crack up laughing.

He does too.

'Oh, Dillon,' I say, tears of laughter spilling from my eyes. 'I've missed you.'

He shakes his head, gathering himself together. 'I've missed you, too,' he replies, sobering. 'Will you stay to watch the gig?'

'I'd love to. Can I come and say hi to the lads?'

'Come on, then.'

Later I find him to say goodbye. He's had a load more drinks by that point, and I stiffen as he takes me in his arms and speaks in a low, gruff voice into my ear.

'If you come to my room with me, I'll tell you which lake I put it in.'

I keep my tone light as I withdraw to look at him. 'I have a boyfriend who I love dearly. You know how I feel about

157

cheating. And, anyway, I think we've been there, done that, don't you?'

'Worth a try,' he says with a wry grin, letting me go.

'Bye, Dillon.' I give him a peck on his cheek and turn away, but he grabs my arm and pulls me back.

'Are you sure you don't want to know which lake it was?'

'Was it on the N71 just past Muckross?' I ask hopefully, giving him a winning smile. I try to ignore the intensity in his dark eyes as he stares at me for a long, torturous moment.

'If you're going to tell me, be kind and do it without strings,' I plead, my tone growing serious.

'Fine,' he snaps. 'Yeah. That's the lake.'

I throw my arms around him and give him a quick, hard hug, our hearts beating together for the very last time.

'Take care of yourself.'

'You too.'

He looks torn as I turn and walk out of the bar.

I'm not sure that he ever threw his part of me away. I'm not even entirely sure that I wanted him to. But we can carry on pretending.

The next morning, I drive the fast route back to Cork. When I write up this chapter for my blog, I'll say I did the journey in reverse, stopping along the way and walking down to the glassy water's edge. I can imagine I found his piece of my heart there in among the stones.

As I say, we can carry on pretending.

Chapter 20

Before I put my key in the lock on Monday morning, the door swings open and Charlie is standing there, smiling.

A warmth bubbles up inside me at the sight of his friendly face.

'Hello!' we both say.

He holds the door back so I can wheel Nicki's bike into the hall.

'How was your weekend?'

'How did it go?'

We speak at the same time.

'You first,' he commands.

'No, you,' I reply, unclicking my helmet.

He shrugs. 'It was fine. Nothing eventful. Adam and I spent Saturday nursing our hangovers. Took April to the beach yesterday.'

I follow him into the kitchen. April beams and babbles at the sight of me, so I go over and pick her up. She presses her cheek against the nape of my neck, clutching onto my shoulders with her little fingers. The radio is on, playing 'Manic Monday' by The Bangles, and the atmosphere is so bright and cheerful that the bubbly warmth inside me expands further.

'Ooh, you're so lovely and cuddly,' I say to April, squeezing her to me.

Charlie hops up onto the kitchen counter and sits there, his tanned legs dangling over the side.

He's in a good mood this morning, as am I. After the upheaval of the weekend, I'm happy to be back into my routine.

'This hug is longer than seven seconds.' I glance at Charlie with a smirk.

He shakes his head, amused. 'That was a good night.'

'Hilarious. I've been giggling about you doing DJ Kool all weekend.'

'I *seriously* don't know how you got me to do that.'

'A deal's a deal.'

He creases his brow at me.

'Don't you remember?' I ask. 'You said you'd do it if I took on Eminem.'

His face lights up with the memory and he throws his head back and laughs. God, that *sound*...

'That was one of the most brilliant things I've ever seen,' he says. 'How did you know all the words?'

'Oh, "Lose Yourself" is an old favourite,' I reply offhandedly.

After a moment, he jerks his chin up at me. 'So how did it go?'

*

160

It's almost ten o'clock by the time I've filled him in on Ireland and made it upstairs to Nicki's office. Soon I'm engrossed in the diary she wrote when she was twenty-four.

Nicki grew up in Essex, but moved to Cornwall in her second year of secondary school because her dad got a job at a top restaurant. When her parents divorced, Nicki's mum wanted to return to Essex, but she agreed to let Nicki finish secondary school first. So, when Nicki set off to university, her mum's new home in Essex became the place she'd return to outside of term time.

But she missed Cornwall, and, even though she also toyed with the idea of emigrating to Thailand, after university, Cornwall won out.

Nicki's diaries became less confessional around this point and more general musings. It was clear she still loved to write, but she didn't seem to feel the need to catalogue every single feeling. It's a shame, because I'd love to know what was going through her mind when she reconnected with Charlie. She seemed excited to see him again: 'JUST BUMPED INTO CHARLIE!' is written in capital letters and is followed by several other references to their catching up. I don't get the impression he held a grudge over what had happened when they were teenagers, and clearly their friendship soon developed once again into something more.

In the next two years Nicki returned to Thailand four times – during the summer and also at Christmas – and she also started to make notes about ideas she had for her novel. There's no mention of Isak, so I don't know if Nicki ever saw him again.

It's not always easy to follow her jumping thoughts,

but I freeze when I turn a page and the words: 'FEMALE BIGAMIST' jump out.

Bigamy…

Dictionary definition: 'Crime of being simultaneously twice married'.

Whoa. Does this mean Nicki *did* intend for Kit to marry both Morris *and* Timo? Was her initial idea to write a book about a female bigamist?

I glance up at the books about Thailand. There are dozens of yellow Post-it notes sticking out of the tops of them. I get to my feet and pull one of the more heavily noted books down, glancing back up at the shelf to see that there's another row of books behind the first.

Something calls on me to investigate.

I drag my chair over and climb onto it. An object is poking out from behind the last row of books – out of view from the floor. I reach up and pull it free.

It's a wooden heart, made of small fragments of driftwood, twisted and kept in place with thin gold wire. A whole section is missing and some of the bits have come loose and need reworking back into the heart shape. It looks like the seahorse, but this creation is half the size – less than a foot in diameter.

I wonder if this is the heart Charlie had planned to finish for April.

I blow on it and a puff of dust fills the air, then I gingerly climb down from my chair, the books on the bookshelf momentarily forgotten.

I feel sick. So sick and sad. I sit there and stare at the heart with its missing piece and suddenly want to cry.

How did Charlie live through losing her? How did he pick himself up and raise a tiny baby when his heart must've been so broken he surely found it hard even to breathe?

The thought of him creating something this beautiful and then hiding it away so he wouldn't have to look at it... Does he even remember that he put it there? Didn't he say that he wanted to find it?

My eyes are drawn to the window. Charlie is outside sawing a piece of wood in half, Nicki's mustard-yellow bandana keeping his hair out of his eyes. My music is still on – I didn't realise it was time for April's nap. I go to turn it down, but then hesitate, looking out of the window again at Charlie. He's totally engrossed in his work.

I get up and quietly walk out of the office, pausing by April's open door to check for any sound before venturing forward.

She's fast asleep, sprawled out on her back. It's warm in her bedroom and she's kicked off her covers, her sturdy baby legs sticking out of the short-sleeved, pink-and-white babygrow she's wearing. Her rosebud mouth is slightly open and her blonde hair is all mussed up and curly. She twitches and I flinch, but her breathing is steady, her little ribcage rising and falling with perfect rhythm.

I glance at her side table, at the white, driftwood picture frames that I now recognise as Charlie's handiwork. There are photographs of April's extended family – I spy Adam and Pat standing with whom I presume is Charlie's dad, and I'm guessing the other people are Nicki's mum, her sister and family, and her dad – but the other pictures are of Nicki. Nicki laughing and dressed up to the nines at some restaurant with the sun setting behind her, and Nicki with her face bare of make-up, smiling down at the newborn baby in her arms.

Something inside me splinters.

The light on April's monitor is glowing green, so I'm careful to make no sound as I place the driftwood heart down beside the photo frames before returning to my office.

Chapter 21

If I didn't know better, I'd say I had my period coming on. I'm trying to understand why I'm feeling so emotional as I walk into Padstow. April was still asleep when I left, but I wasn't sure how Charlie would react when he found the heart in her room, so I thought it might be best for me to be out of the way.

As I sit in a café, barely touching my sandwich, my uneasiness grows. Why did I do that? I don't even know. It just seemed like the right thing to do. It was as though I was on autopilot or something.

But how could I think he'd be okay with my sneaking into his daughter's room and leaving behind something that belonged to his wife – something that had been put well out of the way for a reason?

I hurry back to Charlie's as quickly as I can, full of ready apologies. I listen outside the front door, not sure what I'm expecting to hear. When I hear nothing, I put my key in the lock and step over the threshold.

The hallway leads to a corridor that spills straight onto the kitchen, so I can see right down to the very back of the house from where I'm standing. My gut freefalls at the sight of Charlie sitting at the kitchen table with his back to me. He looks like he has his head in his hands.

I quietly close the door behind me and make my way into the kitchen. April is nowhere to be seen.

'Charlie?' I ask with building nausea.

He jolts at the sound of my voice, but he doesn't reply.

'Are you okay?'

That's when I hear him sniff. *Please don't tell me I've made him cry!*

'I'm so sorry.' I feel absolutely horrified as I approach him. He's staring at the incomplete driftwood heart on the table in front of him, his tears falling in a steady stream, even as he continually brushes them away.

Oh, God!

'Where's April?' I ask softly, placing my hand on his back.

He shudders. 'Living room,' he replies in a choked voice. 'Can you check on her?'

'Of course,' I say quickly, leaving the room.

Bridget, you are such a fucking arse! What the hell were you thinking? He was in the best mood earlier. I can't believe I've shattered his happiness today.

I'm furious with myself as I leave the kitchen, but as soon as I set eyes on April, my anger dissolves.

'Hello, lovely girl,' I murmur.

She's strapped into her Jumperoo – a brightly coloured contraption that allows her to bounce up and down and spin around while playing with the various toys, rattles and lights affixed to the surrounding tray.

She grins up at me and bounces on her feet, then reaches for one of the squashy flowers dangling from the top frame and places it in her mouth, munching up and down. She stops and takes the flower out of her mouth to stare at it, then she looks up at me and lets out a cry of complaint.

'Are you hungry?' I ask. 'I'll get you some lunch. We'll just give Daddy a minute.'

I kneel on the floor next to her and press one of the musical buttons, singing along in a silly voice as the lights flash. It distracts her for a while, but then Charlie walks suddenly into the room, making us both jump. She holds up her arms to him, wanting to be lifted out.

'Come on, then,' he mumbles, complying.

He takes her back into the kitchen while I stay on the floor, feeling utterly wretched.

After a while I head back upstairs to the office, avoiding looking in the direction of the kitchen. I flick through one of Nicki's Thailand books, trying to focus on the pages she'd Post-it-noted, but I can't take anything in, so the exercise proves futile.

I eventually decide I may as well write up my Dillon encounter, but I soon find my heart's not in it. I'm very well aware of the irony of that sentence.

When Charlie knocks on the door, my insides twang with nerves.

'Come in,' I call.

I find it very hard to meet his eyes as he enters the room.

'April's down for her nap,' he says heavily.

'Is it that time already?' I ask.

He nods.

'I'm so sorry,' I whisper, my eyes beginning to sting.

'Stop,' he says quietly, leaning against one of the filing cabinets and folding his arms protectively across his chest. 'It's okay.'

'I don't know what I was thinking.'

'I said I wanted to finish it.'

'Is it the same heart?' I check.

He nods and looks up at the shelves. 'I'd forgotten she threw it up there.'

'*She* put it up there?' I ask with surprise.

'Yeah.' He smiles a small, ironic smile and shifts on his feet. '*Threw* it. We were in the middle of an argument.'

Oh.

'It was a week or so before she died,' he reveals.

This is probably another one of those moments when I should shut the hell up, but instead I ask, 'What were you arguing about?' and prepare for him to tell me to shut the hell up.

He slides down the length of the filing cabinet until he's sitting on the floor, his elbows resting on his bent knees in front of him.

'It was just a stupid argument.' He stares ahead in a daze. 'We were both absolutely knackered. I had a big job I was trying to finish, April had colic and wouldn't stop crying, Nicki wanted peace and quiet to do some writing and I told her she'd have to wait until April was asleep because I needed to crack on. She got so angry at me that she picked up the heart and hurled it at the wall. It landed up there.' He nods at the bookshelves. 'I told her it could stay the fuck up there for all I cared, because I was never going to finish it if she didn't stop being such a bitch, then I walked out and slammed the door and had to listen to April screaming blue murder all afternoon.' He shakes his head and a single tear rolls down his cheek. He brushes it away.

'It *does* sound like a stupid argument,' I say.

'We used to have them all the time,' he replies. 'We were like that. Loved her to hell and back, but, Christ, we fought like cats and dogs.'

I don't know why, but this surprises me.

'How—' I clear my throat. 'How did she die?' I ask cautiously. 'I mean, was there any warning?'

'Maybe, but I wasn't here.' He swallows, running his palm across the carpet and staring at his hand fixatedly. 'I was delivering a playhouse. The doctor said she might've felt a headache – I later found out it would've been the most painful headache ever, like, *unbearable* pain. I found her in April's room, collapsed beside her cot.' He swallows again, tears welling up in his eyes. 'April was fast asleep. Nicki was already gone.' His tears spill over and he brushes them away again. 'Sorry.'

'Don't be,' I whisper, fighting back tears myself.

I feel compelled to go and sit beside him on the carpet. I do it without thinking. He stays very still, very quiet, tears rolling relentlessly down his cheeks.

'I couldn't believe it.' He sounds stunned. 'I couldn't believe what was happening. She was *gone*. Just like that. I don't even remember calling the ambulance. I think I just went into shock. Thank God for Jocelyn. She came over when she saw the ambulance pull up and took April until I'd had a chance to call our parents. I don't remember those conversations either.' He looks utterly bewildered. 'Sorry, I don't know why I'm even talking about all of this to you,' he says, shaking himself.

'I don't mind,' I say. 'I'm a pretty good listener.'

'Yeah, but that's not what you're here for.'

He gets to his feet, but I stay where I am, dazed and wounded.

But, of course, I'm not his friend. I'm his wife's ghostwriter. I'm here to do a job. I'd probably do well to remember that.

Chapter 22

Two days later, Charlie starts rebuilding Nicki's heart. He repairs the fragments that came apart with the force of the blow when she threw it against the wall, and paints the new pieces of driftwood pale pink before fixing them into the missing section with silver wire.

'It's beautiful,' I say when he's finished. I've been sitting on the sofa, rolling a giggling April around on my lap, but I stop when he comes over to show me what he's done. 'Will you put it on her wall next to the seahorse?'

'I don't know. What do you think?' He seems to genuinely want my opinion.

'I think they'd look great side by side.'

He nods and starts to leave the kitchen, the heart in his hands, before halting and looking back at me. 'Will you be okay with April for a bit?'

'Sure.'

A short while later a hammering noise starts up from above our heads. April gazes at the ceiling with interest.

'Bridget?' Charlie calls out.

'Yeah?' I get up and walk to the bottom of the stairs. He's poking his head over the banister.

'Will you bring her up?'

I do as he asks, offering April over as I enter her room, but Charlie just nods at the wall. I turn around and look, April still in my arms.

'Oh, it's so pretty,' I enthuse.

April reaches out her hand, trying to touch it. I step in closer so she can.

'Gently,' I warn softly. She's surprisingly careful as she traces her fingers across the painted and natural wood. 'I love it,' I say, wishing I had one myself. 'You should sell these. I bet they'd go down really well in the gift shops around here.'

He shakes his head. 'Wouldn't be enough money in it.'

He does it for love and love alone.

'How are you getting on?' he asks me, jerking his chin in the direction of the office as he relieves me of April, his warm arms brushing against mine.

'Fine,' I reply, feeling a little jittery as I take a step backwards.

'Fancy getting out of the house tomorrow?'

'To do what?' I ask, immediately perking up.

'I know you want to go to the Lost Gardens of Heligan…'

I smile at him. I haven't stopped bleating on about it.

'But there's also another place I think you'd like. They're not far from each other. We could probably squeeze both in.'

'Are you sure you've got the time?'

'I can work on the weekend if I need to,' he says, kissing April's temple. He returns his gaze to me, concern etched onto his face. 'Are you all right? You've seemed a bit down the last couple of days.'

'I'm okay.' I shrug. 'You?'

'Better.' He nods at me. 'I could do with a day out, though.' He pauses. 'Don't you think?'

I nod. 'That sounds good.'

He picks me up from the campsite the following morning.

'So where are we going?' I ask when I'm safely installed in the passenger seat.

'A place called Lansallos Beach. It's National Trust-owned.'

'Driftwood?' I ask.

'Unlikely,' he replies. 'It's just really beautiful, and it's a nice walk down to the cove.' He checks my choice of footwear: flip-flops. 'Actually, you're going to need walking shoes. Sorry.'

'No worries.' I get back out of the car and go to retrieve my Vans.

I return a short while later and kick off my flip-flops, pulling on my shoes as Charlie drives out of the campsite.

'Was Lansallos in *The Secret Life of Us*?' I've been racking my brain, but have come up with nothing.

'Nicki didn't use the location, but she planned to for the sequel.'

'Oh!' I say with surprise. 'Well, that's brilliant, then. Thanks for taking me.'

'Sure. I only remembered yesterday morning her saying it.'

I wonder what reminded him of that conversation, but decide not to ask.

Lansallos is a small, south-facing cove a few miles west of Polperro. It takes us around an hour to get to the car park in Lansallos village, and then it's a half-mile walk down to the cove. The track is steep and not suitable for a pushchair, so Charlie straps April into her baby backpack, and, after arguing about who's going to carry the sun tent (he wins), we set off.

Sun streams down between the flickering discs of green as we walk beneath a shady canopy of trees, and off to our left the golden fields are bathed in morning light. A brook runs parallel to our path on the other side of a stone wall carpeted with thick moss and ferns, so our walk is accompanied by the music of running water. Every so often, we come across random adventure playground equipment made out of wood, like stepping stones, seesaws, climbing frames and balancing beams. I hop along the stepping stones until April whinges to get out of her baby carrier, so I resist mucking around after that in case she wants to copy me. Charlie says she can play on the way back up – he'll need a break from carrying her.

Eventually, the wooded walk comes to an end and we pass through a stile and emerge onto a grassy hill leading down to the cove. The sea takes the shape of an inverted isosceles triangle, the apex pointing towards the cove where we're headed, and the dark-blue horizon forming a straight line across the top.

The sun is beating down, so I get April's white hat out of my rucksack – that was the trade-off for Charlie carrying the tent: I take her baby things – and pull it over her head. Charlie says he applied sunscreen before we left.

From the grassy hill we go through another gate and then walk down a slippery, sandy, rocky path that slopes gently down in the space carved out between two cliffs on either side. The beach at the bottom is small but beautiful, surrounded by interesting rock formations that curve in on either side. The water itself is pale bluey green as it swells into the cove, darker blue further out.

'Wow!' I say to Charlie.

'Nice, eh?'

'Just a bit.'

I'm in awe as we crunch over the sand-and-shingle mix beneath our feet. The rocks around the cove are unusual in colour – sort of metallic-looking. Charlie erects the pop-up sun shelter, a small blue-and-white tent, while I walk April around. He intends to try to get her to sleep in the tent so that she doesn't kick off from exhaustion.

'She'll be taking her first steps soon,' I say to Charlie, as he emerges from the tent, having straightened out a stripy, coloured beach towel. 'She's very steady on her feet.'

He smiles at his daughter. 'Can you walk without holding Bridget's hand?' He takes her from me and steps back a few paces, then stands her on her feet. 'Go to Bridget,' he says, carefully letting her go. She wobbles and clutches onto his hands. He looks at me, his lips tilting up at the corners, and I suddenly feel a bit peculiar.

'Come on, April.' I kneel down, trying to ignore the niggling sensation in the pit of my stomach.

He lets her go again. 'Go to Bridget,' he says.

'Come on, April,' I repeat.

She takes one step and then grapples for Charlie's hands again.

'Let me try.' I pick her up and turn her around to face him. 'Go to Daddy.'

One step, two steps… Charlie and I glance at each other in delight. *Plonk*. She sits down on her bottom.

'April, that was brilliant!' he says excitedly, picking her up and kissing her over and over again on her cheek. 'You walked two steps! Do you want to try again?'

She shakes her head at him.

'Go on,' he urges, passing her back to me.

'What a clever girl!' I say. 'Go to Daddy.'

She lets out a whingeing sound and grabs onto my forearms.

I don't want to make her cry…

'Come on, darling, you can do it,' Charlie encourages, waggling his hands about.

One step, two steps…

'Good girl!' Charlie says. 'Keep going!'

Three steps… And… *Plonk*.

We both fall over ourselves in congratulating her. I never thought I'd be this impressed by an ankle-biter.

There's a buzzing sound of a mobile phone turned onto silent. Charlie gets his phone out of his pocket.

'Kate,' he tells me, still smiling as he presses answer.

'April just took three steps!' he exclaims into the mouthpiece. Even though he's walked a few metres away from us, I can still hear her overjoyed response.

'Lansallos,' he says. 'Just hanging out.'

I continue to hold April's hand as she toddles around – unwilling to risk letting her go while Charlie's otherwise engaged. With one ear on the conversation, though, it doesn't escape my notice that Charlie comes to the end of the call without once mentioning my name.

I guess I shouldn't be surprised. Kate might think it's a bit off that we're out together like this. I mean, I should really be at home writing her sister's book… But I *am* working, I remind myself.

'Thanks,' Charlie says to me as he stuffs his phone into his back pocket. 'I can take her.'

'I might climb up onto the rocks,' I say, wanting to take a closer look.

'Don't slip,' he cautions.

'I won't.'

I get out my camera and hook the strap over my head, then dig my notepad and pen out of my rucksack.

The boulders by the shore are easy to navigate, so thick with molluscs that there's plenty of grip beneath my feet. As I climb up, I see dozens of rock pools, large and small, full of plants and sea life.

Does the tide really reach all the way up here? I scan the beach for a water line and find it right up by the cliffs.

I peer closer at the rocks surrounding the cove. The colours are incredible – shimmering and metallic, made up of green, mauve and grey, from light to charcoal. It looks like slate – there are millions and millions of shard-thin layers. I step over a gap below and stand on the other side, tracing my hands over the layers. A piece comes away easily in my fingers. I turn to look for Charlie and April and catch him watching me. I wave.

'Careful,' he mouths, looking concerned.

I shrug at him and turn back to the rock face, gingerly climbing further around the corner towards the water. I come across a small, dark cave and sit down, facing the rolling ocean, my notepad and pen at the ready. An idea strikes for a Kit-and-Morris scene, so I begin writing.

After I don't know how long, I hear a voice. 'Excuse me?'

I look up to see a girl in her twenties, wearing a pink T-shirt and shorts. She's standing on the rocks across the gap. 'Are you Bridget?' she asks, her dark hair swinging in its ponytail.

'Yes,' I say with surprise.

'Your husband was worried about you.' She looks back at the beach, waving and giving Charlie, I presume, the thumbs-up sign.

'I'm fine.' I try to keep a straight face at her assumption. 'But thank you.'

'Okay, cool,' she says, turning away and stepping carefully over the rocks. I watch her for a moment, but she doesn't attempt to engage me in further conversation. Who the hell was that?

'Just some random stranger,' Charlie tells me with a smile when I return to the beach. 'She was climbing up onto the rocks so I asked her to look out for you.'

I wonder how he described me and then I wonder why I wondered.

'I couldn't leave April,' he says, glancing over his shoulder. He's sitting in front of the tent with his arms looped around his knees.

'How long has she been asleep?' I sit down beside him.

'Only about ten minutes,' he replies. 'Feeling inspired?' He nods at my notepad.

'Completely. This place is so beautiful, I never want to leave.'

'So you don't want to try to squeeze in Heligan today?'

'Can we go there some other time?' I ask. 'Actually, you don't have to go there with me at all,' I state quickly, remembering who I am and what I'm here for.

'I'd like to, if that's cool.'

'Of course it is,' I say, trying not to show that I'm pleased. I turn and grab a handful of shingle, letting it sift through my fingers. 'Oh look!' I hold up a tiny, smooth piece of bottle-green glass. 'Sea glass.'

'Open your hand,' Charlie prompts.

I glance at him with surprise. He's holding his fist out to me, so I uncurl my palm. He drops a small handful of glass straight into it.

'Where did you get it?' I ask with delight. The pieces range from the size of a fifty-pence piece to smaller than a penny, and come in shades of green, brown, blue, red and yellow.

'April and I were looking for it. I've found sea glass before at this beach.'

'What are you going to use it for?' I dust sand grains off a couple of the larger pieces and then brush the same sand off my legs. I'm wearing my denim shorts today.

He shrugs. 'I don't know. Something.'

The three biggest pieces are green, brown and yellow, in that order. For some strange reason I imagine them being melted together into one piece of polished glass.

And, for an even stranger reason still, Charlie's eyes spring to mind.

God, I'm weird. Why did I even *think* that?

'Look what I got,' I say in turn, emptying my notepad of stone shards onto his hands. 'Aren't the colours stunning?'

'Yeah,' he says with wonder, bringing a piece up close to his eyes and turning it this way and that as he studies it.

'Haven't you ever climbed up there?' I ask.

He shakes his head. 'I've always had April with me.'

'You didn't come here with Nicki?'

'No, she found this place on her own and told me about it. I only visited for the first time a few months ago.'

'Where do you want me to put these?' I ask after a moment, holding out my fist.

'Swap.'

We exchange our finds and I put the shards back in my notebook so they don't get broken. They're very fragile.

'Is your friend coming this weekend?' he asks me.

'Marty? No.'

'Oh.' He frowns. 'I thought you were going to ask her.'

'I did,' I murmur, sifting through another handful of shingle. 'She only got back from holiday last Friday. She wants to chill at home with her boyfriend this weekend before she goes away again.'

I was pretty disappointed when she told me that.

'Have you got any other plans?' he asks, and I know he feels bad for me, which is a bit embarrassing.

'Not yet.' I shrug. 'But I have plenty of work to catch up on.'

'Why don't we do Heligan on Saturday, then?' he suggests.

I give him a small sideways look. 'I thought you needed to work.' We're here on a Thursday, after all.

'I've got ages until my next big deadline,' he replies. 'If you don't want me to come, though, just say.'

'It's not that.'

'What is it, then?'

'No, it's just a bit… I guess it makes me feel… I don't know. I know you're just trying to be kind, but it's not like we're friends, are we?'

He recoils. 'Aren't we?'

'Are we?' My brow furrows.

He looks affronted. 'Sorry, I kind of thought we were.'

Now I feel *really* bad. 'God. I don't know why I just said that. I kind of thought we were too, but *argh*. Something you said the other day reminded me that I'm just an employee.'

'What the fuck did I say?' he asks, alarmed.

Christ, this is awkward. But he seems completely offended, so I force myself to continue. I remind him of what he said in Nicki's office about my listening to him, not being what I was there for.

'I didn't mean it like *that*! I just meant… Well, it's not *any-body's* job to listen to me.'

'Well, *that's* not true. That's what friends and family are for. It's *exactly* their job.'

'I don't really like talking about what happened to Nicki.'

'No, but that doesn't mean you shouldn't. Sometimes talking gets stuff out of your head and makes it easier to deal with.'

'Wait, that's not why you've been quiet the last few days, is it?'

I shrug.

'Did I really upset you?' He's staring at me with growing horror and my cheeks begin to heat up.

'No.' I wave him away, but then sigh and stare at the sky. 'Maybe just a little.'

'I'm so sorry,' he says, wrapping his arm around my shoulder and giving me a quick squeeze. He lets me go again. 'I wasn't with it that day.'

'It was my fault for putting the heart in April's room. I felt like such a frigging idiot.'

He falls quiet. After a long moment, he says, 'I don't know why because I hate losing it like that, but I'm kind of glad that you did.'

Chapter 23

'It's pizza night!' I say excitedly later that evening when Charlie drives up the steep hill leading to the campsite and the green horsebox comes into view. 'I totally forgot!'

'Oh, man…' He stares longingly at the people queuing up for wood-fired-oven yumminess.

'Stay and have one with me?' I suggest.

'Yeah?' he asks distractedly, his eyes following a man carrying four pizza boxes across the road in the direction of the field steps. He looks at me and grins. 'All right.'

I don't have a neighbour at the moment so he parks up next to *Hermie*.

'Do you reckon April will be okay with the salt?' he asks as he gets her out of her car seat.

'I dunno.'

'She's almost one,' he muses.

'A margherita should be fine.'

'Yeah, it should be, shouldn't it?'

I still find it bizarre that he even wants my opinion.

'I'll go and order,' he tells me. 'Do you know what you're having?'

'I might go for the veggie one today,' I reply. 'I'll get the table sorted.'

He comes back with a couple of bottles. On pizza night, a company turns up selling local ales and ciders. He's opted for the latter.

It's such a mild, balmy evening that I decide to dig the second camping chair out of the boot so we can both sit outside in the late sunshine while we're waiting for our food.

'You could do with a camping table, too,' Charlie says. 'I've got one somewhere. I think it's in the shed.'

'Really?'

'Yeah, I'll bring it over at the weekend.'

'That would be cool.'

'Useful for when you have company.'

There's a short, awkward silence.

'I'm sorry your friend's not coming this weekend,' he says.

I blush. 'I do have other friends, you know.'

He chuckles. 'Yeah, *obviously* you have friends, Bridget. Lots of them, I imagine.'

'It's just annoying that my close ones are married with kids or they live in other countries.' Bronte is in Sydney and Laura is in Key West.

'Bet your friends overseas miss you,' he says.

'Probably not as much as I miss them.'

'Why would you say that?'

I shrug. 'They're pretty settled.'

'I bet they miss you as much as you miss them.' He sounds sweetly protective.

'Maybe.'

'Definitely.'

I look at him and grin, loving the fact that we're now officially friends.

He smiles into his cider bottle and then swigs from it.

'Do you reckon she's all right in there?' I ask. April is currently rummaging around in my wardrobe tent.

'As long as you don't mind your clothes being trampled on.'

'Nah,' I reply. 'What time will the pizzas be ready?'

'Six thirty. I'm surprised she hasn't started complaining actually. All those rice cakes, I suppose.'

She polished off half a packet of them on the way back here.

'Do you want another cider?' I nod at the drink he's almost drained.

'I'd love one, but I have to drive home.'

'Couldn't you take her back in her pushchair and leave the pickup here?'

He looks thoughtful. 'I suppose I could. She's good at transferring, actually, so if she falls asleep... Yeah, all right, then.'

I come back a little while later with two more bottles.

'That is *such* a good idea,' I enthuse, jerking my head back at the horsebox. 'It reminds me of Morris's cream-tea business, actually.'

In *The Secret Life of Us*, Morris starts up a business delivering cream teas by bicycle to campsites and village greens.

Charlie laughs. 'That was my idea.'

'*What?*'

'Nicki stole it. Adam and I were going to do it.'

'No way! But it's such a good idea! Why don't you?'

'I can't now, I'd look like a right div.'

'Rubbish! You should!'

'Nah. Anyway, I don't have the time. Adam could if he wanted to.' He shrugs and takes another swig from his bottle. 'This is going down really well,' he says.

'It's almost six thirty.' I grab my purse. 'I'll go.'

I wait in the queue to collect, counting up the amount of money I'll need, only to find that Charlie has already paid for them. He refuses my cash when I try to hand it over.

'That's not fair,' I say. 'I should give you petrol money for today, too.'

He gives me a dirty look. 'Don't be ridiculous.'

'Seriously, if you're driving me to Heligan on Saturday, then I'm paying for the petrol.'

'Bridget, I *want* to go to Heligan. Can you chill out, please?'

'Then I'm paying the entry fee for us all.'

'Whatever. You can if you really want to.'

'I really want to.'

We move into the van and Charlie balances April on his knee while he's cutting up her pizza. It must be tricky for him to eat with her in his arms, but somehow he manages it without spilling cheese all down his T-shirt. She fares less well. Her face is covered in tomato sauce within minutes of tucking in. A couple of weeks ago I would be worried about her getting food on the bench seat, but it doesn't really bother me now.

I know the power of Johnson & Johnson baby wipes.

'Is it her birthday soon?' I ask Charlie from my captain's chair position. I'm in the passenger seat, having not bothered to turn the driver's seat around since I drove back from Bristol airport.

'Two weeks, this Sunday.'

'Are you doing anything for it?'

His voice is loaded when he replies. 'Yeah. My parents railroaded me into throwing a party. I haven't felt much like celebrating.'

'It's a big milestone,' I say.

'Yeah. I know.' His eyes dart up to look at me. 'Will you come?'

'I'd love to.' I'm thrilled that he asked.

'Nicki's mum and sister's family are coming, too.'

'Will they stay with you?' I wonder what they're like.

'Just Valerie, Nicki's mum. The house isn't big enough for Kate's brood. Valerie will only be here for a couple of days, though. Couldn't stand it for much longer.'

'Do you get along with her? You like Kate, right?'

'Kate's fine. Valerie can be hard work.'

'Will Nicki's dad come, too?'

He shakes his head. 'No. Alain is married to his work.' He sounds bitter.

'Do you see him much?'

'I've met him *twice*,' he replies flatly. 'Once at our wedding, and the second time was at Nicki's funeral.'

'Jesus.'

He meets my eyes. 'Nicki and I had talked about going to Thailand earlier this year so Alain could meet April. She wanted them to have a relationship.'

'Have *you* ever been?'

He shakes his head. 'Never. Nicki used to go at least once a year. He glances at me. 'But you know that, right?' There's an edge to his tone.

I sigh. 'Would you rather I wasn't reading her diaries?'

'No. *Definitely* not,' he affirms. 'It's just... It's kind of odd. You understand, right?'

I nod, because of course I do.

'You know so much about me. *Us.*'

Obviously by 'us' he means him and Nicki.

'Not that much,' I reply. 'She didn't really write about personal stuff when you got back together.'

'What do you mean?' He looks confused.

'When you met up again in your twenties. Her diaries weren't so much diaries as notebooks,' I explain.

I can almost see the load lifting off his shoulders – he looks so relieved.

'I'm sorry, I thought you knew that.' I'm bewildered. 'I should've said something earlier. I only know her deepest thoughts from when she was a teenager.'

'So you know all about Isak,' he states.

'Yes,' I reply honestly, glancing down at April. My mouth drops open.

He quickly follows the line of my sight and checks his daughter. She's nodding off.

'Oh, my God, poor baby,' he whispers, trying not to laugh. 'She's so knackered. I'd better change her and put her in her pram.'

'Let me get the table out of the way,' I say as he slides out of the bench seat.

While he's getting April's things from the pickup, a thought occurs to me.

'Why don't you let her sleep in the bed?' I suggest, already making it up for her. 'It'll be more comfortable and, if she's good at transferring, you can still take her home in her pram.'

He hesitates. 'Are you sure?'

'Absolutely,' I insist. 'It'll be warmer, too.'

'I don't know, it's still pretty nice out here.'

'Good. Because you and I are going to be sitting outside.'

He smiles at me and waits while I finish making up the bed.

'I'll get us a couple more drinks,' I say, leaving him to settle April on his own.

Chapter 24

When I return, Charlie is sitting in one of the camp chairs.

'Cheers.' I chink his bottle as I hand it over.

'Cheers,' he replies.

'Is she asleep?' I ask.

'If not, she will be soon. She goes down really well in the evenings.'

'You're lucky, from what I've heard.' I have a couple of friends who can natter to each other for hours about baby bedtimes. I don't know the details because I usually switch off when they start moaning.

'Do you reckon you and Elliot will have kids?' he asks casually.

'Er…' I hate it when people ask this – especially those who already have children. 'Who knows?' I dodge the question. 'I need to give him a call, actually. Haven't spoken to him since Ireland.'

'Haven't you?'

'It's a pain not having any phone reception down here. I don't always fancy climbing up the hill late at night or first thing in the morning.'

'You can always ring him from mine,' he says.

'Oh, no, I wouldn't feel right.'

'Why not?' he asks with a frown.

'I'm there to work on Nicki's book, not chat to my boyfriend.'

'Jesus, you work so hard. Of course you can take a break to call him.'

'All right, maybe I will. Thanks.'

'How is he coping without you?' he asks, brushing a mosquito off his leg.

'He's all right.' I don't really want to talk about Elliot.

'Bet he misses you.'

'Yeah.' I pick the label off my drink.

'Didn't he want to know how it went with Dillon?'

'He did try calling.' I don't mean to sound defensive. 'I missed his call and I haven't really felt like talking the last couple of nights. I emailed him instead.'

'Oh, right,' he says, stretching his legs out and crossing them at the ankles.

'Come on, then, tell me about Seth the Wanker,' he prompts after a while. 'You said you would.'

'Only if you really wanted to know.'

'I really want to know.'

'Urgh.'

We both fall silent. A moment later he says, 'All right, then, tell me more about your mum. Why does she annoy the fuck out of you?'

I can't help laughing.

'What?' he asks, grinning at my reaction, even if he doesn't understand it.

'Those stories are kind of interlinked,' I reply drily.

He looks intrigued. Bugger it, if he wants to know, I'll tell him. It's not like it bothers me *that* much anymore.

'Seth was a Canadian officer on the cruise ship when Mum and I were doing Japan,' I say. 'He and my mum already had a bit of a flirtation thing going on when I joined the cruise. Seth was right smack in the middle of both our ages. I was twenty-seven at the time. He was thirty-eight. When he started paying me attention, Mum sulked. I wrote her moods off as jealousy and thought her behaviour was pretty pathetic.

'Seth was very, very charming and I fell for him hard. I *wanted* to fall for him. Mum almost always had a man on the go, but, at that point in time, she was single. In the past, she'd often prioritised her boyfriends over spending time with me, so I guess I wanted to rub her nose in it. We have a complicated relationship.'

I glance at Charlie, but he's gazing down at his cider, listening.

'Anyway,' I say with a sigh. 'Seth turned out to be a real player. Mum had warned me he had a reputation, but I hadn't wanted to hear it – or believe it. He cheated on me with one of the entertainment coordinators. When I found out, I was crushed, but what hurt even more was how Mum carried on being friendly with him after we'd broken up. I wanted her to be furious with him, but, when I had a go at her for being nice to him, she said it wouldn't be professional for her to get involved in romantic disputes between staff. This really pissed me off, but she just said, in a really patronising voice, "I did warn you about him, Bridget." I was so angry with her – and him – that I got off at Otaru, the next port. Mum managed to convince the big boss not to sue me for breach of contract.'

'That was decent of her,' Charlie says acerbically.

'It took me a while to forgive her, though,' I continue. 'To her credit, she apologised. And apologised. And apologised. But I haven't been on a cruise ship since.' I finish off my drink.

'Want another one?' he nods at my empty bottle.

'Go on, then. Better be quick, though: I think they pack up soon.'

He comes back with four bottles.

'Are you trying to get me shitfaced?' I ask with a laugh.

'You don't have to drink them tonight,' he replies with a grin.

'I definitely don't want a hangover tomorrow.' I take one from him.

He gazes up at the field. The long grass is cast in orange light from the setting sun.

'I remember how nice the sunsets are from up there,' he says. We can't see it from where we're sitting.

'Go and have a look, if you like.'

'Won't you come with me?'

'What, and leave April?' I ask.

'We won't be long. When she goes down, she's out like a light.'

'You can see *Hermie* from up there, actually,' I tell him.

'Come on, then.'

He stands up and stretches his arms over his head. I look away from his exposed navel. I should be thankful that he doesn't take his T-shirt off when he's working – I'd never be able to concentrate.

I lead the way up the steps to the field. I'm getting fitter now, so I don't pant half as much. We turn around and sit side by side on the grass, facing the sun setting behind the trees on the top paddock.

'Don't put your bottle on the grass: it'll roll straight down-hill,' I say.

'You sound like you're speaking from experience,' he replies.

'I am. Sitting up here, drinking on my own.'

He tuts and leans back on his elbows. 'Why don't we go out with Adam again this weekend?'

'What about your other friends?' I ask, turning towards him.

'What about them?'

'Do you have many?'

He shrugs. 'I have a few mates, yeah.'

'Do you catch up with them often?' I haven't met or heard about any of his friends since I came here.

'Not so much recently,' he replies.

'Why not? Do they really collect driftwood for you? They must be good friends to do that.'

'What, to pick up the occasional piece of wood?' He looks at me, raising one eyebrow. 'That's easy.' He sighs and returns his gaze to the view. 'It's the whole bereavement thing they find difficult. They're great "going-out" friends, but I haven't been up for that. I haven't wanted to talk to them about Nicki, but I doubt they'd know what to say or do if I did.'

He's talked about her to me…

'You're different,' he says, as though reading my mind. 'You didn't know her. I think other people find it hard because they lost her too.'

I nod, getting where he's coming from. 'You can talk to me any time you like,' I say quietly, stretching my bare legs out in front of me.

'Thanks,' he replies after a moment.

We sit there in comfortable silence. Well, it's not *that* comfortable: the grass is tickling the underside of my legs.

'Are you sure April's all right?' I ask after a while, nodding down at *Hermie*.

'I'll go and check on her,' he decides, getting to his feet.

I watch as he makes his way back down the hill.

'I was starting to worry you'd buggered off home,' I say on his return approach.

'Paid a visit to the toilet block while I was down there.'

He flops on the grass beside me, barely out of breath. He's so fit.

Yeah, really. It's a bit unfunny, actually.

'April okay?' I ask.

'Out cold,' he replies fondly, leaning back on his elbows again.

'I can't believe Morris's mobile cream-tea service was your idea.'

'Mmm.'

'Are you Morris?'

He grins at me. 'Seriously?'

'Completely.'

He shakes his head, seeming amused. 'It's just a story, Bridget.'

'There are *some* similarities, though,' I point out, rolling onto my tummy and facing him.

'You mean Isak and Timo,' he says.

'Exactly. Timo sounds just like Isak. Do you know if Nicki ever saw him when she went to Thailand to visit her dad?'

His amusement dissolves.

'Sorry, I didn't mean to pry,' I say quickly.

'It's fine.' But it's clearly not fine. 'They used to occasionally bump into each other,' he tells me. 'She claimed it was awkward, but it still freaked me out.'

I nod, sympathetically. 'Why didn't you ever go to Thailand with her?' I ask after a moment.

'We couldn't afford it. We always talked about it. Nicki had every intention of using her book money to take us all there. I've always wanted to go, and, even though I think Alain can be a selfish git, he should have a relationship with April.'

'I'm going to need to travel there myself,' I confide.

'Really?' He looks at me with interest.

'Yeah. I've been once, briefly, but that was almost twenty years ago. It's been so helpful, being here, writing about the places I've visited. Tintagel and Lansallos have given me loads of ideas.'

'When will you go?' he asks.

'Probably October or November.'

'Don't go in October – it rains like you wouldn't believe.'

'November, then. Does Nicki's dad still work at the same resort?' I ask Charlie.

'Yes.'

'I wonder if I'll get to meet him,' I muse.

'Will you stay at that exact place?'

'I'd like to. I want to see the same setting that inspired Nicki.' I elbow him. 'You guys should come with me.'

He raises his eyebrows. 'Think it'll be a long time before we can afford to do that.'

'I get brilliant discounts as a travel writer. I might even be able to wing free accommodation.'

He smiles at me. 'We couldn't even afford the flights at the moment.'

'Fair enough.'

'First star,' he says, nodding at the sky.

'Pretty.' I watch it twinkling. 'I need to go to the loo, but I can't be bothered to move.'

'I should leave in a bit,' he replies.

But we don't leave. We stay there talking for another half an hour until my bladder can no longer stand the pressure. Charlie gets up first and holds his hand down to me.

'I'm okay,' I reply, pushing up onto my feet unassisted and feeling a small, strange stab of regret when his hand returns to his side.

We stagger down the hill and peel away from each other at the bottom.

When I get back from the loo, I find Charlie standing at the foot of my bed inside *Hermie*. He's staring at April.

'I can't bear to move her,' he whispers.

'Don't, then,' I whisper back gently. 'She can stay with me tonight.'

'No…' He frowns, shaking his head.

'Would you miss her?'

'It's not that. I just… I couldn't.'

'Don't you trust me?'

'Of course I do.'

'She'd be all right with me, wouldn't she? You could come back early if you wanted to. Or have a lie-in, if you like. I'll bring her to you in the morning.' We're both still whispering.

He thinks about it, but then he shakes his head again, his mind apparently made up.

'Stay in the tent, then,' I suggest quickly. 'Or' – I come up with another idea – 'you sleep with her and *I'll* stay in the tent!'

He looks at me and grins. 'I'll stay in the tent,' he decides. 'If you're sure.'

'I'm sure. Yay!' I exclaim in a whisper. 'Sleepover!' I'm a bit tipsy.

He chuckles and wraps his arm around my shoulders like he did earlier on the beach, giving me a quick squeeze.

'You call that a hug?' I surprise myself by saying.

He grins at me sideways. 'You after the full seven seconds?'

'Yes.' I jolt. 'I mean, *no*. No. That wouldn't be appropriate. Not now you're staying over.'

He raises one eyebrow. 'You think it's a bad idea for me to take you into my big strong arms?'

I giggle quietly. 'I'm not going to start fancying you, if that's what you mean. It's not that you're not fanciable, because you definitely are. But *I* don't fancy you.'

'Good, I feel the same way about you.'

'What?' I pretend to be put out. 'Why don't you fancy me? I've got a boyfriend – what's your excuse?'

'Er, you're my late wife's ghostwriter? That would be too creepy.'

I laugh. 'You're right. It's good that you don't fancy me.'

'I definitely don't.'

'All right, stop going on about it! I'll get a complex.'

We look at each other and then both crack up, completely silently, clutching our sides. Tears cloud my vision as we stumble out of the campervan. Somehow he manages to close the door behind us before we let rip.

'How do you do it?' he asks eventually, wiping his eyes. 'It's been so long since I've laughed like this.'

'You laughed like this last Friday, didn't you?' I remind him, the memory still fresh and brilliant inside my mind.

'Exactly, that was you again, doing Eminem.'

We've both ended up on the grass, leaning against *Hermie*, our legs stretched out in front of us.

'How am I going to cope when you leave?'

His question – and I think it was rhetorical – sobers us both up.

'Let me get you a blanket,' I say. 'Just shove my clothes off to one side, or sleep on them, I don't care. I'll sort them out tomorrow.'

As I start to get up, he reaches for me and stops me in my tracks. I bump back onto the ground.

'What?' I prompt when he doesn't speak. His fingers are like a red-hot handcuff around my wrist.

'We will stay in touch, won't we?' he asks.

'Definitely,' I reply firmly. 'We're friends, right?'

'Yes. Friends.'

I think he's had more to drink than I have.

'Are *you* hankering for a hug?' I ask after a moment of us still looking at each other. I'm beginning to feel dizzy.

He grins. 'Do you want one?'

I consider this, with his fingers still circling my wrist.

'Maybe.'

'Come on, then.' He gets to his feet and pulls me to mine, and there's absolutely no hesitation before his arms are around me. He's so warm and solid. So broad and… hmm, yes, big and strong. Wow. I am liking this immensely.

'Two,' he says. 'Three, four…'

I start to giggle.

'Five, six…'

'You're ruining it by counting,' I complain over his shoulder.

'Sorry,' he whispers against my hair. A few seconds later, he releases me. 'I reckon that was at least eleven seconds,' he says. 'But, if you need another one, all you have to do is ask.'

'The same goes for you, Mr Laurence.'

Chapter 25

I barely slept last night. April stirred when I got into bed, so I gently placed my hand on her chest for a while, stilling her until her breathing became steady again. But I couldn't relax after that. I was so worried about rolling over and crushing her. As the night wore on, she started to turn in the bed so that her legs were pressing straight into my side, her chubby little feet pummelling me. I tried to curl around her, but there wasn't a whole lot of room. It brought to mind memories of my childhood cat, Murphy, who would make me feel so honoured when he chose *my* bed to sleep on rather than Dad's that I'd do anything to keep him there. Even if it meant folding up into a kinked jellybean shape just so Murphy could have the comfort he so desired.

April is stirring. I lie on my side, facing her, watching as her eyelids flicker open and then close back up again. I wonder what time it is – it feels early.

At least I don't have a hangover – I stopped at three ciders last night, and they were pretty low-alcohol. I wonder how Charlie is faring.

I peek out through the curtains at the tent, but it's still zipped up.

I've been wondering if Elliot would have minded me hugging Charlie last night. He and I have always been tactile with our friends – he'd pull Bronte into his arms without a second's thought, and it was the same with her boyfriend and me. We were like that as a foursome: full of open affection for each other.

I feel a pang of longing for my friends on the other side of the world. I decide I'll mention it to Elliot the next time we speak, just to be on the safe side. In fact, I'll call him this morning. It's crazy that we haven't spoken in almost a week. That's the longest we've gone since we became a couple.

April's eyes have opened up again and she's staring at *Hermie*'s ceiling, blinking slowly. I hold my breath, watching her.

The sound of a zip startles me back to the window. I glance out again through the darkened glass to see Charlie climb out of the tent, but, before I can knock, he heads off in the direction of the toilet block.

April murmurs.

'Good morning,' I say sweetly as she turns her head to look at me.

She murmurs something else, not seeming at all bothered to discover she's in bed with me, rather than in her cot.

'Do you want a cuddle?' I ask.

'Da,' she replies.

'Daddy's just gone to the toilet. He'll be back soon,' I say, not sure if she even understands me.

She seems worried.

'Come here.' I try not to panic as I slide my hand behind her shoulders and pull her little body towards me. She drapes her arm across my chest and settles there, her head tucked under my arm.

'You're such a clever girl, April,' I say to her. 'You took three steps yesterday! Such a clever girl.'

She stays quiet, listening to me.

'Ooh, you're so warm and cuddly. Do you want me to sing you a song?'

Her head moves. I think she's nodding.

I snuggle her closer and sing 'Somewhere Over the Rainbow', the Israel Kamakawiwo'ole version.

After a while, there's a quiet knock on the campervan door.

'We're awake!' I call.

The door opens with a clunk and Charlie peers into the van.

'Everything okay?' he asks, smiling at us both. There's no apparent awkwardness in his demeanour so I relax in turn. I was worried our embrace might've weirded him out.

'Great. Come in.'

He climbs into the van with two takeaway coffee cups and a paper bag.

'Oh, was the coffee van there?' I ask excitedly, sitting up as he places the cups on the counter and closes the door again.

'Yeah.' He sits down on the end of the bed. April whinges, so I hold the covers back from her so she can crawl down to him.

'Hello, baby,' he says sweetly, cradling her small frame against him.

'How did you sleep?' I ask.

'Bizarrely well, actually. I completely conked out. You?'

I shake my head and smile. 'I was too worried about rolling onto her.'

He looks mortified. 'Oh, I'm sorry.'

'No, I didn't mind!' I quickly protest. 'I liked it. I think her hugs are even better than yours,' I joke.

He laughs. 'They're pretty special,' he agrees fondly, looking down at the top of her curly blonde head.

'She's like a teddy bear.'

'Do we need to buy you a teddy bear?' he asks slowly.

'No, you're all right,' I reply.

'You ready for this?' He picks up one of the paper cups.

'Yes, please.' I hold my hands out as he passes it over. 'What is it?'

'A latte. Hope that's okay.'

'Perfect. What a treat.'

He throws me the paper bag. 'Pain au chocolat,' he says.

'Oh, my God, I think I love you. Can you stay over every night?'

He laughs again and kisses the top of April's head. 'So I was thinking…' He takes a sip of his own coffee.

I wait for him to continue.

'How about we do Heligan today? It'll be really busy tomorrow, with it being a Saturday.'

'I should write up my notes from yesterday,' I reply, uncertainly.

'Could you do them tomorrow instead? You could still work from mine if you wanted to.'

'Would you want me at your house on the weekend?' I sound dubious. 'Don't you need your own space?'

He frowns. 'No. You know I like having you around. You make us laugh.' He pulls a funny face at April and a flame flickers on inside me.

'Okay,' I say with a grin. 'Let's do it.'

'Cool. I'll nip home for a shower in a bit and get April's things together. Shall I come back for you around nine?'

'It's a plan.'

After they've gone, I get ready as quickly as possible so I have time to call Elliot. I don't want to waste even five minutes doing my hair, so I leave it to dry naturally, grabbing my phone and traipsing up the hill at eight thirty. That gives me half an hour to chat to him before Charlie returns.

'I've just left work,' Elliot tells me, smiling upon answering. He's walking through the city streets and I can just make out his charcoal suit and silver-and-blue checked tie at the bottom of the frame. He always looks smart when he goes to work. He's a civil engineer at a big consultancy firm and he's quite senior. 'Let me find somewhere to stop and talk to you.' He looks around for a suitable place.

We try to have our longer conversations on weekends so we don't have this problem, but sometimes, with the time difference, we have to make do.

He comes across a deserted doorway. 'I'll perch here for a bit.'

'Hey,' I say warmly, when I have his full attention. 'Long time no speak.'

'Yeah, you've been a bit busy this week, have you?' He raises one dark eyebrow.

'A bit, yeah,' I reply. 'What about you?'

'Still pretty crazy.' He sighs and scratches his chin – he has more of a beard than stubble at the moment. 'Think I'm going to have to go in tomorrow. I'd had it up to my eyeballs with it tonight, though. Had to call it quits.'

'Are you going out?' I ask.

'Yeah, meeting a few of the boys at a bar in the harbour.'

'Nice. Have one for me.'

'I'll have several. Heard today that we're on for finishing this job in early November. There's actually talk about some of us getting a week off before the next project starts.'

'Why don't you come and meet me in Thailand?' I sit up straighter.

'Have you booked your ticket?'

'Not yet, but I'm going to get Marty onto it.'

As a travel agent, Marty has been sorting out my flights for me for years. It might be a dying profession, but she has a lot of loyal clients.

'What dates are you looking at?' Elliot asks.

'I can be flexible around you.'

He shakes his head. 'I won't know until much nearer the time if I can get away.'

'That's okay. I can book mine and, if you can join me, we can get you a last-minute deal.'

'That might work.' He smiles and I'm overcome with the most intense desire to climb onto his lap and hug the hell out of him.

'I miss you,' I say.

'I miss you too,' he replies, his blue eyes softening. 'How's it all going with the book?'

I tell him where I'm at.

'That was nice of him,' he says about Charlie taking me to Lansallos yesterday.

'He's a nice guy,' I reply. 'You'd like him.' I suddenly feel nervous, but I force myself to continue. 'It was funny last night... We were talking about how we both missed hugging – he misses his wife and I miss you. We ended up giving each other one.'

'Oi, oi!' he exclaims, playfully.

'A hug, I mean.'

He smiles. 'I should hope that's all it was.'

I blush and he shakes his head good-naturedly at me.

'You know I don't mind you being touchy-feely, if that's what you're worried about.' He knows me so well. 'As long as there's nothing more to it,' he adds. 'I doubt he'll be looking for a replacement any time soon.'

I wince. 'God, no. It hasn't even been a year since Nicki died. Anyway, can you imagine how creepy it would be if he took a liking to her ghostwriter?'

'Very creepy,' he agrees with a shudder.

It's the same word Charlie used last night.

'How are you getting on with his rugrat?' Elliot asks, pursing his lips.

I shrug. 'She's actually very sweet.'

'You better not be getting all broody on me, Bridgie...' He says it like a warning, but he's only teasing.

I laugh. 'No chance of that.'

'Phew.'

This is one of the reasons Elliot and I are such a good fit. He wants children as much as I do.

Which is not at all.

I know it's a taboo subject, which is why I hate people asking me about it. It's one of the most divisive topics of conversation out there. Most parents don't understand – they think people who choose not to have kids are just selfish, but this makes me quite angry. It's nobody's business but mine. I never take it for granted that Elliot and I are on the same page. So many couples break up over the decision about whether or not to have kids. I know, because I've been there, and it hasn't always been a clean-cut 'for' or 'against'.

It began with Freddie, continued through my time with Vince and came back to bite me squarely on the butt with Liam.

But Liam was the one that hurt the most. I still find it hard to think about him without my stomach twisting into a knot.

I'm so grateful Elliot and I have our 'no kids' policy in common. He's a keeper, that's for sure.

'I read your Dillon account,' he tells me.

'What did you think?'

'It was great. Loved the slowest-horse-in-the-world bit coupled with the chattiest cart driver.'

This comment puts me on edge. It's a slightly unusual anecdote for him to pull out for special attention. 'Did you think the Dillon bit was okay?'

'Yeah.' He nods. 'It was really well written. It'll make a good chapter.'

I frown at him. 'Are you all right?' He seems a bit reserved with his compliments.

'I'm fine,' he insists.

'You *are* still happy about me doing this blog, aren't you?' Worry has begun to eat me up.

'Of course I am,' he insists. 'I don't dig the idea of him trying to shag you, and obviously I'd rather he wasn't still in love with you—'

'He's not still in love with me,' I scoff.

'Sounded like it. But it's cool, I'm not worried.'

'Good, because you shouldn't be.'

He grins at me, and I feel an intense stab of frustration because we can't make eye contact.

'Can you look straight into the camera lens for a moment?' I ask him, desperate for his eyes to meet mine.

He does as I ask, but it doesn't quite work, because he's staring at a black dot, not a person, and there's as much emotion in his expression as you'd expect.

'Thanks,' I murmur. He goes back to looking at my face on the screen.

Charlie is already waiting when I come back down the hill.

'Am I late?' I ask.

'No, I'm early,' he replies, nodding at my phone. 'Elliot?'

'Yeah, finally got a chance to catch up.'

'Everything good?'

'Great.' I smile. 'He was just on his way to Circular Quay to meet up with some mates.'

'What's Circular Quay?' he asks.

'It's the harbour where all the ferries dock,' I explain.

'Right by the Sydney Opera House and the Sydney Harbour Bridge. There are loads of bars there. It's where we first bumped into each other again, actually.'

He wants to know about it, so I fill him in on the drive to Heligan.

'How did you and Nicki meet up again?' I ask after a while.

'I saw her in Padstow,' he says. 'She was in an art gallery, looking around, and I walked past the window. I stopped as soon as I saw her: it was the first time in years. I was so cold with her after we broke up – something I regretted – so it was my chance to make amends. She seemed happy to see me, so I asked her out for a coffee.'

'She always felt bad about the way things ended between you two.'

He falls silent. 'It is *so* freaky when you come out with stuff like that.'

'Oh, God, sorry!' I exclaim as he laughs, shaking his head.

'It's all right, it's just surreal. It's like you actually knew her.'

'Why don't *you* read her diaries?' I ask.

'They're not meant for me,' he says simply. 'I'll never read them.'

'But you wanted to keep them. Was that just for me? For the sake of the book?'

'No. There's no way I could ever bring myself to throw them away. April might want to read them one day. It's a bit odd, because she wouldn't be reading about her mother: she'd be reading about the person who *became* her mother. It's hard for me to know, or even recall, how similar those two people are.'

'I don't know, either,' I reply. 'But I like the younger Nicki a lot. She makes some bad decisions, sure, but she's a good person at heart. She's fun. Funny. I would've wanted to be her friend if I'd known her.'

'I think you would have wanted to be her friend if you knew her in later years, too,' he says. 'She definitely would have liked *you*.'

His comment means a lot. It bothered me, his admission that Nicki would have hated someone else finishing her book. The knowledge that we could've been friends makes me feel more at peace with what I'm doing.

'Thank you for telling me that,' I say quietly.

The conversation gives us both pause for thought.

'Here at last!' I say when Charlie pulls into the car park. 'This had better be worth it.'

Right by the entrance is a series of posters with photographs and the story of Heligan. I already know much of it from *Wikipedia*, but the pictures catch my eye.

The gardens were created between the mid-eighteenth century and the beginning of the twentieth century and are typical of the gardenesque style with areas of different character and in different design styles. There are aged rhododendrons and camellias, a series of lakes fed by a ram pump over a hundred years old, productive flower and vegetable gardens, an Italian garden, and a wild area that slopes steeply down into a series of valleys that ultimately drain away into the sea at the old fishing village of Mevagissey. The wilder area is filled with subtropical tree ferns and includes sections referred to as the Jungle and the Lost Valley.

Many of Heligan's gardeners were killed in World War One, and, in the 1920s, the owner leased out the estate. The gardens fell into a serious state of neglect and were lost to sight until the 1990s, when a huge restoration project was undertaken.

One of the pictures shows a wooden door in a redbrick wall. Light spills through from the other side, and underneath is a quote from archaeologist and Eden Project creator, Tim Smit: 'Wild horses could not have stopped us pushing that door open.'

I'm even more excited to get going after that.

Charlie brings April's pram, and although it makes navigating some of the steeper paths virtually impossible, at least she can nap in peace. He keeps encouraging me to go and explore on my own – I do eventually, because I want to climb the rope bridge over the Jungle – but I meet up with him and April for lunch by the house. We get a couple of burgers from the barbecue hut and sit at one of many picnic tables in the shade of the trees.

'Have you been here before?' I ask Charlie.

'Just once,' he replies. 'Years ago. It's nice to come back.'

'It's unbelievable,' I say. 'I reckon I could stay all week.'

'You'd probably need that long to see everything.'

I tuck my hair behind my ears so it doesn't get in the way of my next mouthful.

'What do you do to your hair to make it wavy?' Charlie asks, studying me from across the table.

'It always goes like this when I let it dry naturally,' I reply. 'The hairdryer blasts all of the curl out. I'm not even trying to straighten it – it does it without a brush.'

212

'It suits you like that,' he says, jigging April gently on his knee.

'Um, thanks,' I reply awkwardly.

'It looks nice the other way, too, though,' he obviously feels compelled to add and now he's the one looking self-conscious.

I grin at him as he rakes his hand through his hair.

'Mine needs a cut,' he mumbles, trying to keep it back from his face.

'I like it long.'

Er, excuse me? Now *I'm* the one giving him *my* opinion about his looks?

'Do you?' he asks inquisitively.

I shrug. 'Yeah.'

'I've been using Nicki's old headbands to keep it out of my eyes.'

'I know,' I say. He gives me a questioning look. 'The little photo of her above her computer log-in,' I explain. 'She's wearing the yellow one.'

'Oh, yeah,' he remembers.

'Very Harry Styles, *circa* 2013,' I say.

He throws his burger down in disgust.

'Sorry, was it 2014?' I ask. 'I might have my dates wrong.'

'Right, that's it, I'm getting a haircut.'

'No, don't,' I beg, and then immediately wonder why I'm bothered either way. 'Do you want me to take her for a bit?' I nod at April. These burgers are delicious but a bit sloppy – it must be a struggle to eat one-handed.

'Have you finished?' he checks.

'Pretty much.' I take one more bite and go around to take her from him.

213

'You sure?' he asks hesitantly, noticing I still have a third of my burger left.

I can't speak, so I nod and make assertive-sounding noises with my mouth full until he smiles and hands his daughter over.

I return to my side of the table and straddle the bench, so April can stand up in the space between my legs.

'Not a baby person,' Charlie mutters after a while, shaking his head at me.

'What?'

'You. Saying you're not a baby person. What a load of rubbish.'

'This one's different,' I reply, returning my gaze to April. She's holding my hands, bending her knees and bouncing up and down while making gurgling noises as if earnestly trying to communicate with me.

'Does Elliot want kids?'

I stiffen at his question. Only last night he asked if Elliot and I wanted children, but he meant us together as a couple and I managed to avoid answering. Now he's getting down to the nitty-gritty and I don't know what to say.

I decide honesty is the best policy.

'No,' I reply flatly.

Out of the corner of my eye, I see him freeze. 'No?' he checks.

'No.' And then I add, 'He's not a baby person, either.'

'So *you* don't want kids?' he asks me, stunned.

'Is that so awful?' I cast him an imploring look.

Please don't judge me…

'No, it's just surprising, that's all.' He seems thrown.

'I don't really like talking about it.'

'Fair enough,' he replies, but I know I've unimpressed him. Is that even a verb?

Maybe it's my imagination, but there's a tension between us after that. I'm gutted. I wish he'd kept his questions to himself.

Chapter 26

If Charlie likes me less after my 'no kids' revelation, then he seems to be over it by the next day.

'Adam's coming this way for a pub lunch. Will you join us?' he asks amiably when I turn up on Saturday morning. 'We're only going into Padstow.'

'I'd love to. Are you sure?'

'Absolutely.'

I exhale with relief. I couldn't get to sleep last night because I was mulling over our conversation at Heligan. I don't know why it got to me – why should I care what he thinks? And why should he care what I want from my life anyway? But I had this horrible feeling that I'd offended him, and, regardless of whether or not it *should've* bothered me, it did. Now I can see that I overreacted.

I go upstairs and crack on with my notes, pausing only when I hear the doorbell ring. It perks me up no end seeing Adam again. He has such a cheerful disposition. He seems happy to see me, too.

Half an hour later, we stroll into Padstow, choosing a different pub from the one we spent most of the evening at last Friday. This venue is further around the corner past the harbour, but it has a beautiful sea view, and we keep getting wafts of sugary cinnamon smells from the donut van just across the road. We got here early enough to snag an outdoor table – a bit of a feat for the last Bank Holiday weekend in August.

'I've been reading your blog,' Adam says, with a nod across the table at me.

'Have you?' I ask, pleased and surprised that he'd bother.

'Jesus, some of those comments are *vicious,* aren't they?' He looks horrified and I'm instantly tense.

I try very hard not to think about the trolls, so I don't like reminders.

'What do you mean?' Charlie asks, whipping his head around to stare at his brother. They're sitting side by side on a bench seat.

'I'm not sure I want to repeat them.' Adam raises his eyebrows at me.

'No, don't.' I hastily shake my head as Charlie looks between us. I don't want Adam to say those things out loud. Not here, not now, not ever, actually.

Slag…

Those men are pathetic for even looking at you…

I inwardly cringe. 'It's fine,' I lie. 'Water off a duck's back.' I wave Adam away. 'I don't even read the bad ones.'

But the ones that catch my eye are ingrained in my mind forever.

You give women a bad name…

Who the hell do you think you are?

'I'm glad to hear it,' Adam says. 'Christ, I was a bit gob-smacked. I expected it to be all hearts and flowers and soppy shit, not like that. People can be *mean*. And it's not even just the girls, is it? The guys are venomous, too.'

Stupid bitch…

Filthy slut……

I'll give you one that shuts you up…

I wish he'd stop talking. I wriggle on my bench seat, uncomfortably. 'Some people don't have anything better to do,' I say with a forced air of nonchalance, looking out to sea at the passing sailboats.

The pitiful comments are the worst.

I feel sorry for you…

You're clearly a very troubled individual…

You should get help…

I return my gaze to Adam and try to inject more confidence into my voice. 'At least the blog's getting attention. People *are* talking about it. That's a whole lot better than people *not* talking about it…'

'Eesh, I don't know,' Adam replies, shaking his head.

Charlie is still looking at Adam.

'What?' Adam asks him. 'She doesn't want me to repeat it.' He nods at me.

'I don't want you to repeat it, either,' Charlie says in a low voice. 'I think you should probably stop talking about it.'

'She says it's water off a duck's back!' Adam exclaims defensively as my face heats up. 'And there are loads of nice comments, too,' he adds. '*Loads* of nice comments.'

That, at least, is something. I may have a lot of

'haters' – another word I despise – but plenty of people rave about my blog, too.

It's so empowering…

Funny how it's easier to remember the malicious comments.

Charlie returns his attention to his daughter. She's making her way through some sandwich fingers he brought with him.

'Anyway,' Adam says, still looking at me. 'I was checking out your website because I wanted to know more about Beau before I saw Michelle, but you haven't written about him yet, have you?'

'I haven't posted anything, no.' Although I started writing about him a couple of weeks ago. 'Have you caught up with her?'

'Yeah, I saw her a couple of days ago. She definitely dumped me for the same guy. Beau Riley.'

'Are you serious?' I perk right up. 'Does she still know him?'

'No, they lost touch. But she has a friend of a friend who used to hang out with him, so she thinks she should be able to find out where he is. She reckons she'd know if he still lived in Bude, though, so he must've moved on.'

I deflate. 'Damn. I was hoping to catch up with him while I'm here.'

'How long were you together?' Adam asks.

'About six months,' I reply.

'After Seth?' Charlie chips in.

'Yes.' I'm surprised he remembers. I thought he was too distracted with April to take in much of what we've been talking about.

'"The perfect antidote",' he adds, repeating what I said last Friday night.

'Beau was lovely,' I say nostalgically.

I'd returned to freelance travel writing after abandoning Mum's Japan cruise. I'd been commissioned to go down to Cornwall and write a piece about the area's best surf beaches and Beau was one of the surfers I spoke to. I was supposed to be in Cornwall for only a week, but Beau and I hit it off instantly. He had crazy red hair and a face full of freckles, with light-brown eyes. He was a real flirt – as was I – so, when he invited me to a party, it was a no-brainer. We ended up going back to his flatshare afterwards and falling drunkenly into his bed. I'd already prepared myself for it being a one-night-stand, but the next morning he woke me up with kisses and asked me to spend the day with him. We only made it out of the house because we were hungry and all he and his flatmates had to eat was mouldy bread.

He was three years younger than I was – twenty-five to my twenty-eight – but he could've been twenty for how sorted he was. He lived with two other über-relaxed surfers who were also content to do nothing more than surf and party.

I went back and forth between Bude and London for the next six months, but eventually accepted that we were never going to work. Beau was so chilled, and in many ways I loved that – I didn't expect him to change, and he sure as hell wasn't planning to – but I didn't really respect him. Sometimes he came across as just plain lazy, and I guess I like guys with more ambition.

We amicably parted ways. But I've always thought of him fondly. He came into my life when I really needed it – a great big plaster for my Seth and Mum wound.

*

We head back to Charlie's after lunch, but Adam sticks around, and in the middle of the afternoon I wander downstairs to get a drink. The telly is on in the living room, so I poke my head around the door to see what's up.

Charlie and Adam are sprawled out on the two sofas watching the Formula 1 qualifying. Charlie cranes his head to look up at me.

'We're going to get a takeaway tonight and watch a movie,' he says. 'You in?'

'Sure!' I love the idea.

'What do you feel like? Indian? Thai? Chinese?'

'I don't mind. Thai?' It feels appropriate.

He glances at his brother. 'That okay?'

Adam shrugs. 'I'm cool with anything.'

Later, Adam heads out to collect the food while Charlie puts April to bed. I'm at a bit of a loose end, so I go and stand in the doorway of the bathroom while April's in the bath.

'Can I do anything?' I ask Charlie. He's kneeling on the floor beside the bath.

'You can pass me her towel. It's the white one hanging behind the door.'

He lifts his daughter out of the bath and I wrap the towel around her. He snuggles her up against him. I lead the way into her bedroom.

'Babygrow?' I ask, going to her top drawer.

'Nappy first,' he replies with a warm smile. I think he likes me helping, and for some reason I've been struck with an unfamiliar compulsion to do just that.

I get a nappy out and open it up, placing it on her change station.

'Can I do it?' I ask, as Charlie lays April on top of the nappy. He glances at me with surprise, but steps out of the way.

I've watched him change plenty of nappies, but it's harder than it looks. He chuckles and comes to my aid after two lopsided attempts.

'She has to go right in the centre, otherwise she'll leak,' he explains. He looks around. 'Where's her babygrow?'

'Here.'

Again, an inexplicable urge to help overcomes me. April looks up at me and smiles, chattering away happily as I insert one foot and then the other into her babygrow. Charlie folds his arms and watches, entertained, as I try to button it up.

No, that's not right…

I furrow my brow, trying to work out where I went wrong. I seem to be out of poppers to press, but there's still a floppy bit of material here.

'You'd better do it.' I admit defeat.

'The ones around her nappy still confuse me sometimes,' he confesses, even though he seems to know exactly what to do.

'She could do with a mobile over her cot,' I note as I fold down her cot sheet. Maybe I could get one for her birthday. And then I have a brainwave. 'Actually, could you turn that sea glass into a mobile?'

He raises his eyebrows, thinking. 'That's a really nice idea. I wonder if I could make it work…'

'Bummer, there goes my present idea,' I joke, looking around her room for more inspiration. What else does she need? I'll have to put my thinking cap on…

'Night-night, then,' I say, leaving them to it as Charlie lays April in her cot.

A cry stops me in my tracks. I turn back and April is holding her arms out to me. Charlie looks from her to me, taken aback.

'Can I give you a kiss goodnight?' I ask April, my chest feeling unusually thumpy.

I walk back over to her cot and, as I bend down to kiss her cheek, her arms fold around my neck.

'Aw, you're such a sweetheart,' I murmur. I can't resist scooping her up for a proper cuddle. 'Sorry,' I mouth at Charlie. I know he's trying to get her to sleep.

He shakes his head with bewilderment as I cradle her in my arms. 'Can I sing her a song?' I ask him quietly, but April interjects.

'Da,' she says.

'You want Daddy to sing you a song?' I ask her.

She stares up at me with her very blue eyes.

'I think she wants you to,' Charlie says. 'I think "da" means "yes".'

'Shall I sing "Somewhere Over the Rainbow" again?' I don't take my eyes from hers. This time she nods and it's such a sweet sight, my heart feels like it's going to burst.

'Just put her in her cot when you're ready. She should settle, but give me a shout if you need me,' he whispers. I wait until he leaves the room before I start to sing.

I'm feeling oddly emotional as I back out of April's room. I placed her down in her cot when I came to the 'lemon drops' bit and sang the rest of the song with my hand on her chest.

She let me walk out of her room without so much as a peep. She's unbelievably good at her bedtime routine.

'It's all down to Kate,' Charlie responds when I gush about how lovely his daughter is. He's sitting at the kitchen table.

'No, I don't believe it's that,' I say decisively. 'She's just a really good baby, isn't she?'

'She's pretty incredible, yeah,' he agrees, distracted by whatever it is he's doing.

'What are you up to?' I ask, moseying over.

He has his toolbox on the table.

'Just trying to find a drill bit that would work,' he mumbles, rummaging around.

'For the sea glass?'

He nods, and then I see it – the small pile of coloured, smooth pieces on the table.

'Could you dangle some pieces of painted driftwood in amongst it, too?' I ask him.

He smiles up at me. 'I had the same thought.'

I grin and sit down. 'Can I help you?' As soon as I ask the question, I backtrack. 'Oh, it's okay, I'm sure it's something you want to do for her yourself.'

'You can help if you want.' He looks at me for a long moment.

God, his *eyes*. They really are unusual. I've never seen a colour like it.

I've had boyfriends in the past who have looked similar to other boyfriends. Jorge had the same caramel-brown eye colour as Felix, and Gabe's were the same dark shade as Dillon's. When Liam frowned, sometimes I'd think I was looking straight at David because their expressions were so similar, and, even though Beau and Freddie looked nothing alike, there was something about the way Beau's eyes creased when he laughed that would bring Freddie to mind.

When I saw *Star Wars: The Force Awakens* I completely identified with that little-old-lady thing with the big, round glasses who said that she's lived so long, she sees the same eyes in different people.

I know what she means. I see the same eyes in different boyfriends, too.

But I've never seen Charlie in anyone.

Chapter 27

'I really want another beer,' Adam announces at nine o'clock.

'You can't, you said you'd drive Bridget home,' Charlie replies resolutely. He's had one too many himself to get behind the wheel.

'I can walk,' I scoff.

'I don't want to drive *myself* home,' Adam cuts off whatever it was Charlie had opened his mouth to say. 'Can't we just crash here?'

'*You* can. Bridget won't want to sleep on the sofa.' Charlie casts me a sidelong glance.

'Are you kidding? This is the comfiest sofa in the world,' I reply. 'I never want to leave.' I'm tucked up under a fleecy blanket that he dragged out of an upstairs cupboard for me. We're sharing the larger of the two sofas, but he said I could lie down. He's right at the other end. I did protest, but he insisted.

'You can stay if you want,' Charlie tells me.

226

'You're not worried about leaving us in the same room together?' Adam chips in cheekily.

Charlie lets out a sharp laugh. 'Nope, not any more. Bridget is more than capable of fending you off.'

'I thank you for your faith in me,' I say to Charlie, mock-sincerely.

'Awesome.' Adam stands up. 'Who wants one?'

I assume he means a drink, so I reply in the affirmative.

'I'll probably still walk home,' I say to Charlie when Adam has left the room, calling out to us to pause the DVD until he gets back. We're watching *Rogue One: A Star Wars Story*. Charlie missed it when it came out at the cinema last December.

He was a bit preoccupied at the time.

'You should stay,' Charlie says, draping his arm across my ankles. I don't know why, but this makes me feel squirmy, until he casually squeezes my toes in such a friendly manner that all I want to do is smile at him.

'Maybe,' I murmur, staring at the paused TV.

'What's he doing?' Charlie mutters after ages of our waiting. 'Adam?' he calls out. He cocks his head to one side, listening. 'Is he on the phone?'

I lift my ear free of the sofa to check. He definitely sounds like he's talking to someone.

'Fuck this.' Charlie unpauses the movie.

A moment later, Adam returns.

'We got tired of waiting,' Charlie says, glancing up at him. The sudden change in Charlie's expression makes me whip my head around. 'What is it?' Charlie asks Adam uneasily as his brother kneels in front of me.

'That was Michelle,' Adam tells me gravely, as I push myself up on my palm, wondering what the hell is going on. All of his cheeky humour has vanished from his face.

'Bridget, Beau died two years ago.'

'What?' I ask, even though I heard him perfectly.

He looks pained. 'It was a drug overdose.'

'No,' I say. 'Not Beau.'

I sit up properly, folding my legs up underneath myself. I'm vaguely aware of Charlie pausing the film again and staring ahead in a daze.

If I were lying on Beau's sofa, he'd somehow manage to squeeze into the gap behind me. He'd wrap his arms around me and pull me tight against his torso so that we'd both fit side by side. We could stay there for hours in that position, watching telly. He was so warm and affectionate. I adored him. I *loved* him. And now he's gone.

I can't believe he's gone.

Despite their attempts to persuade me otherwise, I tell Adam and Charlie that I'm going back to the campsite. I insist on walking – I need the fresh air – but I'm also craving my own space. I'm intensely aware that my sadness might be causing Charlie pain or bringing back memories of his own.

I know that what I'm feeling is minor in comparison with what he went through – is *still* going through – but, even though Beau might not have been my childhood sweetheart, my husband of many years or the father of my beloved child, he still meant a lot to me, and I'm crushed by the news of his death.

My mind is racing as I set off at a fast pace along the

footpath. It was a heroin overdose – a *heroin* overdose! Michelle told Adam that Beau fell in with a bad crowd a few years ago, but, even though he occasionally dabbled in recreational drugs at parties, I never thought he'd go that far.

Who the hell was he when he died? What on earth happened to my Beau?

It hurts so much to think about it.

I hear the sound of footsteps jogging closer on the footpath behind me and I look over my shoulder, preparing to move aside, but instead I stop in my tracks, because it's Charlie.

'Don't argue,' he states firmly when he catches up with me. He knows from the look on my face that I was about to scold him, but then I'm in his arms and he's holding me so tight I can hardly breathe.

'You don't have to be here,' I say in a strangled voice.

'It's okay,' he replies into my ear. 'I want to be here.'

I lose it then, right there on the Camel Trail.

I have very troubled dreams that night. Beau is in them, and Charlie, too, but when I wake up I can't quite remember what they were about.

I have a feeling it's just as well.

Beau is buried in Yealmpton, near Plymouth, about an hour and a half away. Charlie has offered to drive me there. I don't say much in the car. April has her nap and we listen to the radio.

I've brought my camera and my notepad, but I don't feel like putting pen to paper. I sit and stare out of the window for the most part.

Beau's parents chose to bury their free-spirited boy on a

grassy hilltop with far-reaching views of Dartmoor and the Yealm estuary. It's a natural burial site, and, to preserve the environment, his coffin was made of willow, which will return to the soil as nature intended and won't impede the growth of the saplings that will be planted in memory of those who are buried here. One day this entire hill will be covered with trees.

No headstones are allowed, but one of the Woodland Burial Association's employees shows us the site where Beau's body was lowered into the ground.

Charlie takes April for a wander and I'm left in peace.

'I wish you could see the sea, Beau,' I whisper, as I sit there on the grass, surrounded by wildflowers. Skylarks sing overhead as I take time to remember the boy who once took a piece of my heart.

And there is no way now that I can ever ask for it back.

'I can't write about this,' I tell Charlie later, when we're in the car on our way home. My notepad lies open in my lap, the blank pages rustling in the wind from the open window.

'No,' he says. 'No.'

As if it really were that simple.

Chapter 28

'Bridget you *must*,' Sara says the next day. I'm in Nicki's office and she's called me to check on how it's all going. I've just told her I can't write about Beau. 'You absolutely *must*,' she repeats. 'This is exactly the sort of chapter that will bring some grit to your book. It can't all be light-hearted fluff.'

Er, pardon? 'I didn't think it was,' I say narkily.

'You know what I mean,' she soothes. 'There's not a whole lot of depth to your chapters at the moment. They're fun, but, if you really want people to care, I think you need to let them see your emotional side. It needs to be more heartfelt. You can't possibly leave Beau out of it. I thought you'd already written about your time with him.'

I emailed her an update on where I was at with my blog only last week.

'Yes, but—'

'So it shouldn't be too hard to write up yesterday.'

'Well—'

231

'Hard is the wrong word,' she interrupts. 'But remember, the best writers put themselves out there. They *lay themselves bare*,' she says weightily. 'The reason Nicki's book was such a success is because she allowed the reader to see inside her heart. We felt everything Kit was feeling, every painful decision she makes, every butterfly that, I don't know, flaps around her chest.'

Flutters, I think to myself distractedly.

'I'm not the writer,' she continues, 'but you know what I'm saying.'

Unfortunately, I do.

I still don't really understand how Nicki wrote so authentically about her heroine, Kit, being in love not just with one person, but with two. The love she speaks of is so deep, so passionate, I'm not sure I've ever felt anything on that scale before.

Well, not with anyone other than Elliot when we were sixteen. But that was first love. And first love, though ardent, is not necessarily long-lasting; the sort of love that endures.

I still can't believe we found each other again. We've both matured, we're both more experienced. Our relationship this time around really could go the distance.

I don't know why I think about Charlie at that moment, but I do.

I firmly push him out of my mind and slam the door shut behind him.

Somehow Sara manages to convince me that I should write about Beau, but I can't quite bring myself to tell Charlie. I have this horrible feeling he'd be disappointed in me.

On Monday afternoon, I return my attention to the second row of books on Nicki's top shelf. They're very dusty and

I cough as I try to lift some of them down without falling off Nicki's swivelling chair. Frustratingly, most of them are nothing more than old school textbooks.

I have a quick flick through her A-level English language study guide – if only for nostalgic reasons: I used to have the same book myself. A single sheet of paper falls out onto the carpet.

I bend over and scoop it up. It looks like a poem in Nicki's handwriting:

> I am not one thing
> But many little pieces
> Divided but allied
> One of these I gave to you
> Now part of it has died
> Every time you hurt me
> Every time you make me cry
> That little piece of me you own
> Withers up inside
> For now it's still alive
> You haven't lost me yet
> But others have
> Others have
> And that's something
> You should not
> Forget.

I sit down on the chair, shivers ricocheting up and down my spine. My pulse is racing. This is too strange. Too coinciden-tal. When did Nicki write this?

I turn over the page, but there's no date.

> I am not one thing
> But many little pieces

She felt the same way I did.

> One of these I gave to you
> Now part of it has died

Who is she talking about? Who did she give her heart to?

Did she write this poem while she was still at school? Is it about Isak?

Or Charlie?

I'm not sure I should show him – what if it hits him hard like the driftwood heart did? That was such an awful day, but, then, he did seem to feel better afterwards.

And this poem is relevant to my work. This is Nicki, writing from the heart, *about* her heart. I'd like to know when she wrote it. Charlie did say I could ask him anything. I'm hardly going to ring his mother about it.

April is still in the midst of her afternoon nap when I come out of my office, and I think twice about disturbing Charlie while he's working. Eventually, I go downstairs to make a cup of tea and take the page with me, just in case he ventures indoors.

He does.

'Hey,' he says, wiping the sweat from his brow as he comes through the French doors. I notice he's not wearing Nicki's headband today. 'God, it's hot.'

'Do you want a cuppa?' I ask, turning on the radio and filling the kettle.

'No, I need something cooler.' He gets a glass out of the cupboard and opens the fridge, his eyes landing on the piece of paper on the worktop. 'What's this?' he asks as I tense.

'It fell out of one of Nicki's books. Have you seen it before?'

I watch with trepidation as his eyes dart back and forth, reading down the lines of verse on the page.

'No,' he murmurs eventually, turning it over.

'There's no date,' I tell him, relieved that he's not freaking out.

'It looks like her handwriting from when she was at school,' he comments. 'It's pretty melodramatic, which also sounds like Nicki back then.'

'Do you think it's about you?' I ask.

His lips turn down at the corners. 'I don't think so. This has Isak written all over it.'

He sounds on edge. I go and stand beside him, leaning against the counter as he reads the words again.

'I guess I'm one of the "others",' he says drily. 'Along with Samuel.'

'Urgh, Samuel,' I moan. 'He sounded like a right little prick.'

Charlie flashes me a grin and some of his tension dissipates. 'He was. Twat.'

I nod at the poem. 'How do you feel about it?'

'Not great,' he admits, sobering. 'It was a long time ago, but it brings it back a bit, to be honest.'

He pushes off from the worktop and places the sheet of paper face down on the counter, filling his glass with apple juice.

'Sara wants me to publish my Beau account,' I reveal, and then start with surprise because I thought I'd decided to keep that information to myself. For as long as I could, anyway.

'Are you going to?' he asks.

'I think so. She put up a good argument.'

He doesn't say anything, nor does he meet my eyes. After a few moments he says, 'I'd better crack on,' and there's an edge to his voice that makes me feel a little queasy.

'Sure,' I reply.

His disappointment plagues me that night as I write about Beau at *Hermie*'s bright yellow table. I try to put Charlie out of my mind and focus on the job at hand, but it's easier said than done.

I seem to be doing quite a bit of that at the moment where Charlie's concerned.

Chapter 29

'I'm a-coming to Cornwall!' Marty exclaims, laughing down the phone on Tuesday night.

'Really?' I ask with excitement. 'When?'

'This Friday, baby! Ted's got a stag party and I am so there. *So* there.'

I have a feeling she's been watching a lot of American TV recently. She used to be obsessed with US high school dramas when we lived together in our early twenties.

'I can't *wait* to see you!' she cries.

I would like to say thank you here to Ted's friend for being so accommodating. Yay, marriage.

'Will you drive down?' I ask.

'Yep, I'll set off straight after work.'

'Friday rush hour? It'll take you forever!' I say with alarm. 'Can't you come earlier?'

'No, we're going away for a long weekend in early September so I can't really afford to take more time off.'

'Okay.' That's a bit of an anti-climax. 'We'd better make Saturday a big one, then.'

'Hell yeah!'

I bump into Jocelyn on my way to Charlie's on Wednesday morning. She's just leaving her house.

'Off anywhere nice?' I ask her, smiling at Thomas, who's in the process of trying to kick his shoes off from the looks of it.

'Music group,' she replies brightly. 'Thomas *loves* it. I've been trying to get Charlie to bring April along.'

'Oh, she *adores* music,' I say, wondering why Charlie would resist. 'Are you heading there right now?'

'Yep.' Her eyes light up. 'Do you think you could persuade him?'

'I doubt it. Where is it?' I ask as an afterthought.

Charlie is clearing up the breakfast things when I walk into the house. I tell him about my conversation with Jocelyn.

'April would love it,' I say confidently.

He shrugs, less enthused. 'Yeah, probably.'

'Why won't you go? The time would work well with her naps, wouldn't it?'

'Mmm. I guess so.'

'You never take her to any playgroups. Jocelyn's always on her way to one thing or another.'

'You don't have to make me feel bad,' he mutters.

'Why wouldn't you, though?' I persist.

'I don't want to be the widowed dad, all right?'

His sharp tone shuts me up.

'Sorry,' he says contritely. 'I just can't picture myself sitting

238

in there amongst all those mothers. I know it's shit. But I haven't got my head around it yet. It's not like I don't do stuff with her.'

'It would be good for her to socialise with other kids, though, right?' I say this very gently.

'If you care so much, why don't you take her?' he asks childishly.

Something inside me snaps. 'All right then, I will.'

'What?'

'I'll take her,' I say decisively. 'Is that okay?'

He looks totally thrown. 'What, now?'

'Why not? I can get there in time and I can work late to make up for it.'

'You don't have to do that—'

'I want to.' I'm surprised to find that it's true. 'Can I?'

'Are you actually serious?'

'I might even be able to catch Jocelyn up if I hurry.'

We stare at each other for a long moment. He's trying to understand what's got into me. I'm not even bothering to try to understand it.

'Okay,' he says eventually, still slightly thrown.

He helps me get April's things together and watches as I buckle her into her pram, then stands and stares as we set off down the footpath.

Right decision! April is in her *element*!

I giggle as I hold her hands and make them clap together while some madman dances around in front of us with his guitar.

Even *I'm* having fun. Who *is* this guy? He's been playing

The Beatles, The Stones, The Monkeys... We are rocking it, here.

All the mums are singing along, and the babies are going gaga. When the guitar man gets the bubbles out, the kids go bonkers, bumping into each other in their eagerness to capture the tiny popping balls of glory. Even when two of their heads collide, they don't cry for long.

I'm still laughing about it when Jocelyn and I walk back home.

'That was awesome!' I exclaim.

'I *know*!' she replies. 'Do you reckon you'll come again next week?'

'Maybe, if Charlie doesn't want to.'

'That would be great!'

She flashes me a warm smile, and I feel quite touched by her enthusiasm. 'Hey, how's the book going?' she asks.

'Okay. I'm still doing a lot of research,' I admit. 'I haven't got stuck into the writing yet.'

'I can't imagine taking something like that on,' she says. 'It must be so overwhelming.'

'It is pretty daunting,' I agree. 'When I think about all of those readers... It's scary. I'm trying to focus on the story and not dwell on everyone else's expectations.'

She gives me a sympathetic look. 'Well, if you need a sounding board – or even just a break – you know where I am.'

I smile at her as we come to a stop outside Charlie's house. 'Thanks. I really appreciate that.'

'You could always bring April, too,' she suggests. 'It would be lovely for her and Thomas to be buddies.'

'Yeah, it would,' I agree, although a niggling little internal voice points out that it's not my place to take her out for a play date.

Charlie is out the back, working, when I unlock the front door, but he comes straight in.

'How was it?' he asks, still seeming baffled by this turn of events.

'Amazing,' I reply. 'That guy was nuts!'

'Who?'

'The guy who does the music. He was all over the place! Jumping this way and that. He even hung from the rafters at one point and pretended to be a monkey. You *have* to go next week.'

He looks dubious.

'If you don't, *I* will,' I say. 'In fact, I'd probably still go with you if you took her. That was the best thing I've done all week.'

He starts to laugh.

'I'm serious!' I exclaim. 'And April loved it. She was flipping beside herself, I'm not even kidding. I know exactly what I'm getting her for her birthday.'

'What?' Charlie asks.

'Tambourines and stuff. Do you know anywhere around here that might sell musical instruments?'

'There's a toyshop in Padstow.'

'I'll check it out. Otherwise, I'll have to drag Marty further afield on Saturday.'

'Is she coming down?' he asks with interest.

'She is.' I smile at him. 'Friday night. *Late*. Think we'll be saving our big night out for Saturday. Are you doing anything?'

'Aside from sitting here with a takeaway and a movie? Nope.'

'Could you get a sitter? Your mum can't help out on Saturdays, can she?'

'Er, no, and I'm not really sure how I feel about getting a sitter yet. Anyway, you don't want me hanging out with you; you see me all week.'

True.

'I'd like Marty to meet you,' I admit. 'Maybe we could go for a cream tea or something?'

'Okay.' He gives me a smile that has a radiator effect on my stomach, and suddenly my head is singing the opening line of Elton John's 'Your Song'.

Yes, the way I'm feeling *is* a little bit funny.

I go upstairs humming the tune.

'Pizza night,' Charlie says to me the following afternoon.

'You coming over?' I ask eagerly.

'Can I?'

'I'd love you to! You'd better bring a sleeping bag this time.'

'So I can crash in your wardrobe again?'

'Better to be prepared.'

'Didn't April keep you awake?'

'I didn't mind,' I say. 'What?' I ask at the look on his face.

'Nothing,' he replies, but he's pursing his lips, trying not to smile as he turns away.

That afternoon, we walk along the Camel Trail together. I'm pushing Nicki's bike so I can chat to him as we go. April points out the boats and the birds and the dogs and the bikes and anything else that takes her fancy, so we don't talk to each other much.

I've now reached the end of Nicki's notebooks and diaries and have made my way through most of the Post-it-noted pages from the books on her bookshelf. There were two other novels about people leading double married lives up there, and, after reading Nicki's 'female bigamist' comment, I now firmly believe that Nicki intended for Kit to marry both Morris *and* Timo. What I still haven't figured out yet is how it will all unravel.

Because it *will* unravel.

I love Kit, despite everything she's done and is doing, but she's got to pay for mistakes this big.

I'm not sure if that's what Nicki would have wanted, but I'm behind the wheel now and Kit, unfortunately, has it coming for her.

I mean, imagine if she fell pregnant. She wouldn't even know whose baby it was. What sort of person puts herself in that position? What would she do? Would she confess to them both and hope that the father sticks around nine months later when the paternity test is carried out?

I don't think so.

Would she gamble and hide the pregnancy from one of them until she gives birth? Would that even be feasible?

And how could she possibly raise it? *Where* would she raise it? If she chose Morris as the dad – and, let's face it, he would make a *great* dad – then how could she bear to be away from her son or daughter while she's travelling?

That would the most intense double life. Childless with Timo versus being the mother of Morris's child.

Surely she couldn't do it.

Surely she'd never *choose* to do it. She couldn't get away with it, even if she wanted to.

Maybe she discovers that she can't have children... Or perhaps she decides that she doesn't want to!

Or maybe she *does* want to, but that's her penance for falling in love with two men...

I come to a stop on the pavement.

'What is it?' Charlie asks.

'I've just had an idea,' I tell him. 'I'll catch you up, I want to write it down.'

That's it, I think to myself distractedly as I get my notepad out and Charlie continues on, pushing April away along the footpath. Kit has always wanted a family, but, in choosing to marry both Morris *and* Timo, she knows she's making that sacrifice.

And – *oh, my God!* – Morris wants children so much that it kills their relationship when she refuses to relent!

That's it! I've got it.

Morris is the one to end it.

But that leaves Nicki free to have children with Timo...

Would she? Maybe Timo doesn't want children...

This is a total headfuck, that's what this is.

But at least I have some direction now.

Charlie and I end up on the field, watching the sunset again once April is fast asleep in my bed. This time he brought the monitor, so we go only as far up as the signal allows. I've brought a picnic rug to sit on. The grass is too prickly when I'm wearing shorts.

'Justin and Julia are nice, aren't they?' I say.

'Yeah, they're great,' he replies.

They came and joined us for a pizza earlier. They're such a warm, friendly couple. I like how relaxed Charlie is with them.

'Have you ever met Jocelyn's husband?' I ask.

'Edward? Yeah.'

'What's he like?'

'He's all right. A bit strait-laced. Why do you ask?'

'You don't have many friends with kids. I just wonder if it might help to have guys you can talk kid stuff to.'

He shrugs. 'Maybe. So are you going to tell me your idea?'

He's *supposed* to be overseeing the writing of Nicki's sequel, but he barely ever asks me about my work.

'Do you want to know?' I lean back on my palms, my legs stretched out in front of me.

'Yeah,' he replies, looping one arm around his knee.

I'm on edge as I talk him through it. He doesn't show much emotion on his face, but he's taking it all in, his eyes set steadfastly on the sun drifting lower behind the silhouetted trees. I feel thoroughly unnerved by his silence.

'What do you think?' I ask eventually.

'I think it sounds good,' he replies, taking a swig of his beer.

'Really?' My voice is uncertain.

He glances at me. 'Yeah. The readers will like it.' He looks away again. 'I'm not too keen on the cheating, but, hey, it seems to sell.'

245

'Yeah, I guess it does.'

We watch silently as the sun disappears, leaving behind a pinky orange glow that flames back up through the black spindly branches and climbs higher into the sky.

'There it is,' I say as the first star appears, twinkling prettily in the darkening night.

'You up for another?' Charlie asks me, nodding at my bottle.

'Why not?'

'Back in a bit. I'll just check on April.'

'Can you grab a blanket? I can't be bothered to go and put my jeans on.'

His eyes skim over my legs. 'Sure,' he says, turning around and setting off down the hill. I watch him go.

The night wears on and there's still no sign of our moving from the field. We pass the time chatting about silly things – James Bond, old TV shows – nothing of consequence, but enjoyable nonetheless. I have no idea how late it is; I just know that I'm very cosy under my blanket. Charlie claimed he didn't need an extra layer.

'I can't believe you took April to music group,' Charlie says. 'Would you really take her again if I didn't?' he pries.

'Yep.'

'You're so funny,' he says, shaking his head.

'What did I say?'

'You're an enigma,' he states.

I'm liking the sound of this cool, mysterious me until he continues.

'I can't believe you don't want kids. This whole search for proper love – it's crap. You don't even know what real love

246

is until you have kids,' he continues as my smile fades. 'Is it because your mum wasn't very maternal? Has she put you off?'

'No, it's not that,' I reply.

'What is it, then? Elliot?'

'When did the night turn all serious?' I'm wondering how I'll handle it if he pushes this.

'Are you going along with what he wants?' he persists.

'No, I want the same things he does.' I say this with conviction, but, if Charlie takes it much further, I know I'll cave.

He stares at me for a long, uncomfortable moment. 'I don't buy it.' He has a small disbelieving furrow on his brow. 'I don't know what you've been telling yourself, but it's bullshit. You'd make a *great* mum.'

He has no idea of the turbulence raging within me.

'I can't have children.' My admission comes out in not much more than a whisper.

His eyes widen. 'What?'

'Whoa, downer alert.' I throw off the blanket and stagger to my feet. 'Do you reckon the bar's still open?'

'They packed up ages ago. Stay,' he says firmly, grabbing my hand and tugging me down beside him.

I sit with my elbows on my knees, staring ahead disconsolately.

'What do you mean, you can't have children?' he asks me gently, sitting up beside me.

I shrug. 'I can't.'

'Have you tried?'

I let out a bitter laugh. 'It's a long story.'

'We've got all night.'

I turn to look at him. He's staring back at me, his eyes glinting in the darkness. I look away. And then I begin to speak.

Chapter 30

It started when I was with Freddie. Or, rather, it stopped. My periods.

I thought I was pregnant the first time I skipped a period. Freddie and I had the most horrendous argument. He was furious at me for this one time we'd run out of condoms and I'd persuaded him to use the withdrawal method. He was adamant it was my fault, but there was no way Freddie wanted to bring up a kid.

That was how he put it: 'I'm not bringing up a kid. You get an abortion or you do this on your own.'

The pregnancy test came back negative, but there was little relief. Freddie and I had run aground. I loved him – he was wild and free and had taught me so much – but it was too hard to come back from that. He left me soon afterwards.

A similar thing happened with Vince – my periods were patchy, but, when they were late, I worried. Our relationship was very tumultuous. Once he went through my emails and found a message from Freddie, who was simply asking how I was; but, the way Vince reacted, I might as well have been cheating on him. He flew into a jealous rage, punched the wall and kicked over the furniture. When I thought I might be pregnant with his baby, I was horrified. It was obvious we needed to call time on our relationship.

Soon afterwards, my periods stopped completely. I must've been in denial, because it took me way too long to get myself checked out.

I was twenty-four when a doctor told me I had POF – premature ovarian failure. Twenty-four and I had gone through the menopause.

I would never have children.

The news devastated me.

I had already met Olli by this point, but my decision to quit my job at the travel magazine was not as simple as my boss returning from maternity leave and my feeling as if I'd been given a demotion. Nor was my decision to return to cruise ships down to the fact that I could drop in on Olli in Iceland from time to time.

The truth was, I needed to get away. I was running.

I didn't tell anyone about my diagnosis at first. That would have made it more real and, at the time, I think I wanted to pretend it wasn't happening. When Olli and I fizzled out, I consoled myself by playing the field. I'd cruise-coordinate and blog by day, and play hard by night; but sometimes the reality of my situation would keep me awake at night and I'd lie there with tears streaming down my face, picturing a future without children in it. I tried to reassure myself that I could adopt, but I was overwhelmingly sad at the realisation that I would never have a baby of my own.

Charlie was right to some extent – Mum was terrible at being a mum – and, during the Freddie scare, I had asked myself if I'd fare any better. As time passed, I tried to convince myself that I didn't need children – that I didn't even *want* them. Anything to stop the sadness from weighing me down. I couldn't bear it.

Dillon came along – I hopped off the boat and toured Ireland with him and his band, throwing myself into his fun, crazy lifestyle. But going to Dublin with him and staying with his parents showed me another side to him. All of a sudden, I could picture a future with him. I had fallen for him hard, but I didn't trust him, and I hated being out of control. I left before he could hurt me. But it hurt nonetheless.

And then came Liam.

After almost two years of wilderness, I returned to London to take another job at a travel magazine. Liam and I had instant chemistry.

A work trip to San Sebastian in Spain was where it all kicked off. Just the two of us had gone, and we were away for two nights, which was all the time we needed to go from colleagues to lovers.

I told Liam I couldn't have children within a few months of our realising how much we liked each other. I struggled to hold in my emotion when I confessed – I was still coming to terms with it myself – and Liam did his best to be strong for me. Naturally, it was far too early to tell where our relationship was headed.

We were together for almost two years, but Liam came

from a big family and he had always wanted to have children himself. When it sank in that I really would *never* give birth to his baby – this wasn't a case of our being able to have IVF, as he had presumed – it hit him hard. Our relationship wasn't strong enough to survive and he broke up with me.

Liam is now married with two children. I know exactly where he is, but I haven't been able to bring myself to go and see him yet.

I never told Beau about my POF. He was three years younger than I and we just didn't talk about serious stuff like that. Somewhere, deep down, I knew we weren't going to last.

Felix and I were on again, off again, but I was open upfront. I was almost thirty when we met and I'd had a few years to come to terms with everything. Felix reacted well, saying that, if we ever got that far, we could adopt. But we never got that far. After Felix, I avoided getting into another relationship for a long time.

And then Elliot came along. I broke down when he told me early on that he never wanted to be a father. He had split up with his last two girlfriends because they had become broody, so he immediately assumed that my tearful reaction to his confession was a nail in the coffin of our relationship. When I told him about my condition and about what had happened with Liam, it seemed too good to be true that we were on the same page. I allowed him to believe I was crying with relief, but inside I was wrecked. His refusal to have a family sealed my fate. If we stayed together, as I believed we would, no one would ever call me Mummy.

'So when you say those things to me, about me being a good mum… It hurts,' I tell Charlie, brushing tears away. 'I've managed to convince myself that I don't even want children. I don't need to know that maybe I do have maternal bones in my body, because that's just going to cause me more pain.'

'I'm so sorry,' he murmurs sympathetically.

I sniff. 'I think it might be time for a seven-second hug,' I mumble.

He smiles at me in the darkness. 'I can do better than that.'

He lies back and holds his arm out. Without thinking, I follow his lead. His arm folds around me as he pulls me snug against his chest.

'Sorry for bringing the mood down,' I apologise.

'Don't say that. I'm glad you told me so I won't keep putting my foot in it. I'm sorry I kept pushing you.'

'It's okay, don't worry,' I reply tearfully. 'God, I really do want to stop crying now.'

'Would it help if I warned you not to snot on my T-shirt? I get enough of that from April.'

I laugh and he tightens his grip on me. The ache within my chest is easing, but it's being replaced by a different sort of ache altogether.

'Look up,' Charlie whispers.

I try not to dwell on how muddled I'm feeling and turn my face towards the sky. It's lit up with the most breathtakingly beautiful display of stars. It's a completely clear night and the field around us is dark and silent – everyone else is fast asleep. I still have no idea what time it is.

'Thanks for being a good listener,' I say.

'Any time.' He kisses the top of my head, just as I've seen

him doing to April. My scalp prickles. 'Come on,' he says. 'You sound tired. We should probably call it a night before we fall asleep up here and someone calls Social Services. The battery on April's monitor is about to die.'

I don't want to move from his warm, solid arms, but I force myself to sit up.

We meet each other's eyes in the darkness. His expression is serious as he stares back at me. Seconds, minutes, *hours* tick past. *Months, years, an eternity...* And then my gaze drops to his lips and goose bumps shiver into place all over my body.

He looks up at me with surprise. I look *down* at myself with surprise. When did I stand up?

'Whoa.' All of the blood has rushed to my head. I'm confused, unsteady.

'You okay?' He sounds concerned as he jumps to his feet and takes hold of my arm. It's like an electric shock to my skin and I quickly step away.

'Yep.' I feign nonchalance. 'Doing my best not to fall over and roll down to the bottom.' I laugh uneasily. 'That would be embarrassing.'

'Or fun,' he teases.

'Don't tempt me.'

He laughs as we pick up our things and set off downhill.

Chapter 31

Charlie answers a call from Kate as we're going through his front door the following morning.

'I've been calling the landline,' I hear her say. 'Your mobile was going straight to voicemail.' I can tell she sounds accusatory, even from where I'm standing.

'I've been out,' he says. 'April and I have just got back.'

I wonder what Nicki's sister would say if he told her he'd stayed the night at my campsite. I have a feeling it wouldn't go down too well.

Fay has chased me for a detailed synopsis. She wants to check over my ideas before I start tackling the sequel in earnest, so I spend most of the day trying to gather my thoughts together from yesterday. By the time five o'clock rolls around, I feel exhausted both emotionally and physically.

'I don't know how I'm going to stay awake waiting for Marty,' I say as I'm getting ready to leave.

'Where's she going to sleep?' Charlie asks. 'Tent?'

'God, no, Marty's as much cut out for Tent Life as I am. I'm going to make up the bed in the roof space. She's a short-arse, she can sleep up there.'

He looks amused at my description.

'Sorry I've been so out of it today,' I say. In fact, we've *both* been very subdued. 'I'll be back to my perky self by Monday, I promise.'

'Are we not seeing you tomorrow?'

'Of course! I almost forgot. Are you still up for that?'

'If that's cool with you,' he replies.

'Where can we go for a nice cream tea?' I ask, hooking my rucksack over my shoulder.

'I know a good place that you can walk to from the beach. The weather's supposed to be nice. You could hang out there and go swimming, if you wanted to.'

'Ooh, yeah, that sounds great.'

'Have you got a sec for me to show you where it is on a map?'

'Sure.'

He returns a moment later, unfolding a map as he goes.

'This is Harbour Cove.' He presses the map up against the hallway wall. 'You can park up here and walk down this track to the beach.' He traces his forefinger across the image. 'The tide will be out, so you'll be able to walk across the sand to steps here at Hawker's Cove, where the old lifeboat station is, and then along this path to the teashop. Otherwise there's a path up here.' I follow the direction of his finger across the green coastal path. He's standing so close, I can feel the warmth of his body heat beside me. I experience a flashback to lying in his arms last night and feel a prickle of what feels a lot like guilt.

'What's the teashop called?' I ask, stepping away to put some distance between us.

'I think it's called Rest a While or something. They do nice lunches and cream teas with amazing sea views.'

'Sounds perfect.'

'Shall I meet you there at about three?'

'Or on the beach if you can come earlier?'

'Unlikely. I'm catching up with some friends in the morning.'

'Are you all right?' I ask him suddenly. He really has been extraordinarily quiet today.

'Yeah.' He folds the map and hands it over. 'You can take that.'

I look at him with concern. After a moment he meets my eyes.

'I'm fine,' he says softly. 'Nicki's been on my mind a lot today.'

'I'm sorry. Good days and bad days?'

'Exactly,' he replies heavily. 'I'll see you tomorrow, okay?'

I take the hint and leave. He's not in the mood to talk. All my shit from last night probably wiped him out. I feel another stab of what is *definitely* guilt and resolve to cheer myself up by tomorrow.

I am knackered that evening. I get Marty's roof-space bed ready for her, but it's almost one a.m. by the time she arrives. I explained in detail where she could find me – for someone who's a travel agent, she is exceptionally bad at geography and directions – but I'm asleep when she gets here, and it's only her knocking on the window that rouses me. Thankfully, she's as shattered as I am, so she's happy to change into her PJs and go straight to bed.

We both sleep in the next morning, but when I wake up I feel a bubble of excitement.

She's here! My friend is here!

I crawl across the bed and hunchback-creep under the now-low, flat ceiling until I come out in the standing area between the two front seats. I straighten up and turn around, ready to see my pal's friendly face.

She's twisted into a bizarre shape, her legs and arms all caught up in the sheet and blankets. Her mouth is wide open and her dark hair looks matted and crazy. Her new tortoiseshell horn-rimmed glasses are perched on the ledge above the driver's seat – she always looks odd without her glasses on. I giggle and stare at her for a long moment, then remember that she's like a bear with a sore head if anyone wakes her up before she's ready, so I get on with making us coffee. I'm reading in bed when she finally comes to.

'What the— Bridget?' she asks in a muffled voice.

'I'm here,' I reply with a giggle, crawling back across my bed. Her upside-down head appears from over the edge of the roof space, her dark hair falling crazily around her face like something out of *The Exorcist*.

'Fuck, you're scary.' I reel backwards, flinching.

She grins. 'Do I smell coffee?'

'You do indeed. But yours has gone a bit cold.'

'Give it,' she says, waggling her hands at me.

'Come down,' I reply.

'How do I do this?' She scrutinises the area between the front seats.

'Climb onto the driver's headrest, then onto the armrest. Careful, though.'

I try not to laugh as she manhandles her way down to my level, ducking her head under the low ceiling.

I edge backwards into my bed and move the covers so she can sit at the end and pull them back over herself.

'This is cosy,' she says with a touch of sarcasm, taking a sip of her coffee. 'Yuck.' She pulls a face.

'I'll make you another one.' I smile. I am so happy she's here.

We sit and chat for ages about what we've both been up to. She's somewhat surprised to hear that Charlie and April will be joining us today, but she shrugs and accepts it.

'I want to meet this "highly shaggable" person,' she says, raising one eyebrow at me.

'Urgh, stop it. He's lovely,' I say sincerely. 'I feel bad for talking about him as if he were a piece of meat.'

She looks tickled. 'Nevertheless, I can't wait to check him out.'

Luckily, Marty is driving, so I don't have to rely on her seriously useless map-reading skills when we set off to the beach later that morning. It's a bit of a trek from the car park, so it's not that surprising to find that the long, sandy stretch of beach at the bottom of the track is far from crowded.

The beach faces the mouth of the Camel Estuary and is

backed by sand dunes, so it's sheltered from the wind. The tide is still on its way out as we arrive and there are children and dogs alike playing in the shallows.

Every time I visit a place that could become a potential location for a scene in *Confessions*, I do some research, so I know that at low tide the sand here stretches over a mile and a half and is called the Doom Bar – the curse of mariners for centuries. Over six hundred ships have hit the sandbar since records began in the early 1800s.

It's a hot, sunny day – one of the hottest days since I've been here – and ideal for the beach. Marty and I lay out towels and undress down to our swimming costumes, slathering on sunscreen and sunbathing as we used to on holidays years ago. We brought a light lunch to see us by, but at around two o'clock I find myself sitting up and paying more attention to the people on the beach. There's always the chance that Charlie changed his mind.

At two thirty-five, I nudge Marty, feeling twitchy. 'Time to go,' I prompt, standing up and pulling on my skirt.

We walk beside the low cliff edge, dodging boulders and children clambering over the rock pools, until we reach a small, sandy beach. Then we climb up past the old lifeboat station and a row of coastguard houses, winding our way along the track until we come to another row of terraced houses. The gentle clinking of cutlery and cups on saucers mingles with the sound of our feet crunching up the pebbled footpath as the tearoom appears. It's actually an outdoor café that's situated in one of the gardens belonging to the houses, and there's a serving hole in the wall that opens onto the kitchen. There aren't many tables, so it takes me only seconds to determine who's missing.

'Charlie's not here yet,' I note with disappointment. A girl at one of the nearby tables tells us that she and her boyfriend are just finishing up, so we wait off to one side. I absent-mindedly search the path.

We're early.

And Charlie and April are late. By the time they arrive, the table has become free and we've almost finished the cold drinks we ordered to see us by.

'Sorry we're late,' Charlie says, pushing through the gate with April in the baby carrier on his back. I leap up from my seat.

'Hello!' I exclaim, squeezing his arm in greeting.

'Hey,' he replies warmly, smiling at me as he unclips the backpack. I go around to help take some of the weight of the baby carrier as he lowers it to the ground, the muscles on his arms flexing. He unclips April's harness and I lift her out while he holds the backpack steady, then I carry her with me to the table.

'Marty, this is April.' I smile at my friend as I rest April on my hip. 'And this is Charlie.' I glance at him, feeling pecu-liarly proud.

He leans in to shake Marty's hand. 'Hi.'

Yep, she thinks he's hot, too.

'Have you guys ordered?' Charlie's eyes rove between us.

'No, we've been holding off. I'll come up with you.'

'What are you going to have?' he asks me as he scans a menu over by the serving hole.

'Cream tea.'

'Me too.' He rests his elbows on the counter as he places the order for all of us, but I insist on paying.

'Thank you,' he says to me as we turn away, touching the small of my back.

Marty is still watching us and her face is becoming more perplexed by the minute.

'How was your drive last night?' Charlie asks her politely, settling down beside me.

I sit April on my knee and entertain her while Charlie and Marty make courteous small talk.

The view from up here is stunning. The tide is so far out that the sand bank down below in the bay is enormous. It looks like you could almost walk across to Daymer Bay Beach on the other side of the Camel River, but I'm sure the water is deeper than it looks. There's lush green coast over there, and a big white house surrounded by trees. I wonder who lives in it.

'What have you got planned for the rest of the day?' Charlie shifts his body so he's facing me.

'I think it might have to be Rick Stein's tonight. You up for that?' I ask Marty.

'Sure,' she replies, nodding.

'Maybe we could eat along the Camel Trail and watch the tide come in.'

'Have you been to the beach at Padstow yet?' Charlie asks.

'I haven't, actually. Is it nice?'

'It's great. You could take a bottle and watch the sunset. Your fish and chips might be a bit cold by the time you arrive, though. It's about a fifteen-minute walk.'

'How do you get there?'

'You head up the hill past the harbour.'

'I love the sound of that. Will you guys join us?' I ask him hopefully, pressing April's nose and making a 'beep' sound. She giggles.

'Uh, no, we could probably do with a quiet one.'

I try not to show how flat his response makes me feel.

April takes her hat off, but I tell her no, pulling it firmly back into place. The sun is beating down with unusual force today.

'Do you think we should drag that umbrella over and put it up?' I ask Charlie, spying a huge one on a heavy-looking base a few metres away.

'She's got loads of sunscreen on,' he replies. 'But I will do if we're here for much longer.'

The sun's rays are making his dark-blond hair look more golden than usual. It's lightened in colour since the start of the summer.

The waitress appears with our cream teas, so we all get stuck in.

'Okay, what was *that*?' Marty demands to know as soon as we're back in her car.

'What was what?' I ask innocently.

'You. Him. The baby.'

'I don't know what you're talking about.'

'You were like a proper little family!' she exclaims.

'Don't be ridiculous,' I berate her, pointing at the ignition. *Come on, let's go.*

'I'm not having a dig,' she says. 'He's gorgeous. April's sweet, too.'

'Oh, stop,' I wave her away nervily as she starts up the car. 'Don't make it into something it's not. I like him. A lot.'

'That much is obvious.'

'He's a friend.'

'And he likes you, too,' she says significantly.

'As a friend,' I insist, looking over my shoulder. 'Careful as you reverse. It's steep here.'

'You could do worse,' she comments with a smirk, ignoring my driving instructions as the tyres slide across the slippery grass.

'Oh, yeah, and where does Elliot fit into all of this?' I snap. She's being an idiot.

She shrugs, still smirking as she indicates right.

'Er, it's a *left*,' I say sardonically. How can she not remember which way we came into this car park?

'I know,' she replies casually, flicking her indicator to the other side.

'You're a nightmare,' I mutter, rolling my eyes.

She giggles as she pulls out onto the road.

Marty doesn't feel like walking all the way to another beach, so we grab fish and chips and stick with the original plan. The sun is still warm as we sit on a bench overlooking the Camel Estuary, watching the tide roll back in. The air smells a bit pongy, but the view makes it worth it.

'Oh, God, I forgot to say about your Beau account!' Marty exclaims. 'Those comments were incredible – you got so many!'

I'm tense as I top up our disposable cups with Prosecco. 'Yeah.'

'Bet you were beside yourself,' she says, when I hand one over to her.

I posted Beau's account earlier in the week, and Sara texted me a couple of days ago to congratulate me on the response from my readers. I haven't been able to bring myself to look at what people have said. I'm still struggling to come to terms with everything.

'What is it?' Marty asks, seeing my face.

'I didn't want to write about him.'

'Oh,' she says. 'Sorry, I wasn't really thinking. It read so well that I almost forgot it actually happened.'

I don't say anything.

'I'm sorry,' she says again. 'I should have called you.' Her self-reproach has abruptly kicked in. 'I don't know why I didn't. I'm a bit caught up in my own life at the moment.'

'It's fine, don't worry about it. It's just… Beau's death was unexpected, that's all. Sara persuaded me to put it all out there, but I wanted to let him go quietly.'

I fill her in on our conversation.

'She has a point,' Marty says when I've finished.

'I know,' I reply. 'It didn't make it any easier, though.'

We both stare out across the water as we eat in silence.

'I never knew Beau,' she says after a while.

I let out a deep breath. 'I'm not sure I ever knew him either.' My voice is laced with sadness.

She reaches over and squeezes my hand.

'How did that happen?' I ask after a moment. A minute ago it seemed we were looking at sandbanks. Now the estuary is full of water.

'The tide comes in quickly, doesn't it?' Marty goes along with my change of subject.

'I guess so. I haven't been paying attention.'

265

'I wonder how Ted's getting on,' she says.

'Are you missing him?'

'Yeah.' She flashes me a soppy grin.

'Can I be your bridesmaid?' This makes her laugh. Surely it's only a matter of time.

'You can be the matron of honour,' she replies buoyantly.

'Don't you have to be married to be matron of honour?' I gather together our rubbish and stuff it into a bin.

'No chance of you and Elliot beating us to it?' she asks.

'Not when he's on the other side of the world and we're both up to our ears in work.'

She gets up and pats my back empathetically, before grinning. 'Chief bridesmaid, then. Anyway, we're getting ahead of ourselves. He hasn't proposed yet.'

'But you think he will?'

'I think so.' She nods, smiling bashfully.

'How *are* things with Elliot?' Marty asks on our walk back to the campsite, and there's a familiar undertone to her voice that always comes into play when she talks about my boyfriend.

'Fine,' I reply. 'Obviously, I miss him.' Although not as much as I *was* missing him, I realise. 'It's a bit of a bummer because we can't even FaceTime in private here.'

'Ooh-er,' she says.

I smirk at her.

'Yeah, it sucks that you guys have to do the long-distance thing,' she says. 'How long do you think you'll be able to keep that up?'

'As long as we have to, I guess. There's no way I'll make it back to Australia this year and he's so busy at work that he can't get away to come here. Mind you, I wouldn't have time to hang out with him if he did. I'm pinning all of my hopes on Thailand.'

'Thailand?'

'I need to go there in November. In fact, can you look into flights?' I ask.

'Sure. Email me your dates when you know them.'

'I will. Anyway, Elliot is hoping he'll be able to meet me there.'

'That would be cool. I'll cross my fingers for you.'

'Thanks. It'll only be for a week or so, but it's better than nothing.'

She frowns. 'Can't you persuade him to chuck in his job and move here?'

'I'm not sure I'll ever persuade him to do that, but I'll keep trying. If anyone cracks, it will probably be me.'

'No!' she cries. 'Don't do it! You can't!'

I smile and wrap my arm around her shoulders, giving her a quick squeeze.

It doesn't matter how deep in Ted's pockets she is or how little time she even has for me these days, Marty still detests the thought of my moving abroad. She's always been jealous of my boyfriends – even the ones who live here in the same country, the same city, even. The fact that Elliot resides in Australia is a big problem.

She hasn't even met him, but I know she'd love him if she did.

She's not the only one who's worried I'll emigrate. Dad is terrified, too.

To be honest, I don't want to move. I loved Australia, but

England is my home and it is so much easier to travel and see the world from here.

But Elliot, who grew up in this country, has no intention of returning here permanently. He loves his Sydney lifestyle, the harbourside bars, the beaches.

It's a tricky one, that's for sure.

Chapter 32

I'm sorry to see Marty go the next day – much earlier than I was hoping.

'I really don't want to get stuck in traffic,' she says with regret.

'It's okay, I understand. Say hi to Ted for me.'

He called her last night when we were up on the hill, finishing off our bottle of Prosecco. He was right smack bang in the middle of his stag do, but was clearly missing her madly.

She went up the hill again this morning – couldn't go another minute without touching base with him. She came back beaming. They're clearly besotted with each other, and I'm happy for them.

I spend the rest of Sunday doing my washing and trying to get a bit organised, before heading up the hill to catch up on my own work. I haven't bothered checking my emails since Friday, so I'm surprised to see one from a girl at a production company – a former colleague passed on my details. She wants to know if I'd be interested in going on daytime TV later this week to talk about my blog. A romantic comedy with a blogging storyline is about to hit cinema screens and the show wants to do a piece on relationship blogs, generally.

I really don't have any interest at all, but Sara has been urging me from the beginning to do talking-heads stuff, so I write back and say yes, knowing I should feel a whole lot more grateful and excited than I do.

'Good morning,' I call out to Charlie as I let myself in on Monday.

'Hey,' he calls back.

I walk into the kitchen, where he's tidying up a bit.

'How was the rest of your weekend?' he asks.

I tell him what Marty and I got up to. 'I'll have to check out Padstow Beach another time,' I say eventually.

'Maybe we could head there one day for lunch.'

'That would be nice,' I reply with a smile. 'This week might be difficult, though. I have to go to London. I need to be there on Thursday, so that will probably mean leaving Wednesday afternoon and coming back Friday morning. Do you mind? I can make up the time at the weekend.'

'What, you're not going to be here for pizza night?' He sounds mortally offended.

'Oh, shit!' I exclaim. He might be teasing, but I'm a bit gutted.

He smiles. 'Of course, that's fine. Remember it's April's birthday party on Sunday, though.'

'As if I could forget... Oh! You've got Nicki's family

staying, haven't you? I can work from *Hermie* on Saturday, obviously.'

'You don't have to. Kate and Valerie want to meet you, actually.'

'Do they?' This makes me nervous.

'Don't worry, they're not going to bite.'

'Are you sure?'

He smiles at me. 'So why do you need to go to London?'

As I fill him in, I become aware of a shift in the atmosphere.

'I don't want to do it, to be honest,' I admit when I sense he's not impressed. 'But Sara would kick my arse if I said no.'

'You don't *have* to do everything Sara tells you to do.'

'Well, it's done now. I've said yes,' I reply in a slightly snappy fashion.

We fall into an awkward silence. I notice his toolbox is on the kitchen table.

'Did you find a drill bit that worked?' I'm relieved to land on another topic of conversation.

'Yeah, I did.' He's still not quite back to his affable self.

I go over to the kitchen table and after a moment he joins me.

'Shattered a couple of pieces,' he reveals, picking up a piece of yellow glass with a perfect, tiny hole in it. 'Might have to go back to the beach. I'll do what I can for Sunday,' he says. 'I can always add more glass.'

'Don't forget my offer to help paint the driftwood. Unless you want to do it all yourself...'

'Not at all. I was thinking about starting on that tonight.'

'Want some company?'

'Yeah?' he checks.

'Yeah.' I nod.

We smile at each other for a long moment.

'Right, better crack on, I say at last.'

'See you later,' he replies quietly as I walk out of the room.

On Wednesday, Charlie looks harassed when I remind him of April's music group, so I offer to take her again. He feels guilty about it, but I assure him I'm happy to go, and encourage him to crack on with his work.

When we get back, he greets us affectionately.

'Thank you,' he says to me, in such a sincere way that it prompts a bubble of joy to pop inside me.

'It was my pleasure,' I reply.

And then, to my surprise, he pulls me into his arms. The air in my lungs escapes in a rush of breath as he squeezes me against his hard chest.

'Aw,' I say after a moment, extracting myself when my pulse shows no sign of stabilising. 'Are you going to miss me tomorrow?'

'I will, actually.' He looks down at me quite seriously, even though his lips are tilting up at the corners.

'You're used to having me around now. What are you going to be like when I leave?' I clap my hands onto my cheeks and widen my eyes at him in horror.

'I'm dreading it, actually,' he admits, laughing lightly as he gets April out of her pram.

My insides are practically fizzing now.

'Drive carefully this afternoon,' he says, placing his

daughter on the floor. She sets off at a crawl towards the living room. Charlie frowns at me suddenly. 'Actually, don't you think you should leave soon? You'll get caught in traffic.'

'*Now* he can't wait to get rid of me!' I exclaim, mock-affronted.

'Why are you driving at all?' He ignores my attempt at humour. 'Wouldn't the train be easier?'

'Probably. I couldn't be bothered with the bus and the hassle of getting to Bodmin. Just thought it'd be easier to drive the whole way there.'

His frown deepens. 'I would've taken you to the train station.'

'Oh, no.' I brush him off.

'Seriously, I still can. Want to have a look at train tickets?'

'Really?' I have been dreading doing the return journey, if I'm honest. Dad thought I was crazy to not just stay in London for the weekend, but I didn't want to miss April's party.

'Yeah, come on,' he urges.

I'm perfectly capable of checking out my own train times, but I think he enjoys my company as much as I do his.

I go straight from Wembley station to the pub. Dad is working tonight.

'It's my little girl!' he cries as I walk through the door. Several of his punters turn to stare at me.

'Hi, Dad,' I reply with affection as he comes out from behind the bar to gather me up in his arms.

'Ooh, I missed you,' he grumbles into my hair.

'I missed you, too.'

'How's *Hermie*?' he asks, pulling away and looking at me expectantly.

'Great.'

'Really?' His eyes light up.

'Yeah, really,' I laugh. 'I'm used to him now. I kind of like my mini home on wheels. The only thing that's missing is a toilet.'

'I knew it!' he erupts, clapping his hands together once and pointing at me. 'You want to take it back with you?'

I laugh at the eagerness of his offer. He really does love his portable loo. 'Still not quite there, thanks, Dad. It's all right. I won't be in Cornwall for much longer.'

Charlie and April come to mind and I realise how very sad I'm going to be to leave them at the end of the summer.

Dad finishes up soon after I get there, driving us home to the house where I grew up. We moved here when I was eight, when he was still married to Mum, but, although she came here on and off during the next couple of years leading up to their divorce, it never felt like it was hers at all.

There's a photograph of her in a picture frame on my windowsill. She and I are standing cheek to cheek with nothing but the cold blue of the ocean behind us. She's wearing her assistant cruise director's uniform and I'm wearing my cruise-coordinator get-up. She has dyed honey-blonde hair, groomed neatly into a topknot. My dark hair is flowing freely. You can see the resemblance in our navy blue eyes and cheekbones, but, when I smile, people say I look more like my dad.

I still remember the early years, after Mum went back to the cruise ships. At first I cried for her a lot. I was only six, and she was gone. If I fell ill, got picked on at school, or toppled over on my bike, she was the person I called out for. It must've broken Dad's heart.

Eventually I learned that he was the only one who would dish out medicine, talk to my teachers or hold me until I stopped crying.

He was there for me, while Mummy was somewhere in the Adriatic Sea giving manicures and pedicures to rich pensioners. And, what's more, she *wanted* to be there.

I soon learned who my primary parent was.

Despite her lack of maternal instinct, I think Mum struggled with that when we first started joining her during school holidays. I remember one time when I must've been about seven and I had cut my knee slipping down some steps near the pool. She came running, but I didn't want her. I wanted Dad.

It was his name I wailed as she tried to pick me up. As soon as I saw him coming, I stretched out my arms and she had no choice but to step aside and let him be the one to comfort and mollycoddle me.

I looked at her from over Dad's shoulder – I genuinely remember this as if it were yesterday – and she was crushed. I'd hurt her.

I was glad.

Mum and I have always had a complicated relationship. But she's a complicated person.

Sometimes I wonder if I'd be any different if I'd grown up with two stable, happily married parents. Would I have settled down myself by now?

The parallels between Nicki and me are intriguing. Her parents are also divorced, and her father moved to another country when she was younger. Her relationship with him was challenging, just as mine is with my mother.

And there are other similarities between us: her poem, for starters. She willingly gave pieces of her heart to her boyfriends, but she apparently had no issues with commitment when it came to marrying Charlie.

'*If it's right, it's right…*' That's what Charlie said to me when we had that conversation about my blog – about my desire to love wholeheartedly.

It was obviously right between him and his wife.

But so much is right between Elliot and me, I remind myself. He's gorgeous and smart and we have a great deal in common. Fate surely brought us back together for a reason. I miss what we had in Sydney – and I miss what we had with our friends, too. My pining for him hasn't been as intense recently, but that's probably just because I'm getting used to being apart from him.

Right?

Dwelling on it now is futile – there are no easy answers. As soon as this book is out of the way, I need to make some serious life decisions. That much is clear.

Dad and I have a nightcap and sit and chat in the living room for an hour or so before I tell him I'd better call it a night. I need a decent sleep if I'm going to be on TV tomorrow.

When I head upstairs, I see a text on my phone from Elliot: '*Are you FaceTiming me or what? I've got to go to work!*'

Shit. He knows I'm at Dad's tonight, and obviously that means we can finally catch up – *properly* – but I'm absolutely knackered. I couldn't be less in the mood.

'*So tired,*' I text back. '*Tomorrow night?*'

'*Disappointing,*' he replies and my heart plummets.

'*On TV tomorrow. Don't want suitcases under my eyes. Please don't be angry,*' I implore.

He makes me wait for his reply. '*Fine. Tomorrow then.*'

I toss and turn for ages after that. I should've just called him and got it over with.

I'm still feeling shattered and a little all over the place the next day when I trek into the television studios on the outskirts of London. I'm sure the make-up artist spends longer on me than the previous one did when I last went on TV. That must've been a couple of years ago now, and it was at a different television studio. I've been out of the loop since I went to Australia. It's another reason I should be thankful they asked me to come and do this today. I don't know why I'm so reluctant.

At least I'm not too nervous – it's live television and I don't stumble over any of my answers. I get a bit emotional when I talk about Beau, so I try to steer the subject away from him and onto my other exes. The tone lightens substantially after that.

Sara calls me afterwards.

'You are *very* good at this,' she says. 'Very amusing. And you came across really well when you were discussing Beau, too. The presenter loved it.'

This comment makes me feel a bit icky.

'I'll keep an ear to the ground for any more opportunities, but well done,' she says.

'Thank you,' I reply. I'm glad of her praise, but I'm not falling over myself to repeat the experience.

'Who's next on your list?' she asks. 'Seth should be interesting.'

'Er, yeah, Seth would mean going to Canada, so I think he'll have to wait. I've got too much on at the moment with Nicole's book.'

'Is anyone here in London?'

'Vince and Liam are,' I tell her reluctantly.

'Are you catching up with either of them while you're here?'

'I don't have the time.'

'Oh.' She sounds put out. 'Well, don't leave it too long before you post again. You need to keep the momentum going after Beau.'

'Mmm,' I reply noncommittally. Vince or Liam? Neither, thank you.

I looked Vince up online when Elliot first suggested I approach Sara with the book idea. He's still a landscape gardener in north London, but with his own business now. There was nothing on his website about his personal life, but hopefully he's happily married and will welcome the opportunity to put the past to rest.

Or there's the other possibility that he'll fly off the handle when I tell him that I'm writing a book about all of my ex-boyfriends and he has a starring role.

Guess I'll cross that bridge when I come to it.

I'm as keen on crossing that bridge as Billy Goat Gruff.

I don't feel a whole lot more enthusiastic about meeting up with Liam again. As I've said, he's married with two small children, and the thought of his pitying face makes me shudder. *I left you because you can't have children – but I can! Sorry about that…*

I try to push them *both* out of my mind.

'I have some more good news for you,' Sara continues. 'I spoke to Fay earlier, and she loves your synopsis. The baby theme is inspired!'

'Really?' This cheers me up immensely.

'Seriously, Bridget, I am super-proud of you,' she continues as I beam from ear to ear. 'Now all you need to do is write it!'

I feel a flurry of nerves. I have until the end of January to deliver, which is only five months away. Luckily, Nicki had already written a quarter of the book.

I'm itching to return to Cornwall so I can crack on, but unfortunately my train doesn't leave until the morning.

That afternoon I hang out with Dad at the pub, and at dinnertime he joins me at a table. I love gastro pubs – don't get me wrong – but I hope the good old-fashioned British public house menu never dies out completely. There should always be a place for frozen scampi and deep-fried onion rings in our lives.

Elliot FaceTimes me at nine o'clock.

'I'm still at the pub,' I say, turning my screen around to show him the slot machines, followed by my dad behind the bar. 'Look, there's the old man, serving a customer.'

He says something that I can't hear so I turn the phone back around and ask him to repeat it. I have to partly lip-read because it's so loud in here. He wants to know when I'm going back to Dad's.

'Not sure,' I reply. 'Have you just got out of the shower?' His bare chest is coming into shot at the bottom of the screen.

'Yeah. You know I've got to leave for work soon, right?'

He's not at all happy with me, I realise. I sigh dejectedly and get up, going through to the corridor where the toilets are. It should be quieter back here.

'I was waiting for Dad to give me a lift home,' I tell Elliot apologetically when the bar noise has been muffled.

'Couldn't you have walked?' he asks.

'Do you want me wandering the streets alone at this hour?'

He's taken aback by my spiky tone. I've never complained before.

'Are we okay?' he asks after a long, tense moment.

'Yes.' I shake my head, ruffled. 'Sorry, it's just been a bit of a full-on day, that's all. I'm a bit stressed.'

'Why *are* you rushing back to Cornwall?' he asks.

'I've got so much to do...'

'How can Charlie have a problem with you having a few days off? It's a bit rich, considering he made you go all the way there to work.'

'He's not giving me grief about it,' I tell him. 'I *want* to go back. It's his daughter's birthday party on Sunday. I don't want to miss it,' I admit.

At the look on his face, I quickly backtrack, coming to my senses. I'm being a terrible girlfriend. 'What time are you leaving for work?'

'Half an hour.'

'If I walk quickly, I'll be back in fifteen,' I say determinedly.

'Forget it,' he snaps.

'El...'

'Seriously, forget it. I've got to get ready. Speak at the weekend, maybe.'

'Okay. I'm sorry.'

'Yeah.'

His eyes are a lighter, clearer blue than Vince's, but at that precise moment they look just like each other.

That's the last thought I have before he hangs up.

Chapter 33

The closer I get to Cornwall, the happier I feel. Charlie offered to come to Bodmin to collect me, but I know he has Nicki's family arriving today, so he'll have enough on his plate.

I step off the bus at Padstow and take a deep breath of the sea-salty, deep-fried-fish-and-chippy air scented with the tang of vinegar and smile.

I go straight to Charlie's.

Nerves bounce around inside me as I approach the front door. Are they here yet? On impulse, I ring the doorbell.

I hear footsteps and then the door swings open and Charlie is standing there.

'Hello!'

He looks heartwarmingly pleased to see me, and I know that I mirror him.

'Why didn't you use your key?' he asks, stepping aside. *Oi, where's my hug?*

The Last Piece of My Heart

'I wasn't sure if Nicki's family would be here,' I admit.

At that precise moment, a short, stumpy, middle-aged woman emerges from the living room. 'Hel–*lo!*'

'Hi!' I exclaim, feeling instantly on edge at the barbed intonation of her greeting. 'I'm Bridget.'

'This is Valerie,' Charlie says, backing closer to the stairs to make room for his mother-in-law. *Is she still his mother-in-law?*

She has small, round eyes set within a smooth, unlined face, which is framed by lacklustre, medium-length, dark-brown hair. When she shakes my hand, her fingers are cool.

Her expression is cooler.

'When did you arrive?' I ask in as friendly a manner as I'm capable of.

'About half an hour ago.'

I wonder if she's lost the ability to smile, and then I remember that her younger daughter died last year and feel a prickle of guilt.

'Are Kate and her family not here yet?' The house seems very quiet.

'Ian and the boys are checking into their hotel,' Valerie replies. Ian is Kate's husband. They have two boys aged five and seven, if I remember correctly. 'Kate took April with her to get some milk,' Valerie adds.

'Oh, had we—' I glance at Charlie and correct myself: 'Had *you* run out?'

'Yeah. Have you come straight from the bus stop?'

'Yes.' I nod and give him a wavering smile. I can feel Valerie's eyes studying me intently.

'Cuppa?' he asks.

'We don't have any milk, remember?' Valerie chips in tartly. 'Unless she takes it without.'

Who's 'she', the cat's mother?

'Oh, I'm fine,' I say, glancing between them awkwardly, my gaze eventually resting on Charlie. I nod up the stairs. 'I should probably crack straight on.'

'Okay.' He nods and smiles at me.

'Did I hear that right? Does she have a *key*?' I catch Valerie asking impertinently as I push open my office door.

I really missed April, but I'm nervous about meeting Kate, so, when I hear her return, I don't rush downstairs. I'm not playing my music today (as if I could relax enough to do that) and my chest actually aches to hear April's merry little chatter. I can barely stand it, and, before I know it, I'm on my feet and over by the office door. I listen with an odd yearning sensation in my gut as Kate takes April down the corridor to the kitchen. Her husband and sons must still be at the hotel.

I force myself to sit back down. I hope Kate will be more receptive to meeting me than her mother. Charlie told me that she was the one who persuaded him to say yes to a sequel, so surely she'll be pleasant, won't she? She's always nice to Charlie – I've overheard so many of her conversations with him.

I take a deep breath and slowly exhale, trying to calm my nerves. I'll just give them some time to settle in. They're probably having their belated cup of tea. I wonder if Charlie will make me one. When there's a knock at my door, that's the first thing I think of.

'Hey!' I call, swivelling in my chair.

The door opens and a woman enters. She has dark hair like the other female members of the Dupré family, but hers is streaked with lighter, orangey highlights. Her lipstick is pale pink, but thickly applied.

'Hi!' I say brightly.

'Hello,' she replies.

This is not the face of a friend. It looks like the face of an adversary.

'I'm Bridget,' I say, trying to stay upbeat.

'I gather that,' she replies stonily. 'I'm Kate, *Nicole's sister.*'

She puts emphasis on the last two words of her introduction.

She looks a *lot* older than Nicki was when she died, and slightly haggard, as if she's had way too many late nights and early mornings. Only three years separated them, four now, but it could've been ten. Maybe grief has aged her, but it doesn't seem to have had a similar effect on her mother.

'I thought I'd better come to say hello,' she says sourly.

'It's very nice to meet you,' I force myself to reply.

She looks around the room, at my desk, up at the bookshelves, back to my computer. Pain flickers across her features and I soften towards her, despite her frosty reception.

'I was thinking about coming downstairs for a cuppa,' I say gently, saving my work. Earlier on the train, I read through the beginning of *Confessions* again so it was fresh in my mind. I've just started writing a Tintagel-set Morris-and-Kit scene.

'I'd like to speak to you about my sister's book, actually.' She sounds terse. 'Charlie doesn't seem to know anything about it.'

'He doesn't ask me much,' I admit. 'But I'm in regular contact with Fay and Sara, Nicki's editor and agent.'

'Nicole,' she says.

Is she seriously correcting me?

She continues. 'Charlie probably finds it hard to talk about. But he can't *not* pay attention. This is *so* important. I really couldn't believe he had no idea what you've been doing up here.'

'That's not tr—' I start to say, but she talks over me.

'I'll be involved from now on. My sister would've wanted that.'

I'm dumbfounded.

'Is that it?' she nods at my computer, the Word document open on the screen.

'Yes,' I reply. I have no idea how to deal with this. Obviously Kate is still devastated by her sister's death, and I really don't want to upset or insult her, but she has no business coming in here like this and making demands. I'm being paid by Nicki's publisher – they have agreed on the synopsis I've sent them – and I'm more than happy to answer to Charlie. But I won't bow down to Kate.

I need to tread carefully, though. This might be one for Sara or Fay to handle.

Or Charlie.

'I've only just started writing, and I wouldn't feel comfortable giving it to anyone to rea—'

'How have you only just started writing?' she interrupts with astonishment. 'You've been here for weeks!'

'I've been researching,' I tell her evenly, standing up. 'I'm going to make myself a cup of tea. Perhaps we can talk about it downstairs.'

When Charlie's in earshot, I think to myself.

She moves aside grudgingly and follows me down the stairs. My heart is going ten to the dozen.

'There she is,' Charlie says as I walk into the kitchen, trying to mask my unease. 'Valerie, watch this.' He places April on her feet in front of him.

'Hello!' I say to April, my mood immediately improving at the sight of her. I tense as Kate comes to a stop beside me and folds her arms.

'Go to Bridget,' Charlie says, giving April a gentle nudge.

April beams straight at me as she toddles towards me with her arms stretched out.

One, two, three, four, five, *six* steps!

'Clever *girl*!' I cry with delight, catching her and lifting her up into my arms. 'That's the most she's done, isn't it?' I ask Charlie.

'Yeah!' he exclaims, coming over to join us. He glances over his shoulder at Valerie, who's sitting on the sofa in the kitchen extension, taking all of this in with an expression I can't decipher, but it's sure as hell not happiness.

I daren't look at Kate.

Charlie returns his gaze to me, and I feel a pang when I realise that he's lost some of his enthusiasm.

My intestines tie themselves into knots. It's not fair that they're making me – or him – feel like this. I'm incredibly sorry for their loss. But I'm just doing my job. I'm certainly not trying to replace their daughter.

The idea is almost laughable.

'I was saying to Bridget that I'd like to read what she's written,' Kate says casually, coming to take April from me. I feel bereft when she's no longer in my arms.

'Sure,' Charlie replies, nonplussed.

I glance at him sharply.

'If that's cool with you,' he adds quickly, noticing the change in my demeanour.

Kate, beside him, looks smug.

'I'd like to read it, too,' Valerie interjects importantly from her still-seated position.

'You can *all* read it, once it's finished,' I say with forced cheer, trying not to look as hurt as I feel. 'I'll have a fair bit of editing to do first, though.'

I grab a glass of juice from the fridge because the kettle takes too long to boil, and make myself scarce.

Kate's husband and sons arrive soon afterwards, and the noise that travels up the stairs is unbelievable. I hate wearing headphones, but I put them on anyway, counting down the minutes until five o'clock, when I'll be able to leave without anyone commenting on my work ethic.

Charlie sees me to the door. He seems downcast.

'I'm sorry, was that the wrong thing to say?' he whispers when I've crossed over the threshold and he's closed the door against his body to protect us from view.

I shrug at him. 'Bit awkward,' I whisper back, still feeling wounded.

'I'll sort it out,' he promises.

'Don't worry. I'll see you Sunday?'

'You're not coming back tomorrow?' he asks with a frown.

'I'll work from *Hermie*,' I state.

Am I fuck, coming back tomorrow!

'Don't leave me with them,' he pleads in a tiny voice.

His expression raises a smile. 'Bye,' I call over my shoulder as I set off down the footpath. I don't hear the clunk of the door shutting for several seconds afterwards.

I'm dreading being back in Kate's and Valerie's company on Sunday, but there's no way I'm missing April's birthday. The party starts at midday, and I feel a huge wave of relief when Julia tells me that she and Justin have sorted cover so they can come, too. The three of us walk there together – safety in numbers – and their jolly chatter helps take my mind off things.

Adam answers the door to us, further improving my mood.

'Hey!' he says, giving me a hug and turning to shake Justin's hand and kiss Julia. They already know each other well, judging by the warmth of their greetings.

'Oh, hello!' Charlie's mother Pat gushes, coming into the hall. She also does a round of hugs.

If only Nicki's family were this welcoming, I think with a sting.

'What can I get you to drink?' Pat asks us. 'Can I tempt you with bubbles?'

'Ooh, lovely. Yes, please.' I'm the first to reply.

The living room is already bustling with people, old and young. I spy Jocelyn and wave. I'll make a beeline for her in a minute, but first I need to see the birthday girl – and Charlie. I find them together, chatting to a middle-aged couple who move away as we approach.

'Hey!' Charlie greets me with a smile. April turns her head to gaze at me blankly.

'Hello,' I say sweetly, brushing her cheek. Her face

belatedly breaks into a chipmunk grin and she reaches her hand out to touch my mouth. I step closer so she can.

'Happy birthday,' I tell her gently as she flops adoringly against the base of Charlie's neck, her cheek all squashed up against him as she smiles at me. I pass Charlie her present. 'You already know what that is,' I say.

He lifts up the present and shakes it near his ear, his eyes turning expectantly towards the package. Sure enough, the tambourine inside tinkles cheerfully.

'She'll love it, thank you,' he says sincerely.

'There are a few other bits and pieces in there as well. Did she like the mobile?'

He shrugs. 'Hard to tell.'

'Have you hung it up already?'

'Yeah. Go and have a look if you like.'

'Tomorrow.' I tense as, out of the corner of my eye, I see Valerie approaching.

'Here you go, Bridget,' Pat says, materialising with a glass of sparkling wine. 'Cheers.' She chinks my glass. 'Oh, come and meet Barry.'

She drags me away as Valerie appears – I go gladly.

I like Charlie's dad immensely. His laughter lines have been cut so deep into his face that even the tragedy of the last year hasn't erased them. I doubt even Botox would manage it. Pat goes off to answer the door, but Adam replaces her and the three of us indulge in friendly, light-hearted banter. Kate walks past without so much as a hello, but I try not to feel snubbed – there are so many people here, I just want to blend in with the background.

Eventually I make a point of mingling because I'd like

to meet some of Charlie's friends. Jocelyn is here with her husband, Edward, so I go over and introduce myself. Edward works at a museum in Bodmin, and he seems decent, even if he's a bit distracted by his son. I wonder if he'd warm up after a couple of beers.

'How long have you guys lived across the street?' I ask them both when Thomas is preoccupied with one of April's toys, a ball with flashing lights and buttons.

'We moved in only a few weeks before Thomas came along,' Jocelyn replies. 'So that was…'

'Around this same time last year,' Edward chips in.

'That's right! It was just before April was born. Nicki was overdue by a week. She was very fed up,' Jocelyn reminisces fondly.

'Did you know Charlie and Nicki before that?' I ask.

'No, we met Nicki on moving day,' Jocelyn reveals. 'She brought over some cookies. I was heavily pregnant myself, so she and I had a fair few cups of tea in those early days, especially after April was born.'

Her smile is tinged with sadness. It sounds like they got friendly pretty quickly.

'I couldn't believe it when it happened,' she confides quietly, out of the blue. 'Thomas was just a tiny baby at the time.'

'I can't even begin to imagine,' I murmur as her brown eyes fill with tears. It must've felt very close to home for her, being a new mother herself.

Edward squeezes his wife's arm in empathy, even if he does look awkward.

'Gosh, sorry, this is not the time or the place,' Jocelyn

says, pulling herself together. 'Today is a celebration. Charlie...' She shakes her head in awe and we both look over at him on the other side of the room. 'He's been incredible,' she says.

At that moment, Kate's sons tear past us, sending Thomas flying. Edward swoops down and picks up his crying son, as Kate's husband Ian, a short, stocky man with a peculiarly gaunt face, suggests to his boys that they might want to calm down. His tone lacks authority and Jocelyn raises her eyebrows at me.

'I think we might go out into the garden, where it's a bit quieter,' she says.

'I'll probably see you out there,' I reply with a wink.

It's no wonder April looked so out of it when I arrived: the noise in here is deafening.

Where *is* April? I glance at Charlie again. He's chatting to Justin and another man of about the same age, but April is nowhere to be seen. I continue scanning the room, but I can't see her anywhere. Charlie catches my eye and smiles.

'*Where's April?*' I mouth.

'*Kate,*' he mouths back. He jerks his head at me, so I make my way over to him. He's wearing a shirt today and has smartened up a bit. He looks good. But, then, he always does.

'Bridget, this is Gavin.'

'Hey, really nice to meet you,' Gavin says, shaking my hand heartily.

'We went to school together,' Charlie explains.

'We go *way* back,' Gavin chips in. 'Charlie was just telling us you were on the telly last week.'

'Did you watch it?' I ask Charlie with surprise. We haven't

actually talked about it since I got back. I got the feeling he disapproved.

'Of course,' he replies, and his tone isn't disparaging.

'We were wondering why you guys missed pizza night,' Justin explains.

Aah, so that's how the subject came up.

Pat hurries over before I can determine what Charlie thought. 'Darling, where's April? I think it's time for the cake, don't you?'

'Kate's got her,' Charlie replies.

'Maybe she's in the kitchen,' Pat continues worriedly.

'Leave her, Mum, she's probably just having some time with her niece,' Charlie says calmly.

'Okay.' Pat smiles at us apologetically. I think she's a bit frazzled with so many people here.

Valerie is standing nearby, looking lost. 'Another one, Valerie?' Barry calls out amiably, bottle in hand.

'No, thank you,' she replies curtly, but she comes over to join our ever-growing circle.

'Do you remember Gavin, Valerie?' Pat asks kindly. 'He went to school with Nicki and Charlie.'

'Oh, hello.' She eyes him for a long moment as she tries to place him. Gavin looks mildly uncomfortable.

'It's been years, I imagine,' Pat says awkwardly. 'Do you boys catch up much?' She turns to Gavin and Charlie.

'We haven't in a while,' Charlie replies from beside me.

Gavin's discomfort seems to be increasing by the second. At a guess, I'd say he's one of the friends who didn't know how to handle Charlie's bereavement.

'You could really do with a decent sitter so you could go out more, right, son?' Barry says jovially. 'Someone who can work on Saturdays and who won't forget the monitor,' he adds, nudging me conspiratorially and giving Pat a significant look.

I almost clap my hand on my forehead. He's landed his wife right in it.

'What do you mean, someone who won't forget the monitor?' Charlie asks, not missing a beat and giving his parents a quizzical look.

Pat blushes. 'Me, forgetting to bring the monitor down when you were doing that job for the school. Oh, I did feel terrible, didn't I, Bridget? Poor April, she was beside herself, little mite.' She winces theatrically and adds, 'Neither of us heard her.'

Now I'm the one who's cringing. I still feel so bad about it.

Charlie touches my lower back and leans closer. 'Is that why you were turning your music down?' he asks me quietly. He's guessed that I've been covering for his mother.

I shrug.

'Aw,' he says sweetly, squeezing my waist.

I suddenly notice Kate standing in the doorway with April in her arms. Her eyes dart between Charlie and me, her expression grim. I look at Valerie to see she's also staring at us, mutinously.

'Birthday-cake time!' Pat exclaims, clapping her hands together.

I decide it might be best if I go and stand with Jocelyn.

Chapter 34

I drag my heels on the way to Charlie's on Monday morning, walking rather than taking Nicki's bike. I'm pretty sure Valerie will still be there and I'm tempted to go in late or not at all, but I think she already dislikes me enough. I don't want to give her another excuse.

'She's so late! Lazy girl! And after she took all that time off to go and do her own thing, too...'

I decide to open the door with my key – they know I've got one now, anyway – but, as I'm putting it in the lock, I hear a noise from deep inside the house that makes me pause with alarm. Is that crying? It's not April.

The door swings open and Charlie comes out, looking pale and stressed.

'I've been trying to get hold of you.' He hastily ushers me off the front step. In the seconds before he manages to extract my key from the lock and pull the door closed, I hear Kate's hysterical raised voice.

'She's a hussy and a media whore! *I won't have it!*'

I stagger backwards, stunned.

Charlie is stricken. 'I tried to warn you not to come today.'

'Is April all right?' I ask, feeling nauseous.

He clutches his hands to his head, looking a little like he might cry.

'Go and see to her,' I urge, stepping backwards. 'I'll be fine.'

'Bridget!' he calls after me.

'I'll be fine!' I call back, putting my head down and hurrying away in the direction I've just come from.

I've passed the shock stage by the time he comes to the campsite to find me. Now I'm an emotional wreck, and I really *hate* being an emotional wreck.

'I don't want her to see me like this,' I call determinedly through *Hermie*'s closed door. No way am I letting him in. April is in her pram, but she's awake. I can see her chubby little legs kicking from here.

'I'll come back when she's asleep,' Charlie promises, leaving me be.

I watch him walk up and down the internal campsite road, from the lower paddock to the top paddock, over and over again, until eventually he returns.

'She's asleep,' he calls, knocking gently. 'Bridget, please, open up.'

I peer out of the darkened window, and, sure enough, April's legs have stilled.

I open *Hermie*'s side door and sit back down on the bench seat, tucking my hair behind my ears. I'm too mortified to meet his eyes.

'Bridget,' he says quietly, crouching at my feet and resting his bare forearms on my lap.

I shake my head.

He reaches up and brushes my cheek with his thumb. As soon as I meet his eyes and see his devastation, mine fill with fresh tears.

'I'm sorry,' he whispers, sliding his hands around my waist and pulling me towards him. He rests his cheek against my ribcage and my hands automatically cradle his head. It's such an intimate, unfamiliar position to find ourselves in, yet it feels oddly natural.

'I'm sorry,' he whispers again.

I brush my tears away with one hand and stroke his hair with the other.

'It's okay,' I mumble. 'It's not your fault.'

He shudders.

'Charlie,' I say gently, continuing to run my hand through his hair. It's so much softer than I thought it would be. It always looks so dishevelled. As my thoughts drift off on this tangent, I realise my tears have dried up. 'Hey,' I say.

He lifts his head and stares up at me, disoriented, confused, bewildered, as if he's adrift – lost at sea. I force myself to edge over on the bench seat and pat the space beside me.

He slowly, weightily, pulls himself to his feet and sits down, dragging his hands over his face and slumping backwards until his head hits the seat back.

'Rough morning, huh?'

'Just a bit,' he replies wearily.

'What happened?'

He stares at the ceiling in a daze.

'It can't be much worse than what I heard,' I say. 'Can it?' I ask with alarm.

He jolts. 'No. That was bad enough.'

'So Kate thinks I'm a hussy and a media whore. She has a point,' I say with a light laugh.

'Don't.' He shoots me a warning look.

'How bad is it?' I ask gently. 'Do they want another writer to take over?'

'There is *no way* that's happening,' he erupts, shaking his head fervently. 'I'm just sorry you had to hear that.'

'I've heard worse,' I comment philosophically.

This doesn't cheer him up.

'So what's their problem?' I want to get to the bottom of it. I need to understand. 'I thought it was Kate who talked you into doing this book.'

'She did. She's very confused.'

'Is it just because she doesn't like *me*?'

'There's more to it than that.'

'They clearly don't approve of my blog.'

'No,' he concedes. 'They only really started paying attention to it recently. Last night, Kate looked up your TV appearance. Someone had mentioned it to her at the party.'

'I didn't realise it was that offensive.'

'It wasn't,' he tells me. 'I don't think it would matter who you were or what you'd done. Valerie didn't want *anyone* to take over from Nicki. She thought that *Confessions* should be left in peace, as should she. Now Kate's feeling guilty about encouraging me to go ahead with it.'

'Did you remind them about Nicki's readers? About all of those people who were desperate for a sequel? Don't they think Nicki would have wanted someone to see it through?'

'I don't know,' he says with a sigh.

'Maybe if the ghostwriter had been less of a media whor—'

'Stop it.' He cuts me off. 'This is not just about you. They've got it in for me, too. They think I'm over her, that I'm not grieving her enough. They think I've… They think there's…'

'What?' I prompt.

He shakes his head again, seemingly lost for words, but I can guess what he's struggling to say out loud.

'They think there's something going on between us,' I say.

He shakes his head, but it's not a denial. 'It's crazy. I told them that you have a boyfriend, that we're just friends, that there's no way I could fall for my late wife's ghostwriter, but Kate is so damn suspicious!' He shoves his hand through his hair and I wince.

'It doesn't matter what they think,' he continues. 'They don't know anything.'

'They're just missing her,' I point out, trying to be reasonable. 'They're taking it out on you and they shouldn't. You're the last person they should take it out on.'

'No, *you're* the last person they should take it out on,' he says firmly. 'You're just here to do a job. You need to be able to focus. You sure as hell don't need *this* shit. And after you gave up your *whole summer* to come down here!' he exclaims with disbelief. 'I'm sorry. I really am sorry.'

'Okay, stop apologising,' I say. 'That's enough.'

He sighs. 'Yeah, okay.' After a long moment of silence, he says, 'You can't work today. Neither can I. Let's go to the beach.'

'Padstow Beach?'

'Why not?'

'Okay.'

We spend the afternoon making sandcastles and tearing them down again, but, despite the sunny weather, there's no escaping the metaphorical dark cloud that's hanging over us.

Chapter 35

I wonder what Nicki would make of her sister and mother's behaviour, I think to myself the next morning when I return to work. I have a feeling she'd be mortified, but that's not something I'd ever say to Kate and Valerie – they'd probably shoot me for conjecturing.

Nicki used to lock horns with them often, according to her teenage diaries. What was it Charlie said when I commented that Essex was so far away? Something like, *'When Nicki moved back here, she didn't think it was far enough…'*

Nicki might've hated the fact that her dad lived abroad and that he was so busy when she went to visit him, but she loved him and always wanted to go back again.

'At least once a year,' Charlie said, although never with him. Why didn't Charlie ever go with Nicki to Thailand? He said he wanted to, but they couldn't afford to both go. They had talked about using the money from Nicki's novel to visit Alain and introduce him to April, but Nicki died before that

idea came to fruition. Did Nicki suggest the trip, or was it Charlie?

Was there another, non-financial reason that she didn't want to bring Charlie to Thailand with her? Did it have anything to do with Isak?

Charlie said that Nicki used to bump into him occasionally in her twenties and it was awkward, but, as she stopped confessing in her diaries, I have no way of knowing if this is true.

I pick up the piece of paper on my desk and read through Nicki's poem once more.

> I am not one thing
> But many little pieces
> Divided but allied
> One of these I gave to you
> Now part of it has died
> Every time you hurt me
> Every time you make me cry
> That little piece of me you own
> Withers up inside
> For now it's still alive
> You haven't lost me yet
> But others have
> Others have
> And that's something
> You should not
> Forget.

If Nicki did give a piece of herself to Isak, as her poem claims, did it wither up long ago, as she warned him it might? Or was that piece of her still alive when she died?

Nicki's writing is so good that she made cynical *me* believe that it's possible to fall in love with two people. But what if her story is not all fiction? What if it's based in fact? I already know that real things inspired her, like Charlie's mobile cream-tea business idea, and the similarities between Morris and Charlie don't end there.

What about Isak and Timo?

Was Nicki still in love with Isak when she died? No, more than that: were Nicki and Isak *still together*?

Ice trickles down my spine.

Is that why Nicki's book feels so authentic? Was she writing from experience?

I have to know.

I wonder if Isak still works at the same resort as Nicki's dad. What was the name of it again? I'm sure it was somewhere near Krabi…

I bring up Google and do a search for Alain Dupré, French chef, Krabi. The answer is in Nicki's diaries, but this should be quicker… *aaaannnd*… it is.

I recognise the name of the resort as soon as I see it. Going to the website, I scan the top menu for a relevant link. 'Activities & Excursions', that sounds right. As soon as I click on it, a picture appears that shows a muscled man clutching onto a cliff face with his bare hands. I excitedly click to the next picture, but it's of a girl kayaking, so I go back to the rock climber. Is that Isak? You can't see his face. I don't know what he looks like, anyway – it could be anyone. I haven't come across any pictures of Isak since I've been here.

I keep searching the website, but there are no names

mentioned, least of all Isak's. I make a note of the contact details so I can email the resort if I need to. It looks incredible. I must see if I can wing some cheap – or free – accommodation. The hotel looks like it's undergoing some renovations, which means they might want some press to promote their new look... I go to the media centre and jot down the press enquiries email.

Striking while the iron is hot, I then call a friend who works at a wedding magazine to ask if she'd like a honeymoon feature about the resort. She says she'll check with the editor and call me back.

While I'm waiting, I email Marty at work. Elliot gave me a rough idea of the dates he might be able to join me, so I don't have a whole lot of flexibility. Early November is just outside peak season, so the resort should have availability. I ask Marty if she can look into flights for Elliot, as well as me, although it will probably be cheaper for him to do his from Australia.

Elliot and I spoke on Saturday and, at first, our conversation was a bit tense. Luckily he's not the type to hold grudges – he's easygoing like that – so we were pretty much back to normal by the time we got off the phone.

I can hardly believe I might see him in six weeks. The thought makes me feel slightly off kilter. It's probably best not to think about it as it might not happen. I'll call him tomorrow to touch base. For reasons I can't quite fathom, though, I have no desire to tell him about Valerie and Kate.

At that point, my contact from the wedding magazine calls back and, brilliantly, gives me the go-ahead. How I love it when a plan comes together! Now I just need to email the resort and put the idea to them.

In the meantime, I intend to keep my suspicions about Nicki to myself. If she was being unfaithful to Charlie, I'm not sure it's something he ever needs to know.

'What does your dad say about your blog?' Charlie asks me later that week.

It's Friday night and we're in his living room, waiting for our Indian takeaway to be delivered. *Deadpool* is cued up and ready to go, but we've been talking.

I've just confessed that Sara has been encouraging me to visit Vince as soon as I return to London. She reiterated that my blog will lose momentum if I don't post again soon. I can't believe my time in Cornwall is drawing to a close.

Charlie shook his head and stared straight ahead when I told him this.

'My dad doesn't read my blog,' I reply. 'He's under strict orders. He knows I'm no nun, but he doesn't need the details. Anyway, he's always accepted me for who I am. Whatever *that* is,' I mutter.

A slag, slut, hussy, whore, if my 'haters' are to be believed.

I really do hate that word.

Not too keen on the others, either, if I'm honest.

'What about Elliot?' Charlie asks. 'How can he be cool with you going to see Vince after everything that happened? Does he know what went down between you?'

I shrug. 'A bit, yeah.' The truth is, not as much as Charlie, which is weird in itself.

'There's no way I would've allowed Nicki to put herself in that position. I don't understand why you do it to yourself.

How can you stand everyone judging you? *I'm* not judging you – you can live your life however you want to.'

'Thank you very much,' I can't help but quip.

He ignores my sarcasm. 'But when you put it all out there for everyone to read about, then you're inviting criticism.'

'I know,' I say simply, falling quiet. 'The truth is, I never thought I'd be a relationship blogger. I used to detest that sort of thing – people airing their dirty washing for everyone to see. I don't know quite how I got myself into this mess. Oh yeah, that's right,' I say facetiously. 'My boyfriend suggested it.'

I throw Charlie a grin, but he doesn't find it remotely amusing.

'You would like Elliot, you know,' I suddenly feel compelled to say. 'I know you probably think he's a bit of a, I don't know, *dick*, for encouraging my blog, but he's a good guy, really.'

He doesn't seem convinced.

'Honestly, you'd like him,' I insist. 'Everyone does.'

'Hmm.' He picks up the remote control. 'Are we watching this movie or not?'

'Hit it.' We need something to lighten us up.

This week has been all right, considering.

Considering what his sister-in-law and mother-in-law think of me...

Charlie and I have done our best to put brave faces on it. I'm only here for one more week and then my tenants are out of my flat and I can move back home. I've done more than enough research to be getting on with the Cornwall scenes – now it's just Thailand I need to worry about.

My flights are booked, my accommodation is sorted (free – *yes*!) and I've even managed to confirm that Isak does still do rock-climbing sessions for the resort. I was excited when that email came in.

Somehow or other I'll get the truth out of him. I'm still trying to understand Nicki and where her head was at when she wrote this book.

It's been hard keeping Isak out of my conversations with Charlie, but I don't want to distress him unnecessarily. He did contact Nicki's dad on my behalf a couple of days ago and Alain said he would be happy to meet up with me for a coffee sometime. He won't be able to spare much more time than that, from what I've heard, but, if nothing else, the experience will help bring Nicki's diaries to life, and that, in itself, will be fascinating.

I don't know how it happens, because *Deadpool* is absolutely frigging hilarious, but somehow or other I manage to fall asleep on the sofa. When I come to, the room is dark and I have a pillow under my head. The cosy blanket Charlie gave me earlier is still wrapped around me. I squint at the time on the DVD player's digital clock. *Two thirty-five!* I'm not going back to the campsite now. I close my eyes again and try to get back to sleep.

In the morning, the smell of bacon and cinnamon rouses me from sleep. It's just after eight o'clock.

'Hey!' Charlie exclaims when I appear in the kitchen. He's frying up pancakes in one pan and bacon in another. 'Did you sleep well?'

'I did. Thanks for letting me stay.'

'I didn't have a choice: you were out like a light.'

Smiling, I walk over to where April is standing in front of the sofa, jiggling along to the radio. 'Good morning, baby.' She beams up at me.

'MMMBop' by Hanson comes on as I scoop her up. She leans her whole body over to her left and then all the way over to her right, back and forth like a cartoon jumping jack in slow motion.

I laugh and dance around the kitchen with her, singing along to the occasional lyric. When the chorus kicks in, I slide across the floor with her in my socks, but Charlie beats us to our destination, turning the radio up to full volume. We sing along at the tops of our voices before cracking up laughing.

I feel as if I have a balloon inside me and someone is filling it with happy gas. It is the best possible start to the weekend.

Next weekend I'll be back in London. My balloon pops at the thought.

Chapter 36

On Thursday, my last day in Cornwall, we skip work so that Charlie can take April and me back to Lansallos in search of sea glass. He offered to show me another cove, but I wanted to see this beach one more time. While he climbs up onto the rocks to take a closer look at the shimmering colours that I saw the first time we came here, April and I walk barefoot along the shore, getting our toes wet in the cold, clear, light-blue water. I clutch her hands, even though she's growing steadier on her feet every day. The truth is, I just don't want to let her go.

That evening, Pat and Adam join us for one last pizza night.

'Good luck with the rest of your writing,' Pat says to me kindly, when we're saying our goodbyes. She's dropping Adam back to Bude on her way home.

'Thank you,' I reply sincerely.

'I can't wait to read it.' She smiles warmly and gives me a hug. When she withdraws, I turn to Adam.

'Bridget,' he says fondly, opening his arms wide. I grin and step forward and he proceeds to squash the breath out of me.

'Argh!' I gasp, but he just squeezes me tighter and rocks me back and forth for a while before letting me go.

'How was that?' he asks meaningfully as I overegg my efforts to reclaim oxygen into my lungs.

'I'm not sure what you want me to say.' I regard him warily.

He leans forward and whispers into my ear, 'Was it better than sex?'

I burst out laughing and give his shoulder a shove. He's referring to the night we went out in Padstow when I said I missed hugs more than sex. He was unimpressed at the time.

'What did you say to her?' Pat asks her younger son impudently.

'I'm sure you don't want to know, Mum,' Charlie interjects as Adam continues to grin like a loon.

Pat tuts and rolls her eyes. 'You're right, I probably don't.'

After we've waved them off, I turn to Charlie. 'Will you stick around for a bit?'

'I can stay pretty late, but I need to get home.' He sounds reluctant.

'Could we put April to sleep in the van so you don't have to rush off?' I raise my eyebrows at him hopefully.

'Okay,' he agrees with a nod.

He lets me settle her. I lie on my side, facing her, and sing her to sleep, gently stroking her light-blonde curls until her slowly blinking eyes become so heavy-lidded that they close and stay closed. A lump forms in my throat as I stare at her.

Later, we find ourselves back up on the hill to watch my final Cornish sunset. It's the end of September now and the leaves on the trees are already beginning to turn.

I can't believe I've been here for two whole months.

Charlie and I have both been downcast this week. I think he wants me to leave as much as I want to go, which is not much at all.

I am looking forward to sleeping in my own bed and cooking in a proper kitchen and using a toilet that is situated just metres away, but I'm nowhere near breaking point.

I'd stay another month if I could, maybe longer. But there are things I need to do back in London. I'm going to have to force myself to pay Vince a visit so I can write up my next blog entry.

'You should go out with Edward, Jocelyn's husband, after I've gone,' I say to Charlie. 'I thought he seemed nice at April's party.'

'He's pretty quiet.'

'I know,' I reply with a smile. 'But maybe he's shy. Jocelyn is so warm and friendly – he might have hidden depths. Perhaps he needs a baby pal as much as you do.'

He laughs under his breath. 'You really think I'm lacking in company?'

'You will be once I leave,' I joke, but it's not short of the truth.

We sit in silence for a while, but it's comfortable.

'I wish you could come to Thailand,' I murmur. 'It's so sad that you and April have never been, considering Nicki loved

311

it so much. Is there really no way you could make it work? Would Alain help with your flights?'

'He hasn't offered. I couldn't ask,' he replies in a low voice. 'We're just not in a position right now to be able to blow a grand or whatever on flights, however tempting it is. I don't know what's around the corner. I've got a fair few projects coming in at the moment, but they could all dry up. There are no guarantees. I can't risk it.'

'Fair enough,' I reply glumly.

'I was thinking, though...'

Something in his tone prompts me to look at him.

'I don't want you to go and see Vince on your own.'

My shoulders slump. Vince is the last thing I want to talk about.

'I could come to London next weekend and go with you.'

When I don't say anything, he turns his head to look at me. Staring into his green-gold-brown eyes, I get an intensely restless feeling deep in my stomach. It's almost uncomfortable, but I don't want to look away.

Elliot pops into my mind and I jolt, coming to my senses.

'I can't believe you would do that for me,' I mumble, my face flushing as I turn to pull up a handful of grass.

'Of course I would – we're friends,' he replies. 'So is that a yes?'

'Yes,' I say quietly. 'I'm glad tonight isn't goodbye.'

'Tonight isn't goodbye, anyway. We're coming to see you off tomorrow morning.'

'Are you?' It feels safe to look at him again.

'Yeah, I need my tent and outdoor table back.'

I bump against his side, smiling. We both know he could get them back from Justin and Julia at any point.

'Tomorrow wouldn't have been goodbye, anyway,' he says seriously. 'We're staying in touch, right?'

'Definitely,' I reply.

But it won't be the same. It will never be the same. A few days here, a week there... I'll never have an excuse to come and stay for eight weeks of summer again. And, who knows, maybe I'll be living in Australia by next year?

The thought hurts.

That doesn't bode well for the future. For now, I bank my reaction to the idea of moving, but I know full well that it's something I'm going to have to come back to.

Later, we make our way down the hill.

'Do you have to take April home? Can't she stay with me? Can't you just kip over?' I ask the three questions in quick succession, not giving him a chance to reply.

'There's something I need to do.' He answers my third question first.

'That sounds cryptic.' He doesn't want to elaborate so I don't force the issue. He had to mysteriously nip into Polperro on our way home, too – April and I waited in the pickup while he went to get whatever it was he needed.

'April can stay with you if you want her to,' he says.

'Really?' My eyes light up.

'I can come back early in the morning to help you get packed up.'

'Are you worried about me taking down your tent wrong?' I tease.

'No, I'm worried about *you*,' he says categorically, wrapping one arm around my shoulder and giving me a squeeze. I really don't want him to let me go.

The next morning, I wake before April. Dad told me to set off early if I didn't want to get caught in London's Friday rush hour – in fact, he said I should drive through the night if I really wanted an easy journey – but I can't quite bring myself to get up and start quietly packing my things away.

I lie there for a long time, staring at April's little face, so peaceful in sleep. I watch the gentle rise and fall of her ribcage and want to place my hand over her heart, but I'm too scared about disturbing her. I'm going to struggle to leave her today.

I'm going to struggle to leave Charlie, too.

When I'm finally packed up and ready to go, I stand facing Charlie with April in his arms. There's an ugly yellow patch of grass from where his tent has been standing, stagnant, for the last six weeks or so. When I drive away, I'll leave behind a *Hermie*-shaped patch, too. I tell Charlie that he can come back and look at it if he ever misses me, but my comment barely raises a smile.

'Thank you,' he whispers, wrapping one arm around me and pulling me in for a three-way hug with him and his daughter. 'You've done more for us than you know.'

'Stop,' I say, because I don't want to cry. 'I'll see you next weekend, right?'

'We'll be there,' he promises.

I give them both one last hug before climbing into the van. Charlie motions for me to put the window down.

'This is just something small. Open it when you're home.'

He passes me a tiny parcel, gift-wrapped with the same paper he used for April's birthday presents.

'Can't I open it now?' I ask with a smile.

'No.' He shakes his head with determination and his cheeks brighten.

I'm intrigued.

'Bye, Charlie,' I say sadly. 'Bye, Chipmunk.' I wave at April. 'I'll miss you.'

She holds her hands out to me, but Charlie steps back from the car and her face falls. I swallow back the lump in my throat and try to get *Hermie* into gear before I lose it.

I don't make it far. Pulling up outside the big supermarket along the road, I take a deep breath and attempt to gather myself together. I glance at the present Charlie gave me. *As if I'm going to wait…*

As soon as I open it, I see what he had to go home for. He's drilled tiny holes into three of the pieces of sea glass we found yesterday – green, brown and yellow – and threaded them onto a long, silver chain that I'm guessing he picked up from a shop in Polperro. He's made me a sea-glass necklace. I burst into tears.

Chapter 37

I have never been so happy at the prospect of seeing Vince. Seeing Vince means seeing Charlie and April.

The last week has dragged by in slow motion. I've had an ache in my chest that just won't go away and I can hardly believe that they're staying with me for the weekend at my flat. I've borrowed a travel cot from one of my friends and made up the bed in the spare room.

Charlie drives down on Friday night – late to avoid traffic – so April is fast asleep when they arrive. I've been longing to hold her again, but Charlie wants to transfer her to her cot as quietly and quickly as he can. She opens her eyes and looks straight at me as I stand by Charlie's side, so I hurry out of the room and leave him to get her back to sleep. Perhaps she'll think she dreamt me.

Charlie emerges from the bedroom and smiles as he quietly pulls the door to.

'Now we can say hello properly,' he says. I step forward

into his arms and he rocks me back and forth, holding me against his broad chest for a very long time. It is the most beautiful feeling, being in his arms. God only knows how much serotonin is being released by this one.

'We've missed you,' Charlie whispers into my hair.

'I've missed you both, too.' I reluctantly withdraw. 'You look shattered,' I say, gazing up at his weary face. 'Do you feel like a nightcap or do you want to head straight to bed?'

'I'll have a quick one.' He follows me into the kitchen. 'Nice place.' He's looking around slowly, taking everything in.

I live in a middle-floor apartment in a terraced house, a ten-minute walk away from Chalk Farm underground station. There are two medium-sized bedrooms, one bathroom and a light, airy, open-plan living room and kitchen. My favourite thing about my place is the large sash windows that look straight out onto a couple of mature trees. The best time of year is spring, when the leaves start to bud. Sadly, they'll all be gone soon, but autumn brings with it its own rewards.

We take our drinks to the sofa and sit side by side, facing each other.

'Have you spoken to Vince?' Charlie asks.

'I've emailed him,' I reply. 'He said I can go and see him at eleven o'clock on Sunday morning. He's given me his new address.'

'Is that wise, meeting him at his house?' He seems worried. 'Couldn't you have gone to a café or somewhere more public?'

I shrug. 'To be honest, I thought he'd be tricky to pin down so I would've said yes to anything. He won't kick off,' I say assuredly, although I don't really know. 'He might not be happy about me writing about him, but it's been years – he should be over it by now. Anyway, you'll be waiting outside in your pickup if it all goes wrong. My escape vehicle.'

'I'm just nervous about April if he does start anything. I won't be able to leave her.'

'To come inside and be my knight in shining armour?' I tease.

He stares at me, deadpan.

'He won't kick off,' I assure him again, brushing the subject off. 'But I'm still really glad you're here.'

He nods at the necklace dangling from around my neck.

'Do you like it?'

'I love it,' I reply, my eyes shining as I smile at him with affection.

He smiles back at me and then shifts in his seat. 'So, I have some news…' His sentence trails away, along with his eye contact.

'What is it?'

'I've just received Nicki's royalty statement for *The Secret Life of Us*. She's already earned out her advance.'

This means she's sold so many books that she's now being paid extra money on top of her initial payment.

'That's fantastic!' I exclaim.

'Bridget, her royalties are crazy,' he says quietly, disbelievingly.

'Oh, Charlie, I'm so pleased for you both.' I know how much easier that will make things for him and April.

'I'm thinking about joining you in Thailand.'

My jaw hits the floor. 'Are you serious?'

He nods.

'No! You are kidding me!' My happy balloon is threatening to burst right out of my chest. 'Oh, my God! That's amazing!'

He smiles at my reaction. 'I'm glad you're pleased.'

'Of course I am! I can't stop talking in exclamation marks! Look at me!'

He laughs.

'Oh, my God.' I clap my hands against my cheeks, stunned and a little beside myself as I let it fully sink in.

'So, if Elliot comes, I'll get to meet him, after all,' Charlie says pointedly.

Now why does that idea make me suddenly feel so cold?

Charlie hasn't been to London in ages, and April has never been at all, so the next day we go into town to do some sightseeing. April likes the lions in Trafalgar Square and the guards in their red uniforms outside Buckingham Palace, and afterwards we head to Regent Street and go into Hamleys. I buy April a bubble machine for her to take back home with her, remembering how much she liked the music man's bubbles.

Charlie wants to nip into a clothes shop, so I tell him we'll meet up in half an hour. In the meantime, I go and buy April an ice cream, because what the hell, I want to spoil her.

We wander into the White Company so I can check out swimsuits for April – I'd like to get her one for Thailand. Whether or not they still have them at this time of year is another matter, but I can pick up some PJs for her if not – I've bought them for other friends from here before.

We make it to the back of the store before a sales assistant greets us.

'Good afternoon,' she says brightly, looking from me to April. Her mouth gapes open and the blood drains from her face.

'Oh, no,' she says with horror. 'No, no, no, you can't eat in here.'

Another sales assistant spies us and hurries over, just as I crane my neck over the pram to see that April's face and hands are covered in chocolate ice cream. *Oops.*

'No food in here!' the other sales assistant calls, beckoning madly to a third person.

Together the three of them shepherd us out of the shop, their eyes wild and their arms locking us in like a jail, making sure there's zero chance of April's sticky fingers reaching out to brush chocolate goo over their pristine, perfect, immaculate white clothes.

I make it out of the shop and almost keel over with laughter on the pavement.

I've sobered up by the next day. I'm nervous as Charlie follows my directions to Vince's house. We've timed it well with April's nap – she's fast asleep when we arrive in New Barnet, north London, where Vince lives. His house is a tan, pebble-dashed semi next to a brown brick apartment block. There's a white van parked in the front drive with the name of his landscape-gardening business painted on the side: 'GARDENS BY VINCE'.

He's not what you'd call inspiring.

Charlie pulls up outside the house and looks out of the window. I follow his gaze. Eventually, he turns to me. He stares straight at me, but doesn't say a word.

I still haven't made any move to get out of his pickup.

'You don't have to do this,' he says at last.

I shake my head and jolt into action, opening the door and climbing out onto the road. I can feel Charlie's eyes tracking me as I walk around the front of his vehicle and up Vince's drive. I knock on the white, plasticky-looking door.

Through the two frosted panes of seventies-style etched glass, I see the bulk of Vince's frame approaching from down the corridor. He's in no hurry.

He opens the door and regards me coolly. He's broader – fatter – than he used to be, with a bit of a potbelly around his middle. His dark hair is even blacker than it used to be, the tell-tale sign of a war against grey.

'Hello.' I force a smile onto my face, which isn't returned.

'Bridget,' he says in a low, unpleasant voice, stepping back to let me pass. I cast one last look at Charlie over my shoulder. He's staring through his side window, reminding me of a lion about to pounce.

'Who's that?' Vince notices who has my attention and pauses in his move to shut the door.

'A friend,' I reply.

'One of your many men?' he asks nastily, not expecting a reply.

The door closes with a light click, rather than a heavy clunk, but it feels just as threatening.

My head is spinning slightly as he motions for me to go into the living room. At least I can see Charlie from here, I note, albeit cloudily through the muslin curtains. I drag my eyes away from the window and they land on toy boxes. I glance up at Vince with relief.

'You have children?'

'Two,' he replies, curtly.

'So you're married?'

'Four years.'

'Congratulations.' My smile is genuine, but he seems intent on making this painful for me. 'Where's your wife?' I ask.

'She's taken the kids to her mother's,' he replies. 'Do you want a drink or will we be making this quick?' His tone is frosty and abrupt.

'I don't need a drink.' My earlier trepidation returns in force as I perch on the edge of his battered, stained sofa. I try to steel myself and remember my lines, but it's hard to concentrate. 'Vince,' I say calmly, 'do you know why I've come?'

'I've got a pretty good idea,' he sneers. 'The missus saw you on the telly a couple of weeks ago, recorded it for me.' That probably means he's ranted to her about me in the past. 'I can't believe you've actually got the nerve to come here.'

'I need to ask you for the piece of my heart back.'

The words have never sounded more foolish. I just want to be done with it so I can get back to Charlie and April.

He hoots in my face. 'Have you got any idea how ridiculous you sound?' His bitterness runs deep.

'Can I have it or not?' I snap.

He sniggers and relaxes back in the sofa, folding his arms.

'You know what?' Suddenly I see red. 'You're right. This is ridiculous. You never had a part of it in the first place. I was just devastated by Freddie and you were… Well, you were just there, weren't you?' I get to my feet, but he's faster. He looks stunned, as if I'd hit him. As I try to leave the room, he grabs my arm hard and drags me to a halt.

'Get your hands off me or I'll have you for assault,' I warn, meeting his furious glare head on.

'If you dare write about this, I'll sue you,' he threatens in return, practically hurling my arm away.

I back towards the door, then hurriedly open it. I know he wouldn't have a leg to stand on – I change all the details of the men I write about – but I don't bother pointing that out. As I say, he never had a piece of my heart anyway. We're down to eleven.

'Slag!' he calls as I hurry down the path.

Charlie gets out of the car.

'No, don't,' I say firmly, shaking my head at him. 'April,' I remind him. 'Come on. I just want to go.'

Chapter 38

I really am very sorry about Charlie's black mood, but I can't find it in me to stress about what happened with Vince. I'm too excited about the prospect of Thailand.

Charlie hasn't booked his tickets yet, so I put him in touch with Marty. It would be amazing if we could go on the same flight, if not from Heathrow – that would be a bit of a trek for him – then at least from Bangkok.

I try to perk him up as we say goodbye.

'Will you be all right?' he asks, seeming reluctant to leave.

'I'll be fine!' I exclaim. 'Thailand, remember?'

'And you're sure you want us to all be there at the same time? We won't be gatecrashing on a romantic getaway for you and Elliot?' He looks concerned.

'No. He probably won't be able to make it, anyway.'

I go outside to wave them off, my heartstrings twanging as they round the corner, then I return indoors and play Honeyblood's 'Super Rat' as loudly as I can without riling the neighbours through all four walls. When the chorus kicks in, I sing, 'I will hate you forever' at the top of my voice. It's an ode to Vince, but, despite the sentiment, I can't stop smiling.

Sara calls me the next day. She falls silent when I tell her I don't want to write about Vince.

'I'm sorry, but he never had a piece of my heart in the first place,' I say.

'But you can write about that,' she replies emphatically. 'It will make a fabulous chapter.'

'I don't want to.' My voice is sullen.

'That would be a missed opportunity,' she cautions. 'Does Elliot have anything to do with this change of heart?'

'No, I haven't spoken to him. He'd probably tell me to write about it, too,' I mutter.

'Perhaps you should call him, then,' she says boldly.

The fact is, Elliot and I haven't had a *proper* catch-up since I've been back. It's never felt like the right time. He was very surprised to hear that Charlie and April were coming to see me. Surprised *and* apprehensive. I told him Charlie didn't want me to visit Vince on my own and that ruffled his feathers a bit. I had to convince him he was just looking out for me, as any friend would, but it made him suspicious.

'Is there anything I need to know?' he asked me, a wary undertone to his voice.

'No,' I replied.

'Because I've always trusted you.'

'And you are right to,' I said firmly.

He left it at that.

How am I going to tell him that Charlie and April are coming to Thailand? The truth is, he *would* mind their 'gate-crashing', as Charlie put it.

I try not to fret unnecessarily. There are only three weeks until we set off, so, if Elliot hasn't got his act together yet, chances are he never will.

I'm wrong. He FaceTimes me the next morning, wanting to know how it went with Vince. I tell him. Unsurprisingly, he agrees with Sara.

'She's right, Bridgie,' he says with easy nonchalance. 'It *would* make a good chapter.'

I feel a spark of anger. 'You weren't there, you don't know what he was like. I couldn't bear to give the bastard the attention!'

Charlie was there, and he agrees with me... I don't say it out loud.

'All right, calm your tits,' he replies with a grin. 'I've got some news that will cheer you up.'

'What?' I ask, still smarting.

'Guess who's coming to Thailand...'

I stare at his gleeful face and realise that I don't feel a trace of excitement.

His smile falters.

What I actually feel, I realise, is dismay.

That's not right. That's not right at all.

This is *not* a reaction I can bank. This is something that needs dealing with here and now.

Elliot's brow creases into a frown. 'You don't seem that happy about it.'

I shake my head. I can't correct him.

'What's going on?' he demands to know.

'Elliot, I'm sorry.' My voice comes out in not much more than a whisper.

'Why?' he asks guardedly as I force myself to face the truth – it's something I've been avoiding for a while.

'I don't want you to come,' I admit.

'What?' he asks with alarm.

I take a deep breath and make myself say it. 'I think we should break up.'

'*What*?!' He flies to an upright position. He's been sprawled out on his brown-leather sofa, the one on which I've snuggled up with him on countless occasions. 'Does this have anything to do with Charlie?'

'No.' My scalp prickles as I shake my head. 'Yes.' I shake it harder. 'I don't know.' I return my gaze to him on the screen.

'Have you cheated on me?' He's aghast.

'No!' I exclaim. 'Never!'

'But you wanted to,' he says flatly.

'That's not true. At least, I don't think it is. I'm very confused.'

I've always had strict rules about what constitutes cheating. To me, being unfaithful is not as simple as getting physical. Even fantasising about kissing or having sex with someone who isn't your partner is a crime in my books.

I haven't thought about Charlie in that way, but I've been suffocating a far deeper attraction to him. And there's more to it than that. I can no longer deny what my heart has been trying to tell me for weeks.

I am in love with Charlie.

And how he feels about me is irrelevant to the conversation that's going on right now. My admission itself is enough to bring my relationship with Elliot to its knees.

'Do you not think this is just because we've been apart for so long?' Elliot asks me in a wavering voice, and I feel sick to see the pain I'm causing.

Would we be splitting up if I'd never left Australia? I doubt it very much. We *are* good together – we always have been. I still can't believe we found each other again after all these years. There's every chance I'm making a terrible mistake in letting him go.

'I could still come to Thailand.' He puts forward this gentle suggestion. 'We could just see.'

'No.' My chest feels constricted as reality sinks in. I really am breaking up with him.

It's not as if there hadn't been signs: I've been avoiding Face-Timing him for weeks, and, when we have spoken recently, our conversations have often been strained. The piece of me that was his has been shrinking steadily ever since Charlie and I became friends. It's nothing that Elliot has done. It's nothing that *anyone* has done intentionally. My heart is holding the reins, not my head. And it has already carved part of itself off for Charlie.

'It *is* Charlie, isn't it?' Elliot looks stunned.

'I don't know what to say,' I reply, feeling an intense stab of frustration that we're having to have this conversation on the phone and not in person. 'I'm so sorry. I don't even know how he feels about me.'

'You're his dead wife's ghostwriter, for Christ's sake!'

'I know!' I raise my voice, feeling like I'm going to throw up. 'And that's totally fucked up! Nothing might ever come of this. All I know is that when you said you were coming to Thailand, I wasn't happy. That's the undeniable truth of the matter.'

'So this is it,' he says with disbelief. 'We're done?'

I stare with anguish at his face on the screen. The phone camera doesn't care that this moment is poignant – it still refuses to capture our eye contact. I force myself to say it out loud. 'Yes, El. I'm so sorry.'

A thought occurs to him, then. 'Am I going to feature on your blog one day?'

'No.' I shake my head vigorously. 'No.'

'I better not, Bridget,' he warns, and the little devil on my shoulder cries, *'How do you like it when the tables are turned?'*

'You won't,' I vow. 'You won't.'

'That would be really fucking ironic.'

I continue to shake my head.

He sighs and drags his hand over his beard, looking gutted. Tears spring up in my eyes. 'Man. What will our mates say?'

I think of Bronte's disappointed face and wince. She adores Elliot. I'll get a call from her at some point, wanting to know what on earth it is I think I'm doing. I'm not sure myself. Everyone said we were the perfect couple. But is there any such thing?

We end the call, neither of us wanting to draw it out any longer, but that's not to say we won't speak again.

I go back to bed, swiping a box of tissues from the side table as I walk past. I don't know what will happen with Charlie. I know he cares for me, but I'm not sure if his feelings run deeper – or if he'd ever even allow them to run deeper.

The future is uncertain, but right now, I just want to engulf myself in the past. I need time to mourn the death of yet another relationship.

Chapter 39

In the end, Charlie and April take an earlier flight to Thailand, so our flight paths don't coincide, but it gives them a day or so to catch up with Grandpa Dupré before I arrive. I, in turn, will be at the resort for an extra day after they leave. With Alain's contacts and my press credentials, it was no trouble to change our reservations to a two-bedroom beach house that will accommodate the three of us. Charlie simply asked, 'No Elliot?' when I emailed to ask if he was happy with the arrangement. I replied, 'No,' and didn't get a response.

I haven't yet told him that we've split up – I think I want to gauge his reaction in person. The thought of that conversation makes me nervous.

Breaking up with Elliot took some of the shine off my forthcoming trip, but I've put my head down and cracked on with *Confessions*, keen to make serious inroads with the Morris-and-Kit plot before I bring Timo into the mix. I've loved constructing scenes set in the places that Charlie and I visited. The research really helped to bring the book and the characters to life for me, and it's been a joy to let my imagination lead me wherever it wants to go. I've written a novel before, so I'm not inexperienced, but I seem to have more confidence than I did a few years ago, and, as long as I don't think about the pressure or what people are expecting, the words flow freely.

I only hope Thailand will inspire me as much as Cornwall did.

Sara, meanwhile, has given up asking me about my blog. Presumably, she's got bigger fish to fry.

Right now, so have I.

I fly to Krabi via Bangkok and am met at the airport by the transfer team, who take me by taxi to the dock. The resort is a short boat ride away, past several of the ethereal islands that Thailand is so famous for. The weather is warm and humid, a hazy heat hanging over the landscape. It's a complete contrast to the crisp autumnal London I left behind.

I stand on the bow of the boat as the resort island comes into view, and as we draw closer to the evergreen shore, flanked on either side by tall, jagged cliff faces, I see them: Charlie with April on his shoulders, standing on the pristine white beach under the shade of a tree. My heart aches at the sight of them.

April is in a light-blue dress, which is almost, though not quite, the same colour as the water. Her blonde curls have become even more springy in the humidity. I can't wait to hold her in my arms again.

My gaze drops to Charlie. He's wearing khaki green shorts

and a casual, white short-sleeved shirt, unbuttoned at the top.
The sight of him makes me feel breathless.

He smiles at me, keeping his steady hands on April's little
legs when I wave.

As I step off the boat onto the sandy shore, I notice a group
of rock climbers tackling the nearby cliffs, but then Charlie is
approaching and my attention is instantly diverted. He takes
April down from his shoulders to give me a hug.

'It's so good to see you again,' he says after a brief embrace.
Butterflies have crowded into my tummy and I'm finding it
hard to meet his eyes. Three weeks feels like a lifetime when
you realise you're in love with someone.

My awkwardness dispels when I turn to April. 'Hello,
cutie!' I reach out to take her, desperate for a proper baby hug.

To my surprise and disappointment, she makes a negative
sound and turns away from me, burying her face against
Charlie's neck.

'She's tired,' he says apologetically.

'Jetlag?' I ask, trying not to feel too hurt.

'Hellish,' he confirms, grimacing.

The resort staff take me and the other new arrivals for an
induction session so we can hear about the rules and facili-
ties. Charlie waits for me, and, as he walks April around the
open-aired pavilion, pointing out various shiny statues and
ornaments, I sip on my fruit cocktail and try to concentrate.
But my eyes keep drifting to them.

There's no need for a member of staff to show me to my
room because Charlie knows where we're going. My luggage
will follow.

The three of us walk side by side along a winding redbrick

path, its borders thick with ferns and tropical fauna. Vines dangle down from the leafy canopy overhead, and everywhere we look, flowers are in full bloom.

'Look! A monkey!' I shout, spying a small grey fellow up in a tree.

'There are dozens of them around,' Charlie replies.

'Monkey sightings never get old,' I tell him, meeting his eyes fleetingly. It seems impossible, but they're even more beautiful and unusual than I remembered.

I smile at April. 'Are you going to come to me now?' I ask her sweetly.

She shakes her head and looks the other way.

'Oh,' I say despondently, my lips turning down at the corners.

'She was a bit unsettled after we last saw you,' Charlie confides, trying to explain April's behaviour.

'So it's not just jetlag?' That worries me greatly.

'It's okay,' he says. 'She's just got to get used to you again. Here we are.'

I look ahead to what will be our home for the duration of our stay. There are two circular huts, joined together in the middle and surrounded by a high wicker fence. One hut is two-storey, the other single. They each have a cone-like thatched roof that points to the sky. As Charlie leads me around the corner to the gate, I see through a break in other nearby huts that the beach is literally right there.

'Can we go and have a look?' I ask him.

'Sure.'

The long stretch of white sand curves around and out of view to our right. To our left it comes to a stop where it meets an enormous, towering, grey-and-orange limestone cliff. It's as tall as a skyscraper and its very top is thick with jungle-like cover, like a head of resplendent green hair. To our right is a row of moored long-tail boats serving food and drinks, their colourful signage spilling out onto the sand, advertising their wares. The barbecues on board sizzle and smoke with everything from chicken satays and burgers to prawns on skewers. Other boats sell fruit, ice creams and drinks. Behind them is a huge, bulbous limestone island, and, off in the distance, several more otherworldly islands fade away into the heat haze. The still, clear, aquamarine water looks unbelievably inviting.

'You want to go for a swim?' Charlie asks.

'I really, *really* do,' I reply with a grin. I hope my suitcase has arrived at the room with my swimming things inside.

We head back around the corner and go through the gate belonging to our hut. There's a modest private pool with a waterfall running down a smooth slate wall into the pool water, and four sun loungers lined up beside it. A short, but cheerfully winding brick path leads us beneath a heavenly scented frangipani tree to the wooden front door. Charlie unlocks it with a key and pushes the door open.

The pleasant smell of incense wafts out as we enter into a circular living space, complete with a deep-seated sofa, a single armchair, a coffee table, flat-screen TV and a minibar.

'Your room is upstairs.' He nods towards the staircase that winds around part of the living room's outer wall. 'April and I are through there.' He nods to the second, single-storey hut that adjoins this one. 'Nice, eh?' He glances at me for agreement.

'Amazing,' I reply.

'Bet you've seen some incredible places on your travels, though.'

'This is right up there,' I tell him.

He seems pleased by my comment.

'I don't think my bags are here yet,' I say. 'Unless they're upstairs. I'll just check.'

It's also an excuse to see my bedroom. The intricately carved furniture is of dark wood and solid-looking, and the huge bed is made up with crisp white linen. There's an *en suite* bathroom with an oval-shaped spa bath and a large green-tiled shower.

The finishes are of the highest quality, I think to myself with my travel writer's hat on.

A series of expensive-looking toiletries have been set out on the long marble counter. I'll be getting stuck into those later…

When I return downstairs, April has toddled off to their bedroom.

'We need to watch her with the stairs,' Charlie says. 'No bags yet?'

I shake my head. 'Not yet.'

'You want a beer or something while we wait?'

'I'd love one.'

He goes to the minibar and brings out two cans, cracking one open first before passing it to me.

'Cheers,' we say, bumping cans.

I'm still finding it really hard to look at him.

'Have you seen Alain?' I ask with forced casualness, taking a seat on the sofa and sinking right into it.

'A couple of times,' Charlie replies, opting for the arm-chair. He stretches his long, honey-coloured legs out in front of him and crosses his bare feet at the ankles. 'He came to meet the boat yesterday and we had brunch this morning.'

'How was it?' I ask, taking a sip of my beer.

'All right,' he replies downheartedly, studying his own can. 'Obviously, it's hard for him with Nicki not being here. He got a bit tearful around April. She looks so much like her mum.'

'I think she looks like you,' I say without thinking.

He glances at me with interest. 'Really?'

I avert my gaze. 'Except for her eyes.' April's are blue.

There's a knock on the door and I leap to my feet. The porter takes my bags straight upstairs.

'Are you all right?' Charlie asks when I've seen the porter out.

'Yeah, I'm fine. Why?'

'You seem a bit jumpy.'

My cheeks immediately heat up. I press my palms to them. 'I'm okay,' I say in a voice muffled by the pressure on my face. I'm still standing by the door.

'What is it?' he asks with a light laugh.

'I don't know.' I'm slightly mortified. 'I think I'm feeling a bit shy. It's been a while since I've seen you guys.'

'Aw,' he says, seeming thoroughly entertained. He has no trouble at all meeting *my* gaze. 'Do we need a seven-second hug to reacquaint ourselves?'

'Er...' *I'm not sure that will help...*

Too late. He's already up on his feet and walking over to

me. He wraps his arms around me, but this time everything feels different.

The butterflies inside me go so berserk that I feel as if I could take off. It's unbearable. I need to put a more comfortable distance between us.

'Better?' he asks, thankfully pulling back and staring at me.

He has no idea.

It gets worse when I come downstairs in my emerald-green bikini and hot-pink sarong to find that he's wearing his swimming trunks.

And nothing else.

God, give me strength!

So *that's* what he was hiding under T-shirts all summer: slim hips, toned navel and a broad, leanly muscled chest.

My face warms again, so I busy myself looking for towels while he puts April into a swimming nappy.

'What are you after?' Charlie asks me after a moment.

'Towels?' I respond.

'There's a hut down by the beach.'

I should have guessed that.

He sits April up.

'Oh! I have something for her,' I remember, hurrying back upstairs. 'Don't put her in a swimming costume!' I call over my shoulder.

I return with a gift – a navy-blue-and-white-spotted costume, with red trimming and a frill around the middle.

'That's cute,' he says as I help him to put it on.

I hope April is back to herself with me soon, I think with a pang. As if on cue, she looks up at me.

I pull a silly face at her and she smiles.

'There you go,' Charlie says kindly. 'Now you can relax.'

If only he knew the other reason why I'm so tense.

Charlie and I walk April hand in hand down to the beach. The water is unreal – it's so warm. Charlie zooms April to me and I catch her and give her a cuddle until she wriggles, wanting to be zoomed again. I've got to get my hugs in while I can.

'I can't believe we're all here,' he says later, when I'm floating on my back and staring up at the sky.

'Me neither,' I reply with a smile. I've been feeling ever so slightly more relaxed with every minute that passes in his company.

'Where do you want to go for dinner tonight?' he asks.

'Is Alain working?'

'Yes, he's based at the continental restaurant where the boats come in, near the rock-climbing cliffs. They serve breakfast there, too.'

I was too side-tracked by Charlie and April earlier to pay the rock climbers much attention. Isak could've been halfway up the cliff face for all I knew. Maybe I'll go there tomorrow for a look around, but tonight I just want to settle in.

'Shall we go to the beach where the infinity pool is?' I suggest. I think they do a variety of Asian cuisine at the restaurant there.

'Sure.'

We return to our rooms to shower and get ready. I choose a black, lightweight, floaty dress and take more care with my hair and make-up than I would usually.

'You look nice,' Charlie says when I come downstairs. He's reading a magazine in the armchair.

'So do you,' I reply.

'This is what I had on earlier,' he points out with a grin.

I shrug at him and his smile widens.

'Shall I grab April?' I need to get away before he sees me blushing. Again.

'Go for it.'

I find her in the bathroom, coasting around the bath with a yellow rubber duck. She looks up at me.

'We're going to go and get some dinner now,' I say, kneeling down beside her. 'Are you hungry?' She nods. 'Can I have a cuddle?' I open up my arms hopefully. She complies, edging forward into my embrace.

The pressure in my chest as I lift her up and hold her to me is immense.

The restaurant has a bar area with a row of comfy-looking armchairs facing the water, so we decide to sit and have cocktails first, while Charlie peruses the menu for something to eat for April.

'We could just sit here while she eats,' he muses. 'We might even be able to get her to fall asleep afterwards so we can have some peace and quiet.'

'It's lucky she's still young enough to do that in her pram,' I say. 'I bet it gets more difficult as she gets older.'

'Yeah,' he agrees. 'I reckon she'll conk out pretty quickly. She's still getting used to the time difference. How are you faring?' he asks.

'A bit out of it,' I admit. 'But the longer I hold out, the better I should feel tomorrow.'

I choose a lemongrass, lime and Thai basil mojito and Charlie goes for a margarita. He also orders a serving of mini fish and chips for April and some crispy prawns in coconut batter to see us by.

Maybe it's the hazy sky, or maybe it's the company, but I'm sure I'm witnessing the most beautiful sunset I've ever seen. It flows up from the horizon in a wash of intense pink and vibrant orange. It is utterly breathtaking. Charlie goes off to try to get April to sleep in her pram while I sit there, sipping my second mojito and just taking it all in.

'Do you reckon *we* could eat here?' I ask when he returns because I really don't want to move from this position into the main restaurant.

'I don't see why not,' he replies, fixing a mosquito net to the front of April's pram and sitting back down beside me. He stares contemplatively at the sky. 'It's no wonder Nicki loved it here.'

It hurts to hear the longing in his voice.

Ever since breaking up with Elliot, I haven't been able to stop thinking about whether Charlie and I might have a future together. If anything does develop between us, I know it won't – *can't* – happen here. It's too soon, and this trip, for him, is about April connecting with Alain. It's about the wife he loved 'to hell and back' and the daughter she left behind. And for me, it's about doing the best job that I possibly can with Nicki's book. The last thing it is – the last thing it could *ever* be – is a romantic getaway for him and me.

I'd love him to start thinking of me as more than just his friend, but it's not simply a case of small steps here. We're talking teeny-tiny, miniscule, *Borrowers*-style steps. I'll need to tread as carefully with him as if I were walking barefoot on shattered sea glass. This will take time. And we'll have plenty of time once we get back to England and this book is finished. I care too much about him to risk screwing this up by rushing things.

'I'm sorry,' I say quietly. 'I bet you wish she was here.'

He doesn't reply for a long moment. 'Yeah,' he says heavily, but then he smiles at me. 'I'm glad you are, though.'

I take a sip of my drink, feeling apprehensive. 'How did Kate and Valerie react when you told them we'd all be here together?' I ask.

He appears uncomfortable. 'Not well,' he replies. 'I don't think either of them has ever had a friend of the opposite sex before, so they don't get it. I decided not to tell them that Elliot wasn't coming after all.' He flashes me a cynical look.

'What would they do?' I ask suddenly, unable to help myself. I do need to lay *some* foundations. 'What would they do if you and I *were* more than just friends?'

He lets out a single, bitter laugh. 'Never speak to me again.'

My eyes widen. 'Come off it. Did they say that?' I don't believe it.

'They did actually,' he replies.

A bad feeling washes over me.

'"If I ever find out that it's more, I'll never speak to you again." Something like that.'

'Kate actually said that out loud?' I feel sick.

He shrugs. 'Yeah. Obviously, she'd still want a relationship with April, but she'd never forgive me.'

342

'Jesus, am I really that awful?' I ask with a mixture of shock, consternation and hurt.

'Of course you're not,' he replies in a gruff voice, waving me away. 'Just ignore her.' He picks up his menu. 'We should probably order.'

It's no surprise that I'm no longer hungry. So much for laying foundations.

Chapter 40

Would Charlie still love Nicki if he knew that she was being unfaithful to him with Isak?

That's one of the first thoughts that hit me the following morning.

Before I can contemplate it, I hear Charlie talking to April downstairs. It sounds like they're getting ready to go somewhere. I jump out of bed and quickly slip on my robe.

'I was just writing you a note,' Charlie says with a smile as I come downstairs. 'April was getting a bit hungry. You want to come with us to breakfast?'

'Can you give me a sec?' I ask.

'Sure, we'll wait by the pool.'

I'm back outside within a few minutes.

'That was quick,' he comments.

'Figured you'd seen me looking rough on enough occasions,' I say wryly.

'You never look rough.'

Well, *that* makes me smile.

The restaurant by the boat-docking beach is bustling. There are tables outside on the terrace, under the shade of the trees. A female monkey with a baby on its back is running across the thatched roof of the restaurant while a waiter shoos it away. *How can something that cute be a pest?*

'Do you want to go in and get April sorted first?' I offer Charlie. 'I'll wait here with her.'

'That'd be great, thanks,' he replies.

I unclick April from her pram and lift her into the high-chair that has already been brought over by the ever-attentive staff, before taking a seat.

Out of the corner of my eye, a tall, thin man in a white T-shirt approaches our table. When I glance at him, he's already looking determinedly at me. He's in his late fifties, at a guess, and is deeply tanned with thinning, greying, light-brown hair.

'Bridget,' he says, knowingly.

'Yes?'

'Alain Dupré.' He has a very thick French accent.

'Oh, hello!' I stand to shake the hand he offers me.

'Sit down, please.' He pulls up a chair. 'I saw Charlie inside. I thought I would come and say 'ello.'

'It's really nice to meet you.'

'So you're my Nicki's... How do they say? Phantom writer?'

'Ghostwriter,' I correct him with a smile.

He raises his eyebrows. 'Bit strange you are 'ere with her husband and daughter, no?'

Oh, God, not another hater…

Urgh, that *word*!

'That was just the way it worked out.' I'm tense, but I hope I don't sound too defensive.

To my surprise, he smiles. 'Charlie says you 'ave been cheering them up.'

'Really?' Hope replaces some of the tension.

'It is good,' he says. 'What 'appened with Nicki was very tragic.' His face grows sombre as he looks down at the table. 'Very, very sad.'

'Yes,' I agree quietly.

He perks up and strokes April's head. 'But it is good to see this little monkey.'

She stares at him vacantly and he tweaks her nose. She smiles and he smiles back at her. It's a lovely sight.

'Very good indeed,' he says softly, brushing her cheek. 'I 'ave to get back to work, but I maybe see you later, yes?'

'That would be great,' I reply, and I mean it.

He crosses paths with Charlie on his way back indoors, clapping his son-in-law gently on his back. Charlie looks heartened when he rejoins us, carrying a bowl of Rice Krispies and some fresh fruit.

'Okay?' he asks as he places the bowl in front of April.

'Yes,' I reply with a smile.

More than okay…

'I'm just going to nip in here to ask about rock-climbing lessons,' I say to Charlie as we're wandering back past the activities-and-excursions hut after breakfast.

'Rock-climbing lessons?' he asks with surprise. 'Oh, for the *book*!' he realises.

'I'll see you back there?'

'Okay.'

There's a girl sitting behind the desk and a young couple over by the window, flicking through a brochure.

'Can I help you?' the desk girl asks me.

I get straight down to business, booking myself onto Isak's beginners' taster session for this afternoon.

Charlie smiles at me when I return. 'I forgot we weren't just here on holiday, for a minute.'

I wish that *were* the case.

'Are you actually going to try rock climbing?'

'I may as well.' I shrug. 'Nicki's character does it, so it'd help if I could write from experience.'

'When are you going?'

'This afternoon.'

'Maybe we'll come to watch,' he says with a grin.

I can't lie to him...

He notices my hesitation. 'What's wrong?'

'Charlie, Isak still works here,' I say gently. 'I'm doing the session with him.'

He stares at me, his mouth dropping open. 'Are you serious?'

'Yes.' I sit down on the sofa and look at him, pleading with him to understand.

He is not at all happy.

'Why does it have to be him?' he asks me.

'Does it matter?' I reply with a frown. After all, this is me, not Nicki, we're talking about.

'No, I guess not,' he says.

But he's a bit off with me for the rest of the morning.

He takes April to the beach while I make my way back to the activities-and-excursions hut. There are a few people already getting kitted up with harnesses and helmets when I arrive.

I feel a flurry of nerves. *I am actually doing this.*

A good-looking man of about my age comes over with a clipboard. 'What's your name?' he asks.

I tell him and he scans his sheet of paper and crosses me off. 'I'm Isak,' he says and I jolt. His grip is firm and efficient as he shakes my hand. 'Emily here will sort you out for equipment. We'll leave in ten minutes.'

I can barely take my eyes off him after that – it's so surreal to finally meet him in person after reading so much about him in Nicki's diary. It's almost as if he's some sort of celebrity.

He's slim with closely cropped dark hair and interesting grey eyes. He's not much taller than I am, with wiry, lean muscles and freckly, tanned skin. As he talks to the other climbers, I detect a mild Swedish accent. His English is excellent.

There are five of us in the group – two young couples and yours truly – and we walk together past the restaurant where we ate breakfast and down to the beach. There are a few buildings that aren't connected to the resort out here: a café, bar and a shop with colourful clothes and beach toys piled up outside under a veranda. I spy a number of bright orange, green and blue monkey puppets dangling from a stand and think of April, but we're already moving past the building to the rocky shore. We make our way carefully between the sharp rocks, beside the soaring cliffs to a small beach. I look up to see a big overhang jutting out from the cliff face several storeys from the ground. Some climbers are already trying to navigate it.

'Is that where we're going?' I ask Isak worriedly, fixating on a bare-chested, muscled man, dangling from the underside of the overhang. Ropes attach his harness to a hook and his friend is holding his rope at the bottom, but *still*…

Isak glances at me with a smirk. 'No, that's for the more experienced climbers. We'll be tackling this little cliff face, here.' I get the feeling he'd quite like to laugh.

'Thank fuck for that.'

At that comment, he does.

Isak spends some time talking us through the steps before we're finally ready to be hooked up to the safety ropes. I decide to go last, figuring I can check out how the others fare before I make a total tit of myself.

'Okay, Bridget, up you go,' Isak says, holding my rope and belaying me from the bottom. I have his full attention at last, but I don't know quite how I'm going to broach the subject of Nicki when I'm clinging to a rock face with my fingers.

'Good,' he calls encouragingly as I put one hand in front of the other and hoist my entire body weight up. I'm going to ache after this, I just know it. I put all of my attention into concentrating and decide I'll find a way to talk to Isak later once I've really impressed him.

Obviously, I don't really believe I'll impress him at all, so I feel kind of proud when I don't do too badly.

'Well done,' he says with what I think is admiration as my feet hit the rocky, sandy shore. 'Is that really your first time?'

'Yep.' I nod.

'Very good. How long are you here?'

'Almost a week.'

'You should sign up for a course. I think you have a knack for it.'

'Thanks,' I reply, feeling my cheeks brighten. *It's so uncanny that this is Nicki's Isak!*

He turns to the others. 'Guys, that was a great first try. Really excellent. I hope to see you all again while you're here.'

If that was a sales pitch, it was effective. Everyone looks gladdened by his praise.

It's my intention to try to walk beside him on the return journey to the resort, but, frustratingly, he strikes up a conversation with one of the men in our group. After we've taken off all of our equipment in the activities hut, I hang back, hoping to speak to him. One of the other couples are really taking their time, and, to my exasperation, Isak calls out goodbye and leaves before they do. I awkwardly hurry after him.

'Isak?' I call, chasing him down the redbrick path.

He glances over his shoulder and halts with surprise when he sees me.

'Everything okay?' he asks as I come to a stop in front of him.

'Have you got a moment?'

He looks surprised, but not unpleasantly so. 'Sure.'

We move off to one side as a golf cart trundles past with some new arrivals' luggage bumping away inside.

'I haven't been completely upfront with you,' I say. 'I'm actually here researching a book.'

His dark eyebrows jump up. 'Really?'

'You remember Nicki Dupré?'

Now his eyebrows practically hit his hairline. 'Nicole?'

'Yes.'

'You are friends?' he asks me with surprise.

It's the present tense that does it. He doesn't know she's gone.

'When was the last time you saw her?' I check, just in case I'm wrong.

'Oh, years ago,' he replies with a frown, thinking. 'You know we used to be in a relationship?'

I nod.

'We didn't stay in touch,' he tells me, and, despite all of the hours I've spent pondering about whether Nicki was drawing on personal experience when she wrote about being in love with two men at the same time, I believe him. I don't know yet what that means for me, but I'm certain he's telling the truth.

'Is she well?' he asks amiably.

I take a deep breath, feeling troubled that I'm going to be the one to break this to him. But someone needs to. He obviously doesn't speak to Alain. Maybe they just never cross paths. I'm not sure Nicki's father ever even knew the details of her relationship with Isak. He was working so much, she had to occupy herself most of the time. And it was a long time ago that they went out – almost ten years. It probably never even occurred to Alain to tell him.

'I'm sorry,' I say to Isak, my voice wavering. 'I'm afraid Nicki – Nicole – passed away last year.'

He looks crushed, but not utterly devastated, not like he'd look if he were still madly in love with her.

'Oh, no. What happened?' he asks.

I tell him.

Isak doesn't have long to stay and talk, but he'd like to hear more about Nicki and he says he'd be happy to try to help me with my research. I agree to his suggestion to meet up later. He still lives in the village further along from the resort, so he gives me details on where to go.

Charlie is by the pool when I return, sitting on a sun lounger and looking in a right grumpy state. April must be having her afternoon nap. He glances over at me.

'How did it go?' he asks.

'It was fine,' I reply. 'Aren't you going in?' I nod at the pool.

'In a bit.'

'It's so hot,' I say.

'Are you going to tell me about it?' he asks.

'Of course I will, if you want to know.'

'Yes.'

I walk over to him and pull my T-shirt over my head. 'Sorry, I'm too hot,' I say, unbuttoning my shorts. 'Rock climbing is hard work.'

He watches me guardedly as I strip off down to my swimming costume – a blue-and-green polka-dot one today.

I step into the pool and let the cool water engulf me, going right under. When I emerge, Charlie is looking at me, and he's still waiting.

I swim over to the edge and gaze up at him. 'You should come in, it's lovely.'

'Did you meet Isak?' he asks, and it doesn't take a genius to work out that he's jealous.

What went down between Nicki, Charlie and Isak happened years ago, but Charlie still clearly detests the thought of him.

That's because he still loves his wife desperately, I think with a pang.

Regardless of the thought that popped into my mind when I woke up this morning, I don't believe I would have ever told Charlie if Nicki was having an affair with Isak. It would hurt him too much. He deserves to have untainted memories of her, of the mother of his child.

He stands up and pulls his light-grey T-shirt over his head. He's already wearing faded orange swimming trunks.

'What was he like?' he asks as he slides into the water beside me. My breath quickens.

'All right,' I reply noncommittally. 'He had no idea about Nicki.'

'No?' His eyes widen.

'No. He was sad to hear about it.'

Charlie leans his back against the side of the pool and rests his elbows on the ledge behind him as he stares moodily at the waterfall. He looks like a frigging model with his broad chest and bulging biceps.

And I know that's not an appropriate train of thought considering he's struggling with memories of his late wife.

'He said he'd help me with my research,' I reveal.

He glances at me again. 'Yeah?'

'I'm meeting up with him tonight.'

'Oh.' He seems surprised and then put out. 'So we're not going to the Thai restaurant?'

'Tomorrow?' I ask hopefully.

He nods. 'What did *you* think of him?' he asks, and it's a more specific question from the ones that have come before.

'I liked him,' I reply honestly. 'He's good at his job. He's certainly good at encouraging people to sign up for rock-climbing lessons,' I add with a smirk. 'He thought I should go back for a course.'

'Did you think he was good-looking?'

I laugh. Now *that's* a direct question. 'Yeah, in a wiry, rock-climber sort of way. He's not a patch on you,' I say with a grin.

He grins back at me. That comment cheered him up.

'Or Elliot, no doubt.' He obviously feels compelled to belatedly mention my boyfriend.

Ex-boyfriend.

The corners of my lips turn down. Time to come clean. 'We broke up,' I say quietly, my tone losing its humour.

Charlie recoils. 'When?'

'A few weeks ago. After you and April came to see me.'

'Why?' He looks stunned.

'A couple of reasons. We weren't making the long-distance thing work.'

'I'm so sorry.'

'It's okay,' I say. 'I'm okay.'

He reaches out and brushes my arm, leaving behind a trail of goose bumps. 'You sure?'

'Yeah, I'm really fine.' I meet his gaze, but his concern brings ridiculous tears to my eyes. 'God!' I exclaim, brushing them away. 'I really *am* fine. Stop being nice to me!'

'Aw,' he says gently.

I duck under the water and swim to the far side of the pool. When I turn around to face him, he's still watching me.

'Why didn't you tell me before?' he asks with narrowed eyes.

I shrug and push off from the side, swimming back over to him again, but the pool isn't big enough for me to come up with a satisfactory response in the time it takes me to reach him.

'Guess I thought I'd tell you when I saw you.'

He gives me a little frown, trying to work me out.

'So you're single now,' he says in a slightly dry voice. 'How's that going to work out for your blog?'

He catches my arm before I can go underwater again. 'Are you being deliberately evasive?' he asks with a laugh.

His touch sears my skin, but I hate the cold when he lets me go.

'What does it mean for your blog?' he asks again, demanding an answer.

'I don't know,' I reply, looking straight at him. The sunlight hitting the pool is reflected in his eyes, making the shards of green, gold and brown glitter.

'I thought he was your last piece,' he says, and his expression is almost challenging.

My pulse is racing, but I hold our eye contact.

'Guess I was wrong.' I slip under the water again before he can say anything else.

Chapter 41

'Want us to walk you there?' Charlie asks later that evening as I'm gathering my things together. He sounds coolly indifferent, but I'm not sure he feels it.

'No, I'll be fine.' I pick up my camera and slip the strap over my head. 'Catch you later,' I say.

'We'll be here.'

He mentioned that he'd probably get room service later so April can have a proper sleep in her cot. I feel bad for deserting him for the evening.

I click off several photographs as I follow the redbrick path, inwardly singing an adapted version of 'Follow the Yellow Brick Road' from *The Wizard of Oz*. I walk out of the resort gates and turn left, making my way along the concrete footpath adjacent to the shore in the opposite direction to the rock-climbing cliffs. The further away from the resort I go, the less pristine the beach becomes. I pass a few rustic cafés, restaurants and bars, with rickety corrugated-iron ceilings and no walls. The atmosphere seems chilled and the décor unfussy, as laidback punters sit and enjoy the views across the bay.

Everything feels more authentic out here – even the trees aren't as well-maintained.

I pass a couple of resorts, more shops and bars and various huts arranging excursions, activities and tours. Eventually, I come to the bar where Isak said he'd meet me. I go inside and order a beer, then sit down and wait. He joins me after only a few minutes.

'Do you live nearby?' I ask him as he grabs a beer for himself.

'Just around the corner,' he confirms.

'Have you been there long?' I'm trying to work out if it's the same apartment Nicki would've written about.

'Just a year,' he replies.

That's a no, then.

'Do you think you could take me for a look around before it gets dark? Show me the places that might've inspired Nicole? I'd like to take some photos.'

'Okay,' he agrees.

We finish our beers and then set off. There is a whole bustling community right outside the doors of our exclusive, secluded resort. I'd like to bring Charlie and April back here – they should get to see another side of Thailand.

We wander around for ages past vibrant, colourful bars and shops and don't actually end up eating because I'm getting so much material for the book. I'm famished by the time we say our goodbyes. Isak gives me his contact details in case I want to catch up with him again.

On my way back to the hotel, I grab something from a street food stand. It's late and Charlie will have eaten by now. He's probably in bed.

He's not. He's waiting up for me, sitting on the armchair and reading a magazine.

'Hey!' I say, thrilled to see him.

'How was it?' he asks, unhurriedly flipping his magazine shut.

'It was fine,' I reply.

'Where did you go for dinner?'

'We didn't. I just wanted to look around and soak it all up.'

'Are you seeing him again?' he asks as I flop onto the sofa.

'Not sure.' I lie back and stare up at the ceiling fan, whirring around. 'I've got his details if I need them. Not tomorrow night, though. I'm desperate for that Thai.' I turn my head and smile at him. 'How are you guys? What did you have for dinner?'

He sighs. 'We're fine. I got a burger, April had pasta.'

'Were you lonely?' I tease with a grin. 'Did you miss me?'

He rolls his eyes at me.

I'm glad I'm able to joke with him again. I'm getting used to being back in his company, even if my feelings towards him have intensified like you wouldn't believe.

'Did April go to sleep okay?'

'She took a while to go down, actually. I thought she was knackered, so I don't know what was wrong with her.'

'She missed me, too,' I say playfully.

'That did cross my mind.' He's not smiling.

'Isak wanted me to pass on his condolences,' I tell him gently. 'He said he was very sorry for your loss. He remembers you.'

'I bet he does.' He sounds disdainful.

'The last time he bumped into Nicki was when you guys were about to get married. He didn't know you'd had a baby girl.'

'Right, okay.'

I frown at him. This subject is not going down too well.

'Do you fancy doing something tomorrow?' I ask. 'We could do a boat trip to one of the islands maybe.'

'You don't need to do more research?'

'That *is* research. I can write about the places we visit, the things we do.'

'I feel like Isak should be showing you Thailand, not me. That's who Timo is based on, after all,' he says sulkily.

'Hey,' I chide, sitting up and swinging my feet off the sofa and back onto the floor so I'm facing him. 'What's going on?' I demand to know. 'What's wrong?'

'It's true, isn't it? I did Cornwall, he should do Thailand.'

'It's not real, Charlie. You said it yourself, it's only a story.'

'She was obviously inspired by this place, by him. Maybe that's where you should be getting your inspiration also.'

'No, thank you,' I say impertinently. 'I can get plenty of information for the book, regardless of who I'm with.' And then, and I say this without pausing for thought, 'Anyway, if anyone inspires me, it's you.'

We stare at each other for a long moment.

'And April,' I add.

He sits forward and rakes his hand roughly through his

hair. 'Sorry, I don't know what's got into me tonight,' he mutters. 'I'm feeling a bit, I don't know, low.'

'You *did* miss my company,' I say with a grin.

He flashes me a smile at last and I have an almost unbearable urge to go over and straddle his lap.

'I did,' he admits quietly, with a curious look of longing on his face. My breath catches.

There's a cry from the direction of his bedroom. Charlie tenses as he waits to hear if April has woken up. Sure enough, she starts to wail.

'Better go see to her,' he says heavily. 'Think I'll hit the sack now, anyway.'

'Okay. Me too. I'll see you in the morning.'

'Night.'

I watch him edgily as he ambles back into his bedroom.

Chapter 42

Alain joins us again the next morning at our breakfast table. 'Where are you going for dinner tonight?' he asks.

'We were thinking Thai,' I reply.

'Oh, a *beautiful* restaurant.' He shakes his head with incredulity. 'The sunsets from the balcony are stunning. What will you do with my granddaughter?'

'We'll take her with us,' Charlie says.

'Oh, no!' He looks dismayed. 'You can't enjoy the meal and the view with a baby! You must get a sitter.'

'It's all right, she'll fall asleep in her pram,' Charlie replies.

'But our sitters 'ere are fantastic!' he cries. 'We 'ave a lovely girl for you. She is very friendly. April will adore her.'

Charlie looks at me. I shrug. It's up to him.

'I've never left her with a sitter before,' he muses.

'The Thai restaurant *is* very close to our hut,' I point out. 'You could always take April to her room and settle her, then come back. And, if she wakes up, they could call us.'

'What do you say?' Alain prompts. 'I get our girl to come to you?'

'I guess we could give it a try,' Charlie agrees.

'Excellent!' He claps his hands together and gets up from our table. 'And tomorrow night *I* cook for you,' Alain says meaningfully as he takes two steps backwards. 'Yes?'

'Okay,' I reply with a smile.

'Sounds like we have a plan,' Charlie comments as Alain hurries back indoors. He looks at me. 'You and I are going on a *date*,' he says with a smirk.

I suddenly feel very jittery.

Is this too much? I ask myself later, as I eye my reflection in the mirror behind the wardrobe door. My dark hair is down and wavy and I'm wearing the nicest thing I've brought with me, but it's a bit over the top: a silvery, shimmery slip dress with a hemline that floats around the halfway point of my thighs. With heels, my legs look crazy long.

I love this dress. I bought it on a whim, but I haven't had a chance to wear it yet. Fuck it. Seize the day, right?

'Whoa,' Charlie says when I come downstairs, treading carefully so I don't slip on the polished wood and break an ankle. 'I feel underdressed.'

'You still look hot,' I tell him with a flippant grin. He's wearing navy shorts and a green T-shirt.

'Not as hot as you.'

A thrill goes through me, even though he's teasing. I know he still sees me only as a friend, but maybe this dress will help to change that. There I go, trying to lay foundations, again.

'I'm putting a shirt on,' he says, leaving the room.

'Are you serious?' I call after him.

He doesn't reply, but I think that he is.

'This'll do,' he says on his return. He's kept his navy shorts on – they're quite smart, anyway – but he's changed his green T-shirt to a black shirt and he's rolling up the sleeves. 'Still up for cocktails at the cave bar?' he asks.

'Absolutely.'

We plan to feed April first, then pop back to settle her and meet the sitter before going to eat ourselves.

We sip our drinks and watch as the restaurant vendors pack up for the night and the visiting tourists board their long-tail boats to return to their own islands.

'Have you seen anything of Jocelyn and Edward since I left Cornwall?' I ask Charlie.

'Actually, April and I went over there for Sunday lunch before we came away.'

'*Really?*'

'Yeah.' He smiles at my delight. 'I think you're right about Edward. He *is* shy. He was more relaxed at home. Mind you, it might've had something to do with the bottle of red we sank.'

'Do you think you could be friends?'

'Maybe. We'll see.'

'I miss Jocelyn,' I admit. 'I barely knew her, but I liked her a lot.'

'She's still trying to get me to go to that music group,' he reveals.

I wish I could be there to see his face if he does.

'I've finally agreed to take Mum up on her offers to help

out a bit more with April,' he continues. 'Maybe I should ask her to do Wednesday mornings so she can take her.'

'You're missing out,' I warn.

'Yeah, yeah,' he replies with a smile.

Later, I wait by the pool while Charlie introduces April to the sitter, who is indeed a lovely, friendly lady. April seems to like her, but Charlie wants to make sure she's asleep before we leave, and he instructs the sitter to call us if she wakes up.

The resort's Thai restaurant is situated further along the beach near the towering limestone cliffs. We're taken to a table for two outside on the balcony facing the water, and we order a bottle of wine before perusing the menu.

'Is it wrong that I just really fancy a pad Thai?' I ask Charlie.

'No, why?' he replies with a laugh.

'It's so predictable and boring.'

'You should have whatever you feel like,' he states. 'Anyway, it comes with lobster. That's hardly predictable.'

'True,' I say, my mind made up.

The sunset that evening is even more breathtaking than the last. The pale-green water is so still tonight – it barely laps against the white sandy shore. As the light dims, our faces are lit by the candle on the table and the fairy lights in the nearby trees.

'Is that a couple swimming?' I peer further down the beach.

'I think so,' Charlie replies. 'That'll be us later.'

'Shall we?' I ask eagerly. Night swimming!

He shrugs and returns his smile to me. 'Could do.'

The waiter comes over with our food.

'Are you going to see Isak again?' Charlie asks after we've tried each other's dish. This is seriously the best pad Thai I have ever had in my entire life. Charlie's beef curry is bloody good, too.

'Nah, don't think I'll need to,' I reply.

Ladies and gentlemen, that is the right *answer!* The relief on his face is palpable.

'How did you cope reading Nicki's novel?' I'm perplexed. It's obvious he hasn't come to terms with what happened years ago.

'In what way?' he asks, leaning back in his seat and staring at me.

'Well, if you know that Isak inspired Timo, how did that make you feel?'

'Truthfully?' He raises one eyebrow.

I nod.

'Like absolute shit.'

I start with surprise.

'Nicki didn't tell me she was writing a book about cheating.'

'You're kidding me.'

'I'm not. She said that it was about a travel writer and that it was set in Thailand and Cornwall. She told me it was a romance, but she didn't go into details – it wasn't exactly my cup of tea.'

'How did you find out?' I ask.

'When she got a book deal.'

'No!'

'Yeah.'

'You hadn't read it before she submitted it?'

'No. But Kate had.'

I push my food around on my plate.

'Nicki didn't really want me to read it,' he continues, and his expression is full of sympathy when I meet his eyes. He knows how much what happened with Kate upset me. 'You're the only one who knows that, though,' he says.

'Knows what?' I ask with confusion.

'That Nicki submitted her book without telling me what it was about.'

'How did you react when you found out?'

'We had a massive argument. *Massive*,' he states. He shrugs and looks away. 'I don't know, I guess I felt a bit betrayed. It's probably just as well I couldn't stick my nose in. Look how well it did. Women obviously like reading about that sort of stuff.'

I shift in my seat. I liked reading it, too.

'I'm surprised you enjoyed it, actually,' he says. Has he got a telescope into my mind? 'You're so anti-cheating.'

'I am.' I nod. 'It wasn't the cheating I liked reading about – in fact, a lot of the time I was screaming at Kit and wanting to hit her over the head with something hard.'

He smirks.

'It was the falling-in-love part that got me. And this book had *two* love stories. Nicki wrote them so well.' I take a sip of my wine and pause for thought, then throw him a worried look. 'I don't know how I'm going to pull off this sequel, if I'm honest.'

'Is it stressing you out?'

'A bit,' I admit. 'The pressure is immense. All her readers…

I'm not sure what they expect from this story, but I don't want to let them down.'

'You just have to do what you think is right,' he says. 'I have faith in you.'

'Thank you.' I mean it sincerely. 'The thing is, I do believe Nicki was going to have Kit marry both Morris and Timo, so I want to respect her wishes. That's the book that I'm writing. You remember the baby theme I came up with?'

'Yes.' He nods. 'Kit realises she can't bring children into the mix.'

'That's right. And her relationship with Morris breaks down because he wants a family and she doesn't.'

I think of Liam and know that I'll be writing that part from my own personal experience.

'I thought it was a great idea,' he says.

'Thanks.' I smile at him.

'And Timo?' he asks.

'He doesn't even *want* children,' I remind him.

'Maybe he finds out he can't have them,' he says. 'But he refuses to adopt.'

'That's a good idea. Once Kit is his and only his, she realises she'll never be happy.'

'So she ends up sad and alone?'

I regard him warily. 'How do you feel about that?'

'How do I feel about you writing a book about a big-amist who ends up sad and alone?' He checks I'm being serious.

'Yes.' I nod. 'I'm not sure it's what Nicki would have wanted.'

'She's not here, so we can't second-guess her, but I think that ending feels appropriate.'

'Really?'

'Yep. If you're going to bring this story crashing down around Kit's ears, I support that. Nicki built the story up; it's your job to tear it down. But, for God's sake, make it clean, because the last thing we need are readers wanting a trilogy.'

I grin at him.

He smiles back at me and tops up my wine.

'I told you, you were the only inspiration I needed,' I say.

We chink glasses.

Charlie goes back to the hut to make sure everything is okay with April after dinner, but he tells me he'll meet me on the beach. As soon as he's gone, I realise I meant to ask him to bring our swimming costumes back. Hopefully he'll remember.

He doesn't.

'There's no one around,' he says with a mischievous glint in his eye. It's true. The beach is completely deserted.

'Are you suggesting we partake in a spot of skinny dippy, Mr Laurence?' I ask cheekily. We're both a little drunk.

'I'm game if you are,' he replies.

'You first,' I say.

He shrugs and unbuttons his shirt. Thankfully it's dark up here by the cliffs, because I am *blushing*.

I turn my back on him and shiver as I hear the sound of a zip going down.

'See you in there,' he says.

When I hear his footsteps padding away across the sand, I have a quick look over my shoulder at his tall, naked body in the moonlight.

I'm still trying to compose myself when he calls out to me. I turn around and make a spinning gesture with my forefinger in the air. He gets the hint and looks the other way. I slip out of my knickers and pull my slip dress over my head, then wade in.

As soon as I'm submerged nearby, I say, 'Hi.'

'Hi,' he replies, turning around to smile at me. 'Nuts, huh?'

'Ridiculous,' I reply.

The sky is sparkling with starlight, punctuated only by the dark, ghostly shapes of the nearby cliffs and islands.

Charlie looks at the shore, where the resort restaurants are glowing with candles at either end of the beach.

'Was April okay when you went back to check on her?'

'Fine. Hey, how do they say hello again?' he asks me. 'The sitter said it and the other staff say it all the time, but I can never catch it.'

'It's pronounced *sawasdee*,' I tell him. 'Sa-was-dee.'

He repeats it. 'Think I've got it now. Seems to be their go-to phrase here.'

'It is.' I'm about to float on my back when I remember that I'm not wearing anything.

'What did Sara say when she found out about you and Elliot?' Charlie asks curiously.

'I haven't told her yet.'

'Why not?'

I shrug, but don't give him an answer.

'I still don't really understand why you didn't tell me.' He doesn't just sound curious now: he sounds a bit hurt. 'That's a big thing to leave out. I thought we were friends.'

'We are,' I confirm quietly. He's facing the shore, but I've paddled off to his left.

'Is that it?' he asks, giving me a sidelong look. 'Can you really not give me a better explanation? I don't even know if he broke up with you or if you ended it.'

'I ended it,' I confess.

'Why?'

How can I answer him? I sigh, softly. 'I can't talk about this now.'

If I reveal that we broke up because I'm in love with someone else, I'll be laying all of my cards out on the table.

'Yeah, I guess not,' he says gruffly, looking away. 'It's not like I can give you a seven-second hug if you get upset,' he adds, injecting humour into his tone.

I laugh. 'Why not?' Bolstered by how much wine I've had to drink, it comes out sounding a little flirty.

'Do you *want* to get a stiffy against your hip?' he asks with a grin, casting me another sideways look.

I laugh again. 'I thought I wasn't fanciable.'

'I never said you weren't fanciable.' *He remembers that conversation, too.* 'I said *I* didn't fancy you.'

Too well, it seems.

My stomach falls, but before I can swim away, he catches my hand.

'In my defence,' he adds, pulling me back towards him, 'you did have a boyfriend at the time.' He gives me a pointed look and adds, 'You also said you didn't fancy me.'

'I don't feel like that any more,' I whisper, shocking myself. What am I doing?

Unsurprisingly, that comment renders him speechless. I try to extricate my hand, but he grips me harder.

'Bridget?' he questions in a low voice.

'Charlie?' I reply, mimicking his tone. He doesn't smile. He's looking straight at me, deadly serious, and his eyes are glinting in the light from the fairy lights dangling in the trees on the beach.

A shiver ripples through me.

'Are you cold?' he asks, and I wonder if it's an attempt to change the subject. I should be relieved.

But I'm not.

'A little,' I reply.

'You want to get out?'

'No.' *Yes! The answer is yes!* I've had too much to drink. We *both* have. We're not thinking straight.

He brings me closer to his side, so close that I can feel the heat radiating from him. My breast brushes against his bicep and he breathes in sharply, his grip on my hand becoming vice-like. Somewhere in my alcohol–riddled brain I'm aware of just how 'unfriendly' our stance is, but rational thought has completely deserted me.

A long, torturous moment passes when I don't know what's going to happen next. My head is spinning and his gaze is searing as he stares at me in the darkness, and then he turns to face me and slides both of his hands around my waist, slowly pulling me closer until my naked skin collides firmly with his. *Holy shit!* I can feel him down there, pressing against me. My insides turn to liquid.

Without thinking, I slide my fingers up his bare, ripped chest, over his broad shoulders, and into the hair at the nape of his neck. His lips part and an audible groan escapes, and then our mouths come together and the stars above our heads explode with dizzying brilliance.

I gasp into his kiss as his arms lock me hard against his naked, slippery body, shivers spiralling up and down my spine as his tongue strokes against mine. Is this actually happening?

His mouth suddenly slides away. His chest is heaving, but I can sense his hesitation. He meets my eyes again, apprehension beginning to cloud his features.

No… No… We can't go back now.

I press my thumb to his brow and smooth away the lines that have formed there.

This feels too good to stop…

We're obviously in agreement, because suddenly his strong arms are lifting me up, and I'm wrapping my legs around his slim waist, the salty, buoyant water helping to sustain my weight.

We both gasp against each other as he lowers me onto him. It feels so intense, so raw. Our lips stay locked together and the water laps against our skin as he begins to move.

Afterwards, I don't want him to let me go. I stay in his arms, my legs wrapped around him and my face pressed against his neck. He kisses my collarbone.

'We should get back,' he whispers.

I very, very reluctantly let him go.

We wade in silence back to the beach. We didn't bring towels and I feel exposed, but it would be crazy to ask him to turn around after what's just happened. I pull my dress back over my wet body and he does the same with his shorts. Then we pick up our shoes and walk barefoot back to our hut, neither of us saying a word.

I want to ask him if he'll sleep with me tonight, but I sense he might need to gather his thoughts. That was his first time since Nicki died. I only hope he doesn't regret it in the morning.

Chapter 43

When I wake up, all is silent downstairs. I check the time on my phone: nine thirty. *I bet he's taken April for breakfast...*

I lie there for a while, staring up at the ceiling. I can't believe what happened last night. It was incredible, but I feel both blissfully jittery *and* sickeningly nervous at the thought of it. Things got out of hand so quickly. Neither of us had time to stop and think. I know how I feel about him, but how is he coping today? I really hope I haven't messed everything up. So much for taking small *Borrowers*-style steps. That was more like huge, crashing, rampaging, baddies-from-*The BFG* ones.

I feel very unsettled as I get up and go into the bathroom, turning on the shower. I went straight to bed last night and my skin feels tight and dry from the seawater.

I'm dressed and feeling fresher by the time they return, but my nerves are still pulsing away. I watch from the window as Charlie gets April out of her pram, leaving it outside, then I go and open the door for them.

'Hi!' he says with surprise.

'Hi.'

We share a long, lingering look until he breaks the eye contact.

'I brought you some breakfast,' he says as April toddles through the door, into the living room. I gently stroke her light-blonde curls and smile down at her as she passes. Charlie brings out a plate of fresh fruit and pastries from the pram's under-seat basket. 'I didn't know if you'd want something more substantial.'

'This is perfect, thank you.' I take it from him, but he doesn't meet my eyes. I try to exhale deeply to release some of the pressure on my chest as I go and sit on the sofa. 'How are you feeling?' I ask carefully.

'Okay,' he replies, slumping wearily into the armchair. He presses the heels of his palms to his eyes for a long moment.

'You want to talk?' I ask.

'Not now.' He looks at April as she takes pieces of fruit out of the fruit bowl, one by one, and puts them on the coffee table.

Oh, God… He regrets it…

April picks up a bright-pink and lime-green dragon fruit and toddles off to the bedroom with it. I look at Charlie. *Now can we talk?*

'I don't know what to say,' he murmurs.

'You wish it hadn't happened?'

'I don't know,' he says. 'My head's all over the place right now.' He sits forward in his chair, clasping his hands together between his knees. 'This…' He looks around the room. 'This is Nicki's place.' He's not talking about what's within these circular walls: he means the resort. 'She only died a year ago. She *paid* for April and me to come here. It doesn't feel right.' He looks at me directly. 'It feels wrong.'

The blood drains from my face.

He shakes his head, frustrated. 'It didn't *feel* wrong. It *is* wrong.'

'I understand what you're saying.' This is exactly what I feared and I could kick myself for not having more restraint. 'But Charlie...'

'Like I said, my head's all over the place,' he interrupts. 'I need time and space to think, but I don't have time and I *definitely* don't have space.' He casts a significant look at the bedroom, where April is still merrily babbling away.

'I can give you time *and* space,' I say, leaning forward. I'd give anything to be able to take him in my arms, but I know that wouldn't be welcome right now. 'Why don't you go somewhere today? I'll look after April.'

He starts to shake his head.

'I want to,' I insist. 'You could visit one of the caves. Or you could walk up to the top of the cliffs. There's a lake up there. They do guided tours, if you want, or you could just take a map and explore.'

He ponders it. 'What about you?' he asks. 'Don't you need to go to the caves and stuff while you're here?'

'I can go another day,' I reply. 'It's not suitable for children, anyway, so we couldn't bring April with us. Maybe you could take my camera and click off a few photos for me?'

'You're sure?' he asks. He's not taking much persuading – he really does need to get away for a bit.

'Absolutely.'

'Okay.' He stands up and flashes me a small smile before heading into his bedroom.

He hasn't touched me once.

I'd better keep busy today so I don't fret too much. I know exactly where *my* head is at. With a little time and breathing space, hopefully Charlie will see that we can make this work. We have to forge forward now. Going backwards is not an option.

I just hope he agrees with me.

'Bridget's going to look after you today, okay?' Charlie says to April when he re-emerges a few minutes later with her in his arms. He's wearing a hat and trainers, and he has a back-pack slung over his shoulder with two water bottles stashed in the outside pockets.

April stretches her arms out to me and Charlie smiles as he passes her over, all of my hair follicles standing to attention as our arms brush. 'Thank you,' he says, meeting my eyes.

I smile at April. 'We're going to have fun, aren't we?' She smiles back at me and tugs my hair. I tickle her ribs and chastise her jokily. She's still laughing her head off when Charlie goes out of the door.

At lunchtime, April and I wander over to the infinity pool. I order some food and we spend an hour or so splashing around in the baby area. She's fascinated by the older children and I think she'd stay there all day if I didn't have a sleep timetable to stick to. That thought makes me think of Kate.

I know Kate adores her niece – surely she wouldn't let Charlie's love life get in the way of April's happiness? Because any family feud *will* affect her, if not now, then when she's older. I just don't believe Charlie isn't capable of making Kate and Valerie see that we're good for each other; that I could be good for *April*.

Despite all of the inner turmoil I'm feeling about Charlie, the day with his daughter is perfect. My chest keeps expanding with joy – every time April giggles, every time she kisses a baby's face in one of her small cardboard books, every time she does something funny such as splash her face with water and jump with shock. Whatever happens with Charlie, I want to be in April's life. Even if I'm just silly Aunty Bridget.

The thought makes my eyes prick with tears. I don't want to be Aunty Bridget, I want to be more than that. And I really, really mean it, from the deepest depths of my heart. What a turnaround for someone who believed she didn't want to have children.

Charlie returns when April has been down for her afternoon nap for an hour. My heart skips a beat at the sight of his handsome, but exhausted, face.

'Okay?' I ask him cautiously as he comes in the door.

'Yeah.' He nods. 'Thank you.'

'I was about to wake April.' I'm pausing at the entrance to his room.

He indicates for me to lead the way. I set about opening the wooden venetian blinds while he walks over to her cot.

'Baby,' he says softly, leaning in to brush her arm. 'Was everything okay today?' he asks me as daylight begins to fill the room. There are *a lot* of blinds in here.

'It was perfect,' I reply with a smile, nodding at the cot, where April has now woken.

'Hey,' he says sweetly. She makes a sound of annoyance.

'Hello,' I say, going over to peer into her cot.

She glances from him to me, me to him, and then stretches her arms out to me.

'Aah,' I say with delight, bending down to lift her up. As I cuddle her to me, I turn to smile at Charlie. But he doesn't return the warmth of my gaze. In fact, his expression is bleak.

Alain is expecting us for an early dinner at his restaurant tonight. Apparently, he wasn't happy at breakfast when Charlie refused his offer of lining up another babysitter so we could enjoy his full five-star dining experience. Charlie said he thought two sitters in two nights was excessive, so we'd eat early and bring April with us.

I have a feeling he's also trying to avoid a repeat of last night.

We didn't get much of a chance to speak earlier, so I bring my camera with me and, when we're settled, I ask him to talk me through the shots he took up on the cliff top. As the evening wears on, he seems to feel more at ease in my company.

I'm longing to be tactile with him, but, when I touch his hand, he withdraws, putting it under the table. He glances towards the restaurant, and I know he's worried that Alain might see us and draw conclusions. I hope that's all it is.

Later, when April's in bed, I ask Charlie if he'd like to watch a film.

'I think I might be too tired,' he replies, looking at me apologetically from his position on the armchair. 'Sorry,' he adds when my face falls.

I'm trying so hard to return us to a happier, more normal place. Well, normal is the wrong word, but I'd do anything to relieve some of the awkwardness and tension that's vibrating between us.

He obviously feels sorry for me, because he says, 'Do you want to put some music on?'

He knows what will cheer me up. I smile at him and head spiritedly towards the stairs, returning with my speaker. I find the song I want and press PLAY before turning around to catch him observing me.

He realises I've chosen 'Up Where We Belong' by Joe Cocker and Jennifer Warnes from the moment the piano starts to play. It's that instantly recognisable. His lips curve upwards as I raise one eyebrow at him, and then Jennifer Warnes begins to sing.

'*Who knows what tomorrow brings...*'

He laughs under his breath as I melodramatically and earnestly lip-sync to the lyrics from my standing position in the middle of the living space. I nod at him pointedly, urging him to come in when it's time for Joe Cocker's lines, but he shakes his head, smirking at me, so I act out his part instead, clapping my hand to my heart and pretending to climb mountains. He looks amused, but he's still not singing.

I sigh and throw myself into the chorus and he, in turn, throws his head back and laughs. I'm still trying to get him to join in with me – *don't leave me hanging, buddy* – but he resists.

I sway back and forth when Joe Cocker takes on the second verse, sighing dreamily as though I'm deeply in love – which I am, by the way – and then I take over again when Jennifer Warnes sings her part, pretending to be solemn and serious, while also thinking, *Jesus, these lyrics are really fucking appropriate, actually.*

I prompt him again when it comes to the chorus. *Come on, Charlie, meet me halfway here!* And then he does it! He screws up his face and mimics it perfectly. I burst out laughing, so full of love for him.

As the chorus repeats, I walk over to him, no longer lip-syncing along. His eyebrows pull together when I climb onto his lap. *Going backwards is not an option…* He doesn't stop me, and, when the song finally fades away, we're still staring at each other. I slowly bend down and brush my lips against his. He lets me, even though I know he's feeling torn right now. I'm straddling his lap and his body responds beneath me when we deepen our kiss.

'Bridget…' he whispers against my lips.

I try to kiss his worries away.

Chapter 44

I wake up with a start. Through a crack in my blinds, I can see that it's still dark outside. My eyes are stinging and my body is weighed down with exhaustion, so I don't know what roused me. I turn my head to see Charlie, fast asleep in my bed beside me. My butterflies go berserk at the memory of all of the intimate things we did to each other last night.

Then I hear her: *April.*

I climb quickly out of bed and pull on my robe, shutting the door behind me so Charlie doesn't wake up, before hurrying downstairs.

April starts to cry properly as I approach her cot, so I murmur soothingly. She reaches up to me. I know I should probably try to settle her in her cot like Charlie does, but I can't resist. I pick her up and cradle her in my arms and her crying stops instantly.

It's cold in her room – did we leave the air conditioning on? Damn, we did – obviously had other things on our minds. I walk over and switch it off while singing to her quietly. Her eyes are wide and they're staring up at me in the darkness. I brush my finger across her cheek and smile down at her, my heart threatening to burst.

I know I shouldn't bring her into bed with me, but her arms and legs are cold and I want to warm her up. I pull back the covers of Charlie's bed and slide in between the cool sheets, drawing her close and humming until she falls back asleep in my arms.

That's how Charlie finds us the next morning.

'Hey,' I whisper, smiling up at him sleepily. April is still out cold.

'Hi,' he whispers in return, but he's not smiling. He looks deeply apprehensive.

'What's wrong?' I ask with alarm.

The shutters come down on his eyes. 'We'll talk later.'

My insides turn to ice.

'Have you got some work you can do today?' he asks me over breakfast. He did the thing with his hand again, drawing it away when I tried to touch him.

'Yes, why?'

'Alain has some time off. He'd like to spend our last day with April and me.'

'Oh, okay.' I understand why they'd want it to be just the three of them, but I can't say I'm not disappointed.

'I thought I'd see if we can get the sitter again tonight. We could eat at the restaurant in the cave.'

From his detached tone, I have the feeling this is not another date night. Seems like it's time for our talk…

I spend the day exploring the area, taking photographs and making notes, but although the setting inspires me, I can't get rid of the nausea that's constantly churning away.

Charlie returns early that evening and my pulse races at the sight of him, but, when I ask if I can help with April's bedtime routine, he turns me down.

'Just let me get her sorted tonight,' he says, giving me a pleading look before he goes into his room and shuts the door behind him.

Later that night, we find ourselves in one of the most romantic, picturesque places in the world. Our tables are set upon the sand and over our heads, stalactites drip down from the cave ceiling, while out in front of us, Thailand's ethereal islands seem to float away in the distance, on top of the calm, still water.

I can't enjoy a second of it.

'Can you tell me what's going through your mind?' I ask gently.

'I'm still trying to work it out.' His voice is heavy as he stares into his wineglass. 'I just want to do the best thing for April.'

'You think I'd ever hurt her?'

'You're *already* hurting her.' I breathe in sharply at his words. 'She's already developed an attachment to you that's causing her pain.' He leans forward in his seat, pinning me with a disconcertingly hard stare. 'The weeks after you left were *tough*. She didn't just miss you: she *pined* for you. She's getting older now, she's starting to understand. I can't have her thinking you're her mother if you're just going to up and leave us when you get bored.'

'*Charlie!*' I gasp.

'It's true, isn't it?' he asks challengingly. 'It's not like you haven't done that before.' His eyes are glimmering in the candlelight, but he's not upset: he's determined. 'I don't want the next piece of your heart, Bridget.'

I recoil, stunned.

'No.' I shake my head. 'You don't get it. You think this is just another relationship for me.' I don't give him a chance to confirm or deny it. 'You're wrong,' I state. 'I've never felt like this before. I really think this is it.'

'And your blog?'

'To hell with my blog! I'll tear it down. I'm done with it. I'm never going to post another entry again, I swear. I don't want to! It means nothing, Charlie. Not any more. You and April are the only things I care about.'

He averts his gaze, unconvinced.

'Charlie,' I plead. 'What about last night?'

He looks tortured as he returns his eyes to me and whispers, 'I'm just a man, Bridget.'

He might as well have slapped me.

'So you can have sex with me but you can't fall in love with me?' I'm fighting not to raise my voice.

'Argh, Bridget, it was the anniversary of Nicki's death only two weeks ago!' he snaps with frustration. 'Surely you get that it's too soon for me to start something new.'

'I understand, of course I do, but—'

He cuts me off. 'It's not that I don't have feelings for you, because I do, and *obviously* I'm attracted to you, but I need space to come to terms with everything. The best thing for April and me is to go home to Cornwall and try to get back to normal.'

He has my heart in his fist and he's squeezing.

I knew it was too soon for him. I knew nothing could – *should* – ever happen here in Thailand. But it did. And now I have to live with it. As mistakes go, this one is catastrophic.

'You need to put your head down, too,' he says softly as my eyes fill with tears. It hurts so much. 'This book is due in less than three months. We owe it to Nicki to do it right – and her family, too. Let's see how things stand next year.'

'But April will change so much in the next few months! I don't want to go that long without seeing her!'

'I'm sorry,' he says, quietly. 'But it won't do her any good if you just drop in on her from time to time. She needs stability in her life right now.'

I can tell by the look in his eyes that he's resolute. Nothing I say will convince him. This is not our time.

I get up and walk out of the restaurant before I lose it.

They leave the next day, whereas I still have one more day to get through. It's everything I can do not to cry as the boat draws away with April looking at me over her shoulder. I wave at her, and when she flops her little hand back and forth in an attempt to mimic my gesture, my heart shatters.

Whatever happens with Charlie, I know that I'll do my best to pick myself up and glue back the pieces. I don't believe that I'll ever again love anyone else the way that I love him, but I *will* live.

But, if I never see April again, it'll break me.

Turns out it wasn't a man who had the last piece of my heart, after all.

It was a baby girl.

Chapter 45

I'm a mess when I return to London, but I have to pull myself together and focus. I'm determined to do the very best job that I can with this book. I want to do it for April. I want to do it for Charlie. I want to do it for Valerie, Kate and Alain, too.

But, most of all, I want to do it for Nicki.

I *do* owe her that much.

I spend long days at my writing desk, pouring my heart and soul into every single page. Marty comes over occasionally with bottles of wine and attempts to cheer me up, but I'm not much in the mood for socialising. She's worried because she's never seen me like this. My grief feels soul-deep, and I don't know how I'll ever recover.

Marty was both pensive and sympathetic when I told her about what happened in Thailand, but she understands that I have to prioritise my work right now so she doesn't put pressure on me to talk too much about what I'm going through.

It's hard to write about Thailand without thinking about Charlie and what happened there, but Kit's pain feels real, because mine is, too, and I don't hold back. I just hope that my emotion comes across to my – no, *Nicki's* – readers.

Sometimes I call Fay, and Sara, too, when the pressure gets to me and I need help in finding my way through the trees. Fay usually encourages me to take a long walk or to read a book. Once, she even suggested I go and see a movie – anything to get me out of my head and unlock my writer's block. 'Beauty inspires beauty,' she said. Music also helps to motivate me.

I've taken down the blog and have told Sara that I can't write my book. She understood. After all, one day I was supposed to be writing about a marriage proposal from Elliot, so, when we broke up, she saw my happy ending flying right out of the window. I feel terrible for wasting so much of her time, but I couldn't go back to it.

I may write another novel one day when the dust from this one has settled. But, if all I ever do is write travel pieces, well, I'd still count myself lucky.

When I told Fay what I had in mind for Kit, she wasn't at all sure. She thought Kit ending up sad and alone sounded like a real downer, but she told me to go with my heart.

I'm a little surprised when my heart leads me in a different direction…

Morris does divorce Kit because he wants children and she continues to pretend that she doesn't. She's determined to stick to the vow she once made to herself: that she won't bring a baby into the mess she's created.

She's devastated to lose Morris, but she finds some relief in being just with Timo. Finally, she can live a normal married life.

She moves to Thailand permanently, but she soon discovers that she doesn't know Timo as well as she thought she did. Their relationship was built on rocky ground and worked because it was so highly charged – every time they parted ways, the anguish over Kit returning to England for long lengths of time would drive their passion. Eventually, that passion levels out and, within the course of three years, Kit's desire for a baby overcomes her. But Timo is adamant that he doesn't want one, so their marriage ultimately breaks down, and Kit returns to Cornwall.

Kit has missed Morris terribly and she's crushed to learn that he's now married to someone else, with a baby of his own on the way. He's where he sought to be in life and she's happy for him, but inside she's tormented. She still loves him, but she also wants the best for him, so she vows to herself that she'll keep her distance from him and his family.

Then she finds out that she's pregnant with Timo's baby and he is *furious* when she calls to tell him. He asks her to terminate the pregnancy, but she refuses, saying that she'll raise it herself.

She pours all of the love that she has into her baby – a little girl she names Aubrey.

As the years pass, Aubrey starts asking questions about her father, and Timo eventually comes around to the idea of having a relationship with his daughter. Kit and Timo become friends, and, when Aubrey is old enough, she visits Thailand on her own to spend time with her dad.

Kit loves being a mother more than anything else in the world.

But it's not enough.

She has short-lived romances, but her feelings for other men pale in comparison to what she felt for Morris and Timo. She experienced the deepest kind of love – *twice*. If only it hadn't been at the same time.

Cornwall is a small world, and sometimes Kit sees Morris from afar with his beautiful wife and three sons and wonders how things might've been if she'd never met Timo on that work trip to Thailand.

But, if she'd never met Timo, Aubrey wouldn't exist, and having her daughter is something she will never regret.

When I finish writing the last page, I burst into tears. It's a long time before I've composed myself, but, once I have, I pick up the phone and call Charlie. He's the first – the only – person I want to share my news with tonight.

My heart thuds dully as his mobile rings out and goes to voicemail.

I send him a text: *'Just finished the book. Wanted to say hello.'*

He replies almost straight away and I'm crushed, knowing that he likely let his phone ring out on purpose: *'Well done. I'm proud of you.'*

It's been two and a half months since Thailand and he still won't speak to me. When will he agree to *see* me? April is growing and changing with every week that passes – how much of her life am I going to miss out on before he comes around? What if he doesn't? The more time that passes, the more terrified I feel.

What if the next time I see them is at the launch party for Nicki's book? It will have been almost a year. April will be speaking. She will have grown so much. She won't even remember me. Charlie will be distant, detached, just getting on with his life and putting the past behind him. The pain I feel upon conjuring up this image is colossal.

I can't let it come to that.

My phone buzzes again with another message from Charlie: '*April and I are visiting Valerie and Kate in a few weeks – maybe we could catch up for lunch on our way to Essex?*'

'*I'd love that,*' I text back, my spirits rising. Does this mean there's still hope for us?

Or does he just want us to be friends?

A few weeks away feels like a lifetime. It's already been so long.

Somehow I've got to convince him that we'd be good together. Charlie is like no one else I've ever known. He's so determined and driven and he's always set on doing what's right.

But this time he's wrong. How can I make him see that? I've never been in this position before so I don't know what to do and I'm not sure who I can ask.

'*You can always ask me…*'

I jerk as a memory comes back to me. Pat. Charlie's mother. What was it she said?

'*Charlie's not much of a talker. And he finds it very hard to talk about Nicki. So, if there's anything you need to know about her, them, whatever, then you can always ask me… I'll give you my number so you have it if you need it.*'

At the time, I thought that, if it didn't feel right asking Charlie something, I wouldn't feel comfortable asking his mother. I didn't even need her help because he opened up to me himself, despite not being 'much of a talker'.

Without thinking about it, I search for her number in my contacts and call her.

'Hello?' she answers warily.

'Pat, hello, it's Bridget!' I say, hoping that the caution in her tone is just because the caller ID displayed an unknown number.

'Bridget!' she exclaims. 'Hello there, love, how are you doing?'

I exhale with relief. She genuinely seems pleased to hear from me.

'I'm okay, thank you,' I reply, wondering if Charlie has told her anything about us. 'I've finished writing Nicki's book.'

'Oh, that's fantastic! Well done! Are you happy with it?'

'I think so. I only reached the end tonight, so obviously no one's read it, yet, but hopefully Fay will think I've done a good job.'

'I'm sure she will.'

Nerves crash through me. 'Um, do you remember once offering me your help if I ever needed it?'

'Yes. Is there something you'd like to know?'

'I need to ask you a question.'

'Okay...'

I take a deep breath. 'I'm in love with your son,' I blurt. 'I love Charlie. And I love April. And I think that Charlie might love me, but he's scared. He's scared that this is just another relationship for me – and *I don't blame him for coming to that conclusion*,' I say quickly. 'But he's wrong. Please, he's so wrong.'

I'm panting, clutching my hand to my chest.

'Are you there?' I ask.

It's gone very quiet at the other end of the line.

'I'm here,' she says. 'But you haven't actually asked me a question.' She sounds amused.

I laugh. 'Oh, God, okay. Do you think that he loves me, too?'

She chuckles under her breath. 'I think that, in this instance, Bridget, this really *is* a question for Charlie…'

'Oh, Pat, I *want* to ask him! But I'm not sure he'll admit to it! He was so steadfast in Thailand about doing the best thing for April, but I believe I could be good for her – for him. We could make this work.'

There's a long moment of silence. 'I agree with you, love. Charlie was broken before you came along. He was lost. You made him laugh again. You brought joy back into that house. He was crushed when you left Cornwall. You're right. He *is* scared. He's scared of giving his heart away and never getting it back again.'

Whoa, she used to read my blog?

'I want his heart,' I say firmly. 'I want it forever.'

'You'd better come and get it, then,' she replies.

I drive through the night, not wanting to miss another minute without Charlie and April in my life. If I have to become a mad stalker and camp in his tiny front garden for the foreseeable future, then so be it. I'd even stand there and play my music to him, like John Cusack at the end of the eighties classic *Say Anything*. I might need a more powerful speaker but, fuck it, I'll try anything.

It's four thirty in the morning when I pull up on his street. The sun is still several hours away beneath the horizon, and as I sit there, staring at the quiet, dark house, I wish I'd thought through my timings a little better.

Dad's right: it *is* quicker to drive through the night. But what am I going to do now?

If only I had…

Oh, my God! I *do* still have a key! Charlie never asked for it back and I completely forgot to give it to him!

I lie. I kept it on purpose, like the crazy stalker that I am.

I dig around in my bag and pull it out, triumphant. Then, with my pulse going haywire, I get out of the car, walk up the path and insert the key in the lock.

If the alarm goes off, I'm busted.

I hold my breath, hoping he's not about to come downstairs brandishing a baseball bat.

But nothing. Phew.

I very quietly close the door behind me and stand there, letting my eyes adjust to the darkness. My heart contracts, knowing that the two people I love most in this world are upstairs, fast asleep. I really don't want to completely freak Charlie out by appearing in his bedroom like an apparition, but I can't – *I just can't* – go any longer before seeing him again.

I head upstairs, pausing outside April's room before deciding that, *no*, standing over her cot really would be too creepy.

I walk further along the corridor and halt again.

What am I doing? I'm probably going to give him a heart attack. For a moment I consider going back downstairs and waiting in my car until the sun comes up, but I decide to press on.

I take a deep breath and walk into his room. The sound of his steady breathing fills the air. I go and kneel at the side of his bed and look at his tranquil face.

'Charlie,' I whisper, brushing my hand over his arm. 'Charlie?'

He jolts awake, his eyes widening as they turn from hazy to sharp.

'Bridget?'

'I don't mean to terrify you, but I've driven all through the night to get here. Please don't throw me out.'

He stares at me for a long moment, obviously surprised, but then he edges over in his bed and lifts up the cover of his duvet for me.

I'm filled with hope as I slide in next to him. We face each other in the darkness, pillow to pillow.

'What are you doing here?' he whispers.

'I love you,' I say. 'And I'm not giving up, because I believe you love me too.'

He doesn't deny it.

'I've missed you so much.' Emotion suddenly overcomes me and my eyes fill with tears. I cup the side of his face with my hand. 'Please let me be a part of your life, Charlie. You have my *whole* heart. You and April. I've never loved anyone more. I'd give up my flat in London in a heartbeat and move to Cornwall tomorrow, if you'd let me. I want to be with you forever. I want us to be a family.'

A beat passes. 'Come here,' he says gruffly, drawing me against his body. He kisses me gently and a shiver runs down my spine, but I'm scared of this just being sex. Perhaps he senses my reticence, because he pulls away. 'I love you too,' he says, tucking a lock of hair behind my ear. 'I've loved you for a long time. I don't even know when I started loving you because there've been so many moments that made me love you. Does that make sense? I just needed time to come to terms with everything. I had to be sure. I needed *you* to be sure.'

'I *am* sure.' A tear slides from my eye.

'I'm sorry I hurt you,' he whispers, pulling me into the crook of his arm. 'I'll try not to do that again.'

I wrap my arms around his neck, wanting to get as close to him as possible. He tightens his grip on me so our bodies are completely flush to each other.

'You really do give the best hugs,' I say after a while.

'One…' he murmurs, 'two… three…' – I smile and kiss him – 'four…' he says against my mouth.

'Seven seconds won't be enough, you know,' I warn.

He smiles at me in the darkness. 'I'm okay with that.'

Epilogue

We get married in Lansallos church and make the whole congregation walk half a mile down the steep hill to the beach for a picnic reception. Marty, my mum and Wendy are just three of the women who openly complain to me about both the walk *and* not being able to wear heels, but I think even they accept our decision when they see the view.

Charlie proposed to me on this same beach, the week after April's second birthday. April is a couple of months short of three years old when we tie the knot, and she makes such a beautiful flower girl.

Adam is Charlie's best man and gives the funniest, most heartfelt speech any of us have ever heard. Even my friend Bronte confirms it, and she's a wedding photographer, so she's heard plenty. She comes all the way over from Australia for me to do the photos, and she brings with her a card from Elliot, wishing me all the love and luck in the world. Despite her fondness for Elliot, she hit it off with Charlie immediately. How could she not?

Marty is my chief bridesmaid, not my matron of honour. I'll have that title when she marries Ted later this year; she's piqued that I beat her to it, but she wanted a longer engagement than I did…

Our friend Laura comes, too, bringing with her a brand-new baby boy. Jocelyn, Edward and Thomas – our now good friends – also join the celebrations, and Charlie's other pals arrive in force, seeming genuinely happy that he's found love again.

I wish I could say the same about Kate and Valerie. Relations are still strained, but Charlie and I won't give up trying to build bridges. A few months after I moved to Cornwall permanently, which wasn't that long after I had finished writing the book, I drove to Essex to speak to them both. I wanted them to know how much I love April, and how I will always respect Nicki's memory and make sure April does, too. They were still very saddened at that time about Charlie moving on, but they did extend an olive branch by coming to April's second birthday party. They say they'll be at her third, too, but they declined our wedding invitation. We understood, of course, but at least they knew that they were welcome. Alain wished us all the best and encouraged us to go back to Thailand soon to see him. We said we'd certainly try.

Confessions of Us was an immediate bestseller, but the reviews were mixed. Some journalists loved the book; others thought Kit should've been brought to justice. As for the reader reviews, many wished Kit had ended up with Morris, with one girl even claiming that she hurled her book across the room when he demanded a divorce. I think I might've poured more passion into him than Timo. It's no surprise why.

I'm still not sure if my ending was what Nicki had foreseen for her story. But, as Charlie said, maybe even *she* didn't know where it was going.

I can only hope that I've done her proud.

Charlie, April and I still live in Cornwall and our new house is warm, happy and full of love, laughter, hugs and music. He still creates beautiful things with his hands; I'm now writing a novel of my own, which Sara and Fay say they're looking forward to reading. I also still write about the places I visit – albeit with my family, most of the time.

As for my darling adopted daughter April, she still has the last piece of my heart. And I'll never ask for it back.

Ever.

Bridget's Playlist

'Tainted Love' by Marilyn Manson

'U Can't Touch This' by MC Hammer

'The Sun Always Shines on TV' by A-ha

'It's Still Rock and Roll to Me' by Billy Joel

'Ice Ice Baby' by Vanilla Ice

'Unbelievable' by EMF

'Pour Some Sugar on Me' by Def Leppard

'Frankie Sinatra' by the Avalanches

'Hold Tight!' by Dave Dee, Dozy, Beaky, Mick & Tich

'Downtown' by Macklemore & Ryan Lewis

'A View to a Kill' by Duran Duran

'One Piece at a Time' by Johnny Cash

'Lose Yourself' by Eminem

'Let Me Clear My Throat' by DJ Kool

'Somewhere Over the Rainbow' by Israel Kamakawiwoʻole

'MMMBop' by Hanson

'Super Rat' by Honeyblood

'Up Where We Belong' by Joe Cocker and Jennifer Warnes

Acknowledgements

The first person I want to thank is YOU! I truly believe I have some of the loveliest, most passionate readers in the world, so thank you to anyone who's shared my books with their friends or taken the time to let me know what they think of my stories on Twitter, Facebook or Instagram. (Find me under PaigeToonAuthor if you haven't already.)

There are so many fantastic people working behind the scenes at Simon & Schuster, but I've got to know the following well, so heartfelt thanks to my wonderful editor of eleven years, Suzanne Baboneau, her awesome wing-woman, Emma Capron, and also the brilliant Jessica Barratt, Dawn Burnett, Sara-Jade Virtue, Jo Dickinson, Dominic Brendon, Joe Roche, Sally Wilks, Laura Hough, Rumana Haider, Richard Vlietstra, Louise Blakemore, and last but not least, Pip Watkins, for yet another beautiful cover design.

Thank you also to the team at David Higham and my agent, Lizzy Kremer, for her spot-on suggestions and advice.

Thank you to my friend and fellow author Ali Harris, who has always been a great sounding board for my books (in fact, I came up with the ghost writing element of this story when Ali and I were on our way to an event and another car almost crashed into us. I was writing *The Sun in Her Eyes* and approaching a particularly juicy scene, and thought, if anything happened to me and S&S brought in a ghost writer, I'd come back and haunt them until they got my story exactly right! Anyway, this book comes minus the ghosts – I think I'll leave supernatural thrillers to others, for the time being...)

Thank you also to my lovely friends Jane Hampton and Katherine Reid for their proof reading and suggestions – your help is always deeply appreciated.

The Last Piece of My Heart is set mainly in Cornwall and Thailand, and a tiny bit in Ireland, and many of the scenes and locations are inspired by actual events.

Heartfelt thanks to our good friends, Georgie, Lewis, Betty and Wilf Barnes for our amazing Cornish camping holiday (Hermie is actually real, FYI – I penned part of this story sitting in him down the back of our garden).

And thank you to my parents, Jen and Vern Schuppan, and Kerrin, Miranda and Ripley Schuppan. I had one of the best holidays of my life at the Rayavadee Resort in Thailand, and it made me smile when my editor suggested it all sounded a little too perfect. Honestly, it was.

Thank you also to Clodagh Quinn and her family for inspiring some of the Ireland-set scenes. Such a beautiful country.

I'd also like to give a special mention to the real-life music man, Jeremy, who is not based in Padstow, but North London. The memories I have of taking my kids to his music sessions are priceless (check out Jeremy's Music Session on Facebook if you're local to the area).

Thank you to my husband, Greg Toon, who never lets me gush about him in my acknowledgements anywhere near as much as I'd like to. He is incredibly (controlling – ha!) supportive and creative and I am grateful to him in countless ways.

And finally, thank you to my children, Indy and Idha, who will one day read this story and realise just how much of it they inspired. I love you so much and couldn't do any of this without you.

(Please remember though, when you *are* old enough to read this book, it wasn't Mum swearing, it was Bridget.)

To find out more about Paige or her characters, visit her website, www.paigetoon.com where you can sign up to receive free extra content and short stories via her newsletter, *The Hidden Paige*.

www.paigetoon.com
#TheHiddenPaige
Twitter @PaigeToonAuthor
Facebook.com/PaigeToonAuthor
Instagram.com/PaigeToonAuthor

Turn the page to read an extract from

the **ONE**
we fell in
LOVE with

Prologue

Angus

She's here. I'm instantly tense. The people around here are mistaken. They *don't* all look alike. She's special. She's different. She's the most beautiful girl I've ever seen.

I watch her in a daze through the crowded, smoky air as she gets herself a beer from the makeshift bar. I want to go over to her, but I stay where I am, leaning against the door-frame. After what happened last night, she has to come to me. But I don't know if she will. I've been worried she wouldn't even turn up.

She swigs from her bottle, then looks around the packed living room, taking everything in. She's late and everyone else is well on their way to oblivion. Turning up at a party alone at this hour is brave. It wouldn't surprise me if she walked right back out again. That thought messes with my head, and it's already messed up enough. I can't believe I've let her get to me like this.

I watch, fixated, as she puts the bottle back to her lips and then suddenly her eyes lock with mine. I force myself to stare back at her.

She smiles at me and the relief is instant. I jerk my head backwards, willing her to come over. Still smiling, she slowly makes her way through the packed space, squeezing through bodies until she's right in front of me.

'Hey,' I say, reaching down to touch my fingertips to hers.

'Hi.' She closes her hand into a fist.

Okay, so we're not cool. Her gorgeous eyes are wide as she stares up at me. My gaze drops to her lips. They're shiny, like she's just applied lip gloss. I want to lick it off her.

Bloody hell, I'm drunk.

'How was dinner?' I ask.

'It was fine!' She shouts. I can't hear her next words because the music is too loud.

'What did you say?' I shout back, cupping her head with my hand and pulling her closer.

'I said it's noisy!'

'Yeah,' I reply with a grin. 'Sorry, I'm a bit pissed.' I speak right into her ear.

'Lucky you.'

She is so sexy. Her hair is soft under my fingers. I run my thumb across her temple and she puts her hand on my chest. I think she's trying to keep me at bay, but it's not working. Her touch almost does me in.

I take her hands and pull her closer.

'Angus?' She sounds uncertain as I touch my forehead to hers. I know I'm making her uncomfortable in front of all these people, but I need to be with her. I want her so much. *Too* much.

Determination surges through me. 'Come with me,' I say firmly, putting our beers on a nearby table. I grab her hand and tug her out of the living room. My head is spinning as I push open the door to the cloakroom under the stairs. I pull her inside and hear her gasp as I slam the door shut behind her. Then my mouth is on hers. I hear her sharp intake of breath as my tongue pushes her lips apart. She hesitates only a little before kissing me back. I could kiss her forever.

'I want you,' I murmur into her mouth, pressing myself up against her so she can feel how much.

Her breath quickens as I slide my hand up inside her T-shirt.

'I want you,' I say again, and then she silences me with fast, hungry kisses and I know that I've got her. She's mine.

Someone turns the doorknob and I whip my hand out from under her T-shirt and slam my palm against the door, keeping it shut.

'Go upstairs,' I shout, locking the door. 'Whoops.' I laugh under my breath as I pull her body flush to mine. But she's tensed again. 'It's alright,' I tell her, my hand returning to the hem of her shirt. But this time she catches it, stopping me in my tracks.

'What… We… What are you doing?' she asks, even more breathless than before.

'What do you think I'm doing?' I ask in a low voice, kissing her neck. We're picking up from where we left off last night. She needs to know what she does to me.

'Angus, stop!' she says loudly.

Oh fuck. Ice freezes my stomach and I jerk away from her, reaching for the pull cord to flood the room with light. She flinches at the brightness, instinctively lifting her hands up to block it. She squints at me from under the shade of her fingers and I stare back at her with horror.

Same greeny-gold eyes… Same light-blonde hair… *Not* the same girl. 'Oh…' I say. 'I thought you were—'

Rose

Phoebe

Eliza

You could say we're freaks of nature.

We look exactly the same with our blonde hair and green eyes, and we all carry the same genetic material. One of us could literally commit murder and blame it on the others without our DNA giving us away.

Identical triplets are formed when a single fertilised egg splits into two, and one of the resulting two eggs splits again. The odds of this happening could be anything from 1 in 60,000 to 1 in 200 million, but one thing's for certain: identical triplets are very, very rare.

When our parents brought us home from the hospital, they were *terrified* about mixing us up. Apparently we wore our hospital armbands until they grew too tight, and even after Mum snipped the bands off, she painted each of our little fingernails a different colour. Sometimes she's still baffled about who's who in our baby photographs.

But even though we look the same, and even though we came from the same, single, fertilised egg, we were separated into three before our mother even knew she was pregnant.

And here's the crux of it: we were born three *completely different* individuals.

As time passed and our personalities began to shine through, Mum and Dad came to realise that we actually had very little in common.

Yes, we could all scream very loudly.

And yes, we were all extremely stubborn.

But that was about it.

Until we were seventeen, that is. Because when we were seventeen, Angus Templeton moved in next door. And unfortunately, all three of us fell head over heels in love with him.

Part One

Chapter 1

Phoebe

When people say they're living in the shadow of the mountain, it sounds kind of ominous. But there's nothing ominous about this. The mountain is so close, I feel like I'm *in* it. I can't even see the top unless I sit down on the sofa, and then my eye line reaches right up to the snowy peaks. What I wouldn't give to be up there...

'Why are you sighing?'

I jolt at the sound of Josie's voice, glancing over my shoulder to see my best friend gazing down at me. 'Nothing. I'm just happy to be back.' I smile warmly.

It's been almost ten years since we first came to Chamonix together at the age of eighteen.

'What time did you get up?' Josie asks, belatedly noticing that I'm fully dressed.

'An hour or so ago,' I reply, tightening my ponytail high up on my head.

'What's wrong with you?' she grumbles, not expecting an

answer as she flops onto the sofa beside me and yawns. Her medium-length dark hair is all tangled and her blue eyes look half asleep. She's still gorgeous, though.

'Coffee?' I ask, bounding to my feet and heading into the small kitchen.

'Yes, please,' she replies.

We only arrived yesterday, and last night we hit an old haunt and drank one beer too many. To Josie's irritation, I rarely suffer with hangovers, but then again, *I* managed to avoid being roped into the shots she did at midnight.

I switch on the radio and set about making the coffee, humming along to the music while she chills out.

'What do you want to do today?' she calls.

'Climb a mountain.' I poke my head around the door and flash her a hopeful grin.

'Noooooo. No, no, no, no, no.' Josie shakes her head adamantly and I continue with my task, chuckling to myself.

'Sorry,' she says, taking her cup from me when I reappear. 'I don't want to spoil your fun.'

I frown at her. 'Don't be silly.'

I'm getting married in two weeks, and all I wanted to do hen-wise was to come back here for a few days with my closest friend. I've thought a lot about Chamonix over the years, and as Josie and I experienced it together, it felt right that we should return, just the two of us.

My sisters were a little put out at not being invited, but now they've made other plans. Eliza and I are going to see a band in Manchester and Rose has organised a spa day. It'll be great to have some one-on-one time with each of them. We don't get to do that nearly enough these days.

'So, aside from climbing a mountain, what else could we do?' Josie perseveres.

'Paraglide off one?' I ask hopefully.

She pulls a face. 'You know I don't do extreme sports. I'm a boring mummy these days.'

Josie has a one-year-old son, Harry, back at home and this is the first time she's been away from him.

'How about we go on the Aiguille?' I suggest. 'You haven't seen the top at this time of year.'

She went home towards the end of the winter season in March all those years ago, but I managed to secure a contract working on the Aiguille du Midi cable car. I loved life here so much that I ended up staying on through the summer.

'Okay, sure,' she agrees, nodding. 'Guess I'd better get cracking then. I assume we'll have to queue for ages like all the other tourists?'

'Mmm, unfortunately. I don't know anyone who works there any more.'

The thought makes my heart squeeze.

A couple of hours later, we're nearly 4,000 metres above sea level on the highest and most famous of the Aiguilles de Chamonix.

I feel giddy with elation. Or maybe it's the altitude. Whatever it is, I'm ecstatic to be back.

'Wow,' Josie murmurs as we stand in quiet reverence on the panoramic viewing platform. 'I'd forgotten how beautiful it is up here.'

I gaze around at the jagged browny-grey peaks of the surrounding mountains. Mont Blanc is ahead of us and carpeted with snow, nonchalantly indifferent to the fact that it's summer. It looks deceptively close, but the way from here to its summit is one of the more technical climbing routes. I know because I've done it, as well as another route that is slightly less challenging, but not to be underestimated.

'I can't believe you climbed the White Lady twice.' Josie appears to be reading my mind.

'Neither can I,' I reply, as another of Mont Blanc's nicknames comes back to me: *White Killer...* It's hard to keep track of how many people have lost their lives trying to reach the top of Western Europe's highest summit, not to mention those who have perished coming back down again.

'*Getting to the top is only halfway*', my dad used to say. The thought of him here, now, brings with it a sharp sense of loss.

Dad died of a heart attack eight years ago, and I miss him so much, especially here in the mountains. He was the person who taught me how to climb.

Josie snorts with amusement, oblivious to the dark turn my thoughts have taken. 'You are such a jammy git. Did you really get paid to stay overnight up here? What a view to wake up to!'

I can't help but smile again. 'Well, there are no windows in the staff apartment,' I tell her. 'But yeah, it was pretty ridiculous walking outside in the morning.'

When Josie and I first came to Chamonix, we started off as chambermaids, but when she went home, I set my sights higher — a *lot* higher.

I'd made friends with a few locals, and one of them, Cécile, worked here on the Aiguille du Midi. The likelihood of a non-Chamoniard securing a contract on the cable cars was so low that it barely seemed worth applying – once you got a contract, you didn't let it go. But my French was fluent and Cécile promised to put in a good word for me, so I sent in my CV. When a couple of full-timers unexpectedly quit citing personal reasons, I got a lucky break.

It's hard to convey how much I loved it. I had to do everything from manning the cable cars to picking up litter, but the icing on the cake came once a month, when two of us would be guardians of the top, staying overnight in the staff apartment three floors down from where Josie and I are standing now. We were the last people to see the sun set at night and the first to see it rise the next morning. The experience was unforgettable.

My thoughts flit away from me again and suddenly I'm on the footbridge, the sky tinged orange and the mountains jagged silhouettes all around. For a few moments, I let my mind drift, before gathering myself together.

'Let's go to the ridge,' I prompt Josie, bumping her arm.

Soon afterwards we're in a shiny, dark, hollowed-out, frozen tunnel and, as I breathe in the cold air, I hear the familiar scritch-scratch of crampons on boots digging into densely packed snow. In the oddest way, I feel like I've come home.

There are three climbers ahead, preparing to set off down the ridge, and as they make their way through the gate, I move out of the ice cave and into the light. I watch as they set off down the narrow snow track, tethered together by rope.

'Freaking nutters,' Josie says under her breath, casting me a look. 'And you're a nutter as well.'

I smile a small smile. 'It feels like a long time since I did that.'

'You don't really go climbing much these days,' she observes.

'Hardly ever,' I reply quietly.

'Do you miss—'

'Yes,' I interrupt, then smile at her properly. 'I need to get my act together.'

She smiles back at me. 'Plenty of time for that. What do you reckon, lunch?'

'Good plan.'

BANYAN TREE
-VABBINFARU-

WIN A HOLIDAY OF A LIFETIME AT BANYAN TREE VABBINFARU IN THE MALDIVES!

Included in the prize:

- A seven night stay at Banyan Tree Vabbinfaru in a Beachfront Pool villa for two people

- Full board basis, incl. soft drinks, excl. alcohol

- Return transfers from Male to Banyan Tree Vabbinfaru

- Two × return economy flights from London to Male up to a value of £700 per person

- Trip to be taken between 1 November 2017 and 30 April 2018
  Blackout dates include 27 December 2017 – 5 January 2018

To enter the competition visit the website
www.simonandschuster.co.uk

Entrants must be resident in the UK only